MW01146172

This book is dedicated to my wife for her invaluable input, and inexhaustible patience. Enjoy, Missy.

Guardians of The Hyless
Prologue

"Milord!"

Lord Kinzin jumped and nearly dropped the book he was reading. He turned to face a guard clad in black armor jogging toward him. He slid the tome behind his back, clearing his throat.

"What is it?"

The guard bowed at the waist, his hand propped on his claymore. "Begging your pardon Milord, but it's your wife. She has fallen ill."

Kinzin stared at him, alarm pecking at the back of his mind. "Ill? How? What do you mean?"

"She speaks to herself, her eyes rolling wildly and her mouth foaming white," the guard said, his face turning green. "It's bad, Milord."

Kinzin dropped the tome on the library table behind him and hurried past the guard.

He shoved open the library doors and ran briskly down the brightly lit stone hall, thoughts of what could possibly have happened running rampant through his mind.

It wasn't long before he reached the door to his wife's chambers. The guard caught up to him, stopping and staring at the door queasily.

"I will go in alone," Kinzin said.

"Thank you, sir," the guard gasped, bowing and hurrying away.

Kinzin slowly pushed open the door and stepped inside. The room was dark, a single shaft of light tracing across the floor of the room from a small window above his wife's bed. The smell of scented candles hung thickly in the darkness. The cradle by her bedside was as still as death, the small pink blanket hanging out the side of it unmoving.

"Telyn," he said softly, stepping over to her bedside.

The beautiful woman lay still, her head pressed firmly into her pillow. Her face was fair, narrow cheekbones resting beneath slender eyes. Her body was taut as a bow string, as though she had been convulsing, her golden hair framing her pale face like a battered halo, soaked in sweat. Her belly was swollen with child, nearly a full nine months, her lips a sickly white color. A small bit of foam traced down the corner of her mouth.

"Telyn!" he said again, louder this time. He reached out and seized her shoulders, panic washing over him. She couldn't have passed already! "Telyn!" he cried, running his fingers through her damp hair.

"I'm afraid she is gone, Milord," a cold voice said from behind him.

Kinzin wheeled around, his sword flashing out its scabbard. "Who's there?" He scanned the darkness for a sign of movement.

An armored figure stepped out of the gloom, its eyes glistening from behind its helmet. "Our master has finally succeeded," it said in a rasping voice, obviously male.

"What master?" Kinzin snapped, leveling his sword at the man's throat. "What do you speak of?"

The armored man drew his sword from its scabbard, the metal ringing across the chamber. "I think you know. The *Havi Ut Gahdness* will once again be celebrated across the continent: The Years of Mourning have begun. There is nothing you can do to stop it now."

A chill crept down Kinzin's spine. "Where did you hear that name?" Kinzin hissed. "Who are you? How does a simple guard know of such things?"

The man looked to his right and six more armored men melted out of the shadows, their weapons drawn. The steel glinted like submerged pearl in the faint light from the window. "We are the ones that serve your better," he said. "A man fit to rule Glaistoff and harness the might of the Prisms, a man with the stomach to use their power."

"Guards!" Kinzin yelled at the door. No answer came from the other side of the door. The room was silent, save for his own breath.

He was alone.

He lifted his chin proudly. "I am Lord Kinzin, rightful ruler of Miasma City and Keeper of the floating Prisms of Glaistoff. I am your King! You would not dare challenge me."

The guards lifted their blades, and charged.

Chapter One
By Any Means Necessary

"Haze, milord."

A voice pecked at Haze's consciousness, trying to force him awake.

"Milord, ten o'clock is truly very late for an elite general of the royal force," said the voice again.

"Good grief, man," Haze groaned, rolling onto his stomach and pulling his pillow over his head. He had stayed up entirely too late the previous night and may have had just a small amount too much wine as well, given the fact that his head was pounding with a vengeance.

"If there is such a thing as a good grief, I have yet to have seen it, Milord. I suggest you simply up and get, so I may begin with my duties."

"Why are you here? What time is it?"

"Ten o'clock, as I said, and it is high time you awoke and faced the day, no matter how much you loathe the idea."

"What did I do to deserve being cursed with you?"

"You hired me, sir."

Haze sighed loudly and slowly pulled his knees up under himself, his face still buried in the blankets under his pillow as his behind rose slowly into the air. "Who made mornings and why?" he groaned.

"Mornings are so the sun can rise once more and banish the night, filling the world with beauty in place of darkness."

"Beauty?" came Haze's muffled voice from under his pillow. "I should think you need to reevaluate your definition of that word."

His blankets were yanked off of him without warning, his pillow snatched and thrown to the floor.

"Ugh," he groaned, flopping back down onto his stomach. "You have no decency, man," he muttered, swinging his legs over the side of the bed and sitting up. He yawned as he rubbed the grit out of his eyes.

Standing in front of him was Rageth: his personal butler, his servant, and his best friend. He was perfectly groomed, as usual, and looked as though he had been up since four in the morning. Which, Haze thought disgustedly, was probably true.

"There we are," Rageth said, laying neatly folded clothes on the bed next to Haze. "You have a guest waiting for you in the breakfast hall." He smoothed down what looked like a dress shirt and laid an ice blue pendant on it. "I suggest you wear these, as it is a royal gathering and the King will be present."

Haze wrinkled his nose at the finery. "I will take that suggestion under advisement." He rubbed his eyes again as Rageth strode across the room.

The butler yanked the curtains open just as Haze lowered his hand, allowing sunlight to flood into the room and assault his already pounding head.

"Moron," Haze muttered, squinting his eyes in the light.

"Waking up is only such a battle because you insist on staying up until all hours losing yourself in the pub. Should you get yourself in bed at a reasonable hour, this wouldn't be so devastating."

Haze glared at the man, who looked back at him innocently. "Out," Haze said flatly. "I need to change."

Rageth spun on his heels with a smile, and exited the room. The door slammed shut behind him.

Haze remembered the meeting for today. Some wizard or other was coming to meet him and the King. It was something about a way into the Elliset Mountain Range. So many people came to them with ways to get into the Mountain Range, all failing miserably, most dying in the process. However, the King was obsessed with getting into the Mountains and never turned anyone away. His feverish attempts to enter the Range had led him to a conflict with a strange group of magicians known as the Druids of Val Ek Song. They proclaimed themselves to be the keepers of the Mountain Range's secrets and refused to allow Orlivan anywhere near them. The old King had not taken kindly to this, and immediately turned to violence. Haze personally headed the invasion of the foothills of the Range, wiping out every druid he came across, per the King's orders. It wasn't until after they had all been killed that they had found the Range to be blocked off by a cold so fierce it killed men in moments. The secret of entering the mountains had died with the druids of "The Song," as they were called, and the King had nearly abandoned hope that he would ever discover its secrets.

Personally, Haze disliked magic users. It was a group of sorcerers that took his family, leaving him an orphan at a young age. Orlivan had pitied him and taken him in, raising him as his own son. Had it not been for the old King, Haze would likely have died at the foothills of the Range, the same place he later launched one of the most brutal attacks in history.

He yawned again as he stood up and pushed the fancy shirt and pendant off his bed and onto the floor, staggering over to his closet.

God, how his head hurt.

Besides, everyone knew wandering into the Mountains was suicide anyway. The circular Range took up eighty leagues of the center of the continent, the peaks so high you couldn't see the tops. They were tight together, not a space large enough to fit a mouse anywhere between them. Trying to go over them was impossible; they were so cold that they froze men solid less than halfway up the side.

He opened the door and poked half-heartedly through his meager supply of tunics. He chose a dark blue one and pulled it off the shelf, grabbing a pair of black trousers and shuffling back over to his bed without closing the closet door.

The more work he could leave for Rageth the better.

Yawning again, he dropped his night clothes to the floor and slid into his tunic and trousers, buckling his silver Wyvern belt around his waist.

His belt was something the King had gifted him personally after a battle in which he had faced and defeated thirty-three enemy Malgonians single-handedly.

Malgonians were the King's most resilient foe thus far, and some of the oddest creatures one would ever see. They were very much like armored swine that stood on their hind legs like men, and wielded an assortment of weapons. Couple this with their uncanny ability to breath fire, and they were a real handful. The King's military had defeated their kingdom, but they still had scattered pockets of resistance here and there. It was one of these pockets Haze had an unfortunate run in with while he and three other guards were on patrol along the eastern borders. They were ambushed in the early morning hours, and two of the others were killed instantly, the third wounded. Haze and his wyvern had faced off against the entire horde and defeated them all, after which the King had gifted Haze with a new lance, belt, and dubbed him the general of his elite flying force, the Winged Demons. The battle had cost him his left arm, and he had been forced to train in a special fashion that resulted in him being able to manipulate his lance over his back and around his neck so that he could still fight.

Heading over to the stand which held a small mirror and wash basin, he splashed cold water on his face. The cold caused the pain in his head to flare suddenly.

11

Groaning miserably, he dried his face with a towel and studied his reflection.

Light brown hair was cropped short over a broad brow and green eyes, his jaw square and set. A small scar just touched his hairline, a tiny white line formed by the edge of a training sword.

He quickly ran his fingers through his hair and grabbed a small dagger hanging on his bed post.

Flicking the belt around his back, he pinned it to the front of his silver buckle and clasped it deftly with two fingers. He had become accustomed to working with one hand.

Shrugging into a heavy outdoor cloak, he strode towards the hall, leaving his night clothes in a pile on the floor. He grinned wickedly at the thought of Rageth having to pick them up later.

Opening the door, he stepped out into the hall, looking left and right down the white stone hallway. Rageth was nowhere in sight.

Chuckling to himself, he left the door open and strode down the corridor towards the breakfast hall, holding his hand up to the windows to shield himself from the light cascading in through the pale green panes.

He rounded a corner and heard laughing and talking in the chamber ahead of him. Apparently, breakfast had already begun.

Opening the door to the hall, he peered inside cautiously, looking for the King and any unfamiliar faces in the crowd, but saw neither.

"Must not be here yet," he mumbled to himself, pushing the door open just a little farther and edging his nose into the crack, trying to catch a whiff of what was being served for breakfast.

"Ugh," he groaned to himself as the scent of oatmeal reached his nostrils.

Closing the door, he turned and headed down the hall towards the wyvern pens. He might as well visit Salezz until the King sent for him. The King's guests were never on time anyway.

Hurrying down the corridor, he pushed open the giant double doors at the end of it and stepped out into the courtyard, wincing as the sunlight hit him with full force.

"I'm never drinking again," he swore to himself as he staggered across the cobblestones towards the high iron fence on the west side of the courtyard. "Never."

"I've heard that many times in my day," said a gruff voice on his right.

Haze grinned as he looked to his side. Alovere was catching up to him, a small smile on his face.

He was a larger man, standing perhaps two inches taller than Haze. His eyes were a steel gray, his hair shoulder length. It was grayed from time and age, but still thick and full. His face was speckled with the beginning of a silver beard, his jawline square and tense. Dark red armor covered him from his shoulders to his toes. An ornate helmet was tucked under his left arm, a black plume decorating the top of it.

Alovere was a Dragon rider in the King's elite military as well, though not as decorated as Haze. He was skilled, however, and Haze took great pains to stay ahead of the other man, as he was older and had more experience. While the Riders got along fine, their mounts had a thriving rivalry. Alovere's fire dragon picked on Haze's wyvern mercilessly, usually besting the young beast and giving Haze countless wounds to treat. Haze couldn't always understand the pecking order of the wyrms, but he hated it nonetheless. He always argued that it wasn't his wyvern's fault that he lost, as the dragon was nearly five hundred pounds his senior and at least four feet taller and broader. Not to mention, dragons were in general larger than wyverns, and didn't have the same growth rate. Wyverns tended to grow in spurts: sudden, instant, and complete. Each wyvern was expected to experience about five growth spurts in its life time, and Salezz had been due for his final spurt for around three years now. Most believed he would never get it, but Haze wouldn't admit it.

Despite his dragon, there was no one Haze would rather have fly at his back than Alovere. He was ridiculously reliable, and Haze trusted him with his life.

"Going to visit Salezz, are you?" Alovere asked, glancing in the direction Haze was heading.

"If I can get there without falling on my face."

Alovere caught up to him, falling in by his side. "I've been told that the King is considering sending me with this new sorcerer into the Mountains of Elliset," he said. "Has he asked you yet?"

"No." Haze frowned. "I imagine that must be why he asked me to meet him in the great hall. Yet another brainless mission into the Mountains."

"At some point it's going to work," Alovere stated. "You know that's true. There is only so long that mystery is going to hold out."

"I suppose, but I am not going to be the one that dies solving it, I guarantee you that."

Alovere grabbed his arm and pulled him to a stop. "Are you going to refuse to go?"

"Absolutely," Haze replied stubbornly. "I have watched countless good men go into that Range and never return. I am not joining those ranks, and I certainly won't have anything to do with a sorcerer."

Alovere rubbed the back of his head. "I don't suppose you would mind suggesting me to His Majesty?"

Haze stared at him. "You *want* to go?"

Alovere glanced at his boots. "I want to prove myself. You are young. I have nearly twenty years on you, and somehow you made General before me. You are a sell sword! You aren't even a sworn soldier of the Kingdom."

Haze flushed. "I am also the adopted son of the King," he said bitterly. "That makes him favor me and you know it. You are a fine soldier. You have nothing to prove."

"I have a temper," Alovere said flatly, "and it can get out of control sometimes. I get that. But my wife looks to me when I come home for food and security. How much of either of those can a mere commander provide?" He shook his head. "I need a promotion. I want this mission."

"Alovere," Haze said quietly, "you will most likely die on that mission. No one has ever come back. Ever. Do you really want to leave your wife behind like that?"

"What's this? A lover's quarrel?" A greasy voice slid into the conversation.

Haze rolled his eyes as he looked to his right.

A burly man clad in black armor leaned against the corner of the Wyrm Pens. His hair was dark, and slicked straight back. His puffy eyes were nearly as dark as his hair and narrowed to a pair of dangerous slits. His face was clean shaven, a blunt nose that looked as though it had been broken multiple times mashed into the front of his face. Two straight swords were crossed on his back, the tips of the black blades showing on either side of his hips.

"Zaajik," Haze sighed.

"What's this I hear about going into the Mountain Range?" Zaajik asked, spinning a tiny blade on the back of his hand. "And why wasn't I invited?"

"Because you are a murderer," Haze spat. "What do you want?"

The man shrugged, standing up straight and sheathing his knife. "Nothing at all. I simply want to be filled in on the goings on, same as the rest of you."

"Your commanding officer will brief you when it becomes necessary."

"Yes, I know," he sighed exasperatedly, "but it always takes him so long. You know, age and all." He glanced meaningfully at Alovere, who growled under his breath.

Zaajik was a new hire, coming to serve his Majesty shortly after Haze had returned from his time as a mercenary. He was a sell sword that wandered the continent honing his abilities, and had recently signed on as an aerial soldier in Haze's Winged Demons. He didn't get along with any of the other men in his score of fliers, and was well known for his merciless and cruel treatment of his opponents on the field. Haze also believed he was after court position, and was constantly vying for favor with His Majesty. King Orlivan, for some reason unknown to Haze, liked Zaajik. He had promised him a promotion as soon as the year was out. This angered Haze, because the only promotion that was available was to a commander, Alovere's position.

"Return to your score," Alovere snapped. "I gave you specific orders before I left. You are supposed to be running dive drills."

"Boring," Zaajik drawled. "Besides, I would rather hear the latest gossip."

Alovere turned to Haze. "Don't forget what I asked you." He then turned and stalked towards Zaajik. "Let's go! Back to the training yard." He shoved on the younger man's shoulder, knocking him off balance for a moment and turning him around. The other two marched off towards the training grounds, leaving Haze alone.

He shook his head and continued on his way to the Wyvern Pens.

Alovere had a mysterious past. No one really knew where he came from, or what he had done before he showed up in Beril. Haze was just a child when he arrived and signed on as an aerial soldier for His Majesty's Sky Force. He was a power to be reckoned with on the battle field, his movements that of an excellently trained soldier, yet completely unique in style. He used nothing but a plain double-edged sword, never changing his weapon or carrying a shield. He was, in fact, one of the only Riders that didn't use a longer weapon, such as the lance that Haze used. He had a thirst for promotion, quickly accepting any mission the King asked of him and carrying it out without fail, no matter what the cost, lending him a fair standing. But this also bled into his reputation of being violent and carrying out even the most gruesome of orders without question, some of which even Haze had not known the details of. He believed that may have had something to do with Alovere's disdain of Zaajik. Zaajik was not only competition, but also younger, and willing to go even farther than he was.

Haze reached the gate of the Wyvern Pens and looked up. The massive domed structure rose high into the air, its clear glass ceiling glinting at the sky like transparent scales. Its walls stretched as far as he could see in either direction, sweeping far out of the city and into the wilds. It was built entirely from Malogarian steel, metal mined from the depths of the Boar Mountains. It was the only material known that could withstand the searing heat of dragon fire. He looked back down at the familiar dragon's head handle, and grabbed it. He grunted and turned it hard to the right, straining to move it with his one hand. With a thunderous clanking sound, the giant door swung inward and he hurried through and into the outer edge of the pens. He turned around and heaved with all his might, returning the enormous steel gate to its previous state of airtight closure.

The Pens were the pride and joy of Beril. They rose high into the sky, enormous perches of Malogarian steel reaching out into the open expanse like metal fingers. They covered a distance of twenty leagues, more than five hundred dragons and wyverns calling it their home. It was rife with rolling pastures, rocky canyons, frozen tundra, and anything else dragons would need to keep themselves entertained.

"Good morning, sir," said a friendly voice to his left. "How is your day so far?"

Haze turned to face Horkus, one of his own soldiers. He stood about an inch shorter than Haze, his face round and friendly. Brown eyes that matched his hair were settled in a freckled face nearly always creased with a smile. Horkus was skilled with a lance, trained by Haze personally. He was one of Haze's best friends, and doubled as the Dragon Keeper as well as one Haze's Winged Demons.

"Bright," Haze said gruffly, rubbing his temple. "Very bright."

Horkus smiled. "Ah. I see."

"Seen Salezz around?"

Horkus pointed up. "Yup. Right where he usually is."

Haze shielded his eyes with his hand and looked up, scanning the crowd of shimmering scales and talons that whirled like an armored tornado all around the enclosure. He spotted Salezz, high above the rest of the fire breathing creatures, hovering by the very top of the cage.

He stepped over the bones of what looked like a cow and whistled shrilly.

The reaction was instant.

Salezz whipped around and plummeted towards the ground, a big brown dragon Haze recognized as Vixen, Zaajik's storm dragon, hot in pursuit. Haze knew Vixen could neither keep up with nor maneuver well enough to outstrip Salezz, but occasionally he had to land, as in this case. That was when Vixen set on him, usually beating him to a pulp and leaving him for the other dragons and wyverns to harass while he was weak.

As the Wyrms got close to where he was, Haze noticed Salezz tuck his wings even closer to his sides, his eyes narrowed to nothing more than blue slits in his icy scaled face. Vixen began to slow her descent as they neared the bottom of the pens, spreading her wings out. But Salezz leaned forward even more, his beady eyes fixed on his master. Haze felt his heart thrumming in his chest as Salezz drew closer and closer to the ground, refusing to slow his fall.

He always hated watching this.

Moments before the Wyvern collided with the hard-packed earth, his wings billowed out. They filled with the cold October air and sent him skimming a few feet above the ground towards Haze. The massive storm dragon pursuing had veered off a good while before and was winging towards the other side of the pen.

Salezz floated gently down onto his claws, landing just in front of Haze and making a pleased barking sound.

He hopped clumsily towards Haze one step and rubbed his thorny scaled head against his master's chest, still making small barking sounds deep in his throat.

Haze stepped back and stared at his friend proudly. He never failed to be impressed with Salezz, who was one of the rarest creatures in the realm.

He was born a runt, smaller than the rest of his litter, but Haze always thought he was special somehow. In Salezz's third year he found out he was correct; the wyvern sneezed on the fountain in the town square and froze it solid. He was the only Wyvern in history that was capable of breathing ice instead of fire, and the only wyvern in it to have colored scales, instead of the standard dull gray. His were a transparent ice blue color that matched his eyes perfectly.

He always seemed a little pitiful on the ground, limping around on his wings and ungainly legs, like when a sea creature washes up on land and loses most of its mobility, but in the air...he was miraculous. He could fly circles around every other dragon or wyvern in the Force.

"Hey big boy," he said, scratching the top of the Wyrm's head affectionately.

"He is one of the smartest we have in here," Horkus put in, patting Salezz on the neck. "Arginox may be the biggest, but that doesn't mean a thing. Little Salezz out spins him all the time."

Haze smiled. Horkus was a huge fan of Salezz, never missing a moment to talk the little wyvern up.

Haze wiped a bit of dirt off the beast's wing and stepped back, facing Horkus. "How about letting me take him for a ride?"

Horkus grinned broadly. "Don't see why not. He needs a good breeze under his wings anyway. I'll grab your saddle."

As the dragon keeper went to go retrieve Haze's saddle from the tack barn, Haze noticed Vixen snarling and edging towards their position.

He grabbed one of the dead cow's ribs and threw it at her, the ivory bone bouncing harmlessly off the dragon's scaly snout. "Beat it!" he yelled.

She turned away and trundled off, barging through a crowd of smaller wyverns and snapping at their haunches.

Haze shook his head. Vixen behaved much like her master; rude and cruel, her only gift being hurting those around her as much as possible. He hated that it was possible for people to pollute the behavior of their animals so much.

There was a jarring collision with Haze's rib cage as Salezz nuzzled his nose into his side, begging for attention.

"Alright, alright," he laughed, rubbing the Wyverns forehead affectionately. "Take it easy. Horkus is coming."

"Milord?" a voice said from behind him.

Haze sighed and turned around.

He wasn't surprised to see Rageth standing in the doorway to the Wyvern Pens, a steaming mug in hand.

"What?"

"The guest I mentioned earlier is still awaiting you in the great hall," Rageth said, holding out the mug of hot liquid. "I brought you some coffee to ease your transition back into the light," he added with a twinkle in his eye.

Haze glared at him. "Tell the guest I will be a moment." He took the mug and sniffed it. It smelled like freshly ground heaven. "But thanks for the coffee."

"Milord, his Majesty insists that you come at once," Rageth said. "He said I was to use whatever means necessary to bring you to the hall."

"Tell him I will only be a moment," Haze said again. "I need to take Salezz for a spin."

Rageth cleared his throat. "Milord, that would be unwise. His Majesty is in a foul temper this morning and it wouldn't do to anger him further."

"'His Majesty' can take a breath!" Haze snapped. "And what does he mean by 'whatever means necessary'? What does he think you're gonna do? Wrestle me to the palace? I could beat you with one hand behind my back."

"You only have one hand, sir," Rageth pointed out.

"My point exactly."

21

"Very well sir, enjoy your coffee," Rageth sighed, turning on his heels. "Do let me know if there is anything else I can do for you." He strode out the door, leaving it open behind him.

Haze raised an eyebrow. That was odd. Rageth never gave up that easily. He couldn't count how many times he had stood and argued with his butler over something like what he should wear, or why he was going to be late for something. Rageth had the tenacity of a bulldog and the cunning of a cobra; it was next to impossible to win an argument with the stately servant.

He shrugged, dismissing the thought and gingerly sipping some of the boiling liquid from the cup. Grimacing, he swallowed the horribly bitter substance. "Rageth!" he bellowed. "Where's my cream and sugar?"

The butler's head immediately appeared around the door. "They are waiting for you in the Great Hall, Milord."

Haze stared at him incredulously. "You know I can't drink my coffee without cream and sugar."

"Whatever means necessary, milord," Rageth said smugly. "Shall I go inform his Majesty you will be arriving shortly?"

Haze grumbled and stormed towards the door, patting Salezz on the head briefly. "You are brutal, Rageth. Entirely ruthless. Completely lacking in common courtesy or the vaguest sense of remorse. Have you no shame?"

"Whatever means necessary, sir. His Majesty's orders."

Chapter two
Galnoron

Haze pushed open the double doors leading into the main hall with his elbow, trying not to spill his coffee. The sound of chatter and raised voices reached his ears. The voices belonged to the King, and one other man whose voice he did not recognize.

The hall was lit with more blinding light from the open windows, cascading across the dark stone floor and sparsely set table. Chandeliers hung cold and lightless from the high ceiling, giant chunks of wax drooling down from their holders.

The King was seated in his customary chair at the head of the table, his rich crimson robes draping down to the floor. The crown of Elliset rested on his head, adorned with a scatter of rubies and emeralds.

A man sat a little way down the table from him on his right, long black robes covering him head to foot, a drawn hood hiding his face.

Rageth cleared his throat loudly. "Ahem. General Haze to see you, Your Majesty."

"Excellent! Come here, boy," the King said, beckoning Haze to come closer. King Orlivan was a giant of a man, towering above the tallest of his soldiers. Haze himself was a full two heads shorter than he, measuring in at just six feet. Orlivan had competed in the Battle of Ascension to rule as King the first time at seventeen; a grueling battle of wits, strength, and sheer cunning. Dozens of lives were lost in the Battles of Ascension every decade, and those that Orlivan had taken to secure his throne were no exception. He had won, of course, and had been winning every ten years for the last four decades. He was slowly aging, however, no one being impervious to the wear of time. He was now in his sixties, and approaching the next battle where he would once again fight to defend his right to the throne.

"Yes sir," Haze said, striding over and bowing low to the King. "What is it you need of me?"

"Haze, meet Galnoron," he said, gesturing to the man in dark robes.

Haze faced the man. His face was cloaked in a dark shadow, making his features difficult to discern. Haze thought he saw a hooked nose over tightly drawn lips before the man bowed his head, further obscuring Haze's vision. "Pleased to meet you, sir," Haze said.

"Likewise," Galnoron replied cordially, his voice smooth and high. "What an honor it is to meet the most esteemed soldier in King Orlivan's military. They say you could defeat a thousand men without breaking a sweat."

"I'm flattered," Haze said, bowing slightly, "but those tales are vastly exaggerated."

"Haze is being modest," the King interjected. "I don't know about *any* thousand, but a thousand Malgonians he could certainly handle. He is my one-armed miracle! My Lord of Winged Demons! And the son I never had," he added proudly.

Haze was always ashamed when Orlivan spoke about him like a trophy. He cared greatly for the old man, and was grateful that he had taken him in as a child, but always wished the King would tone down his praise a bit. He had dubbed Haze his "Lord of Demons" upon making him General, an honorary title Haze always felt was a bit heavy. Couple that with the way Orlivan talked him up, and it made for a crippling sense of duty. This wasn't helped by the fact that Orlivan was constantly bragging about Haze's abilities to anyone that would listen for more than three minutes.

There was a time Orlivan had tried to marry him off to an eligible princess from the neighboring kingdom of Lalogat. He had gone about it all wrong, however. To Haze's horror, Orlivan had regaled her for two hours of all his greatest missions and exploits, finishing with the phrase: "And you will get used to him only having one arm. One less thing to worry about, after all."

"I've heard that you have something of a special Wyvern?" Galnoron asked, dragging Haze out of his embarrassing memory.

"Salezz is...different, yes." Haze answered. "How did you hear tell of it?"

The hooded man laughed softly. "It's hard not to catch whispers of General Haze and his infamous Wyvern these days, is it?" he said. "Tell me, does he breathe fire like usual?"

Haze frowned and shook his head. "No, he breathes some form of liquid ice."

Galnoron remained motionless, his face shadowed. "Hm."

"Well, Haze," King Orlivan said, "I have a proposition for you."

Haze bowed low. "Anything, Milord."

"I want you to accompany Galnoron into the Mountain Range of Elliset."

Haze felt his heart sink as his suspicions were confirmed. "Pardon me?"

The King laughed. "You heard me, boy. I'm thinking it's time you got some real wind under your wings."

Haze struggled to find something to say. In his mind, conquering two kingdoms in His Majesty's name was wind enough under anyone's wings, not to mention traveling the entire continent from one end to the other hunting druids. "But milord, the Mountains are colder than ice itself. We would die," he said hesitantly.

The Elliset Mountain Range was the one place Haze had never wanted to go. He had seen it many times, and heard the stories. Never one time had he so much as considered going there. Just battling the druids at the foothills was enough for him. The idea of trying to summit the freezing peaks and going inside them made his skin crawl.

"Galnoron here claims he has a way to keep you and him warm during the journey. Salezz will be impervious to the cold due to his unique make-up."

"Surely Alovere and Arginox would be a better choice, Milord?" Haze said hopefully. "I know Alovere has a personal desire to see beyond the Mountains. I'm sure—"

"It's done," the King said, raising his hand. "Alovere is aging. He is skilled, yes, but for things like this, I need someone I can trust to perform adequately. And besides, Arginox is a fire dragon. He would be killed by the cold of the Mountains, and Galnoron only has enough magic to protect two of you." He stepped forward and laid a hand on Haze's shoulder. "And there is no one I would like better to discover the secrets of the Range than my son."

Haze stepped back. "Magic?" he hissed. "I will have no part of this Sorcerer. Find someone else."

Orlivan rolled his eyes as Galnoron rose to his feet, his face rank with disdain. "You will do as your King commands you! What sort of kingdom is this, that subjects defy their superiors?"

Haze glared at the wizard. "I am a mercenary that has sold my lance to King Orlivan for many years, and his son. I am not his subject."

The room fell silent, Galnoron staring incredulously at the young rider. The wizard's face was still clouded in shadow, only his eyes visible. They shone a bright, iridescent yellow in the cold light of the hall.

"Alright," King Orlivan said lightly, settling into his chair. "Let's take a break and discuss this in a moment, shall we Galnoron? I need to have a word with Haze here."

Galnoron took a step away from Haze and bowed to the king. "Yes, your Majesty."

Turning away from both of them, he exited the hall, the great double doors crashing closed behind him.

Orlivan sighed, looking at Haze exasperatedly. "I would have expected such an outburst from Zaajik."

"And for once, I would have agreed with his reaction," Haze retorted. "What are you doing? Consorting with a sorcerer to gain access to a mountain range so deadly it would be suicide to enter it?"

"I do what I have to do to keep us on the top of the food chain," the King said stubbornly. "It's not as if I haven't exhausted every other option. I have marched into the Mountains myself! I froze and nearly died, but it was the only thing I had not yet tried. There is a power that sleeps in those mountains that has not been touched in over five hundred years. We are soon to be at war, Haze, and I don't want our enemies to possess a power we cannot face."

Haze gripped his dagger in frustration. "But Milord, you don't even know what this power is! How can you hunt something you have never seen? This is foolish!"

"You will *not* speak to me like that!" Orlivan snapped, drawing himself to his full height. "I understand what is at stake here better than you. Tell me, Haze," he said, coming around his chair and standing in front of the rider. "Do you know how the relations are between myself and Miasma City?" He shook his head. "They aren't good. And now I hear tell that the Mountains are open! I must find the power hidden in them before Jaelyn does. What would happen to our kingdom if she discovered the power first? She is ruthless! Lord Kinzin is dead, and the only thing standing between her and world domination is me!"

Haze knew what Orlivan was speaking of. The waning peace between the Kingdom of Beril and the Empire of Glaistoff was tenuous, at best. Queen Jaelyn had made several mild threats that Orlivan took as a prelude to all-out war. Haze didn't believe their relations were as volatile as Orlivan thought, but he agreed that if Jaelyn obtained this mysterious power from inside the Mountains, they could be. That is, if there was any 'power'.

"How do you know the Mountains are actually open?" Haze asked skeptically. "Some wizard just came to you and claimed he can get in? Do you know this man? Is he trustworthy?"

"Yes, he is," Orlivan said immediately. "He has been into the Mountains before, and he survived."

"How do you know that?" Haze asked incredulously. "He's lying. All these fools claim amazing discoveries and deliver nothing. Can you believe Alovere asked me to put a word in for him? He wants you to send him to his death. Just like everyone else you have sent in there! When will you learn, your Majesty?"

"I will learn when I succeed in entering the Elliset Mountain Range!" King Orlivan's face reddened as he smashed his fist on the long dining table, the dishes rattling loudly at their places. Haze fell silent, watching Orlivan closely. "I am king in this land! All of it! I will not have Jaelyn's power hanging over my head like an axe. I *will* be the first one to the center of that mountain range, even if that means I must consult the powers of mysticism myself!" The exasperated King took a breath, closing his eyes briefly. "You must understand, Haze. I have been everywhere in Elliset. I have conquered every kingdom that there is, and ruled over every race and province. Except," he frowned deeply, "this one behind the Elliset Mountains. I do not know what lies beyond that range, but I will find out if it costs me my very life."

Haze stared Orlivan. He was trembling a bit, his hand grasping the hilt of his ornate sword tightly. Something about the King's urgency to discover a way into the Mountains had changed lately. Right now, his face was betraying a different sort of emotion than the normal excitement that came when someone presented a way into the Range. It almost seemed like fear.

"Your Majesty," Haze said quietly, "I do not think you are well. Perhaps let Rageth—"

"Nonsense!" Orlivan waved his hand dismissively. "I am just fine. Galnoron!" he yelled.

The double doors swung open with a loud creak, Galnoron's hooded figure stepping into the archway. "Milord?"

"Haze will escort you into the Elliset Mountain Range." Haze opened his mouth to protest, but the King lifted his hand. "You will do this for me. I need someone I trust implicitly on this mission. You are that person, General."

Haze felt a twinge of pity for the man. His robes hung on his thinning body like dying skin, dark circles under his eyes marking nights taken by lack of sleep. He looked at his general almost imploringly, searching for acceptance.

Haze sighed. "I will travel with Galnoron," he said. "On two conditions: I see proof that he has been in the Range, and you pay him upon his successful return and not a moment before."

The wizard and Orlivan looked at each other for a moment, before Galnoron cleared his throat. "General, it seems as though there is a misunderstanding." He bowed to Haze. "I do not wish any payment. I will be paying *you* to accompany *me*."

29

Haze frowned. Something about Galnoron's manner caused his insides to twist. He had only known the man for five minutes, and already wanted nothing more to do with him. "Why?"

"I needed the best of the best to come with me into the Mountains. You see, I've been there before. They are not very..." Galnoron rubbed his chin thoughtfully. "Welcoming." He said the word carefully, as though afraid of offending someone. "There is a personal reason I wish to return, and in return for me giving your king a way into the Mountains, he has agreed to allow only the finest of his men to accompany me as a bodyguard. You will also receive ample compensation for your time."

"Are you saying they are dangerous?" Haze snapped, "because we knew that already."

Galnoron suddenly lowered his hood, revealing a narrow, hook-nosed face, his lips drawn together in a thin white line. His head was shaved, shining in the light from the torches. But his face was what sent a chill down Haze's spine. The skin was disfigured and melted, frozen mid-drool halfway down his left cheek. Open cavities and angry red blisters speckled his features like a disease that consumed one's flesh. "And just how dangerous do you think the Mountains are, General?" he said softly, his yellow eyes wide.

Haze cleared his throat quickly. The burns were bad, that much was certain, but the wheels had already set to turning in his mind. "This is hardly proof that you have been in the Mountains, if that's what you think it is," he said stubbornly. "You could have been caught in a simple house fire or angered the wrong end of a Dragon. These are common problems."

Galnoron flipped his hood back up, once again covering his scarred face in shadow. "That's true, except no matter how bad my injuries are, they are not the proof I am presenting today." He reached inside his robe and pulled out a small leather satchel. "Tell me, General," he said, untying the top of the leather bag, "have you traveled much of Elliset?"

Haze nodded, staring at the satchel. "Yes."

"Nearly all of it, I would presume?" Galnoron said confidently. "As General of the Winged Demons, surely you have been from one end of this continent to the other?"

Haze sighed impatiently. "Yes. What point are you trying to make? Speak your mind."

Galnoron smiled and reached into his bag, pulling out a broad ice-blue feather easily as long as Haze's right forearm. "In all your travels, have you ever seen anything like this?"

Haze stared at the feather.

It looked as though it was made from pure ice, sculpted by only the finest of craftsmen and polished to an almost luminescent shine. A faint mist rose from it, as though it was combating the heat in the great hall. "No," he murmured, shaking his head. "I never have."

"This is something I retrieved while in the depths of Elliset, just before I sustained my injuries. About twelve days ago this morning."

It was nearly the same color as the scales that covered his Wyvern from head to toe, glinting an iridescent blue in the torchlight. He felt as though he had seen it before, in a dream perhaps. Or maybe when he was young, before his memories had formed. He shivered slightly as a sense of cold radiated from the feather. Something about it cast a feeling of dread over him. Not fear of the object, but fear of where it came from. It felt as though the feather was warning him to stay away, as though it didn't want to be discovered.

31

Haze glanced at Orlivan, who was staring at him intently. Returning his gaze to Galnoron, he lifted his chin slightly. "I changed my mind. Find someone else."

Orlivan sighed in frustration and shook his head.

Galnoron looked on in utter shock. "You cannot disobey the direct order of your King!" the sorcerer said indignantly. "You have been ordered to accompany me, and so you shall!"

Haze glanced at him. "I take orders from no one. Title or not, I am my own master, and no one in this kingdom will stand against me," he said calmly. "Find someone else."

He turned on his heels and strode towards the door, making it halfway there before Galnoron called for him to stop.

He paused in the doorway, not facing the other man. "What?"

"Don't you want to know why your wyvern is the way he is?" the wizard said quietly from behind him. "Don't you want to know why he breathes ice and not fire? Where he came from?"

Haze stood still. He didn't answer.

"Just bear this in mind: my wounds didn't come from fire. They came from ice."

Haze silently exited the Great Hall, letting the doors crash closed behind him.

Chapter Three
Departure

Alovere patted Arginox's flank, the massive beast turning his head to fix his master with his crimson gaze. He grinned, tightening the strap on his saddle.

It hadn't taken long for His Majesty to come to his senses and send him along with the new sorcerer instead of Haze.

He frowned. It shouldn't be this hard to gain favor in the eyes of the King. He was the more experienced soldier, and up until recently, had held the higher rank. Still, the favor went to Haze and his Wyvern. He had been denied his promotion to General and left at captain for a long time, before being promoted to a commander. Haze was given the position he had wanted.

He synched up the saddle tighter.

Haze was a good soldier. He couldn't deny that, or hate the young man. But there was something about taking orders from someone younger than himself that made him itch. He smiled, swinging himself into his saddle. At least it wasn't Zaajik giving orders. Had that been the case, he was certain he would have been hanged by now for murdering the snake.

Alovere spurred Arginox in the ribs and the great beast leaped into the air.

The wind whistled in his ears as his mount surged higher, his wings beating the air with force fit to shame a hundred wyverns.

Dragons possessed real power, far above a wyvern, in Alovere's opinion. They were taller, wider, and had a foul disposition that made them ideal for combat. They may lack the razor-sharp intelligence of their smaller counterparts, but they made up for it with their prowess in battle.

He soared above the city of Beril, looking down on its grey stone streets and brown houses.

It was the center of the world. Beril, home to the great King of Elliset, conqueror of all. In it dwelled the greatest of craftsmen and warriors: rulers of men. None stood against the might of King Orlivan and his Winged Demons. Save for Jaelyn, that is, and even she, with her airships and cannons, did not challenge him in open war. Denied acts of sabotage and skirmishes were the closest she came to challenging him. Were it not for her taking the throne in Miasma City, Alovere didn't think the two kingdoms would ever have quarreled; Lord Kinzin was a far better ruler before he faced the tragedy of losing his wife and child, and shortly thereafter, his own life.

Alovere sighed to himself in frustration as he guided his mount down towards a small house on the outskirts of town.

He believed that if King Orlivan was not the one to obtain the power that lay hidden in the Mountains, there would no longer be a City of Beril. The confrontation between Jaelyn and Orlivan had been on the wind for five years now, the first incident arising when Jaelyn asked for troops to defend her home against a mysterious adversary she was challenging at the time. She never elaborated on what the conflict was about, but in support of her new leadership and to bolster relations, His Majesty sent her the troops.

They never returned.

Orlivan had grown wary of her after this, and had sent spies into her kingdom to learn what had happened to his soldiers. Unfortunately, she discovered the spies and became enraged. She struck out violently with an act of war: In a brutal raid, one of the eastern-most villages on the continent was attacked and burned to the ground. Women and children were slaughtered by the dozen, and the entire village wiped out. King

Orlivan responded in kind and sent a force of his Winged Demons to assault the floating fortress of Lorrik Kihl, one of her border strongholds. The battle was gruesome, over three thousand dead soldiers between the two of them. But Queen Jaelyn had learned that His Majesty was not to be trifled with, and ceased all further attacks on Elliset.

But as time went on and her power grew, tensions grew as well.

Arginox drew them closer to the house, a small stone cottage just outside the busy district of the lower part of the city. Smoke curled lazily from the chimney, etching a small cloud of mist into the crisp morning sky. Freshly tilled earth surrounded the house in a field of brown. His wife, Enial, would soon be planting the winter bulbs, spring flowers that bloomed after the last frost of the year.

Arginox widened his wings, filling them with wind and slowing their descent. They drifted to a graceful landing in the front yard, a dozen paces or so from the door of the cottage.

Alovere swung down off his dragon, his sabatons sinking a good three inches into the soft dirt. The smell of freshly baked bread drifted from an open window, floating lightly about the yard.

He marched over to the door and pushed it open.

The welcoming sound of Enial humming reached his ears, the fire at the far end of the cottage blazing merrily as a tea kettle hanging above it whistled dutifully. A small table sat in the very center of the room, littered with an assortment of things ranging from wooden bowls, to small leather bags, the contents of which he could only guess. In the center of the table was a basket heaped with all manner of food. Tucked into the far corner of the room was a large bed, draped with various colored blankets.

His wife stood by the fire, lifting the tea kettle from the flames and pouring the contents into a large clay jug resting on a stool by the fire.

35

She was small, not quite five feet. Long brown hair streaked with grey fell in wavy curls nearly all the way to her waist, tied by a small red ribbon at the back of her neck.

He walked gingerly across the room, careful not to let his metal boots clank on the wooden floor.

Creeping up behind her, he leaned on the mantle above the fire place, standing so close behind her he could smell the ginger perfume she wore hanging lightly in the air around her.

As she turned to replace the kettle on the fire, she cried out and stumbled backwards. The kettle flew into the air as she flung her hands up in front of her.

Alovere leaned forward and caught the pot deftly, losing only some of the water onto the stone hearth.

She glared at him, her blue eyes flashing dangerously. "Alovere, how many times have I told you not to sneak up on me?" she said crossly, snatching the kettle from his hand and returning it to its hook above the fire, the lid now propped open to prevent the whistling.

"A few times now, minimally," he admitted, "but aren't you glad to see me?"

Enial's mouth twisted into a begrudging smile as she took a step forward and wrapped her arms around his middle. "You know I am."

"I have something for you," Alovere said, stroking her hair. "It's something I got while out on patrol yesterday."

"You always have something, dear."

"Quite a find, actually."

"Oh?"

He pulled away from her and reached into a small bag at his waist.

She gasped as he pulled out a shining golden pendant, about the size of the tip of his thumb. Fine engravings traced a dragon into the metal in a glowing red hue, flames billowing out of its mouth.

"Where did you find this?" she asked, reaching out and grabbing the dainty yellow chain from his fingers.

"In the market," he said vaguely.

"But you said you found it on patrol!" Enial said, clasping it behind her neck and staring down at it as it rested over her thick blue blouse.

"Patrolling the market, yes," he said with a wink. "I got home yesterday, actually. The King wished to see me this morning, so I had to wait around for a while. I decided to go hunting for a gift."

"That is so sweet. Thank you," she said, standing on her toes and kissing him lightly. "It's beautiful."

Alovere cleared his throat. "Enial," he said hesitantly, "there is something I need to tell you."

Enial's brow dipped towards her chin. "What is it?"

"The King is sending me back out right away. There are some special circumstances, and I will be traveling with someone else. I could be gone for a long time, I'm not sure yet."

He regretted saying the words the moment they left his mouth.

Enial turned away from him and put a lid on the clay pot.

"Enial."

She ignored him and began pulling food out of the basket on the table, her movements rushed.

He stepped forward and grabbed her wrist, causing her to drop a bowl to the floor with a loud clatter.

She whirled on him. "Why so soon? You have been gone for three weeks! Now you come home just to tell me you are leaving again? When do you leave?"

"In the morning," he mumbled.

She covered her mouth with her right hand, tears springing into her eyes. "When do I get you back from the King? When do I get you back from this foolish desire to seek his favor?"

Her words burned like a branding iron, churning his stomach. His first reaction was anger; anger that she would call his drive to get a promotion a foolish desire. Yet there was a certain truth to her words. Many years ago, they had married after a horrible tragedy that took her only living relative from her. In the time since they had left their homeland and come to Elliset, Alovere had been absorbed in his duties. Always for good reason; to put food on the table, and a roof over their heads. But in truth, Alovere was uncertain he could stop working. He was nearly sixty years old now. It was true, he was blessed with the look and health of a younger man, but he could feel the wear of age. He feared that if he stopped, he would waste away and become nothing more than a cow farmer barely able to scrape by on his taxes.

The thought bit like acid. He had to serve. He had to achieve a higher rank so he could retire with his coffers full of gold. He couldn't watch his wife go hungry.

"It is what it is," he said bitterly, turning away from her and striding towards the door. "I will return. In the meantime, I must serve my King."

"Alovere!"

He paused in the doorway, not turning around.

"I love you," she said, her voice trembling.

"I love you too," he replied flatly, stepping through the door and closing it behind him.

Hurrying over to Arginox, he swung himself into the saddle and spurred him in the ribs.

With a massive leap, the great beast threw them into the sky and surged towards the clouds.

Chapter Four
The Drunken Druid

The sound of chatter and laughter filled the pub, coursing from one end of the small wooden establishment to the other. The smell of alcohol lingered on everything; the entire table Haze was seated at glistened with spilled spirits.

The King had sent Rageth to tell him that Alovere had been chosen to accompany the wizard into the Mountains after all. Haze had convinced himself it wasn't his duty to warn Alovere of the wizard. Besides, it was nothing but a hunch he couldn't prove anyway. Galnoron had not done anything directly wrong or suspicious, he just seemed...off.

He lifted his goblet and swallowed a mouthful of the bitter liquid inside it.

It didn't matter. He wasn't going anywhere with that snake, and if Alovere wanted to go, he wasn't going to try and stop him.

He closed one eye and waited for the burn in his throat to pass.

"That swill you're drinking. Is it any good?" a drawling voice said from beside him.

Haze looked to his right.

The stranger was tall and lean, bright blue eyes gleaming out at him from behind a scruffy face in need of a shave. His dark hair was ruffled and unkempt, perhaps a bit longer than it should have been. A long silver coat was draped over his shoulders, flowing around his ankles like liquid metal. He slouched casually against the bar, a golden flask hanging loosely in his right hand.

"It's alright," Haze said, looking him up and down. "Not the best."

The man rolled his eyes. "Ugh. Unbearable. Is there nothing decent to drink in this forsaken land of ice?"

Haze raised an eyebrow. "Forsaken land of ice?"

The man nodded, running his fingers through his hair and fluffing it up a little. "Buckles and broomsticks, you haven't got an idea what I'm talking about, do you?" he sighed and shook his head. "Have you ever been outside this little town of misery and frost? Sunshine? *Living* plants? Ever seen those?"

Haze frowned. "Not in October! How much have you had to drink?"

The man's eyes opened a little wider and he leaned back slightly, taking in Haze as though seeing him for the first time. "Perhaps I should get your name, yes?"

Haze stared at the man warily. "You first."

"My name is Glassworn," the man said, flicking his hair out of his eyes and extending his hand. "I am a Druid of rare talent," he winked shrewdly. "I drink a lot. You may call me Glass."

Haze scowled at him. It seemed he wouldn't be able to escape magicians today. "Haze. General to His Majesty's Winged Demons. And I don't consort with your kind, so you would do well to leave me be."

"My kind?" the man raised an eyebrow, his eyes twinkling. "And what kind is that?"

"You practitioners of magic," Haze snapped bitterly. "You dabble in things that others pay for."

"You sound like someone with experience in magic."

Haze swallowed the last of the mead from his goblet and stood up, dropping a coin on the bar. "Enough to know I don't want anything to do with you." He turned and strode toward the doors of the pub, leaving the gentleman standing with his mouth hanging open in either shock or confusion.

He pushed open the swinging doors and stepped out into the darkness. He took a deep breath as the smell of the cool night air filled his nostrils like a sweet breeze.

41

Maybe the night wasn't gone after all. It was clear, the stars gleaming down like tiny lanterns scattered throughout the heavens.

He shoved his hand into his trouser pocket and shuffled awkwardly down the street.

It would be a fine night to take Salezz for a turn around the city. There were few things he enjoyed more than soaring as high as he could above Beril, until the lights from the buildings looked like their own kind of stars, winking up at their distant cousins high above them. He felt it was like being caught between two heavens, surrounded by nothing but beauty.

He whirled around suddenly as he heard a loud scuffling noise behind him.

Glassworn was jogging towards him, his coat swirling around his legs.

Haze rolled his eyes and resumed his walk down the street.

"Please, I wish to discuss something with you!" the man caught up to him, panting loudly.

"Go away," Haze mumbled, waving his hand tiredly. "I don't talk to lunatics and magicians."

"Lunatic?" Glassworn said, taken aback. "Excuse me, but I am of the finest breeding! Not a single maniac runs in my family bloodline. Though we have had a few eccentrics and one or two alcoholics."

Haze raised an eyebrow.

"Alright," The Druid exclaimed, crossing his arms dramatically. "*Several* alcoholics. Are you happy now?"

"Who are you?" Haze asked, blinking furiously. The light from the open door of the bar was shining around the man, accenting his silhouette and demolishing any hope of seeing the rest of his features. "I can't see you too well. And you are...a little weird, aren't you?"

Glassworn flinched, then scratched his head. "I will pretend you didn't say that."

"You do that." Haze said, turning away from him and continuing across the street.

"Wait, wait!" The man ran past him and cut him off, blocking his path. He put his hands together and opened his mouth to say something, then closed it. Then opened it again. Then closed it.

Haze squinted at the druid.

This guy looked like a fish caught out of the water. Or maybe he had really had too much to drink this time, and just couldn't hear what he was saying.

"How did you lose your arm?" Glassworn finally blurted, covering his mouth with his hands and drawing a quick, gasping breath.

Haze raised an eyebrow. At least he wasn't deaf yet. "You came running after me just to ask me that?"

"Well, it's not every day you get to see a battle-hardened warrior with one arm and nasty scars seated at a table in a bar, is it? Besides, everything else so far has been just dreadfully dull. I do believe you are the first color I have seen in this place since I arrived."

Haze closed his eyes and raised his hand. "Okay, wait. Where are you from?"

"Miasma City," the man said shortly. "And how I wish I was there now, drinking my *Bimogne Felai* and sleeping—"

"Stop!" Haze said sharply. His eyes snapped open and he frowned at the other man. "You're one of Jaelyn's spies, aren't you?"

Glassworn looked genuinely offended. "Me? Work for that horrible woman?" he shook his head violently. "Not for all the wine in the world."

Haze stared at him warily. "And you simply expect me to believe..." he trailed off, swaying unsteadily.

It felt as though the ground had lurched under his feet. The buildings along the street suddenly started leaning in towards the cobblestones, the light from their windows twisting into leaping shadows that danced across the street like flaming minstrels.

He yanked his dagger out of its sheath and pointed it at Glassworn. "You drugged me!" he wheezed hoarsely.

Glassworn took a step towards him, grabbing his shoulders with an iron grip and lowering him to the ground. "Technically, the barkeep did. Sorry, old chap," he sighed, "But there is someone that very much needs your help. I would hate to disappoint him."

Haze's world clouded, and the druid's face slowly faded away as it was replaced by the darkness of unconsciousness.

Chapter Five

A Heavy Heart

Alovere pulled the collar of his cloak higher around his neck, blocking out the biting cold wind that whipped in his face as they trudged east towards the ridge of the Mountain Range.

Galnoron seemed impervious to the cold, his hood blowing down repeatedly and exposing his bare face and neck to the elements. He wore no gloves, and did not shield his hands from the ice as he walked, standing straight as he was buffeted by the subzero temperatures.

They were in a barren tundra, nothing but drifts and icicles as far as Alovere could see in any direction. There were no hills or hollows: only a flat expanse of ice speckled here and there with the occasional frost-bitten pine, leaning away from the gusts as though trying to flee from the relentless onslaught of biting wind. The air was thick with white, the visibility lower than he had ever seen it. The wind picked up clouds of snow and rolled it across the open ground in sudden storms of miniature blizzards. They had been walking for nearly two days, the weather too rough for flying on Arginox.

Alovere looked behind him.

The great dragon's breath came in billowing puffs of steam, floating back in the wind to collect on his tightly folded wings and forming large, luminescent blue icicles that stretched towards the snow packed ground.

The Wyrm snorted a jet of blue flames and shook a dusting of collected snow from behind the horns on his head.

Galnoron had come this way before, supposedly. His telling of the landscape differed greatly, however, from the miserable whiteout they were trudging through now. According to the wizard, this was supposed to be a massive forest that stretched from the base of the Mountain Range all the way to the borders of King Orlivan's kingdom itself.

"This was a forest before," Galnoron said, leaning forward in a sudden gust.

"Yes, you said," Alovere snapped. "Keep your crazy stories to yourself, wizard. Just keep me from freezing, and I will keep you from being killed."

Galnoron glanced over his shoulder at him briefly, and Alovere thought he saw a thin smile under the sorcerer's hood.

They marched on in silence for another hour, before Alovere suddenly smelled smoke.

He sniffed quickly several times, looking around them. Spying a trail of gray to their immediate left, he pointed at it. "There!" he called ahead. "That must be the village."

Galnoron stopped and turned around. Looking at the small line of smoke in the sky, he nodded. "I was slightly off in my calculations, but it appears you are correct. We must see what they have for food. Entering the Mountains before stocking would be disastrous."

Alovere stomped quickly in the direction of the smoke, his vigor restored with the thought of a warm fire and hot food. It was a good distance away, and it was a full three quarters of an hour before they reached it.

They arrived outside a tall wooden wall, built from giant logs buried end up in the ground and bound to the log next to it. A massive gate comprised of hewn boards tilted precariously on its hinges in the front of the wall. Black scorch marks speckled the dark brown door, one or two still smoldering lazily.

"What happened here?" Alovere mumbled to himself, drawing his sword from its sheath as quietly as he could.

"Sh!" Galnoron held his finger to his lips. "Whoever did this may still be here."

Alovere froze mid draw, his sword halfway out of its scabbard. His heart hammered in his chest with the familiar rush of adrenaline that accompanied the possibility of a fight.

Galnoron leaned forward around the corner of the gate, his left hand balled into a fist by his side. A small glowing ember shone through the cracks between his fingers.

"What are you thinking, wizard?" Alovere whispered.

Galnoron shrugged, taking a slow step through the open gates. "Bandits, maybe. Hopefully."

Alovere placed his gloved fingers on either side of his blade and pulled it soundlessly from its scabbard, following the sorcerer through the gates.

The sight that greeted them was as horrifying as anything Alovere had seen on the battlefield.

Bodies were scattered about what looked like a market place, several produce carts at random placements in a small courtyard. Blood soaked the white snow like a crimson blanket of death across nearly the entire courtyard. The smell of burning meat and hair singed his nostrils.

Alovere tripped on something and sprang back in horror.

Staring up at him through lifeless eyes was a young boy, not more than ten years old. His face was pallid and still, eyes wide in his final moment of terror. Clutched in his hand was a small kitchen knife, stained with blood.

"Damn," he muttered.

"Dragon Rider," Galnoron called from farther ahead. "I think I found the source of our smoke."

Alovere looked where the man indicated, and saw a small house tucked away against the far side of the wall, a tiny wisp of smoke curling from its chimney.

Alovere clenched his teeth. "So, that could be good or bad," he stated, licking his lips.

"I am going to go out on a limb and say bad," Galnoron said jovially. "Being as the gate is open, logic would state that this is not one of the locals. If I were alive after a bloodbath like this, I would certainly have closed the gate after my attackers left."

"Unless all your attackers are dead and you won the battle," Alovere snapped. "What are you so cheerful about, anyway?"

"Oh, nothing. A nice, bloody mystery always keeps my spirits where they're supposed to be," Galnoron said happily, trudging through the field of dead bodies and snow towards the house. "What's the worst it could be, at any rate? An Algid? Bandits?"

"Which one of those is worse?" Alovere asked warily, following the wizard with his sword up. "What is an Algid?"

Galnoron laughed loudly, causing hairs to rise on the back of Alovere's neck. "Oh, they are a special sort of creature. Lots of cold and frost. Touching one can freeze you solid."

"Then why is the village in flames?"

"The villagers would have used fire to counter its attacks, I would think. They burned their own home to the ground trying to protect themselves."

"Great," Alovere muttered, gripping his sword tighter and glancing around himself warily. "One Algid can do all this?"

"Oh, certainly," Galnoron said. "They are some of the most powerful magical creatures I have ever encountered. I would hate to meet one in the dark somewhere. But still, face to face they aren't terribly difficult to defeat if one stays on his toes."

Alovere looked down at Galnoron's hand and saw the glow between his fingers change from a red to a bright yellow. "Why have I never seen or heard of one? I have been all over Elliset and never run into a creature like that."

"Because they aren't from Elliset, exactly," Galnoron said, slowing his pace as they neared the house. "They are from inside the Mountain Range. They are a side effect of someone leaving the Range without permission from the Keeper."

Alovere froze in his steps. "Wait, you mean this thing is hunting you?"

Galnoron stopped just outside the door of the small house and faced him. "Yes, it probably is." He smiled and winked. "I hadn't thought of it that way. Very clever man you are."

Galnoron spun back around and shoved the door open quickly, his fist blazing so bright Alovere had to turn away from the light.

"Hey!" he yelled, as Galnoron vanished through the doorway.

He leaped over a fallen cart and bolted into the house as quickly as he could, his sword held in front of him.

He stumbled into a small room with an overturned table facing the door, broken pottery and torn books jumbled all over the floor. The smell of burned clothing hung in the air like a vile perfume, the stench causing Alovere to gag slightly. The body of a man lay on the ground by the leg of the table, his clothes covered in a thick white frost. He looked to be about thirty, a little older than Haze. His hair was dark, and long, a small sword at his waist. A light mist rose off of him as he lay there, likely from the ice on his body evaporating in the heat.

The entire scene sent a chill crawling down Alovere's spine.

"Is this the work of an Algid?" he asked, pointing to the man with his sword. "Hello?" he said impatiently, looking up at Galnoron.

The wizard stood beside the table, staring silently at the fire crackling merrily in the corner of the room.

Seated by the table was a young girl, perhaps six or seven years old. Her brilliant green eyes were wide with terror as she shrank back from them, a hatchet gripped tightly in both hands. Dirty blonde hair fell in greasy curls down to her waist. She wore a simple green dress stained in blood and soot. A ragged hole was torn in the coarse fabric just above her right knee, showing a small scrape on her leg.

Alovere glanced at Galnoron. The wizard's face was an interesting mix of emotions, anger and exasperation being the dominant ones. He paused for a moment, then turned and strode wordlessly from the house.

"Hey!" Alovere hollered, "what are—we can't just leave her here!"

"Watch me," Galnoron answered from outside.

Alovere stared at the girl for a moment.

She was shaking violently by the fire, her eyes barely visible around the corner of the axe as she stared at him in terror.

He resisted the urge to cross the room and ask her name. He knew there was no way he could help her; they barely had enough food for themselves. Besides, there had to be someone else left in this village. Why would a seven-year-old girl be the only remaining survivor of this tragedy?

He shook his head.

Putting her out of his mind for a moment, he looked around the room. It seemed as though they were not in a house at all, but a store of some kind. Or at least, what used to be store.

Shelves lined both sides of the fire, covered in all manner of odds and ends, including small leather bags marked "Dried Frost Hen." A few others marked "Powdered Snake Scales" and "Ground Boar Tusk" sat on the shelves next to them.

He stepped over to the shelves and pulled his bag from his shoulder.

Grabbing handfuls of the dried frost hen, he dumped them into his pack. He also grabbed two extra waterskins and a tinder box off of a lower shelf.

Wandering over to the east side of the store, he poked through the garments for a moment before coming across a tightly rolled wool blanket bound with leather straps.

Picking it up by the straps, he swung it over his shoulder with his bag and turned to walk out of the building.

Pausing by the door, he glanced over his shoulder at the young girl.

Her gaze was fixed up at him, the axe now lowered to the floor. Her eyes were wide as she stared at him hopefully.

Turning away, he closed the door and started after Galnoron with a heavy heart.

Chapter Six
Tarian Ddu

A loud humming, followed by a rhythmic chugging sound snapped Haze out of his dreams and he shot bolt upright. His brow was slicked with sweat, and his head spun violently.

He blinked furiously, his eyes blurring in and out of focus. He winced as his head pounded fit to shame the worst hangover he had ever had. Placing the palm of his hand on his temple gingerly, he took stock of his surroundings.

He was in a large room, made entirely out of a dull grey steel. Shiny silver studs speckled the floor and the walls. The humming was coming from a giant crystal floating in the center of the steel room, its smooth surface glowing a bright gold. It was the size of a small dragon, suspended magically between the ceiling and the floor as it rotated steadily clockwise.

He seethed inwardly as he recognized it as one of the Prisms of Miasma City.

"Curse that druid!" he yelled, smashing his fist into the floor. "I knew he was working for that woman!"

The people of Glaistoff used mysterious prisms to power their giant aircraft called Vurekans, or Airships. Haze didn't fully understand it, but he was under the impression it had something to do with magic. This was why he steered as far away from it as he could, and never accepted any missions that led him and Salezz near Miasma City.

He heard a low groan coming from the other side of the Prism.

Leaning over until he was on his hand and knees, he shuffled as quietly as he could around the right edge of the glowing stone, his stomach in his throat.

The groaning grew louder and louder, a rattling, gasping sound that echoed off the steel walls and rebounded in his ears.

He rounded the corner and gasped. "Salezz!" he cried as he leaped to his feet and hurried towards the wyvern.

Salezz was laying on the steel floor, a small film of ice on the metal in front of his mouth. His eyes were rolled back into his head, his breath coming in ragged gasps. His saddle was twisted awkwardly on his back, his mouth tied closed by a thick black muzzle.

Haze fell to his knees beside the beast, running his hand over his neck. "What happened to you?" he breathed. "What's the matter?" He looked the Wyrm over as well as he knew how. There was no sign of injury, so he had not been attacked. He had slight chaffing around his neck where it looked like someone had fastened a rope or chain.

He growled to himself. If he ever saw that drunk again, he was going to wring his neck.

A loud crash sounded as a door flew open behind him.

Leaping back to his feet, he reached for his dagger. His hand grasped empty air. Clenching his teeth, he lifted his hand in front of him and braced his feet. He stumbled slightly as the room spun around him.

A small woman stood in a doorway that had appeared in the middle of the wall. She stood perhaps five feet tall, her black hair tied back in a tight bun and her arms held firmly behind her back. Her face was pinched in a severe expression, her eyes a cold blue. A dark uniform dress fell to just below her knees. She stood rigidly in the doorway, framing the light that filtered in from behind her.

"Welcome to the *Laudlin*, General Haze," she said, her voice sharp. "I hope you slept well."

"Who are you?" Haze demanded. "What happened to my wyvern?"

"Your wyvern is fine," the woman stated. "He was given a sleeping draft, same as you. Due to his explosive nature, it seems my crew panicked and overestimated the dosage. He will recover. As for the second question," she said, lifting her chin, "my name is Moxie. I am captain of the *Laudlin*, finest warship in his Majesty's Armada."

Haze's mind spun. His Majesty? Did she work for Orlivan, then? He didn't know Orlivan had airships. "I thought only Queen Jaelyn possessed the secret of airship flight?" he said warily.

Moxie's expression changed to something like disgust. "We should take a walk, Haze. Salezz will recover in time. I promise you that he will be well looked after."

"I'm not going anywhere," Haze retorted. "You had me drugged and taken from my kingdom. King Orlivan will have your head for this."

Moxie stared at him blankly. "I think not. Orlivan is too busy with his preparation to march into the Mountain Range to come looking for a single crippled Rider."

Haze glared at her. "I am General of His Majesty's Winged Demons, the finest airborne force in the world. He will come for me with every Demon he has at his disposal."

Moxie stepped to the side, gesturing out the door with her hand. "Shall we walk?" she said patiently.

"No!" Haze snapped. "I don't want to hear anything you have to say. You are a puppet for Queen Jaelyn and everyone knows what she wants. I will not help you bring about the fall of Orlivan's kingdom."

Moxie glared at him. "You can walk with me, or I can call for my first mate and have him drag you topside. Choose."

Haze hesitated. He glanced at Salezz, then back at Moxie. "Salezz comes with me."

"Your wyvern is drugged out of his mind. I promise you he won't wake for another three hours at least, and unless you intend to carry him yourself, he stays here." She paused and sighed. "I know you don't trust me, and you have every reason not to, but I swear to you on my life, you and Salezz are in no danger."

"How do you know our names?" Haze said shortly.

"We have been watching you for some time."

"Who is we?"

"Me, and my entire crew. Specifically, Glassworn."

"The druid!" Haze hissed vehemently. "He is the one that drugged me!"

"He is," Moxie admitted, "but it was under my orders. You must forgive him."

"Lying, cheating snake," Haze muttered. "Fine! Let's take your walk."

He pushed past her and stepped through the open door. It led into a long hall; the floors, walls, and ceiling were covered in a dark stained wood. Windows lined the right side of the hall, bright light gleaming in through the glass and casting shafts of yellow on the glossy woodwork.

"Whoa," he exclaimed.

"We are heading forward," Moxie said briskly, moving past him towards a set of winding stairs that led steeply upward. "There are a few people I would like you to meet, and some things I would like to show you."

Haze glanced at her. "Forward?"

"Towards the front of the ship," she explained. "Aft is the back, starboard is the right side, and port is the left side. Topside is on deck, below is where we are."

Moxie rattled them off so quickly that it sounded like she was talking a different language. "Why do I need to know all this?"

"Because you will be on the ship for two days," she said, "and in that time, you will be required to find your own way around and get your own food, etc. I will not give up one of my crew members to escort you around like a child."

Haze's temper flared up immediately. "Had you not kidnapped me I wouldn't be here at all! If you do have to give up one of your precious crew for two days, it's your own fault. Wait, two days?" he said quickly, suddenly realizing what she had said. "What happens after two days?"

"You will be leaving on a mission that you will accept," Moxie said shortly, "the details of which I will explain to you once I have introduced you to some of my crew."

Haze laughed bitterly. "If you think I will accept any mission you try to give me, you are sorely mistaken. I am loyal to his Majesty, and I would rather die than commit treason by working for your queen."

Moxie didn't answer him, but stopped at the base of the stairs and gestured silently for him to begin climbing. Her eyes were cold and flat as she stared at him.

He glared at her as he started up the stairs towards a small door he could barely make out at the top.

They were silent all the way up, Haze pushing open the small oval door that stopped them at the peak of the steps. A gust of wind blasted into the opening, shortening his breath and whipping his hair wildly. Grey light from an overcast sky was draped over the steel deck of the massive warship, the sky thick with darkening clouds. Men wearing dark black trousers topped with puffy-sleeved white shirts and knee length leather boots hurried across the deck, some shouting orders at others. Looking up, Haze saw a massive balloon made of black canvas suspended above the ship by chains running from the rails. Pulleys and cables were twisted around ornately made metal pegs at the base of each of the chains, each one molded in the shape of a hawk's head. The wind tore across the deck, whistling through the chains with an eerie shriek.

"Rhys!" Moxie yelled over the howl of the wind from behind Haze.

Haze jumped to the side as she pushed past him and stepped out onto the deck, her dark black dress whipping in the wind.

One of the men broke free from the mill of soldiers on deck and jogged over towards them. He was roughly the same height as Haze, but thicker than a dragon. His face was broad and clean shaven. He wore the same uniform as the rest of the men on deck, save for a black tailcoat with a high white collar that rose up behind his neck. A large broadsword was strapped on his left side, the hand guard composed of a mesh of steel wires nearly as thick as Haze's little finger. His brown hair was cropped short and neat.

"Aye ma'am," he said, bowing low to her when he reached them.

"This our guest, Haze," Moxie said, pointing at him. "I would like you to get the boys together so we can brief him on the plan."

A smile crept across the man's rugged face. "Very well, Ma'am. I'll gather the boys 'round, then."

He glanced at Haze, then turned around and cupped both hands around his mouth. "Alright, ye floatin' sky dogs! Her ladyship's wantin' a gatherin', so let's make it right and tidy over 'ere 'bouts!" he bellowed, the sound deafening even over the wind.

All the men immediately ceased whatever they were doing and started jogging in their direction. One leaped down from one of the chains that led up to the balloon, another hopped out from behind a strange metal tube pointing off the side of the ship, and still more came pouring out of different trap doors and deck levels that Haze couldn't even see. Finally, around forty men stood in front of them on deck, murmuring quietly to each other and straightening their hair in the wind.

"These men are my crew," Moxie said, gesturing to them. "We have a very specific favor to ask of you."

Haze frowned at her. "This is what you wanted to show me?" he said incredulously. "Your crew? What is this supposed to be convincing me of?"

Moxie pointed to the large man she had called over first. "He is my first mate. His name is Rhys. He lost his brother in the attack on Lorrik Kihl four years ago. They were killed by your Winged Demons, of whom you are so proud."

Haze glanced at her, a twinge of fear rising in his stomach. "I am a soldier. I don't remember every life I take. I have lost those close to me as well."

She ignored his comment, and pointed to another man in line. He was younger, perhaps early twenties. "His name is Myrick. He lost his father in that same attack. And this," she said, walking over to an older gentleman in line and patting him on the shoulder, "is Evyn." It was comical to see her march around her men so confidently, even though she was nearly half their size. The amount of respect they treated her with was astounding, however, and gave Haze the feeling that she was not one to be crossed. "He lost all four of his sons in the attack on your eastern village down on the continent."

Haze glared at her. "Then your queen should not have attacked it. What do you want from me?"

"I completely agree, as we all do." Moxie crossed her arms and fixed him with a calculating stare. "You are the best soldier in Orlivan's military, yes?"

Haze shrugged. "Maybe. That sort of thing is impossible to know."

58

"But you are his general, his favorite. You have survived things most men would die at the thought of." Her eyes strayed to the stump of his left arm.

"What's your point?" Haze snapped impatiently. "What are you getting at?"

"We want you to take your wyvern into the Mountain Range and find this power that is said to sleep there," Moxie said shortly.

"I would rather die than supply your queen with that kind of power."

Moxie glared at him. "You misunderstand me, Haze. None of these men serve Jaelyn. She is a warmongering child intent on driving the kingdom into the ground, and has cost each one of these men dearly. We serve our true King." She lifted her chin proudly. "We do not ask you to help Jaelyn. We are asking you to help *us* dethrone her. We fight for Lord Kinzin himself, Keeper of the Prisms of Glaistoff and rightful ruler of Miasma City."

Haze stared at them blankly. "What?"

"Lord Kinzin was banished from the kingdom for murdering his family. The truth is, they were killed before his eyes by Queen Jaelyn's henchmen," Moxie explained. "He has patiently awaited the day he could return and retake his throne from her. Now is that time, but we need your help."

Haze shook his head. "Wait, so Lord Kinzin is alive? Right now?"

"Yes, and we serve him loyally still, hiding right under Jaelyn's nose. She believes that we will fight for her in the upcoming battle for the Mountain Range, but we have every intention of preventing that battle from happening. If we can get Lord Kinzin back on the throne, he can bolster the peace between Miasma City and the City of Beril. Perhaps the battle for the Range will not consume the world in fire."

59

Haze's mind choked on the sudden rush of information. "You are mad to oppose her with one ship of men!" he said in bewilderment. "Common soldiers cannot stand up to her entire Armada!"

"We aren't common soldiers, Rider," Moxie said quietly. "We are his personal bodyguards." She lifted her chin, her eyes flashing. "We are the Tarian Ddu, the Black Shield of Lord Kinzin."

Chapter Seven
The Man of a Thousand Deaths

Alovere stared into the flames of the campfire. They danced merrily in the soft breeze that blew in the mouth of the cave they had sheltered in for the evening. Small bits of dry weeds dangled from the ceiling here and there, like massive cobwebs strung out across a stone attic. Galnoron had enchanted them to glow a faint, incandescent green color that shed a soft luminance across the cavern.

Arginox was too large to fit into the cavern, and so laid patiently in the mouth of it. His massive frame took up nearly the entire opening, blocking out the majority of the gusts that were still tearing across the plains outside. He was quiet, occasionally yawning, but otherwise silent.

The young girl from the village was seated on the other side of the fire, her gaze fixed on his. Unable to battle his conscience, he had turned back and brought her with them. Galnoron had sworn it was the biggest mistake Alovere had ever made, and was making a point to harass him about it every ten minutes, despite Alovere's multiple threats and warnings. She hadn't said a word since they left the village. The only communication she seemed to be capable of was staring at him intently whenever he spoke to her about anything. It seemed like she understood him when he spoke, at least mildly. She ate the food he gave her ravenously, as though she hadn't eaten in days.

"We should leave her," Galnoron's voice echoed from the back of the cave. The wizard was bent on staying as tucked away in the dark as possible, only the glow of his yellow eyes visible in the fire light.

Alovere choked on a Frost Hen bone and spat it into the fire. "She's sitting right here," he hissed at the sorcerer.

"Afraid she'll think I don't like her?" Galnoron shrugged. "Either way, she can't come with us. I don't have the magic to protect us all from the cold, and we don't have nearly enough food. You shared your rations with her this evening, but that isn't going to last, as we both know." He chuckled quietly. "She would last a while in this cave. Who knows, someone might even find her."

Alovere shook his head. "You're sick."

"And you are soon to be dead," Galnoron countered. "You're letting your feelings get in the way of completing the mission. If you keep feeding your food to a worthless little stray you're going to starve."

"All we have to do is make it to the next village and resupply," Alovere protested, looking at the girl. She was sitting with her knees pulled up tightly to her chest, staring at him silently.

"There is no other village. We just went through the last one before we head into the Mountains."

"Well we aren't just leaving her," Alovere said quietly.

Galnoron sighed from the darkness of his corner. "You are truly making this more difficult on yourself. And in the process, you are making it harder on me as well! Don't you understand she has nothing to—"

"Yes, the mission. I know!" Alovere snapped. "I am under no obligation to explain myself to you, and I have no intention of doing so! She will share my rations, and you will eat yours. Now please leave me in peace."

They fell silent for a moment, nothing but the crackling of the fire bounding across the empty cavern.

"I know why you insist on keeping her," Galnoron finally said.

"Leave me be, wizard." Alovere grumbled, poking at the flames with a stick and sending up a shower of sparks.

"The 'Man of a Thousand Deaths,' isn't it?"

A cold chill ran through Alovere and he looked over at Galnoron. The man's eyes glinted from the darkness of the corner. "Where did you hear that name?" he whispered hoarsely.

The sorcerer sat as still as death, not the slightest movement detectable in the gloom of his corner. "A little continent called Jiikk," he said nonchalantly. "Apparently there was a horrible man wanted for the murder of dozens of people. An assassin, they say. A paid killer. One so brutal, those that witnessed his killings called him the 'Man of a Thousand Deaths.' The legends claim that his victims felt that they had died a thousand times before he finally allowed them the peace of passing." Galnoron shrugged. "You were a handsome young lad, estimating by the picture."

"Picture?" Alovere said weakly. "What picture?"

"Someone drew up a likeness of you. Rather striking, I must say. You cut a fine figure in your blood-red armor back in the day, didn't you? It's a shame it was a wanted poster and not a portrait."

"Where is this picture?" Alovere growled.

"Safe, back at the palace," Galnoron said quickly, "and that's where it will stay, as long as we stay focused on the mission at hand." He leaned forward, his face coming into the light. His marred features twisted into a wicked a smile. "Tell me, Alovere. What did that poor man do to you to make you drag him out into the middle of a town square and cut all his fingers off? And burning him alive?" He clicked his tongue and shook his head. "Exquisite. Exactly how I would have handled it myself."

"Be quiet!" Alovere snarled. "We are nothing alike, you and I. What I did as a boy is none of your concern. Leave me be."

"You know, when we return from this mission, I will have a very lasting opinion of you." Galnoron said ominously. "I will then have to decide whether I like you well enough to keep this business of your youth to myself."

Alovere glared at him. "Tell the King, then. I don't respond to threats."

"Oh," Galnoron laughed, "I'm sorry, you misunderstand me. I have no interest in telling the King, but your wife? That would be interesting."

Alovere stared at him. "What could you possibly hope to gain from that?" he said in disgust. "You would ruin a man's life and for what? The sweet satisfaction of it?"

"Oh, no," Galnoron said in mock horror. "I never do anything without a very important reason. See, that's why I recognize you keeping this girl must be some attempt to remedy your past sins." He cocked his head. "Not that it works that way, but I find it interesting. Familiar, even. No one does anything without a reason, as I said."

"You don't know what you're talking about," Alovere grumbled, poking furiously at the fire and sending up more sparks.

Part of the wizard's words rang true. He boiled in rage at the thought, but there was nothing to be done about it. He had indeed kept the girl because he believed it was what Enial would have done.

"I know well what I speak of, Rider, and you would do well to listen to what I have to say. A time may come when your reputation may be the death of you."

"Enough!" Alovere snarled, glancing at the girl. She stared at him through the crackling flames, her eyes wide. "She can understand us. I am sure of it. Now what do you want with me? Out with it!"

Galnoron leaned back into the shadows, his face falling once again into darkness. "Nothing just yet, Rider. Nothing just yet."

Chapter Eight
The Havi Ut Gahdness

Haze stood in front of Moxie's wooden desk as she rummaged about in one of the drawers. Her quarters were far more luxurious than he had thought they would be. A plush red carpet lay across the entire floor, blanketing it in crimson. A few chairs were set out in front of the ornate and glossy wooden desk she sat behind. An enormous dresser stood against the port side of the cabin, sporting a mirror large enough to use as a lighthouse reflector. They were both thick with dust, cobwebs strung across them in a fine lace. A canopy bed rested by the starboard wall, the black blankets draped across it contrasting heavily with the light purple canopy and skirt. A plain trunk sat at the foot of it, beaten and marked by years of being hauled on and off of airships.

"Do you spend much time in here?" Haze asked, looking around curiously.

"Yes, I do," she answered, still digging in one of the drawers. "These are my quarters."

"I only ask because, well, it doesn't seem like you do," he said, looking at the dresser.

Moxie looked up at him. "These are my mother's old things. She used to captain the Laudlin before me. I took over when she was promoted to Armada Commander." She glanced at the dresser. "I am a simple person. I have everything I need in my trunk, and I sleep on the bed. I don't use the dresser, and I don't care for flashy colors. So, I use my own bedroll." She pulled a handful of papers out from the drawer and slapped them down on the massive desk. "Ah! Here we are."

Haze looked down at the parchments, but was unable to read the foreign scrawl penned across them.

She gestured at the seat across from him. "Have a seat. I am going to fill you in on what is going on between our two kingdoms. I have no doubt that you would like to know."

Haze nodded and seated himself. "I might as well, since escaping doesn't seem like an option."

"Not until your wyvern wakes up, and by that time, I don't think you'll want to." Moxie thumbed through the papers for a moment. "Now, I am not going to read you this entire story because it is exhausting, and the language is dreadfully complicated, but I will give you the gist of it: A long time ago, Elliset was very different than it is now. It was dry and desolate. It was ruled over by the Malgonian swine, who mined ice from the depths of the Boar Mountains. With the greatest commodity on the desert-like continent being water and ice, they held an iron fist over the other warlords of Elliset. But one day, they mined too deep into the Mountains and struck a sensitive vein. They released the heart of Elliset, a creature born of frost and ice. Cold washed over the land, freezing it solid overnight and wiping out nearly the entire population. This was called the *Rhew Mawr*, or 'Great Frost.'"

"I have never heard this story," Haze said, raising an eyebrow.

"That's because it has been carefully hidden," Moxie answered. "At any rate, this creature was known as the Ice Hyless. Lucky for Elliset, it felt badly about what it had done, and thawed the world back out, returning life to its citizens. Not only did it remove its cold, but it added things like rivers and plant life. It also created a giant Mountain range that rose in the center of the Continent in a massive circle."

"The Elliset Mountains," Haze said.

Moxie nodded. "Yes. It was unable to return to its home in the depths of the ice mines. The cold it needed to survive had been washed away when it was released into the world. So, it created a body for itself and sealed itself away in the Mountain Range, the peaks so cold no one has ever been able to enter them. At least, that's what we have been led to believe."

Haze frowned. "You mean people have been in the Range before?"

"Oh yes. Many times. Every one hundred years, in fact. Save for the last five hundred years when the legend of the Hyless remained jealously guarded."

"Why would it need to be guarded?"

"Every one hundred years, the Hyless is reborn in a new body," Moxie explained, "but when it is first born, it is weak, and its powers lie dormant. Until it is about seven years old, it is vulnerable and the cold falls away from the peaks of the Range. These first years are known as the 'Years of Mourning.' That is when the Hyless is in the greatest danger."

"Why?" Haze interrupted. "Shouldn't a creature of life being born into the world be something to celebrate?"

Moxie nodded and sighed. "Well, you and I may think that, but unfortunately that is not how the warlords of Elliset viewed it two thousand years ago. After witnessing the great power the Hyless controlled when it was first released into the world, they wanted it for themselves. They launched an attack on the Mountains in an attempt to kill the Hyless and steal its power. It became a famous game, in fact. Every century, the sons and grandsons of the first warlords organized a great search for the mystical creature known as the *Havi Ut Gahdness*, Hunt for the Hyless. During the Years of Mourning, the Hyless is forced to fight for its survival. Fortunately, the hunts were never successful. Fifteen centuries of the greatest warlords to ever rule never killed the Spirit. Five hundred years ago, the legend vanished entirely. It is said that the first Spellcasters of Miasma City still knew the legend, and wrote it down in a tome that was lost in the royal libraries of Glaistoff. They did this in hopes that the Hyless would never again be hunted."

"And the hunts stopped?"

Moxie looked at him over the top of the paper. "After a fashion, yes. Lord Kinzin tells me the Hyless was blessed with a handful of guards. They were called the *Aurrau von Gahdness*, or Guardians of the Hyless." Moxie paused. "Should these Guardians exist, you would do well to pray you never meet them. They were something to be reckoned with, by the stories Milord tells. According to Lord Kinzin, the last warlord to enter the Mountains was utterly destroyed, along with his entire army. It was a catastrophic defeat, over ten thousand deaths in the blink of an eye. The legend says that his force attacked the walls of a great city deep within the Range and that four Guards came out to meet him. They clashed outside the gate, and the Guardians decimated his entire military and himself."

Haze cleared his throat. "A little difficult to swallow, that one."

"Nonetheless, one must be wary. To venture into the Mountains believing that they didn't exist would be foolish."

Haze nodded. He knew where this was going. "Let me guess: someone found the tome, right? The one with the legend?"

Moxie nodded. "Queen Jaelyn found the book that tells the legend, yes. She counted the star charts provided within the book and discovered that the Years of Mourning were just beginning. That was over six years ago."

"Right about when she asked Orlivan for forces," Haze said bitterly. "Now we know where they went."

"They were taken to Miasma City for exactly the reason she said," Moxie explained. "to defend the city. When Jaelyn had sent her army into the Mountain Range to hunt for this creature, they encountered dangerous spirits." Moxie paused. "I was there," she said quietly, her eyes distant. "They had the same look as a human, though they had no faces. No mouths, or eyes, or ears. Their bodies were made from a perfect union of ice and metal, shining blue and silver. A faint mist rose off of them wherever they went. They wielded blades of frost and steel that couldn't be dented no matter what we tried. They killed dozens of us." She stopped for a moment. "We retreated, but Jaelyn had angered them. They followed us to Miasma City in an airship made of ice and laid siege to it for weeks before Orlivan's forces arrived and drove them away. We call them the Rime Born, as Kinzin told us they were named."

"Why did our men never return?" Haze asked. "Why did she keep them?"

Moxie shook her head. "There were none left. They had all been killed."

A chill ran down Haze's spine. "You want to send me in there? Why, exactly?"

Moxie looked up at him from the papers. "I believe Orlivan is going to launch an attack on the Mountains. I have received word that a wizard gave Orlivan news that the Mountains are open to travelers. That is because the Hyless has not yet discovered the use of its powers, and the cold that usually protects the Range is weakened. He will be able to march right in."

"You have spies in Beril!" Haze cried in disbelief.

"Yes," Moxie snapped, "but it is for Lord Kinzin, not for myself. I am trying to prevent a war! Now if what my informant tells me is true, that is about to become a lot harder."

"I was there when the wizard told him," Haze admitted, "but he claims he has to scout it first and bring back news of what lies inside."

"Yes, I know." Moxie said. "Jaelyn is also sending in more scouts right now. Soon, it will be armies."

Haze felt his stomach sink. "And you want me to be your scout?"

Moxie shook her head. "No. I want you to find the Hyless and protect it from these two lunatic warlords."

Haze blinked. "What?"

"I serve my Lord, Haze," Moxie explained. "He is a direct descendant of the original spellcasters that hid the tome containing the secret of the Hyless five hundred years ago. He doesn't believe that the Hyless is a creature that should be tampered with, and neither do I. The first time it was disturbed, thousands of people died and the world turned into an iceberg. It is now stuck here in this world with us, and while it is, it provides us with water and life. If the Hyless dies, the cold that once swept across the land may return. Or worse, life could snuff out entirely."

"How does this help you restore the throne to your King?" Haze asked warily. "I don't see the connection."

"I do not know," Moxie admitted. "He has not told me. He simply said to trust him, and to do as he says. He is my Lord; I do not question him."

Haze rubbed his chin. "One could argue that this is nothing but a child's tale."

Moxie nodded. "Yes, but the Mountains have been frozen for a hundred years. Now, they are suddenly thawed out once again. That was written in the text. It was also written that there would be people who try to steal the power of the Hyless. Orlivan may not know that the power is controlled by a Hyless, but he is bent on getting to it regardless." She frowned. "Haze, this is the Hunt for the Hyless."

Haze swallowed. "Why don't we speak to him? He is not an entirely unreasonable man. He will listen to me."

"He cannot be trusted. Lord Kinzin knows him, and says he will pursue the Hyless in hopes that Jaelyn does not find it first."

Haze nodded in agreement. He believed that is exactly what Orlivan would do if he told him. He could imagine the conversation right now, in which Orlivan says that he won't use the power, but must find it before Jaelyn so *she* can't use it either.

"Alright, now for the question that has been bothering me the most," he sighed. "Why me?"

Moxie smiled. "Lord Kinzin has watched you closely. He has deemed you more than worthy of performing this task, and for some reason beyond my comprehension, would allow no other to do it. Also, the borders of the Mountains are crawling with these ice men that chased us out the first time. We believe that your wyvern is native of the Range and could fly in without being detected by them."

"You believe?" Haze asked incredulously. "And you think your belief is enough to get me to do this? Really?"

Moxie frowned at him. "We have no one else we can ask or trust. Lord Kinzin is a very..." she paused and cleared her throat, "*spiritual* man. He spent three years looking for the person he believed was 'the one' supposed to find and protect the Hyless. You are that person. Is the security of the world not important to you?"

"I didn't say I wouldn't do it," Haze said, "but it sounds to me like these Guardians have it under control. Wouldn't you agree?"

"Times have changed," Moxie said quickly. "Five hundred years ago, there were no Boltcannons. There were no molded steel weapons. The Guardians did not face the deviousness of sorcerers; They faced gangs of warlords and their thugs. They would be hard pressed to fight against Orlivan and Jaelyn."

He nodded. That was true, at least. The more modern invention of cannons was rivaled only by the discovery of Arcane magic five hundred years ago. The amount of carnage that could be unleashed from a single airship was staggering if targeted correctly. Orlivan himself was only able combat the combined forces of magic and airships by way of his Dragon Riders; The Guardians wouldn't have that luxury. They would, in fact, be facing not only the airships and magic, but the Winged Demons as well.

He swallowed nervously as he realized he was slowly convincing himself to do as Moxie asked. Part of him was disgusted with himself; disgusted that she so easily predicted his reaction. The other part was impressed with her knowledge of him, and the matter at hand. She was obviously an incredibly clever woman. He sighed and thanked the stars she was on his side. Maybe if he got to the Hyless before either of them, he could find a way to prevent this war from happening.

"I'll do it," he said suddenly, before he could change his mind.

Moxie smiled broadly. "Excellent! You are doing us a great service, Haze."

The door banged open suddenly, and the drunken druid staggered into the room with a tray on his arm, two wine glasses perched precariously in the middle of it.

"'Scuse me, Milady," he slurred. "I brought the wine you wanted."

He started into the room, but his feet got tangled in the bottom of his long silver coat and he tripped, the tray flying from his hand and landing on the desk miraculously. The glasses weren't nearly so blessed; they toppled over, emptying onto Haze's lap.

Haze cried out and leaped to his feet, swiping uselessly at the drink.

The man looked up at him from his position on the floor and sniffed, wiping his nose. "H'llo Gen'ral."

"You oaf!" Haze bellowed, wiping at the sticky red brew that now coated his tunic. It was no use; it was going to be permanent.

Moxie gestured at the man exasperatedly. "One more thing, Haze. Glassworn will be traveling with you. I hope you don't mind."

Haze froze and stared at her in shock. "He what?"

"Lord Kinzin requests that Glassworn accompany you into the Range," Moxie sighed.

"You're joking."

"I wish I were," Moxie muttered.

"Great," Haze said crossly, glaring at the drunkard as he finished wiping the wine off his trousers. A large red stain had seeped into the front of the blue material. "I don't suppose there is any way for me to change his 'Spiritualness's' mind regarding this idiot?"

Moxie shrugged. "You could kill him."

"Captain!" Glassworn cried out in dismay.

"No, really," Moxie snapped, glaring at the druid. "If it wasn't for Lord Kinzin, I would have killed you myself by now. I must admit," Moxie said, shaking her head. "I wonder at Milord's choice of soldiers. A cripple and a drunk..." She sighed. "Such are the burdens of fealty."

Chapter Nine
The Elliset Mountain Range

"Now, you'll want to steer clear of the rudder," Rhys yelled over the wind roaring in their ears.

Haze's two days on the Laudlin had gone much faster than he had anticipated, and he had actually come to enjoy much of it. Rhys was a comical genius, always lighting up the galley with colorful jokes that caused the entire crew to burst into laughter. Evyn was a wild old man that had a knack for loading Boltcannon's quicker than anyone else on the ship. He had fired one off at Haze's request, soot blackening his face and his rampant white hair standing on end. He laughed wildly, black grime caught in his myriad of wrinkles. Moxie had run up on deck with a sword in her hand and sleep in her eyes, staring around the deck in a panic. Haze had laughed at this, but he was the only one. The rest of the crew had fallen silent until she had finished her ranting and yelling, and then chuckled nervously amongst themselves when she had gone below. Moxie commanded much more than just the common respect a crew would give its captain, and Haze believed it was because of her standing with Lord Kinzin.

Lord Kinzin's name carried a certain weight with it. Haze had only ever heard it mentioned in hushed whispers and behind closed doors. To be the one Lord Kinzin trusted with his life, lent Moxie a distinguished level of respect that no one would even dream of challenging.

It wasn't that they didn't enjoy her company: The crew often invited her to the galley in the evenings, and she would join in the laughter and games same as the rest of the men. She obviously enjoyed these sorts of evenings, likely because she had precious few moments where her crew treated her as anything but a feared and revered captain.

Haze couldn't help but feel warmed by the kindness and generosity of the warships troop. They were a familiar sort to him, as he had spent most of his life as a soldier. They had all lost something or someone close to them, and this brought them together in a unique kind of way.

But in spite of this warmth and cheer, he could sense a deep-seated feeling of dread. They knew their kingdom was at a turning point. If Kinzin didn't take back the throne before Jaelyn got her hands on the power of the Hyless, it would never happen. Haze thought it was because of this that they treated him with much the same sort of reverence as Moxie. He was the one Kinzin had chosen to enter the Range, and they believed he was their greatest hope of returning their King back to his throne.

Unfortunately, this mission didn't start quite how Haze thought it would.

He and Glassworn sat on Salezz's back, their saddlebags packed. The wyvern stood at the edge of the airship, his wing talons clinging tightly to the metal rail as he peered anxiously over the side into the swirling vortex of white below them. Moxie had remained in her cabin, insisting Rhys was more than capable of seeing them off. She had informed Haze of as many details as she could, as well as provided him with a map she had begun making when she had first ventured into the Range herself.

"What do you mean steer clear of the rudder?" Haze yelled back at the burly man, the wind whipping in his ears.

"Ye're jumpin' off the side of a movin' ship, mate," Rhys hollered. "When you get out into open air, we are going to pass you up. You want to be clear of the rudder or we'll knock ye with it."

"Why can't we just jump off the back?" Haze exclaimed.

Rhys winked. "Where's the fun in that? We placed a wager on whether or not ye can pull up in time." He leaned in closer. "My moneys on ye makin' the dive like a champ."

"Great," Haze gasped, leaning forward as Salezz stumbled slightly. Apparently, "anything for Lord Kinzin" only went as far as a good wager.

"What are you worried about?" Glassworn drawled from behind him. "I haven't flown on a wyvern before at all, so what could be worse than voluntarily jumping off the side of a safe haven into a swirling blizzard on the back of a temperamental creature with a mind of its own?"

Rhys grinned broadly. "Bein' pushed!"

Haze blinked. "Wait, what?"

He yelped as Rhys shoved his massive shoulder against Salezz's flank. They pitched down as the creature tucked his wings and plummeted towards the whirling snowstorm.

Glassworn's arms latched around Haze's middle and crushed the air from his lungs as they plunged through the icy tornado, ice chips and frost biting into Haze's face and numbing it instantly.

A gust blasted them from the side and sent them spinning wildly; Salezz opened his wings like great chutes and paddled them furiously to regain control, but it was no use. The storm battered them back and forth, Haze gritting his teeth and hanging onto the saddle with fierce determination. Another gust hit them, driving them downward even quicker than before. Salezz was forced to tuck his wings back into his sides and freefall.

Between their rapid descent and Glassworn crushing his ribcage, Haze was robbed of breath entirely, his vision beginning to fade.

The wind whistled loudly in his ears, drowning out thought and concentration, his only awareness the smooth leather of the saddle in his hand. Squeezing it tightly, he forced himself to take a breath. He could see light beneath them, a thinning in the swirling clouds. Leaning forward, he urged Salezz on.

Just before they reached it another gust buffeted them, knocking Salezz to his side. Glassworn was torn from the saddle, his arms losing their grip on Haze's waist as he was pulled from the wyvern's back.

"Glassworn!" Haze yelled into the squall, the sound of his voice vanishing in the howling storm.

The druid's body whipped in the wind like a loose sail as he shot above them, vanishing as he was seemingly consumed by the stormy grey clouds.

Salezz spread his wings slightly, and Haze pitched forwards towards the wyvern's neck as their descent slowed dramatically. The creature's entire body trembled with the effort as his wings strained under the load.

Glassworn suddenly appeared again, falling a little distance to the right of him. Haze leaned out, reaching towards the Druid as his body came closer and closer. He caught a glimpse of the drunkard's face as it whirled past; his eyes were rolled back into his head, lids partially closed. Salezz spread his wings even further, screeching in pain as the great appendages filled with air.

Glassworn's body suddenly spun towards them, crashing into Haze and knocking him from the saddle. He cried out as he fell, seizing Salezz's foot just before he was separated from his wyvern. He closed his eyes and held onto the scaly foot as hard as he could as they were whipped relentlessly by the raging wind. He willed the storm to pass, and for them to fall through the bottom of it and into clean open air.

He had barely thought the words when they burst through the bottom of the cloud formation and into steady air.

The screaming wind stopped abruptly. The howl of the storm died away, replaced by the soft rhythmic flapping of Salezz's wings as he glided slowly through the sky.

Haze opened his eyes, scanning the cloud-patched sky for Glassworn, but didn't see him anywhere.

"Salezz!" he called.

The great wyvern squawked a brief reply, before arching his tail around and hooking the back of Haze's tunic on the large silver barb adorning the tip of it.

Letting go of Salezz's foot, he allowed the creature to lift him to his back.

He breathed a sigh of relief as he saw Glassworn draped across the saddle. Apparently, he had become lodged there when he had collided with Haze.

Settling down behind the saddle, he unhooked his tunic from Salezz's barb and patted the creature's tail gently.

He shook Glassworn. "Hey."

There was no answer. The man's eyes were now clenched firmly closed, his right hand clutching something under his shirt.

Haze grabbed his shoulder and shook him hard. "Glassworn!"

The man gasped, his eyes flying open as he shot up straight, his eyes rolling around frantically.

"Take it easy," Haze said crossly. "We are on Salezz. We made it out of the storm."

Glassworn panted loudly, wiping the back of his sleeve across his forehead. "Where are we?" he asked, his voice cracking.

Haze looked around them, trying to see through the small patches of clouds. "I'm not sure. We have to go lower to find out. I would guess somewhere over a river, seeing how thick the clouds are, not to mention that storm."

Glassworn nodded, his face relaxing slightly. "I see." He then looked down at the saddle. "Say, aren't you supposed to be sitting here?"

Haze glared at him and didn't answer. He squeezed Salezz's left side with his leg, and felt the great creature begin to descend.

After a few moments, they passed through the wisps of clouds and into a sight like none Haze had ever seen.

Giant snowflakes fell all around them, the smallest ones the size of Haze's hand. Small wisps of clouds and mist were draped over the ridges and peaks of thickly wooded Mountains that towered above them on all sides like timeless sentinels.

Haze felt tiny in comparison to the crags; they were so tall he couldn't even make out their peaks. They plunged into the clouds above them like great spears, vanishing into the milky-white fog. Valleys and canyons stretched as far as they could see, etched into the ground as though carved out by the fingers of a giant. A river wound its way through the bottom of one of the nearest valleys, shining a brilliant sapphire in the overcast light. The entire scene was covered in boot-sized snowflakes that blanketed the landscape in white.

"Um...Glassworn?" he said slowly.

"Yes, I know," the druid muttered, brushing large droplets of water off his cloak. "We are in the Elliset Mountain Range."

Chapter Ten
The Assassin and the Girl

Alovere stopped in his tracks, shook his head, and squinted at the Range.

"What is it?" Galnoron said, stepping up beside him.

"I could have sworn I saw something go down just through that cloud," Alovere said, pointing towards the point of the tallest peak, veiled in a faint mist.

"Impossible," Galnoron said, lowering his eyes and marching forward towards the Mountains. "It's nothing but your imagination playing tricks on you. Things do not simply fall into the Range."

Alovere nodded slowly, staring at the peak. "I understand, it's just..." he trailed off, searching for the right words. "I swear it was a wyvern or dragon over that ridge."

"Please!" the sorcerer grumbled, pushing past him and stomping through the snow packed hillside.

Alovere adjusted the young girl who was riding on his back, and resumed his endless trudging. "Are you comfortable?" he asked her. "Are you warm?"

She didn't answer, as usual, but stared straight ahead of them blankly.

He had wrapped her in his blanket to stave off the biting winds that whipped across the frozen wasteland they had been traversing now for a full four days.

Biting his glove, he pulled it off and put his hand up under the blanket. He touched the bare skin of her feet, wrapped around his middle. They were cold even to his frigid fingers, and he could feel her shivering violently on his back.

"We need to stop and warm her again," he called to Galnoron, slowing to a stop and whistling for Arginox.

"We should have left her in the cave," Galnoron snapped as he turned around, the blowing snow packed into sleet on the left side of his hood. "This is taking too much time. This isn't the sort of journey you take children on."

"We have had this conversation already today," Alovere growled, lowering the girl to the ground and turning around. "We will not be having it again."

Scooping her up in front of him, he wrapped her tightly in the dull brown blanket and scanned the skies for Arginox.

They had sent the great beast ahead to check for danger, as well as to stay warm. Walking on the ground was too cold for the fire dragon, who was used to much warmer climates. The workout of flying through the storms was keeping him warmed sufficiently, though Galnoron swore that it wouldn't work once they were inside the Range itself. The cold draped over the peaks and ridges of the Mountains of Elliset was frigid enough to burn your skin on immediate contact, according to the sorcerer. He had the scars to prove it, which he was all too ready to show Alovere any time the Dragon Rider questioned his story.

Snow whipped up in a sudden frenzy a dozen paces away as Arginox flapped his wings vigorously upon nearing the ground.

Dropping down to the snow, the dragon snorted a jet of blue flames as steam hissed from where his claws sunk into the tundra. His crimson eyes scanned the area until they met with his master's. He took two massive strides and was by Alovere in an instant, his elegant features creased with concern.

"It's alright," Alovere said soothingly. "We just need to warm the girl again."

"Hurry it up, Rider," Galnoron said impatiently, crossing his arms and facing away from the others. "We don't have all the time in the world. Jaelyn is no doubt sending her own scouts into the Range. Orlivan would hate to be left behind."

Arginox snarled, baring rows of silver teeth that glistened like daggers. Alovere grinned smugly as Galnoron backed away a step.

"Easy, 'Nox," Alovere said, patting the dragon on the head. "Let's have the wings, boy."

Arginox bowed his head and lifted his massive red wings, wrapping them around Alovere, curling them over the top of his master like a scaly canopy. The cold and wind were closed out, silence falling on Alovere and the girl.

The great Wyrm arched his long neck over his back and tucked his head down into the tiny space with them, his glowing red eyes dimly lighting the miniature room.

"Fire," Alovere said.

The dragon drew in a deep breath and opened his mouth, a tiny blue flame springing into life in the back of his throat.

The effect was nearly instant: small heat waves shimmered in the air in front of the Dragons mouth, the snow they were standing on glistening with moisture as the little room filled with warmth.

Alovere pulled the blanket off of the girl and dropped it on the packed snow. Setting her bare feet down on the blanket, he held her arm to steady her as she stood on wobbly legs.

Her dress was soaked from the snow melting through the blanket and clung to her tiny frame in wet wrinkles and dirt.

He cleared his throat. "Go around the back of Arginox's leg and take your dress off," he said gruffly. "It needs to be cleaned and dried."

She stared at him silently, her eyes wide.

"I won't look," he said shortly, "but you can't be wandering around in this thing all wet. We need to get it dried off."

She blinked, cocking her head at him. She showed no inclination of removing it, either in front of him or behind the dragon.

He sighed and moved towards her, grabbing the hem of her dress. She flinched as he yanked it up and over her head, leaving her in her shift. Removing his red cloak, he dropped it over her shoulders and pushed her gently towards Arginox's makeshift furnace.

Pulling out his sword, he dug a small hole in the icy floor of their room and dropped the dress into it.

"Arginox," he said.

The dragon leaned forward and breathed gently on the hole in the ice, the edges melting into tiny streams and rivulets that trickled down to fill the bowl Alovere had dug. The dress drifted up in the tiny pool, flecks of dirt floating off of it.

He scrubbed the dress against the edges of the icy bowl, slowly working the blood and grime out of it. The water in the hole gradually darkened until it was nearly black with dirt and filth.

Lifting it out of the hole, he wrung the befouled water out of the cloth as best he could. Shaking it out, he turned around and held it in front of Arginox's mouth, steam billowing from the damp fabric as it began to dry.

He turned and looked at the girl.

She was watching him curiously, her eyes flicking from the dress to his face.

"I'm just getting it clean and dry," he explained. "It will be warmer."

She didn't answer, but stared at him silently.

"What is your name?" he asked, turning the dress around and putting the backside to the flame. "You have not said a thing since we met. How did you survive the attack on that village?"

She cocked her head at him in confusion, her blonde curls tumbling down in front of her face.

She either couldn't understand him as well as he thought, or was the strongest silent-type he had ever met.

Alovere sighed and shook the now dry dress in the hot air before holding it out to her. "Here you go. Put it on."

She looked at the dress for a moment, then dropped the coat to floor and lifted her hands above her.

Alovere rolled his eyes and slipped the dress over her head, pulling the hem as far down around her ankles as he could.

Straightening, he pulled on his cloak and lifted the blanket from the ground. Holding it in front of Arginox's breath again, he waved it in the blazing heat for a moment until it was dry, then wound it tightly about the girl.

"Now, you have to tell me when you get cold again, alright?" he said. "You can't just be freezing on my back and not say anything. I know you don't like to talk, but let me know somehow, alright?"

She stared at him blankly, her eyes flicking back and forth between his quickly.

With no answer, he glumly turned around and scooped her up, wrapping her legs around his waist again.

"Alright, Arginox," he sighed.

The dragon unfurled his wings and launched immediately into the air with a loud growl, nearly knocking Alovere off of his feet as he kicked up a miniature blizzard with his take off.

"Geez," the Rider grumbled, shifting the girl on his back a little.

"We have to get moving," Galnoron said shortly. "You continue to waste precious time on that child. Exactly what do you think our mission here is?"

Alovere groaned in aggravation. "Enter the Mountain Range, scout it out, and return with intel on the layout of any structures or civilizations. I know."

"And where in all that did you hear, 'drag along helpless little girl so she may be the cause of all our deaths?'"

"Just let me worry about the girl, alright? You worry about keeping us from freezing to death when we finally make it inside," Alovere said, pushing past the sorcerer and stomping towards the Range.

Chapter Eleven
A Noble Titan

Haze clicked his tongue quietly, signaling Salezz to slow their descent. They had fallen below the tree line now, and were nearing the snow-dusted forest floor. It was ridden with fallen trees, their limbs curled and dead. The trees that still stood were straight and strong, their needles a vibrant green-blue. Boulders and rocks were scattered randomly about the floor of the forest, all coated in a dense layer of ice and snow.

Haze kept his eyes peeled, watching for any sign of movement. The entire forest was dead silent, the sound of Salezz's wings beating the air the only noise echoing across the wilderness.

The wyvern touched down, whipping up a small cloud of snow as he settled into the small clearing they had chosen to land in.

Glassworn immediately swung off, clutching his stomach as his face slowly returned to a normal color, as opposed to its previous shade of green. "Never again," he moaned. "Wings are for birds. Not for men. Ugh..."

Haze ignored him and dropped to the ground by Salezz, rubbing his mount's head affectionately. "Good job, boy. You did great."

Salezz wriggled his neck happily, snorting a jet of frost. He yawned, showing rows of razor-sharp blue teeth.

"I know. As soon as we find a good place to set up camp, we'll rest. Alright?" Haze patted his neck and turned towards Glassworn. "Tell me you didn't just pack a bunch of alcohol into that bag on Salezz's saddle."

The druid looked up at him, his hands on his knees as he balanced himself. "I packed food, mainly. I threw an extra blanket into your bedroll so I had something to use. Whatever you packed is your business."

Haze looked back at his wyvern.

Glassworn's small blue rucksack was tied to the side of his larger saddlebags. Stepping over the Wyverns tail, he reached up and unbuckled the saddle bags, letting them fall to the ground. Untying his bedroll from the top of his saddle, he unrolled it and pulled Glassworn's blanket from the middle of it. He tossed it at the other man, hitting him square in face. "You carry your own stuff when you fly with me. I don't need any extra weight, and neither does Salezz."

Glassworn blinked. "It's one blanket!"

"Then you shouldn't mind carrying it."

"We are flying on the same dragon! What difference does it make?"

Haze glared at him. "First of all, he is a wyvern, not a dragon. Secondly, when we are traipsing through the forests, we will be walking, not flying. During these times, you will be carrying your own gear, and even when we are flying, keeping it separate."

The druid grumbled loudly and bundled the blanket up into a roll.

Haze returned his attention to the saddlebags. Reaching inside the one closest to him, he pulled out the small map Moxie had given him.

"What's that?" Glassworn asked, pointing at the small piece of parchment.

Haze picked it up and unrolled it. "A map Moxie gave me. Incomplete, by the look of it. It stops at the edge of Tundra Falls?"

Glassworn leaned back and sighed. "Oh, I know what that is. Tundra Falls was the farthest she had ever made it. The Rime Born were very concentrated in that area. There was one other spot as well, though I can't remember what it was called." He rubbed his chin, adjusting his blanket under his arm.

Haze dropped the map and looked up at the man from his position on the ground. "Have you been here before? How much do you know about this place?"

Glassworn lifted his hand, lowering his gaze. "Now, let's not get too upset about this, but yes. I have been here before."

Haze glared at him. "Speak."

"I was Moxie's personal bodyguard. For a while, that is. Until my drinking got carried away, and she had me replaced with some other oaf that can barely tell the difference between a sword and—"

"Leave out your personal problems!" Haze snapped. "What sort of danger are we in? Where should we go or not go?"

Glassworn clenched his lifted hand, an expression of forced patience flashing across his face. "We are in no danger should we avoid Tundra Falls and the tunnels beneath the ice. They are crawling with Rime Born for some reason, but we had not found out why by the time I was removed from Moxie's detail. The rest of the Range seems fairly hospitable, even magical."

"And what about those spirits? Do they know we're here? The Rime Born?"

Glassworn shook his head. "I don't think so. The way we came in was different. That storm was violent. We dropped directly into the center of the Range. It's a good long way from the Ridges, so let's hope we didn't alarm any of them."

Haze rolled his eyes. "Hope?"

The druid picked at something in his teeth. "Any other ideas? We will just have to wait and see if they know we entered. Give it a day, maybe two, and we will have algids chasing us. That will tell you everything you need to know."

"What is an algid?"

"You don't want to know."

"Yes I do, you idiot! I am likely to be chased by one if you are correct!"

Glassworn glared at him. "They are like clouds of frost and mist. Only they have teeth. Will that be all?"

Haze took a deep breath and scanned the map. "What is this?" He pointed at what looked like a poorly scribbled collection of buildings.

Glassworn leaned over and squinted at the paper, rubbing his right eye. "Don't know. That wasn't on there when I was with Moxie."

Haze sighed in frustration. "You aren't much use, are you?"

Glassworn shrugged. "'Worthless replaced drunk,' remember? Besides, I was rarely allowed to see the map anyway, even when I was part of her regular detachment."

"She didn't allow you to see the map?"

"Sometimes, to ask if I remembered something specific, like you just did. But not usually, no."

"So, she didn't trust you?"

"Oh, heavens no. She didn't trust anyone. It wasn't exclusive to me. Though I imagine my drinking didn't help my case."

"You don't say?" Haze returned his attention to the map. "That's where we're going to go," he said, pointing at the collection of buildings and poorly scratched marks. "It looks like it could be some kind of old ruin. Maybe it will serve as shelter if we can make it there before nightfall."

Glassworn nodded vigorously. "Wonderful idea. Let's go see about that. What could possibly go wrong?"

Haze raised an eyebrow at the drunk, who was standing with his arms wrapped around his blanket and a sour look on his face. "Is there something you don't like about this plan?"

"No! No, I think it's wonderful. We should definitely go spend the night in a dilapidated ruin that could possibly be haunted, and that has almost certainly become home to wild beasts of the Range. Which, I might add, are not friendly after any fashion. Oh, and they aren't really afraid of much, either. Like fire?" he said, chuckling nervously and shaking his head. "Doesn't bother them."

Haze folded the map deftly between his fingers and his leg, and began packing things back into the saddle bags. "So, you want to camp out under the stars in the Elliset Mountain Range, vulnerable to anything that strolls by, because you are superstitious?"

Glassworn rolled his eyes and opened his mouth to say something, then closed it. "Yes?" he said hesitantly, frowning in confusion.

Haze swung the saddle bags onto Salezz and tightened the strap down quickly. "Well while your being delusional, I will be sleeping indoors by a warm fire with hot food."

He swung onto Salezz's back and turned the wyvern away from Glassworn.

"Wait!" the druid called. He hurried over and climbed on behind Haze. "If I'm gonna be eaten alive by something, it might as well be indoors, and not outside in the cold."

"That's more like it," Haze smiled, spurring Salezz into the air.

The wind rushed past them as they climbed above the trees, the forest shrinking to a sea of green and frosted white beneath them.

They rose on a sudden draft. Salezz glided upwards on still wings, the Mountains dwarfing them on all sides.

"All we have to do is find what looks like a canyon a little to the north-east of here. The ruins are directly in the center of it, all the way at the bottom," Haze called over the wind. "I'm not sure how large this map is or how far away the canyon is, but I'm hoping it isn't far."

"Hope, huh?" Glassworn mumbled irritably.

"What's that?"

The druid cleared his throat and leaned forward. "Nothing. It shouldn't be too far. The Range isn't very large. It changes around sometimes, though." He burped loudly in Haze's ear, the smell of alcohol wafting across Haze's nose.

He swatted at the man's face, dropping the reins briefly. "What do you mean it changes around?"

"One day the canyon will be an hour away, the next day it will be three hours. Sometimes it's only a few minutes. It's always the same scenery, always the same place, it just seems to take longer to get there."

Haze frowned. "Is that some sort of magic?"

"Well, it's possible, yes, but it would have to be a form of Time magic. That is something very difficult to control. It's the most dangerous kind of magic there is. If that's what is going on, I would hate to meet the caster."

Haze urged Salezz into a faster gait, the trees whipping by below them. "Time magic? I thought there was only one magic? The arcane stuff?"

"Oh no. Time, Ethereal, Druidic, Arcane, Celestial, Astral, and more that I am sure I have not heard of yet."

"And time is the most dangerous one of all? How does that make sense? What about Celestial? Isn't that god-like or something?"

Glassworn shook his head and shifted uncomfortably. "Celestial is difficult to obtain, and often requires you to commit some horrid act of violence and thievery against the spiritual being you take it from. Unless it is bestowed upon you, that is. It has much raw power, but it doesn't have the consequences or finesse of time magic. Time magic is thought to be useless in duels and battles, and so the teaching was abandoned in most schools and traditions. But true masters of time?" He shook his head. "They are the deadliest spellcasters you will ever see."

Haze ground his teeth together. He didn't care how deadly any sorcerer was. They were the cause of his family's death, and he would have nothing to do with any of them. If this Mountain Range was somehow enchanted, he wanted nothing to do with it either. Magic seemed to be the cause of all of his misery. Magic took his parents. The hunt for the Druids of Val Ek Song took his arm. It was magic that now had him flying into the most dangerous place in the world, and magic sitting behind him on Salezz.

"I really don't care how dangerous a time wizard is," he spat. "If he gets in my way, I'll cut him down. Now tell me what I'm watching for."

Glassworn sighed. "The canyon is marked by a large stone outcropping that Moxie and I spotted on our first day. It seems as though the it cannot be entered from any other direction. If you try to climb, fly, or walk into it from any other place, it will just not be there."

Haze rolled his eyes. "That's an enchantment if I've ever heard one. Just what I wanted to spend the next few days right in the middle of."

Glassworn chuckled. "Yes, I'm fairly certain that's what's going on there, but it's better than running into the Rime Born again. I would sooner have a little dealing with an enchantment than a run in with a horde of faceless, steel wielding machines."

"Fair enough." Haze mumbled. "What lies inside?"

Glassworn shrugged. "Not sure. We only went in once or twice that I recall, but we never went that deep because of some odd looking creatures clinging to some of the rock formations."

"Did they look dangerous?"

"How can I put this in a way you'll understand?" Glassworn said, rubbing his chin. "Everything is dangerous in the Range. The only friendly creatures you will find in here are the ones that share *you* with their friends." Glassworn leaned back and crossed his arms behind his head. "If it's all the same to you, I might grab some shut eye before we get there. I don't really feel like fighting for my life on half power."

"Too late," Haze said quietly, nodding his head below them.

Glassworn sat back up and sighed. "Wonderful."

They were gliding over a massive fissure carved out of the ground. It was jagged and long, as though someone had taken a giant axe to the earthen floor. Boulders perched precariously on the upper edge, threatening to roll in on the slightest incitement. Green slopes bounded down the sides of the canyon, leading to a snow packed floor speckled with rocks and fallen trees. The canyon wound through the steep mountains like a dry river, vanishing from sight around the bottom of one of the massive crags.

"There is the pillar!" Glassworn said, pointing to a large outcropping of rock almost directly beneath them.

Haze pulled on Salezz's reins, turning him in a slow circle above the pillar.

There was a narrow trail leading into the canyon on the east side of the rock, vanishing under the large rock outcropping.

"I don't know," Haze said. "It doesn't look to be crawling with any creatures right now, does it?"

"I don't see any," Glassworn said, gripping the back of the saddle and leaning off the side of the wyvern. "But that doesn't mean they aren't here."

Salezz wriggled his neck and hissed uneasily.

"I know, mister." Haze patted the creature lightly. "Let's take it a little lower."

They descended slowly towards the large rock, bringing the ground closer and closer.

They scanned the floor of the canyon, but were unable to see anything aside from the scattered rocks and trees.

"It looks alright," Haze said. Small eddies of wind carried a thin mist through the canyon, faint, and low. Sunlight soaked into it from above, creating an undappled light that filtered down to the canyon floor, glowing a warm yellow. Salezz was chirping loudly, the sound deadened by the density of the clouds.

"Excellent. Shall we land?"

Haze narrowed his eyes. "I don't see anything. What creatures do you remember exactly?"

Glassworn leaned forward, his face next to Haze's as he scanned the ground below them. "Nothing spectacular. Little scurrying things that were tough to make out in the dark. Because of course, that's when Moxie brought us here." He cast a sidelong glance at the Wyvern Rider. "Think dog. That's what it looked like."

Haze put his hand on the Glassworn's forehead and pushed him back into his seat. Shifting in the saddle, he rubbed his face and stared down through the swirling mist. He couldn't see anything that made him think danger, but Salezz was uncomfortable. He had learned a good long while ago to trust his mount's instincts. They had saved him on more than one occasion, and the one time he ignored them was the day he lost his arm.

A sudden image flashed before his eyes; a massive armored swine, fire seeping from the corners of its mouth, lifting its blade in preparation to strike his arm from his side.

94

He swallowed and shook his head, clearing the memory. "We will land somewhere else. Salezz doesn't like it."

Glassworn moaned quietly. "Fine. Not that I mind, as I was against the idea to begin with. What other place do you have in mind?"

Haze turned in the saddle, straining to look back at the man. "Me? What about you? You're the one that's been here before! Do you have any ideas of where we should go?"

"Hey, I was drunk nearly every time I came down here," Glassworn drawled, taking a swig from his flask. "I don't remember much."

Haze rolled his eyes. Of all the people he had to get stuck with, it had to be the worthless drunk that couldn't tie his own boots.

A loud screech sounded directly above them, causing Salezz to veer suddenly to the right. Haze cursed and gripped the saddle tightly, swaying atop the wyvern. "What was that?"

He heard Glassworn gulp loudly behind him. "Okay, *that* I remember."

"What is it?" Haze asked, scanning the skies above them. He could see nothing but swirling grey clouds draped in the sky like drawn curtains, cloaking whatever lay behind them.

"I remember the screech," Glassworn exclaimed. "That doesn't mean I remember what it is!"

Something collided with the back of Haze's head, knocking him forward and jolting his vision.

He whipped his lance out of its sheath on Salezz's side and sat back up, looking around them anxiously.

As he turned in his saddle and looked above them, he saw it.

Diving towards them was what looked like a bat, its body glistening ice blue in the faint light. Its eyes were a vivid yellow, glowing like miniature suns in its crystalline skull. It had to be at least the size of a large dog. It's mouth opened wide to reveal rows of white teeth.

"Dive!" he yelled to Salezz, who immediately began dropping towards the canyon.

The wind whipped in their ears as the canyon floor grew closer and closer, the sound of the bat shrieking behind them joined by a multitude of other screams as more of the creatures gave chase.

One of them appeared at his right, and he struck out with his lance. The creature shattered into pieces when the tip struck it in the side.

"Okay, now I remember what they are!" the druid shouted over the screeches and wind.

"Shut up, Glassworn!" Haze hollered, striking at another bat as it gnawed on Salezz's reins.

He veered Salezz hard to the right around the top of the rock outcropping, diving beneath it and sliding to a jolting stop on the canyon floor.

He spotted a cave beneath the outcropping. "There!" he yelled, swinging off the wyvern and pulling the creature towards the cave.

Glassworn tumbled off of Salezz and picked something out of his pocket. Tossing it into the air, he murmured something quietly and a tiny glimmer of silver buzzed angrily around his head. He flicked his wrist and the miniature silver fleck hissed through the air, zipping through three bats and vaporizing them into dust.

The sky was alive with fangs and wings, the bats making regular dives at them before veering off and climbing back up out of reach. The screeching of the creatures intensified as they got closer and closer to the cave mouth, surrounding them like the squeal of a thousand rusty wagon wheels.

Haze sprinted as fast as he could, pulling hard on his wyvern's reins.

They reached the edge of the cave and stumbled inside, Haze turning around to see Glassworn just outside. He was scrambling frantically on all fours, whimpering quietly.

Haze dropped his lance and hurried out, grabbing him by the shoulder and hauling him to his feet.

"Wait!" the druid cried. "My flask!"

"For the love of life, man!" Haze exclaimed, trying to drag Glassworn back into the cave. His hand slipped on the smooth fabric of his coat and the drunk fell back to his knees, his hands flying across the ground desperately.

Haze ducked as a bat shot towards his head, and heard it shatter on the rock outcropping behind him. Several more wheeled around and dove straight for them.

"Glassworn!" he yelled, stumbling backwards.

The man shot to his feet, his flask clutched to his chest. His eyes rolled wildly as he bent low and hurried towards the cave mouth.

Haze took a flying leap and landed on his side just through the opening of the cave, Glassworn staggering in behind him.

"Salezz!" Haze yelled, pointing at the open cave mouth. The bat-like creatures were pelting towards them at full speed, fangs bared.

Salezz roared, the sound like thunder trapped in a bottle. A jet of bright blue light shot out of his open maw, hitting the cave ceiling. Under the steady stream of the wyvern's breath, a glowing blue barrier of ice slowly extended down towards the ground. It hung like a frigid curtain in the entrance of the cave, the sound of bats crashing into the outside of it echoing in the darkness of the cavern. After several moments of screeching and repeated thuds into the wall, the sound died away. Haze held his breath, his heart thrumming in the silence. After a moment of quiet, he let it out in a whoosh.

He turned and glared at Glassworn.

They were plunged almost completely into darkness, the only light coming from the makeshift wall Salezz had created. It cast a faint blue glow on walls and floor, illuminating Glassworn's face as he stared at the barrier in amazement.

"Maybe I had too much to drink," he began, pointing at the curtain of ice.

"Yes, you have," Haze snapped. "Do you realize that going back for that stupid flask could have cost all three of us our lives?"

"Precisely why I went for it," Glassworn said jovially, all traces of terror gone from his eyes. They were once again half lidded and empty. "Heavens forbid you have to deal with me after I have gone too long without a drink."

Haze looked at his pocket. "What did you do to those bats out there?"

Glassworn stared at him silently for a moment, then reached into the pocket of his long silver coat. He pulled out a tiny metal insect. It was not even as large as the tip of Haze's little finger, with miniature metal wings fixed to its back. It looked to be made of the same material as his coat. "This is a very special creature," he said quietly. "I told you I am a druid. Well, druids have a connection to nature that most people do not understand. I have learned to use that power to connect to very special things, such as certain creatures, or metal. In this case, a mixture of both."

The druid's eyes glowed briefly, a bright blue color.

The tiny insect's wings suddenly fluttered, and it rose buzzing off his palm.

"What is it?" Haze asked, staring at it warily.

"It is called a Noble Titan," Glassworn answered, staring at the object floating in front of him. "Named in irony of its size, yet great prowess in battle. It is friendly, and serves me loyally. I saved it from being melted in the forges at home and made into an arrow head. It was mixed in with the metal scraps. He may well be the last of his kind."

Haze frowned. "It's alive?"

"Not exactly. He is brought to life through me, but cannot live without my power. They were created a long time ago by master craftsmen of Miasma City. They are an old weapon of the druids, along with the coat I wear. Both can be manipulated to great effect by my spells."

"Do me a favor," Haze said impatiently. "Tell me now if there is anything else I need to know about you. This instant."

Glassworn snatched the little insect out of the air and dropped it back into his pocket, pulling his flask out of his belt. "I drink."

Haze growled and shook his head. "Ugh!" He stood up, brushing himself off. "Help me find out where this tunnel leads."

Glassworn nodded as he lifted his flask to his lips.

"Do not drink that in front of me!" Haze snapped, slapping the bottle from the man's hand and sending it skittering and clanking across the cavern floor.

Glassworn's mouth hung open as he watched it bounce off the cave wall and fall still, liquid pouring slowly from the tip.

"You have had enough of that! I need to be able to rely on you. I can't have you drinking yourself to oblivion on this mission. Moxie is counting on us to find and defend the Hyless at any cost."

Glassworn licked his lips and fidgeted, his eyes fixed on his flask. "Absolutely."

"Which adds a new objective to said mission: keeping you alive!" Haze said exasperatedly. "I can't do that if you are staggering around in a drunken stupor."

Glassworn drew himself up to his full height, eyeing Haze defensively. "I may spend the majority of my conscious hours fashionably inebriated, but I *certainly* do not stagger!"

Haze glared at him. It was all he could do to keep himself from slugging the drunkard directly in the eye. "You are going to run out eventually anyway," he breathed through gritted teeth. "So, when we stop for the night, I suggest you make the most of it and chug the whole thing, because I don't want to see you nursing on it for the entire trip."

"Actually, it's an enchanted flask."

"What?"

Glassworn gulped. "Uh, it has a minor enchantment on it. It holds about three kegs worth of whatever you put in it."

Haze's jaw dropped. "And you filled it with alcohol?"

"Well, yes." Glassworn blinked, his expression puzzled. "What else would you put in it?"

"Water, you dunce!" Haze bellowed.

There was a resounding crack, and a fracture suddenly appeared in the curtain. It started at the top, zigzagging its way all the way to the bottom of the makeshift wall. A small chip popped out onto the stone floor at its base.

Haze and Glassworn looked at each other.

"Let's go," Haze said shortly, picking up his lance. He marched over to Salezz and grabbed his reins. "Our only option is to go further in. I don't want to try and face off against a hundred bat things with nothing but a lance and the local boozer."

100

"They are called Verglas Bats," Glassworn said, scooping his flask up off the ground gingerly. He closed the lid and inspected it thoroughly. "At least, that's what Moxie says Lord Kinzin calls them. I could be wrong."

Haze turned and stared at him incredulously. "You knew what they were the entire time? Right down to their name?"

Glassworn looked up from his flask and swallowed. "N-no, I couldn't remember at first. It came to me though."

Haze turned and stalked down the tunnel, pulling Salezz with him. "It came to him," he muttered under his breath. "Of course, it did. Not like it would have been helpful to identify these monsters *before* they 'came to him.' Worthless idiot. I should have just let him die looking for his flask. That would have been the easier thing to do, I'm sure of it. Less trouble. Less stress. Less—"

"Haze." Glassworn's voice drifted up from behind as his armored boots clanked down the stone cavern. "Can I still finish what's in the flask tonight, or…?"

Chapter Twelve
Tell-Tale Evil

Alovere leaned back, trying to see through the mask of wool he had wrapped around his face.

They had been in the cold of the exterior Range for a full day now, Galnoron having had to renew the enchantments on him and Arginox every three hours. He had refused to enchant the girl, so Alovere had her wrapped tightly in his blanket and was stopping to let Arginox warm her every hour.

He grinned to himself slyly. If they kept stopping, he knew it was only a matter of time before Galnoron tired of waiting and simply enchanted the girl.

The sorcerer had not yet mentioned it, however, and was now standing at the edge of a cliff that barred their way forward. The bottom was out of sight, hidden by a sudden drop off that vanished into a sea of swirling snow and ice.

"How far down do you think it is?" Alovere yelled over the noise of the constant storm.

Galnoron turned and faced him, his hood frozen around his neck. Ice coated the stubble of a beard he had grown in the last few days. "No way to tell. Too far in this storm to fly your Dragon, I can tell you. His wings would break in the gusts. The distance changes dramatically, and randomly. It is most likely the work of a time magician."

"So how do we get down there?" Alovere snarled, shifting the girl's weight on his back. Her fingers were cold against his neck, like little icicles wrapped around it. "You can't seriously expect me to climb down a sheer rock face?"

Galnoron glanced at him and smirked, reaching under his robe and pulling something free from inside.

It was a rough brown rope, a little bit longer than Alovere himself. Fastened to one end was a large metal grappling hook.

Alovere pointed at it and chuckled. "You have the right idea, bringing a rope. I think it's missing a couple a hundred feet, though."

Galnoron didn't answer. He simply bent down and fastened the hook on the protruding edge of the stone cliff, tugging on it to make sure it was secure. Turning around, he then lowered himself over the edge and began a slow descent into the storm.

Alovere hurried over, leaning carefully out over the precipice. The sorcerer had vanished into the snow and ice, the taut rope magically extending in size and stretching down in the vortex of white.

He watched it anxiously as it swung back and forth, quivering under the strain of the other man's weight as he lowered himself into the abyss.

After several long moments, the rope went slack, blowing wildly in the wind. A few seconds later, it steadied and shook twice in quick succession.

Alovere lowered the girl off his back and turned around to face her. "I am going to go down first. I don't think the rope will hold both our weight combined. You will have to climb down after me. Okay?"

The girl's face was mostly hidden behind the wool blanket wrapped tightly around it. Her eyes glistened like emeralds behind it as she cocked her head at him curiously.

Alovere sighed. Standing up, he pointed at the rope, then grabbed her hands and shook them, pointing at the rope again. Her expression remained quizzical, scanning his face for an answer.

He groaned and turned away, heading for the rope. "Meet you down there, 'Nox," he called to Arginox.

The mighty fire dragon roared in response, belching a cloud of blue flame.

Grabbing the rope, Alovere began his descent.

He sucked in a breath as wind buffeted him from all sides, sleet blasting down his collar and freezing against his bare chest. He tucked his chin and slid quickly, the coarse rope digging into his hands and causing them to burn, even in the frigid temperatures.

He grabbed lower on the rope, but ice had frozen in a glass-like sheet on its surface, and his hand slipped. His heart leaped into his throat as he plummeted downward, his hands sliding over the line with an unwanted efficiency. He squinted, trying to keep the sleet from pelting his eyes.

He glanced below him and saw a dark shape protruding from the cliff face like a crooked dagger.

His heart sank when he saw it was a large rock outcropping, and he was speeding helplessly towards it. He realized with sudden dread that he was moving too fast to change his course. His hands burned like fire as he squeezed the rope harder and tried to slow his descent.

Seconds before he collided with it, he kicked at the face of the cliff in desperation. His boot made contact with the rock wall and he swung away from the outcropping. He rushed past it, the sharp point of the stone ledge missing his eye by mere inches.

He jolted painfully to a stop as his hands reached a part of the rope that had not yet been frozen.

Panting heavily, he turned and looked down. He could see Galnoron's dark silhouette in the blowing snow.

He let out a breath of air and slowly climbed the rest of the way down to the sorcerer, dropping the last four feet or so onto the snow packed ground.

Galnoron looked him up and down curiously.

Alovere self-consciously straightened his wool mask and brushed packed snow from around his collar. "What?" he snapped. His hands smarted hotly, the skin on his palms and fingers torn from the rough line.

"You look disheveled, Rider," Galnoron said in amusement. "It's a rare treat to see you in this state."

Alovere turned away from him, sighing to himself. He shook the rope hard twice.

"You really think she is going to climb down that rope on her own?" Galnoron laughed. "You are truly one of the most naive people I have ever met. She is a young girl who clearly can't speak our language, if she can speak at all, and is obviously traumatized by whatever horrible event happened to that village we came across. Somehow, you are obsessed with the idea that you can...what? Redeem yourself of past wrongs by caring for her?"

"It's none of your concern, Wizard," Alovere snapped. "Mind your magic spell that's keeping us alive and quit harassing your bodyguard."

"My bodyguard?" the sorcerer scoffed. He folded his arms and glared at Alovere. "The man who is guilty of so many things that he feels the need to seek redemption in the form of an orphaned girl? The man who runs from his past because he doesn't have the ability to face it and bring himself to justice? Is this man my bodyguard?"

"Quiet!" Alovere growled, focusing on the rope as it swayed gently back and forth.

"No, I don't believe you have the luxury of quieting me, soldier. Your failures and misguided youth have turned you into a man that hardly has the power to push through day to day life, let alone protect me." Galnoron smiled wryly. "Or even worse, to compete against such a competent warrior as Haze. No wonder the King hardly acknowledges your presence. Haze's shadow is cast on everything you do, everything you say. He will forever be his Majesty's favorite."

Alovere felt his rage boil over. Before he could stop it, his sword flashed out of its scabbard. He pressed its tip against Galnoron's heart, the wizard's robes drifting around it in the cold breeze.

"One more word," he breathed, his heart racing and teeth clenched, "and I will take your life so slowly you will wish you had never been born."

Galnoron smiled broadly and nodded, waving his hand lightly in the air.

Alovere heard a high-pitched scream, followed by a resounding crack high above them.

He whirled around and saw a short length of rope coiled at his feet.

"You bastard!" he roared, wheeling on Galnoron. "What have you done?"

"I simply unhooked the rope," Galnoron shrugged. "It seems as though your precious little girl met with that ledge you narrowly avoided on your way down. Pity. I think she was starting to like me."

"You killed her!" Alovere bellowed, leveling his sword at Galnoron's neck.

"Yes," the wizard said quietly, "but you are no stranger to that, are you? Why should one more death bother you?"

Alovere blinked, rage clouding his vision. He knew he couldn't kill Galnoron; his Majesty was relying on him. Enial was relying on him. He couldn't betray either of them like that.

"If it bothers you so much," Galnoron shrugged, "go ahead and kill me. Or," he added, bending down and picking up his rope, "we can continue with our mission the way we should have from the beginning, and forget the girl ever happened."

Alovere was sorely tempted to remove the wizard's head right there. His sword arm twitched like a charger waiting to be loosed by a battle horn. He thought of what he could tell Orlivan: Galnoron had died upon entering the Range, that he had been beset upon by wild beasts and there was nothing Alovere could do. There would be no one to say otherwise; no one had ever been in the Range before. As far as the general populace knew, there were all manner of beasts inside the Mountains.

A vision of Enial smiling at him brightly suddenly flashed into his mind, and his heart melted. He couldn't let her down. He couldn't.

He lowered his sword slowly, glaring at the sorcerer. "Be silent," he seethed, sheathing his sword and turning away. "My patience has reached its end. Keep me alive, and I will do the same for you."

Chapter Thirteen
An Angered Algid

Haze walked as softly as he could. The sound of his boots clicking on the stone floor echoed off of the walls of the cave, reverberating in his ears and filling the entire cavern with the sound of a thousand scurrying insects. He tried to stay as quiet as possible, not knowing what creatures might live in the depths of the tunnels.

From behind him, however, thundered Glassworn. He staggered and belched his way through the cavern like a drunken dragon, occasionally belting out a terrible tune that made the Wyvern Rider wince in physical pain. Even Salezz had taken to whining and attempting to tuck his lizard-like head between his wings when the drunkard began to moan out the first lines of what he must have thought was music.

The cave got darker and darker the farther away from the ice curtain they went, and so Haze had taken the lamp out of the pack. While it was a sound plan to bring a light source, Haze had noticed with irritation that Glassworn had not packed any fuel source for the lantern. After the first three hours of their trek into the cavern, it had gone out and plunged them into darkness.

After Haze had ranted and thrown a terrible fit about Glassworn's scatterbrained packing job, the drunk had a moment of genius and opened the lantern. Holding it in front of Salezz, he coaxed the wyvern into breathing his magical ice onto the wick. It then glowed much like the ice curtain at the mouth of the cave, magnified by the glass shade and casting a brilliant blue light on the three of them and the surrounding walls.

Haze had snatched the lantern without thanking him, muttering angrily to himself as he stomped deeper into the cavern. He had briefly entertained the idea of losing Glassworn in the tunnels, but thought better of it when he imagined the drunk panicking if they came upon each other in the shadows and shooting him with his metal bug by accident. In the end, they traveled together in relative silence. The only conversation was when Glassworn would begin to sing, and Haze would tell him to shut up.

This went on for some time until they came to a fork in the tunnel.

Haze stopped abruptly. Glassworn crashed into him from behind and sent them both tumbling to the ground.

"Watch it!" Haze snapped.

Glassworn stumbled precariously for a moment before regaining his footing and squinting at Haze. "What's going on?"

"There's a fork in the tunnel," Haze said, climbing to his feet and pointing out the obvious.

Glassworn narrowed his eyes at the tunnels. After a moment, he shrugged and looked back at Haze. "If you say so. I thought there were two the entire time."

Haze stared at him flatly. "Of course you did."

Glassworn burped, the sound echoing off the walls and repeating itself a myriad of times before fading into the distance.

Haze glared at him. "You truly lack all forms of intelligence."

"I've known plenty of people who were sharper than whips and were miserable company," Glassworn said carefully, as though choosing his words was quite the workout. "At least I'm not an unpleasant person."

"I'd prefer miserable company if it were useful!" Haze hissed.

Glassworn looked up at the ceiling for a moment, his mouth hanging open. "Fair enough," he shrugged again, looking back down at Haze. His eyes were slightly crossed.

"Ugh," Haze groaned in exasperation. He randomly chose the right tunnel and started his way down it, whistling shrilly for Salezz.

"So! Right it is," Glassworn said cheerfully, strolling after him.

The caverns leaped and twisted in every direction, forcing Haze to keep close track of every side jaunt they took. He didn't want to get too deep inside them and find out they didn't actually open up at some other entrance.

Haze frowned and tried to block out the racket of Glassworn's latest composition from behind him, scanning the walls and ceiling of the cavern warily.

He was letting the druid get on his nerves, and it was destroying his attentiveness to his surroundings. He was now fuming at Glassworn, and afraid that they would be attacked by wild beasts that he neglected to notice due to his anger. He had already nearly thrust his lance through Salezz's eye when the wyvern crept up behind him and nudged him in the side.

After a while, the druid quieted down and strolled behind the Rider silently, the only noise being the bubbling sound of his drinking.

Haze slowly relaxed as the time slipped past, his nerves frayed to their last edge.

It was two blessed hours of silence before Glassworn spoke again. "I say. Do you smell that?"

Haze stopped and rolled his eyes. "If you start singing a song about smells, I am feeding you to Salezz."

The wyvern seemed to rather like this idea, as he chortled and wriggled his neck delightedly.

"No, not at all." Glassworn mumbled. "This smell's truly interesting. Sort of like..." He paused, rubbing his chin. "You know what, I'm not sure."

Haze turned his head side to side, trying to smell whatever it was that the drunkard was smelling.

Taking a deep breath, he caught a whiff of the odor. It was like a cold winter morning, or a frozen pond with a fog hanging low above it.

Something inside him clenched tightly, his instincts warning him against the powerful odor.

He wrapped his fingers around the hilt of his sword. "Glassworn, didn't you say Moxie avoided these caves?"

"Yup," he answered nonchalantly. "She was scared enough of the things we ran into above ground. She didn't want to risk venturing into the deeper parts of the Range. Her words were, 'I will not wander into the bowels of an obviously perilous land with the foolish belief I will return unscathed,' or something of the sort. She always uses such big words."

Haze didn't hear most of what Glassworn had said. The words "she was scared" were the ones that lodged firmly in his mind. He had known Moxie only briefly, but in that short time he had learned a valuable lesson: Anything Moxie was afraid of, he wanted nothing to do with.

He turned around and started marching back down the tunnel.

"H-where are you going?" he heard Glassworn call from behind him.

"Back to the fork in the tunnels. We will go the other way."

"But we are a good distance down this side already," Glassworn whimpered. "Are you sure you don't want to continue down this way?"

"I'm sure."

"But Haze—"

"We are going back to the fork. It's not up for discussion."

"Are you sure? I like discussions. They can be enlightening. We should talk about it."

"I don't want to talk about it. I don't want to talk you. In fact, I don't really like talking at all," Haze grumbled. "Now please, stop making noise and just follow me quietly."

"Well, fine!" Glassworn bellowed suddenly.

Haze's stomach dropped into his feet and he wheeled around. "Be quiet!" he hissed.

"I don't know what it is you are afraid of down here," Glassworn continued in his elevated volume, "but I am going to go this way." Glassworn spun on his heels, heading further down the tunnel, the sound of his voice echoing off of the walls and spiraling through the darkness.

"Glassworn!" Haze said angrily, taking a step towards the other man. "Keep your voice down!" Panic rose inside him and he scanned the tunnel around them, the eerie blue light from the lamp casting dancing shadows on the grey rock.

Glassworn ignored him and continued his lurching stagger through the cavern, lifting his flask into the air and belting out a horrible tune:

> *"Oh, a happy heart is ne'er awry,*
> *Through thick and thin I bring it 'long,*
> *In hopes that though the bottle's dry,*
> *My life will carry on!"*

The next few moments of Haze's life became vastly more interesting than he would have liked. First, Glassworn tripped. While that in itself was not out of the ordinary, what he tripped *on* was.

A small chunk of ice-coated rock lay on the floor, a faint mist drifting off of it.

Glassworn squinted down at it. "What's that?"

Haze swallowed. "I don't know, but you just kicked it."

112

Glassworn leaned down and rubbed his fingers through a thick slime on the floor. He brought them to his nose and sniffed. "Ugh!" he cried, holding his hand as far away from his face as he could. "I found the nasty frozen water smell." His face brightened. "Oh! I remembered what—"

He was cut short as the ground exploded in white from underneath him, launching him screaming into the cavern ceiling. He crashed into it with a yelp and fell back to the floor, landing flat on his back.

Haze covered his face with his arm as the white mist slowly faded away. He realized it was powder snow, drifting in a small breeze coming from the direction that led back to the entrance.

Glassworn sat up, his legs spread wide in front of him and his eyes spinning. A dusting of snow covered him from head to toe. "What was *that*?" He exclaimed. He coughed and turned to face Haze, swatting at the buildup of sleet on his jacket. When he looked up at Haze, he shrank back in terror. "Oh," he said weakly, looking at something over Haze's left shoulder.

Haze stared at him. "What?"

He flinched as a wave of frigid air washed over him from behind. It felt like he was being chilled from the inside out, an icy floating sensation reaching into his boots.

He turned around slowly, his hand sweating on his lance.

A cloud of glistening blue mist hung in the middle of the cave behind him. It swirled like a miniature blizzard, writhing and twisting in the air like a banner caught in a high wind. A tortured moan escaped it as it eddied in the tunnel ahead of him. It sounded like the moan of an animal caught in a trap.

Placing his lance in its sheath on his back, Haze reached around behind himself for Glassworn. He didn't dare take his eyes off of the cloud as he seized the druid's collar and hoisted him to his feet.

"An Algid, right?" he whispered hoarsely.

Glassworn whimpered pathetically in reply.

"Great," Haze muttered. He could see Salezz on the other side of the beast through the mist. The wyvern seemed as shocked as he was, snorting jets of frost and pacing back and forth behind the cloud in confusion.

"We are going to walk slowly backwards," Haze said to the druid. "Do not make any sudden movements. Maybe it will just leave us alone." He held little hope for this, but decided it was his best idea. At any rate, he guessed he wasn't going to be able to hurt it by stabbing it with his lance.

Taking a deep breath, he took one slow step backwards.

The Algid erupted in a chorus of shrieks and moans so loud Haze clapped his hand over his right ear and pinned his left to his shoulder. The creature shuddered painfully for a moment, and a dark line began to appear in the middle of the cloud. It spread across the front of the vaporous creature, slowly taking more and more shape. Haze felt a sinking feeling as it began to take the shape of something he recognized. A moment later, the cloud convulsed violently and the thin line erupted in a shower of drool and snow. It spread open, bared in a wide snarl and showing rows of ice-blue teeth. Fangs the size of Haze's forearm protruded from the cloud like icicles from a fog bank, lines of saliva stretching between the razor-sharp incisors.

"Run!" Haze yelled, dragging Glassworn deeper into the cave.

"I think it's angry," Glassworn mumbled incoherently as Haze dragged him along the cavern floor.

A loud crash from behind them announced the beast's pursuit.

"Yes, I would say so," Haze answered, "because you kicked it in the head, or whatever that was."

"I tripped on it. That's—"

"You kicked it!"

"Tripped is not the –"

"It is the same, and you know it!"

"All I'm saying is that it wasn't intentional, and that makes it less my fault as opposed to me purposefully wandering over and ringing the chap on the bell."

"This is still your fault, Glassworn."

"Yes, but not as directly. And it hardly even has a head, now that you mention it."

Haze cried out as the ground under their feet shifted suddenly, heaving them into the air and sending them careening into the wall to their left.

They struck it at full speed, the lantern flying out of his hand and skittering across the floor. Glassworn landed almost completely on top of him, the ornate buckle on his boot digging into the corner of Haze's eye.

"Get off! Get off!" Haze snapped, shoving the drunkard off of himself and leaping to his feet.

He ducked quickly as the beast drifted around the corner, twisting angrily in the air.

Heaving Glassworn to his feet, Haze shoved him towards the lantern. "Come on!" he yelled. "Go! Go!"

They both jumped suddenly as they felt a blast of air shoot past them, narrowly missing their noses. The wall beside them froze instantly, small sequins of frost etching themselves across the stone.

Haze swallowed. He didn't want to find out what would happen if they got hit by that.

He grabbed Glassworn's arm and yanked him to the side as another blast of whitish-blue air shot out of the Algid's mouth, accompanied by strings of frigid saliva.

They dove to the ground as it lunged forward, maw opened wide. It vanished into the wall with a piercing shriek.

They clambered to their feet and bolted down the tunnel.

"Salezz!" Haze yelled over his shoulder as they ran. He couldn't hear the wyvern, nor did his mount answer him with his customary bark. He gritted his teeth and ran faster, still dragging the stumbling druid along behind him, but it was no use.

The Algid leapt out of the smooth tunnel wall ahead of them, moaning miserably as it opened its mouth once again to freeze them solid.

They slid to a stop and Glassworn grabbed onto the edge of his coat. He pulled it in front of both of them, just as the beast let loose an explosion of freezing air.

The cold bit through the coat like a frozen viper, stinging Haze's hand and numbing his entire arm before Glassworn pushed them to the side and out of the beam of ice.

They were now back against the wall, the Algid advancing on them slowly. Its mouth drooped open, an icy blue tongue creeping between its teeth.

Haze swallowed. "Glassworn?"

"Yes?" The druid answered, his gaze fixed on the beasts dripping fangs.

"I am killing you if we survive this."

"We won't."

116

"Yes, but if we do—"

"We won't."

Haze squeezed his eyes shut as the beast swelled suddenly, taking in what must have been a breath. He waited for the frigid air that would be his end.

Moxie had sent him to his death. He wouldn't be surprised if she was working for Queen Jaelyn after all. Perhaps she had sent him here simply to be sure he couldn't lead the Winged Demons himself.

A deafening roar filled the tunnel, rebounding off of the stone walls like the blare of a battle horn.

Haze's eyes snapped open. "Salezz!"

The wyvern stumbled around the corner in the cave, his mouth held open. He slid to a stop a dozen paces away from the Algid and let loose a torrent of liquid ice. It hit the strange creature directly in the mouth, shoving it away from Glassworn and Haze.

"Good boy!" Haze said happily, leaping to his feet. He left Glassworn cowering against the wall and hurried over to stand by his mount. He brushed some of the snow off his tunic as he went.

The beast was trembling with effort, the beam of ice pouring out of his mouth pounding into the Algid like a storm. It writhed and hissed angrily, pulsing different shades of blue as Salezz pummeled it relentlessly.

Haze's smile faded. It was writhing, but not in agony: It grew larger and larger under the stream of the wyvern's breath, it's fangs growing longer and mouth wider. It swelled to a size proportionate to Arginox, flashing and convulsing violently.

"Uh, stop. Salezz! Stop!" he yelled.

The wyvern didn't listen. The Wyrm took a step forward, his eyes tightly closed.

"Salezz! Hey!" he snapped, seizing the beast's reins and pulling his head to the side.

Glassworn ducked as the torrent of ice coming out of the Wyrm's mouth shot over his head and streaked across the wall, exploding with small pops and hisses as it seeped into small holes and crevice's.

Salezz finally took a breath, the beam of ice vanishing and his eyes opening. He smacked his lips contentedly and looked at Haze.

Haze, however, wasn't returning his gaze.

The Algid had grown to five times its normal size under Salezz's assault, now so large it filled the entire tunnel with its vaporous body. Its moan morphed into a roar as it turned and hissed at them angrily.

"Uh, Haze?" Glassworn said.

"Yes, I know. Run."

Chapter Fourteen
Reunion

Alovere and Galnoron walked in a tense silence. Galnoron had not had to keep up his spell against the cold; they had left it behind in the higher reaches of the Mountains. They now traveled across a damp hillside, the weather much more like spring or fall than deep winter. Dewdrops draped the ice blue needles of tall trees that rose out of the valleys and hills, decorating them in a fine raiment of glittering crystal. A few shrubs were littered around the bottoms of the trees, their few leaves and flowers pulsing different colors of green and blue.

It had been nearly a full day since they had left the bottom of the cliff where they had lost the girl. Not a word was spoken between them, save for the occasional command Alovere gave his dragon.

Galnoron was now leading them towards a dark cave, claiming that it led out into a canyon on the other side. He walked with a cold surety, positive of every action he made.

His very demeanor sickened Alovere; he could hardly stand to look at the other man. He was walking twenty paces or so behind the sorcerer, his hand on his sword and his teeth set.

The image of the girl shivering by the fire where they had found her haunted his every step. Something about that girl was special. He couldn't say why, but he knew it. From the moment he saw her, he knew she was different. She had survived an attack on her village, and most likely watched her parents die. She was hurt and traumatized, but something about her seemed warm. Everything from her eyes to her hair seemed to glow. She had made him feel like he was doing something good for once. He had been glad that he had not decided to leave her there alone in the village.

And Galnoron had killed her.

His fist tightened on the hilt of his sword. His mind drifted to Haze. He knew why the Wyvern Rider had refused to work with the man. Haze had always been a better judge of character than he was. He must have sensed right away that the wizard was trouble, or perhaps it was as simple as the General refusing to work with a spellcaster. Haze couldn't abide magic users of any kind; it had something to do with his family.

He shook himself out of his thoughts as Galnoron turned to face him.

The wizard had stopped a little way into the mouth of the dark cave he was leading them into. Lowering his hood, he stared hard at Alovere. "I need you to understand something, Rider."

Alovere glared at him silently, stopping ten paces away from the other man.

"I know you resent me," Galnoron said, his voice colder than ice, "but this isn't the time for you to be harboring an anger that may sway you from your responsibility. Remember, it's your duty to keep me alive. I'm not confident you can do that with your current attitude."

Alovere didn't answer, but narrowed his eyes slightly. How this man thought he was justified in having this conversation with him at all, he simply couldn't grasp. Every word that passed through the sorcerer's lips fueled his rage, pulling him closer and closer to removing the other man's head.

"To be clear, I expect you to do your job regardless of any misgivings you may have about me personally. Do you understand?"

Alovere remained silent, fixing the man with as threatening a stare as he could muster.

"Very good then," Galnoron said, turning and striding deeper into the cave. "Stay close. This land is filled with horrors you can't even imagine."

Alovere shook his head and started after the sorcerer. Misgivings indeed. He had more than a few "misgivings" about Galnoron, particularly his willingness to kill children and threaten members of the royal court. He also had a feeling Galnoron had plans of his own that didn't involve His Majesty's orders. The way he spoke about the Range was unsettling. He sounded obsessed, even deranged when he spoke of the power that lay inside the mystical Mountains. He had been there before, yes, but the way he spoke of them sounded more like a man fearful of a past experience, or bent on revenge.

Alovere stepped into the shadow of the cave mouth, a small breeze gently lifting the end of his scarf. It smelled wet and cold, as welcoming as a graveyard in late fall. The feeling radiating from the darkness ahead of him sent a shiver down his spine.

He licked his lips. He hated caves. He always had. There was something about running into a place where he couldn't safely take to the skies on Arginox that made him uneasy.

Every hair on the back of his neck rose straight up as a piercing scream echoed up from the depths of the cavern. Galnoron backed toward Alovere a few steps, narrowing his eyes.

"Run!" someone yelled from inside the cave.

A moment later, Haze's wyvern appeared. He was galloping as fast as he could on his wings, froth built up at the corners of his mouth. He was followed closely by what looked like a sloppily dressed gentleman hanging on Haze's shoulder.

He smiled broadly as his wing-man came into view. The mission was about to become infinitely easier.

His smile vanished. Haze was sweating heavily, heaving the other man along as best he could. Both the men's clothing and hair were dusted in a brilliant white powder that glistened in the sun. Alovere narrowed his eyes at the gentleman. Was he drunk?

"Run!" Haze yelled, dragging the other man along like a ragdoll.

Alovere whipped his sword out of his sheath as the two stumbled past him.

"It's a beast larger than Arginox!" Haze bellowed, shoving past Galnoron and knocking the wizard to the ground. He stared up from the hard-packed snow, seeming shocked that Haze had completely failed to notice him.

"What beast?" Alovere asked the Wyvern Rider. "What are you talking about?"

"Massive," the gentleman mumbled, his eyes rolling wildly. "Quite large. Dangerous. Horrible breath."

"Who the hell is this?" Alovere gestured to the drunk now laying on the ground.

"Never mind that!" Haze gasped, squinting his eyes as they adjusted to the light.

Alovere had never seen him so disheveled. His clothes were hanging in torn disarray, his hair grimy and blown wildly on top of his head. The little metal plate he usually had covering the stump of his left shoulder was knocked askew, showing a small bit of the mangled scar tissue underneath.

The shaken Wyvern Rider pointed at the drunk on the ground. "It's your turn to carry him. Come on, we have to go! That beast is not far behind us."

"Oh, no way!" Alovere spat. "I am *not* carrying that degenerate. If you want to keep him so badly, you carry him."

Galnoron brushed past both of them at a quick pace, his robes billowing in the wind. "We need to move."

Haze turned and walked away from Alovere and the other man, climbing onto Salezz. "I suggest we fly. Immediately."

"Hey!" Alovere protested, pointing at the drunkard. "You can't just leave me with—"

He was interrupted by a deafening roar that shook the very ground, bits of snow falling from the ledge above the cave.

Turning around, he squinted into the cave.

A massive white storm cloud drifted around the first corner of the tunnel, dagger-like fangs glinting in the light from the entrance. It hissed, a miniature blizzard jetting out of its mouth.

"Oh," he exclaimed.

Alovere whirled around and heaved the drunkard to his shoulder, whistling for Arginox.

The great dragon landed a few paces away, his crimson eyes fixed calmly on the beast emerging from the cavern.

Alovere slung the drunk over the back of Arginox's saddle and heaved himself up, shouting the command to fly.

The beast rushed forward, its mouth opened wide as it glided silently over the frozen ground.

The dragon unfurled his wings and leaped into the sky, the creature's teeth snapping shut on empty air merely inches from the tip of Arginox's tail.

Alovere looked over his shoulder at the massive beast as it roared in frustration. It circled once, its eyeless face turned up towards them.

He turned his attention forward and scanned the sky for Salezz. He spotted him flying just a little bit higher than he was, about twenty lengths ahead.

Urging Arginox faster, he fell into pace next to Salezz and Haze. Galnoron was seated behind the younger rider, gripping the back of the saddle with a look of utter terror painted across his face.

"What are you doing here?" Alovere called over the noise of the wind whipping through their ears.

"It's a long story," Haze answered. He stared straight ahead, his eyes scanning the clouds around them.

"Well, I want to hear it," Alovere demanded, "seeing as you disobeyed a direct order from His Majesty and still ended up in the Range!"

"I will explain later when we land. Trust me, I don't want to be here any more than I did when I refused to come. Now, do you know of any place we can settle safely for the night?"

"Ask him," Alovere jerked his chin at Galnoron. "He seems to think he knows where we are."

"I do not know where we are, because that is not possible in the Range. There is a powerful—"

"Time magician. Yeah, I know," Haze interrupted him, "but where can we land for the night? I don't fancy being eaten by anything in the dark, thank you very much."

"If we can fly over the mountain that tunnel leads through, there is a canyon on the other side that has a collection of ruins at its center. We should be able to camp there."

"Do you hear that?" the drunk mumbled groggily from behind Alovere.

"What did he say?" Haze called back to the Dragon Rider.

"Nothing," Alovere snapped. "He's bloody incoherent."

"No, I heard something." The drunkard insisted, sitting up and wiggling his finger in his ear.

Alovere's ears perked as he heard what sounded like a low whistle. It grew steadily louder, until it suddenly turned into a scream.

A ball of flame shot past them, narrowly missing Arginox's head. Alovere hauled back on his mount's reins, pulling the dragon to the right.

"Ballistae fire!" his passenger yelled.

A loud humming Alovere had not heard since the last battle with Jaelyn filled the air, and the silvery bow of an airship thrust through the cloud bank to their left. The rails of the ship flashed several times with more cannon fire, followed seconds later by fire balls hissing towards them.

"Dive!" Haze yelled.

Alovere leaned forward, urging Arginox into a dive. The wind screamed in his ears as they fell through the sky, the mist of the clouds filling his eyes. He lost sight of Salezz and Haze in the gloom, the soupy clouds blocking his view.

Their descent was halted suddenly as an enormous metal net fell around them. It tangled in Arginox's claws and wing talons, pulling the dragon upside down in mid fall. Alovere heard Salezz screech loudly as the same thing happened to them.

He cried out as Arginox's full weight pressed him into the bottom of the net, crushing his arm into the metal strands. He struggled to worm his way out from under the Dragon, but it was in vain. He managed a half inch in the desired direction, before the dragon struggled violently, trying to free himself from the net. The Wyrm's scales pressed into his chest, robbing him of breath. He could hear the drunk yelling something on the other side of the beast, but his vision was fading quickly. He struggled to take a breath, his lungs screaming for air. The world slowly faded into an inky black, the thrumming of his heart filling his ears.

****

Alovere gasped, sitting bolt upright. His back was cold, as though he had been laying on a bed of ice. He blinked and rubbed his eyes, trying to adjust to the sudden light.

He grunted and leapt to his feet, his sword flashing out of its scabbard.

He was surrounded by people. Or were they?

They were humanoid, at least. They stood about six feet in height, long blades of curved metal held in their hands. Mist flowed off of them in a damp cloud, drifting to the ground and creating a small fogbank around their ankles. Their faces were empty, nothing but smooth ice where their eyes and mouths should have been. They cocked their heads and stared at him, their weapons at the ready.

"Arginox!" he yelled, scanning around himself. He sucked in a quick breath when he saw they were on the deck of the airship that had attacked them, open sky stretching out from the frigid rails of the vessel.

One of the creatures moved towards him, its weapon raised.

Alovere acted instinctively: His sword danced up, severing the beast's head and sending it rolling across the deck.

"Arginox!" he yelled again, bringing his sword around in front of him.

The rest of the creatures charged, drifting across the deck as silently as a creeping frost. He countered one blow after another, his sword sparking against their iron-like bodies. They whirled around him like a tornado of ice and steel, their expressionless gazes fixed on him. He cried out as he felt one of their cold blades bite into his ribs, driving deep into his body. He pulled away, raising his sword. Another head rolled across the deck. A sudden blow came from behind, driving him to his knees. This one sank into his side, sliding through his skin like a

126

frozen razor-blade. Multiple blows caught him on the shoulders, the flat sides of the creature's swords ringing on his head. He fell forward, crying out in pain as another cut bit deep into his sword arm and he felt his fingers sag. A sharp rap to the back of his head made his vision spin, and he fell back into darkness.

****

Haze's eyes snapped open, the sound of dripping water filling his ears. He shot up straight, crying out as his ribs screamed in pain. He blinked wearily and rubbed his eyes. Looking down, he saw a dark purple streak along the right side of his rib cage. He touched them gingerly and winced. They were badly bruised, if not fractured. Also, whoever had taken them out of the sky had taken everything off of him except his trousers and shoes.

He took stock of his surroundings. He was in a cell, obviously. Most likely subterranean, given the amount of water that poured in from under the door. The floor and walls were made of a white stone. The door was a dull, non-reflective steel. A small slat was cut diagonally across the middle of it, a metal plate bolted over the top of the hole. He was laying on a cot, suspended from the ceiling by a set of rusty chains. Another cot just like it dangled from the ceiling across the room from where he was. The only light he could see was leaking through an imperfection in how the plate was fixed across the middle of the door.

He lifted his hand and scratched the back of his head.

The walls and ceilings suddenly burst into life. Tiny, glowing blue sparks danced like stars and spun along the smooth white stone. They flowed softly towards the door as though the walls themselves were moving with light.

"Whoa," he muttered. He groaned as his head flashed with pain. After a moment, the lights began to dim, then faded back out entirely.

127

He sighed and swung his legs over the edge of the cot, resting his shoes on the damp stone floor.

The walls and ceiling once more exploded with radiance, drenching the room in the same blue glow.

He jumped to his feet, looking around for anything that could be causing the sudden bursts. The room was empty, save for his cot.

He stepped over to the door. Leaning down, he slid his fingers around the metal hole. The plate was fastened firmly over the top of it, the gaps near the edges barely large enough for the tip of a knife to slide through.

He stood up. "Hey!" he yelled, banging on the door. He flinched as his ribs throbbed painfully, but continued banging. "Hey! What's going on! Where am I?"

Silence answered from the other side of the door. There was no sound, save for the rhythmic drip from the back of his cell.

"Hey!" he yelled as loud as he could, his voice echoing off the bare walls. He rolled his eyes. "I know someone is out there listening."

The metal plate in the bottom of the door swung open, and something dropped in through it.

He took a step backwards and stared warily at the floor. A small wooden bowl lay on the white stone, heaped with rice.

"Eat," a cold voice said through the slat.

"Who are you?" Haze yelled immediately.

The slat slammed shut, plunging him back into darkness.

He sighed and bent down to pick up the bowl, the room exploding in blue light again.

Sitting down on the edge of the cot, he set the bowl on his lap and dug his fingers into the mass of white grains. They were hot and sticky, clinging to his skin as he lifted them to his nose. The rice smelled fine, at least. A little pungent perhaps, but that was expected of prison food.

Haze dropped the sticky substance back into the bowl and set it on the floor by his cot.

Rising to his feet, he strolled around the room twice, looking for any sort of weakness or inconsistency in the walls and floor.

The room was solid rock, thin gray lines marking the seams where the square stones were sealed together. The tiny blue lights that scurried across the surface illuminated every tiny crack and joint in a thin glowing line, making it easy for him to come to the conclusion that there was no way out of the room.

He plopped back down on his cot and sighed.

He wondered if his companions were in a similar predicament. He doubted any of them were together, as he was imprisoned alone. He had to assume they had all been separated. Not that it mattered, as this was more than likely a trick on Jaelyn's part. He would be shocked if they weren't somewhere in Miasma City right now. It was the only place he knew of that would have the kind of magic to create light in a room like this.

The door suddenly banged open, the blue light winking out and torch light flooding the room. Glassworn stumbled into the cell, catching himself on the other cot.

"Glassworn!" Haze exclaimed.

The druid lifted his hand, his eyes squeezed shut. "Please," he said weakly, "not so loud. I beg you. My head..."

"What did you do to him?" Haze whirled on the open door, and swallowed. A giant of a woman filled the doorway. She stood at least seven feet tall, clad from head to toe in a brilliant ice blue armor that glinted in the torch light. Her hair was dark and fell to just above her shoulders in smooth waves. She was more attractive than not, or would have been were it not for the severity of her expression. Her slender jaw was clenched tight, her brow pulled down into a grounding frown. Her features were angular and pale, an angry red scar tracing a crimson furrow from her left eye to the bottom of her chin. Her eyes flashed a dangerous green as she stared at him coldly. Her hand rested on the hilt of a massive battle sword hanging at her waist.

"I did nothing to your friend," she said, her voice carrying across the cell like thunder. "He is in pain because he drinks too much wine, and we have taken his possessions."

"She took my flask," Glassworn muttered from behind Haze.

"Who are you?" Haze demanded. "Why are you holding us here?"

"Don't ask me questions," the woman said flatly. "I'm not allowed to answer them, and I wouldn't even if I were. I am going to take you to someone who can."

"Who?"

She glared at him. "No questions. You can either follow me, or I can restrain you and drag you to where we're going. Choose."

Haze looked her up and down for a moment. Given the rock-melting stare she had fixed him with and her sheer size, he decided it would be best to simply follow her. "Alright," he said. "Let's get this over with. Do I get some clothes?"

She threw him his blue tunic. "Let's go."

Sliding his tunic over his head as he walked, Haze stepped out of the cell beside the massive woman. She closed the door with a loud crash and turned to walk down the hall. He followed her down the torch lit corridor, the flames casting a dancing orange glow on the white stone. Doors were spaced evenly along the walls, each made of the same dark metal, and each with a small slat in the bottom. At the end of the

130

corridor, they were met by yet another door, this one larger than the cell doors and locked shut with a massive silver bolt.

The woman pulled the bolt to the side and opened the door, revealing another corridor identical to the first. She looked at him expectantly, and he hurried through. Closing the door behind her, she bolted it from the side they were on and continued down the corridor.

They walked in silence, the only sound being the tap of their feet on the stone.

Haze cleared his throat. "So, I noticed my cell lit up when I moved. How do you do that?"

She didn't answer for a moment, and Haze had begun to think she was ignoring him when she finally said, "We don't do that. There is a Yobe infestation in the Mirror Wood prison."

Haze blinked. "Yobe? Mirror Wood?"

"No more questions."

"I'm sorry, it's just that I have never heard of those names before," Haze said quickly. "Is this some sort of secret prison Jaelyn set up?"

The woman ignored him, pulling open another door and ushering him through it silently.

"Are you going to ignore me now?"

She stopped and turned to face him. "Yes, and you should be thankful for it!" she snapped. "If I had it my way, you never would have woken up."

"Why is that?" he said immediately, almost regretting it.

She glared at him, then spun away and continued down the hall.

Haze's mind spun wildly, trying to grasp what this was about. The more he thought about it, the more he knew this was some nasty trickery on Jaelyn's part. She had no doubt taken himself and Alovere so they couldn't fight her in the upcoming battle with Orlivan. If the

Winged Demons were left without their commanders, they would be severely weakened.

The rest of the walk was in silence, the only noise being the opening of the last two doors before they burst into sunlight. Haze lifted his hand over his eyes as they adjusted to the sudden flash of light. The smell of burning wood reached his nostrils, along with the overwhelming scent of wonderfully fresh air. The only air Haze had smelled that was this clean was in the Boar Mountains during Orlivan's march on the Malgonians.

They stood in a dense forest, sunlight filtering down through the branches of the trees and trickling in shafts of gold radiance onto the moss-covered floor. A strange bird call he had not heard before sounded from his right, and the bubble of water announced the presence of a nearby stream. He looked up and squinted at the branches. Unless his eyes were failing him…

He shook his head. There was no way. Were they blue?

"Here he is, Vlaire," the woman said shortly, stepping past him.

Haze looked down and was surprised to see a man standing in front of him. He had not been there a moment ago when they had exited the prison, and now he was standing in front of Haze in the same sort of armor the woman wore: blue and silver steel etched with decorative, leaf like patterns that reminded him of October frost on the palace windows. His hair was dark, like the woman's. It was nearly as long and tied back, a few stray wisps framing his square jaw and pale, blunt features. His eyes were the same shade of green as the woman's, but twinkled with a different kind of light. He was every bit as tall as the woman, and a good deal broader.

"Haze," the man said, bowing his head respectfully. "As you can see, I would like to begin our relations on stable footing. You are not bound, and I have done all that I can to give you the same respect I would ask of you."

"How do you know my name?" Haze asked, glancing at the enormous hammer hanging from the man's belt. Just the head was at least the size of Haze's torso.

"Your friend told me all of your names," he answered. "He is a decent person, if not a little weak to the finer sides of life. Also," he added, smiling kindly, "my name is Vlaire, and this charming lady is Oaina, my sister."

Haze found the woman to be many things in the short time since they had met, and charming was certainly not on the list. "Why am I here? Where am I?" Haze asked. "And why are the trees blue?"

Vlaire and Oaina exchanged looks. "You are in the Elliset Mountain Range, as your people call it. We call it The Range of Spirits. As to why you are here, I was hoping you could tell me. That was the one thing your friend refused to tell me."

Haze almost sighed in relief. At least Glassworn had the forethought not to give away their entire mission to strangers. "We are here to scout the Range," he lied. "We were actually sent here in two different groups, but that's something of a long story."

Vlaire narrowed his eyes. "Scouts? For a military?"

Haze's mind scrambled as he tried desperately to think of some peaceful reason for scouts being in the Range. "Well, not exactly. Sort of, yes." he rolled his eyes as he listened to himself bumble pitifully. "We are here for a reason I cannot tell you," he said simply. "I know that I am not exactly in the sort of position to be refusing you anything, but I simply cannot tell you. The mission is incredibly sensitive and much hangs on its success.

Vlaire lifted his chin. "I will respect that for the time being, but I will have you know that had my sister been given her way, you would have been killed when the Rime Born took you out of the sky."

"Rime Born?" Haze asked quietly, his stomach clenching. "The Rime Born are the ones who ambushed us?"

Vlaire cocked his head. "Met them before, have you?"

Haze cleared his throat. "No, not personally. I have heard of them, though. They work for you?"

Vlaire smiled. "I think that is enough questions for now. I need to show you something."

He turned abruptly and walked away from Haze, heading towards a small tent that was tucked away in the trees.

Oaina glared at him and he hurried after Vlaire. She didn't seem like the sort of person he would want to cross.

Haze cast his gaze around the clearing as he walked, taking stock of every detail. Three guards leaned casually against the trees around them, chatting merrily and puffing on pipes. Two more guards stood by a path that led out of the clearing, winding into the wood. They were at attention, spears planted firmly in the ground. Should he need to escape, he couldn't go that way. He would be forced to dash into the woods and hope for the best. He could return for Alovere once he had gathered his bearings.

Vlaire lifted a large flap draped over the front of the tent and gestured for him to enter.

Haze glanced at him for a moment, then obliged.

All thoughts of trying to escape vanished from Haze's mind when he saw what awaited him in the tent.

He gasped when he saw the man lying on the small cot inside. "Alovere!"

He was poorly bandaged, blood leaking from a massive gash in chest. His right arm and leg were also wrapped in crimson stained cloth. His eyes were squeezed shut, sweat beading on his brow.

"What happened to him?" Haze cried.

"He resisted spectacularly when the Rime Born attempted to bind to him," Oaina said. "It took ten of them to finally take him down. He is a remarkable warrior," she added, her tone traced with awe.

Haze pulled back the bandages on the other Riders chest and his heart fell. He had seen plenty of wounds in his time on the field, and this was serious. "This is bad," he said quietly. "He isn't going to make it."

"He will make it," Vlaire said. "We simply need to get him back to the City. We have an amazing healer there that can work wonders with wounds like this."

Haze heard a slight hesitation in the man voice and looked up at him. "Why do I feel like there are conditions to this?"

Vlaire and Oaina glanced at each other. "We can heal your friend," Vlaire said, "but we cannot trust you. Should you return to the city with us, you will be accompanied by a guard everywhere you go. There is no exception to that, and it will not change for the duration of the time you are there. You have not committed any act against us, so we cannot treat you as an enemy yet, but we must handle your sudden appearance with great caution. You aren't the first stranger to wander into the Range over the years."

Haze shook his head.

By all rights, they should be treated like enemies: In prison, in chains, or executed, at least based on what Moxie had told him the last visit went like.

135

"Why aren't you simply chaining me in a dungeon somewhere and letting Alovere die?" he asked warily. "Why are you helping us at all?"

"Excellent question," Oaina said shortly, glaring at her brother.

"My reasons are my own," Vlaire answered calmly, "but understand this; should you draw a weapon on any of the guards, wrong me in any way, or be discovered as a spy for this 'Jaelyn' that came here before, I will not hesitate to kill you or your friends."

Haze swallowed. The man's eyes were soft, but stern. He had no doubt Vlaire was telling the truth. "Alright." He stood up from Alovere's side and bowed respectfully to Vlaire. "I greatly appreciate your kindness. It is unwarranted."

A small smile slipped across the man's lips. "Kindness is never unwarranted, Haze."

He then whistled shrilly, and the two guards outside the tent hurried in, each grabbing an end of Alovere's cot. They marched him out into the daylight, Haze following Vlaire behind them.

"We will take the airship back to the city," Vlaire explained. "It is only a little way from here."

"What about Glassworn and Galnoron?" Haze asked immediately. "Aren't they coming?"

Vlaire nodded. "Yes, but I'm afraid they will remain in prison once we reach the city. Once you prove yourself to be trustworthy, perhaps you can all wander freely. Until said time, you will be their representative." He smiled, his eyes twinkling mischievously. "I suggest you stay on your best behavior. How comfortable your friends are over the next few days depends heavily on it."

Haze nodded silently. Vlaire did seem as though he was a reasonable person, but not one to be meddled with by any means. Although he appeared kind, he spoke with a cold conviction born of a lifestyle Haze was all too familiar with; war.

He followed Vlaire and his sister along a narrow path that wound between the oddly colored trees, the trail overgrown in thick turquoise moss and speckled with a variety of strange looking mushrooms, some taller than Haze himself.

It was a short time later that the trees began to thin more and more, the moss fading from the ground and being replaced by a gray stone floor until the greenery and trees faded away entirely. The trail emptied out onto a ledge overlooking a giant cliff. Sapphire grass lay sparse over the rock, mounds of moved dirt making way for a massive wooden ramp that was leaned against the side of a blue airship.

It made the *Laudlin* look like a child's toy. Its hull glistened a brilliant silver-white, etched with the same sort of blue, leaf-like patterns that decorated the armor of the guards he had seen so far. It was different in the design from the other warship in few ways. It did not have a balloon floating above it. Instead, it had two separate masts rising high into the sky, much like Orlivan's ships on the eastern sea. Sails were rolled down atop the spreaders, tied off with dark black ropes. Its prow was longer, and more intricate in design. A carving of a wyvern's head was mounted at the tip of the bowsprit, its mouth opened in a toothy snarl. The rails were lined with giant crossbows, the tip of each bow carved in the shaped of a wyvern's head, mouth open wide with the tip an ice bolt glinting inside. Cannons protruded from trapdoors in the sides of the hull, tips blackened from recent cannon fire.

"Magnificent," he breathed. "I've never seen anything like it."

"What?" Vlaire said, looking back at him.

"The airship," Haze said, pointing at it. "It's beautiful. Even for a machine of war, that is a remarkable sight."

"Indeed," Vlaire agreed. "It is something that has been a part of the Rime Born for as long as I can remember. It is called the *Rhewddraig*, or Ice Dragon in your tongue. It patrols the Range in search of intruders. Not unlike yourself," he added cheerfully. "Lucky it found you before my sister did."

Haze nodded. "I believe you," he muttered. "She seems to be quite the serious person."

Vlaire laughed. "I can see how you might think so. She isn't that bad, really. She just has a very specific idea about what things should be allowed and what things shouldn't. She is under the impression that *you* should not be allowed."

"What do you mean 'I' should not be allowed? Shouldn't be allowed what?" Haze asked in confusion.

Vlaire shrugged. "I'm not sure. I didn't ask her. My advice to you is that you don't ask her either."

Haze glanced over his shoulder at the massive woman. She stalked behind him like a wolf on the prowl, her hand resting uneasily on her battle sword.

"I think you're right," he mumbled. "I won't ask her anything at all, if I can help it."

Chapter Fifteen

Hallovath

Haze looked down as they walked past the Rime Born guards and boarded the *Rhewddraig*. Their expressionless faces glimmered at him coldly as they passed, a faint mist rising off of them and into the sky. Their frozen hands grasped the hilts of wickedly curved swords at their waists, suspended by their sides without so much as a belt. Cold seemed to waft off of them as Haze passed, sending a shiver down his spine. They radiated a clean, fresh smell, something like the first breath of winter in the air after a long summer.

He passed the two that were standing guard by the ramp and stepped out onto the deck.

Vlaire kindly showed him around the ship over the next thirty minutes or so, as they waited for the silent crew to finish their preparations and cast off. A large cabin stood to aft, a stairwell leading down into a midships galley that came near to putting the Palace kitchens to shame. Several more doorways and stairwells led to compartments used for storing things like ammunition for the crossbows, while others led to small armories. Haze was bewildered to find them nearly empty of weapons, only a few dented shields and a broken sword hanging on the walls. When he asked why it was that there was no weaponry on board, Vlaire said that the Rime Born didn't need anything but their own weapons, and that the armory was for an old crew that used to run the ship before them.

Soon after they had settled Alovere into one of the beds in a dusty set of crew quarters, a loud horn sounded from the deck and they hurried up to it.

Rime Born milled about on the glistening ice, pulling on ropes and heaving the ramp off of the rail. With a resounding creak, the *Rhewddraig* drifted away from the cliff and out into open sky. A low rhythmic chug began to sound across the ship, growing steadily in speed until it was coughing at a stable pace. The *Rhewddraig* floated out into the blue, the ground falling away from them as they rose slowly higher. At length, the chugging died away, and the sails fell down from their spreaders. They billowed out as they filled with wind, and the *Rhewddraig* groaned as it heaved over to one side.

It slowly picked up speed, and in no time the ancient ship was soaring through the sky. Clouds wisped past them like damp feathers as they hurtled across the Range towards their unseen destination, the sails stretched tight and the masts bent under the load.

"I see you have been on an airship before," Vlaire remarked, seeing Haze relax contentedly on the rail.

"Only once, but it was enough."

The giant man fixed him with an intense stare. "Why don't you tell me why you're here?"

Haze swallowed. "I can't tell you that. Not yet."

"You wait to see if you can trust me," Vlaire said, a small smile creeping across his face. "Ironic, as I only ask because I do not yet trust you. I suppose this puts us at a stalemate, doesn't it?"

Haze nodded, looking up at the other man. "I agree to adhere to whatever rules you may have in return for Alovere's treatment," he said politely, "and I swear I will cause no harm or trouble to anyone. Beyond that, I cannot give away why I am here without sufficient reason."

Vlaire stared at him for a moment. "That will have to do, then. Tell me, is this different from how we would be treated if we invaded your kingdom?"

Haze laughed out loud, then coughed and scratched his head. "Uh, yes. I'm afraid so."

Vlaire looked out ahead of them at the open expanse of the Range. "Well, I hope you do not abuse our kindness."

Haze marveled at how well he was being treated by his "captors." Apart from Oaina, who was responding much more like Haze would have expected, he was being treated with courtesy. There were no chains or shackles. He was being offered something very close to freedom in exchange for mutual respect. He had never even heard of such a place, let alone dreamed he might be in one someday.

The *Rhewddraig* rocked suddenly to the left, causing Haze to sway violently and seize the rail for support. When he looked ahead, he saw dark shadow in the clouds beneath them, just beneath the milky white mist. Had they not swerved, they would have struck whatever it was with the hull.

"What was that?" Haze asked in alarm.

"A Banyeet," Vlaire said simply, still staring ahead as though nothing out of the ordinary had happened.

"A what?"

Vlaire glanced at him. "A giant tree. They grow in the Mirror Wood, and some of them are tall enough to pierce the clouds. We sometimes miss them in the gloom and strike them with the hull."

Haze swallowed. Trees tall enough to grow above the clouds? Things were getting stranger by the moment.

Most of the flight over the next two hours was silent and uneventful. Haze spent most of his time below decks with Alovere. He had not been permitted to see Glassworn once they boarded the ship.

He shifted as the Rhewddraig rocked slightly. He was sitting by Alovere's bed, staring at the fever-stricken man. His face shone with sweat, his steel gray hair clinging to his neck and brow in damp mats. His breath came much too quickly as he gasped for air.

Haze gritted his teeth. One thing was for certain, he was not going to trust any of them. Not Vlaire, not the Rime Born, or anyone else in this wretched place.

His frown melted away when he remembered why he was here.

The Hyless.

Just the name sent a wash of calm over him. Yes, the Hyless. That was what he would do. He would find the Hyless and fulfill his part of the bargain he made with Moxie. Not that she had a part, he reminded himself bitterly. He was doing this entire thing to prevent a war between two raging Kingdoms.

He smiled to himself. Soon, he was going to be in the heart of the Range. He was probably the first person from outside to see that far into it in five hundred years, let alone live there for weeks while Alovere healed.

He lifted Alovere's bandage, examining his wound. He noted that the wound was beginning to clot, large black curds of blood forming around the edges of the gash.

"Haze."

Haze pushed the bandage back into place and turned around. Vlaire stood in the doorway to the crew quarters, his hand on the door. "Yes?"

"We are about to begin our descent," Vlaire said. "You should get ready."

Haze stood up and shrugged. "I am as ready as ever. I don't have any of my possessions, so there is nothing I have to gather." He shrugged. "May I join you on deck?"

Vlaire nodded. "If you want to, that would be fine."

Haze rose and followed him up the stairs and out into the frigid air.

The Rime Born hurried around busily, all seeming to move at exactly the same pace as their neighbor. Haze couldn't help but think that their orderly behavior and tidiness would have made Orlivan weep with joy.

He followed Vlaire back over to the bow of the ship. Oaina stood facing forward, her hands resting on the rail. They joined her, standing as near to the edge as the railing would allow them.

The ship pitched forward, Haze's stomach rising into his throat. There was a loud creaking noise as the Rhewddraig shifted, and they picked up speed. The deck began to shake under Haze's feet, the masts groaning loudly as the ship heeled over violently. The wind whipped past as they plummeted down through the clouds, mist soaking Haze through to the skin.

Suddenly, they burst out the bottom of the cloud banks. The ship leveled out into an easier descent, floating softly with a gentle breeze in its sails.

Haze's breath left him as he saw what lay ahead.

Massive trees larger than small mountains rose up out of the ground in front of them, towering hundreds of feet above even the *Rhewddraig*. A dozen or more of the majestic growths were spread out evenly across a wide forest that stretched from his left to his right as far as he could see. Behind them was another giant tree, blocking the way they had come, its sapphire blue boughs catching the light of the sun and casting shadows on the land below.

Beyond the trees in front of them, a frozen waterfall tumbled down the face of a cliff. It was at least three times as large as Beril City, the sheer size being enough to take anyone's breath away. Carved into the side of the falling ice was a shining white city, reflecting the suns rays in a blinding radiance. Pillars of ice supported street after street, layers of white cobblestone roads weaving across the face of the blue like tiny streaks of clouds across a clear sky. Houses and buildings of many different sizes stood along the streets at regular intervals, stained green windows glistening out at them like emeralds. At the bottom of the waterfall, a pair of gates opened out onto the barren surface of the frozen river. At the top, a shelf of ice curled out over the city, stone pillars extending down from it and supporting a large flat platform. A pyramid shaped white building rose up from the form and buried its peak in the bottom of the shelf. It was wide and round, easily the size of the *Rhewddraig*. The entire structure hung from the bottom side of the shelf like a giant white bat, hanging guard over the city.

Vlaire glanced at Haze, a smile spreading across his face when he saw Haze's expression. "Welcome to Hallovath, City of the Hyless."

Chapter Sixteen
The Range Keeper

The *Rhewddraig* settled against the edge of the of the odd structure with a weary moan as the Rime Born began throwing ropes over the rails. In moments, they had the ship tied off to the edge of the platform.

Haze looked above them with his mouth hanging open. The ice swept overhead as though it had frozen in mid fall, icicles the size of entire houses reaching down at them from above. He felt tiny in comparison to everything he was seeing; even the building was half the size of the palace. It was wide at the base, tapering to a sharp point that buried into the bottom of the ice above it. Wyvern statues guarded either side of the double doors leading into it, each sitting back on their haunches with their tails curled around themselves elegantly. Blue gemstones were embedded in the white rock for their eyes, staring down on the city watchfully.

"Help me with the other end of your friend's cot, would you?" he heard Vlaire say breathlessly.

Haze tore his eyes away from the incredible sight to find Vlaire standing behind him. Alovere's cot had been carried up from below decks by the Rime Born and left by the ramp leading down to the stone platform. Vlaire stood at one end of it, his hands resting on the wooden frame.

Hurrying over, Haze lifted on the other end of the cot. Together, they walked the wounded man down the ramp and out onto the stone platform.

"Where is Salezz?" he asked Vlaire suddenly, realizing he had not once asked what had happened to his Wyvern.

"He could not be captured unfortunately," Vlaire said. "But I did see him behind the airship a few times on the way over here, if that makes you feel better."

Haze nodded. Salezz was determined. He was sure the wyvern would find his way to him.

He turned to his left to see a young man not much older than twenty jogging towards them. He wore the same armor as Vlaire and Oaina, and an elegantly curved sword hung at his hip. His hair was a flaming red, his round face clouded by freckles. He smiled broadly when he saw Haze. "Hello," he said breathlessly, bowing his head briefly. "We haven't met, have we? I'm Lox."

Haze glanced at Vlaire, who smiled. "Lox, this is a prisoner of ours, Haze."

Lox's smile vanished. "Oh. A prisoner, eh?" He looked Haze up and down. "And what did a one-armed man do to deserve imprisonment?"

Vlaire cleared his throat and stared at the young man. "Also, we have a patient for you." He gestured to Alovere, who laid as still as death. "He resisted the Rime Born and they exacted their toll."

Lox looked down at the injured warrior. "And you want me to heal him?" he asked warily, "a man that the Rime Born have dubbed an enemy?"

Vlaire ignored him. "I don't know who they are yet, and I have reason to believe they are important to us. So, Lox," he said quietly, "you have a patient."

Lox smiled cheerfully, all doubt gone from his expression. "Alrighty then! I will get him down to my place. Malya and I will have him on his feet in no time."

He whistled shrilly, and a screech returned from somewhere above the white gallery. A moment later, an ice wyvern at least half again the

146

size of Salezz whirled around the corner of it. The beast glided down to where they were and landed gently by Lox. It snorted and shook its head, scattering a few water droplets off of its back. Its legs were almost twice as thick as Salezz's, its neck half again as long. Its wings made Salezz's look like bird's wings in comparison. Its eyes were the same sapphire blue, only rounder and more kind than his own mount's.

"Been playing near the nests, have you?" Lox said kindly, rubbing the wyvern behind its scaly ears.

"Remarkable!" Haze exclaimed. "I have never seen another ice wyvern before."

"His name is Bard," Lox answered amiably. "He is the largest wyvern we have here, actually." He patted the great creature once and strolled around behind him. Lifting Alovere unceremoniously from the cot, he slung him over Bard's back and clambered on in front of the injured man. "I will be at my place should you need me for anything," he said to Vlaire. "Pleasure to meet you Haze," he added, spurring his Wyvern gently.

With a sharp bark, Bard unfurled his wings and hurled himself off of the edge of the stone platform. Haze watched as they glided gently down towards the City below.

"*He* is your healer?" Haze asked skeptically. "Isn't he a bit young? Alovere's wounds are serious. This isn't something to trifle with."

Vlaire nodded. "Oh, don't worry. Lox is a remarkable healer. I would trust him with my life. Someday, when I am wounded on the battlefield, it will be Lox that I ask to care for me. Not to mention, he has a kind heart. It's in his nature to feel the pain of others as his own. Alovere couldn't be in better hands."

Haze nodded reluctantly as the massive blue Wyrm winged down towards the houses and streets, vanishing into the radiant white city.

"What are we going to do with him?" Oaina spoke up suddenly from behind them.

They turned around to see her standing behind them, her hand still fixed to the handle of her sword.

"I must visit the Range Keeper," Vlaire said. "He will accompany me. After that, we will settle him with quarters in the Gallery."

"The Gallery?" Oaina hissed. "You can't put him in our sacred hall!"

"I can, and I will," Vlaire said calmly. "It is the only place I know he cannot escape without his wyvern. He will be safe and unable to leave until we come for him."

"But the spare room is for honored guests!"

"Until he has proven himself to be an enemy, he is nothing less than that. Would you have them treat us like prisoners should we wander into their home unaware?"

Oaina grumbled loudly, twisting her fist on the hilt of her sword. "Fine!" she snapped, "but I insist on staying with him. I will not leave him alone in the Hyless Gallery."

Haze's ears perked up. "The what? The Hyless Gallery? What does that mean?"

They both turned and looked at him. Oaina looked as though she were near to beheading him, and Vlaire looked confused.

"Have you never heard of the Hyless?" the man asked.

Haze swallowed.

He wondered if he should tell them that he had. Should he tell them that was why he was here, and that he believed the Hyless may be in danger?

He shook his head. "I have heard of it," he said slowly, "but not in great detail. And I have certainly never heard of this Gallery."

Vlaire laughed. "It? Do you know what the Hyless is, then?"

148

Haze frowned in confusion. "A creature released from the depths of the Boar Mountains that now provides light and life to the world. At least," he added quickly, "that is what I have been told."

Vlaire nodded, his smile giving way to a more solemn expression. "Yes," he said quietly. "I suppose that is close enough for now." He looked at Oaina. "Resume the patrols on the Banyeets. We found a few Hela that had wandered into the bottoms. Their movements cannot go unchecked."

Oaina hesitated, glaring at Haze. She grunted reluctantly and strode over to the edge of the platform. Whistling loudly, she hurled herself off the edge and into the sky.

Haze cried out and hurried over to the side of the stone, just in time to see a flashing white wyvern swoop down and catch her gracefully on its back before whirling off in the direction they had come in.

"Let's go," Vlaire said from behind him. "There is someone I must take you to."

Haze tore his eyes away from the odd woman and turned back to Vlaire. He was walking steadily towards the Gallery.

Hurrying to catch up, he fell into stride beside the man. "Does she do that a lot?"

"I'm afraid so. If there were ever any person who was one with the sky and wind, it is my sister."

"You sound disappointed in that."

"You mistake indifference for disappointment." Vlaire smiled. "I have seen her antics for so many years, that I have become calloused to their wonder."

"I see. What is a Hela? Does everyone in the city have a wyvern, then?"

Vlaire smiled. "In answer to your first question, you are a Hela. It means Hunter, people from outside that invade the Range in search of the Hyless. In answer to your second question, no. Not everyone has a wyvern, but most of the City Guards do."

"What about you?"

"I do," he said fondly. "His name is Boar. He is a calm, perceptive beast, given to great prowess in battle."

Haze raised an eyebrow. "Battle? Are the invasions really that bad?"

Vlaire's expression turned grave. "I am not able to tell you, unfortunately, until we speak to the Range Keeper." He stopped at the doors of the great Gallery and heaved them open. They groaned in protest as they swung outward, opening up into the massive building. "Please," he said, gesturing for Haze to enter.

Haze stepped through the doors and was greeted by the most beautiful craftsmanship he had ever seen.

White pillars supported a massive domed ceiling, draped in cobwebs of gold and sapphire chandeliers. The floors were a polished black marble, reflecting the light of the chandeliers onto the pillars and walls in a dark blue glow. A white carpet stretched from the double doors all the way to the other end of the Gallery where it was met by a white stone statue, twice as tall as Haze himself. The stone was carved into the shape of a young woman, perhaps twenty years old, holding a small book in her hands and smiling down at them kindly. Between each of the pillars that lined the sides of the white carpet were more statues, shining white against the dark floor like pearls nestled on the sea floor. All but the first were children, perhaps seven or eight years old. They were young girls, each of them varying in height and features, but all with the same kindness beaming out of their eyes.

Vlaire strode down the carpet, Haze in tow. Making a sharp right in front of the statue of the woman, he headed towards a small door in the back of the hall. It was tucked neatly away in the corner, nearly out of sight from the Gallery doors. Opening it, he started up a set of circular stairs.

They wound up at least two stories before the stairwell turned to ice. The steps were draped in a fine mist, the walls lit with torches that flickered in the breeze from the open door below. The stairwell emptied out onto a landing where their path was blocked by a black door set into the blue ice. It was made of a wood Haze was unfamiliar with, and had strange letters etched into it in bright silver letters. Graceful arches and swirls were scrawled across the wood to shape a single, glowing word.

"What does it say?" Haze asked immediately.

"It says 'Lorgalith,'" Vlaire answered, raising his fist and knocking on it sharply. "He is the Range Keeper."

Haze glanced at him as a latch sounded from the other side of the door and it swung inward slowly, allowing a draft of cold air to blast over them through the opening.

Vlaire ducked his massive frame through the door and out into an open gazebo, a bright red carpet covering the icy floor from edge to edge.

Haze followed him out and was once again astounded by the beauty.

They were under a small building on top of the ice shelf the Gallery was built under. It had no walls, but vertical beams held up a small domed roof of transparent ice. A large bed sat in the center of it, emerald blankets piled in a jumble on top of it. A desk made of the same dark wood as the door was settled by the entrance on his left, a quill resting by an open bottle of ink. Parchments were scattered about the desk with what looked like star charts scratched onto them in dark ink. A flower pot was placed in the far-right corner of it, a tall flower of purple and blue blooming brightly in the cold. Its petals seemed to flicker with light similar to the Yobes, flowing up and down the length of the odd blossom. A high-backed chair stood in front of the desk, its strange wood carved with images of the stars and moon. A potbellied stove stood on his right, with a kettle whistling dutifully on top of it. It had no chimney, and yet a fire crackled merrily in the open grate, hardly a wisp of smoke emptying into the room. A set of stairs led down out of the small gazebo at the opposite end, carved right into the ice floor. They led out onto a ledge that overlooked the City, a view of nearly the entire Mountain Range visible from the edge. They were just below the clouds, nearly eye level with the Banyeet trees they had flown past on the *Rhewddraig*.

"How did we get up here?" Haze asked in disbelief. "There is no way we walked the distance."

Vlaire laughed. "It is a bit of time magic, I suppose. Something the keeper is sort of gifted at."

Haze stared out at the expanse. "Amazing. I have never seen such a sight."

Vlaire nodded. "I always enjoy coming up to see him. The view is beautiful from here. You can see our entire home and beyond."

"So, who is the Range Keeper?"

Vlaire folded his hands behind his back. "I suppose I should let him tell you himself," he said slowly. "I would hate to speak for him and get it wrong. He can be a little sensitive about certain details."

"Only the ones you get wrong," a high voice cackled from their left.

Haze looked to see a stooped old man hobble into the gazebo from the east side. He leaned on a dark staff with an emerald embedded in the top, tendrils of the black wood wrapped protectively around it. The man wore black trousers and a long gray coat that fell to just below his knees, silver buttons lining the front seam. He was entirely bald, waterfalls of wrinkles marking the age in his face. A light scruff covered his face due to lack of shaving. A tiny clean-shaven spot with a small cut marked where he had tried and quit.

"Because that is what you always do," the strange old man chuckled, hobbling over to them slowly. His gait was stiff and uneven. He leaned heavily on his staff, his right arm trembling under his weight. "It's the little details that often are the most important, like the fact that your young friend here has lied to you."

Haze felt his insides freeze as Vlaire glanced at him in alarm, his hand floating to his hammer.

"No need for all that," the old man said, waving his hand at Vlaire. "He lied to you, but not in a bad way. Just in the little details," he said wryly, his eyes twinkling.

Vlaire looked as though he were ready to throw Haze off the edge of the ice shelf. "What exactly did you lie to me about, as I treat your friend's wounds and honor you like a guest?"

Haze opened his mouth to speak, but the old man spoke for him. "He isn't a scout," he sighed. "He is the General of King Orlivan's army. Leader of the Winged Demons, to be precise. Which," he added with a chuckle, "is a much higher rank than scout, if you didn't know."

"I know," Vlaire snapped, his face reddening. "So, why is he here?"

The man looked at Haze silently for a moment. "Well, I think that is yet to be seen," he said mysteriously.

Haze relaxed. He didn't know why he was here. Maybe this could be salvaged after all. It is a known fact that if Jaelyn could kill him, she would. To eliminate the head of the Winged Demons would bring her a great advantage in battles to come. That would serve as an excuse for why he had lied.

"*What* he was sent here to do," the old man added, "is quite simple; he was sent here to protect the Hyless."

Vlaire's mouth nearly dropped open. "Pardon me?" he said weakly.

The man smiled, showing a row of cracked teeth the color of old cheese. He lowered himself into his chair with a weary groan. "Yes, I know. Rather confusing, isn't it?"

"Confusing?" Vlaire exclaimed. "A military general here to guard the Hyless? She has enough guards!"

"She?" Haze asked quickly.

Vlaire's face paled. "It."

"No, you said she," Haze said. "What is the Hyless?"

"That is none of your concern," Vlaire snapped. He looked back at the old man. "Lorgalith, tell me what is going on."

Lorgalith sighed. "Well, I only know parts of it myself. The rest we will have to wait to understand fully."

"Then tell me the parts you know," Vlaire said. "Surely you can do that."

Lorgalith looked at the guard for the first time. "I can tell you what you should do. You know very well I cannot tell you everything I know. That is the burden of the Range Keeper."

Vlaire cleared his throat in forced patience. "Very well then, *what* should I do?"

"I am in need of my hot water bottle on the shelf above the stove," Lorgalith said cheerfully. "My back has been in a frightful state today. You may begin by fetching me that."

Haze had to stop himself from laughing as Vlaire stared at the old man silently for a moment, his face slack in bewilderment. Finally, he

154

spun on his heels and strode over to the shelf. Haze heard objects clattering to the floor as he dug through the jumble looking for this hot water bottle.

"So, Haze," the old man said. "I am Lorgalith, as you know. Tell me, what are you here for?"

Haze blinked.

Lorgalith's eyes sparkled mysteriously. "I know what you were sent here to do, as do you. I mean the question on a more personal level. Why are *you* here?"

Haze lifted his chin. "First, tell me what you are. A Ridge Keeper? What is that?"

"It's Range Keeper," the old man corrected him. "I am the time magician that warps time in the Range. I am also responsible for monitoring the Rime Born and keeping watch on all things inside the Range, and some things outside that may affect it. I am also the one that told Vlaire to prevent Oaina from killing you, and to bring you here instead. Now again; why did you come here?"

Haze struggled to understand what the old man meant. He seemed to know everything already. Why was he asking him the same question he already knew the answer to?

"Let me explain better," Lorgalith said. "I know what you are here to do: Protect the Hyless. That is a mission, plain and simple, but I want to know why the General of the Winged Demons would go on a mission such as this one," he said quietly, his beady brown eyes fixed on Haze. "Why did *you* come? I know your king did not command you."

Haze swallowed. He didn't even know himself why he had done it. To prevent a war was a lie. From the way these people marched their Guards around, it seemed as though they expected a war regardless. "I honestly don't know why," he answered truthfully. "It has something to

155

do with the name of the creature I am supposed to be protecting. I know it sounds foolish," he added quickly as the old man's wrinkled face broke into a smile.

"On the contrary, that was exactly what I was hoping to hear."

"What were you hoping to hear?" Vlaire asked shortly, appearing at Haze's right with the small metal bottle.

"Oh, thank you Vlaire. Would you mind filling it there with the kettle?" Lorgalith said, pointing at the pot whistling on top of the stove. "Please and thank you."

Vlaire glared at the old man before turning around and walking away again.

"You see," Lorgalith continued, settling comfortably back in his chair, "there is an old story you have probably heard about the Guardians of the Hyless. It's amazing, and written by a great story teller. Unfortunately, it is not entirely true."

Haze raised an eyebrow. "How so?"

Lorgalith eyed him for a moment. "Do you believe in fate?" he asked.

"I do not," Haze said flatly. "I believe it is a misconception of consequence."

Lorgalith nodded slowly, rubbing his chin. "Fascinating. What a well reflected statement." He leaned up and ruffled through some of the papers on his desk absently for a moment, then leaned back and crossed his arms. "Fate is something not entirely understood, I think. You don't believe that it exists, and that there are only actions and consequences?"

"I don't think any man is born with a fixed purpose," Haze said. "I think we are the masters of our lives."

"I quite agree," Lorgalith said cheerfully.

"So why did you ask me?"

156

"Because I wanted to know whether or not I should tell you what I believe," Lorgalith said, "but since you don't believe in fate, you won't believe what I believe, and that, I believe, would cause you to believe that I am insane." He winked. "So instead, I will ask you a simple question on which you may reflect for as long as need be: If fate is nothing but the consequences of our actions, then why should we not be fated to accept or endure them?"

Haze blinked. He couldn't tell if what the old man had said was profound or mad. "What do you mean?"

The old man laughed. "Never mind. You will figure it out soon enough. For now, I need an honest answer: Are you a danger to the Hyless?"

"If I were, would I tell you?" Haze asked incredulously.

"Yes." He smiled. "It is not possible to lie to me. I would know if you tried, and have Vlaire stove your head in with a hammer."

Haze cleared his throat, glancing over his shoulder at the hulking man cursing at the tea kettle. "Right. I am not a danger to the Hyless," he said truthfully. "I mean her no harm, and I am here for exactly the reason you said I was to begin with. I mean to protect her."

Lorgalith smiled at him, his eyes twinkling. "I am inclined to believe you. Please don't make a fool of me. It's hard enough for me to be taken seriously around here."

"Alright, Lorgalith." Vlaire walked over, shaking his hand. "Here is your hot water bottle. Half the kettle ended up on my hand, so it had better be worth it."

Lorgalith stood up slowly, leaning on his staff and catching his breath. "Oh, thank you Vlaire. Just set it on my desk there. I am feeling better after all. Young Haze here is an inspiring young man."

Vlaire stared at him, his face turning the color of a sunrise. "Now will you tell me what to do?" he said through gritted teeth, dropping the metal bottle down on the wooden desk.

Lorgalith smiled and nodded. "Yes, I think so. You must introduce Haze to the Hyless. I believe they need to meet."

Vlaire coughed. "What?"

"He is here to protect her," Lorgalith said, "and that being the case, he will need to know where she lives."

"Lor, I think you are making a mistake," Vlaire said slowly. "We don't know him. He could be dangerous."

"No, I am not," Lorgalith said sharply, "and you know I hate it when you call me that. It makes me sound like a foreign delicacy." He sighed and waved his hand. "But no matter. Take him to Lox and see that they are introduced. Be sure he gets his weapon."

"His weapon?" Vlaire cried.

"You heard me. And make sure your sister doesn't kill him," he added sharply. "That would vex me greatly. If I spend one more day looking for the bodies that woman hides in the Mirror Wood, I may well die there myself. I'm not the youngest man in Hallovath, you know."

Haze swallowed nervously. It seemed Oaina was just as bad as she presented herself.

Vlaire grumbled to himself for a moment. "Can I put him under a regular watch at least?"

"I would expect nothing less. Now take him to see her already. She should be waking up from her nap any time now."

Haze raised an eyebrow and glanced at Vlaire. "Nap?"

Lorgalith smiled. "Yes. The Hyless isn't some beast like you have been told, enter the false part of the story," he chuckled. "She is a little girl."

Chapter Seventeen
Ki

"Is he insane?" Haze asked as they exited the Gallery and strode towards the *Rhewddraig*. An ice wyvern sat contentedly by the wooden ramp that led up into the ship.

"Sometimes I wonder," Vlaire said, shaking his head. "He has a tendency to come across in two ways, either very wise, or completely mad. This was the mad day."

"So where does the Hyless live?"

"She lives with Lox, the red-headed guard who is caring for your friend. All of us Guards are her surrogate family. She looks to us for guidance."

"I see. Tell me something, why does Lorgalith trust me?"

Vlaire glanced at him quickly. "Lorgalith sees things the rest of cannot. He speaks to the mountain peaks around us, communicates with the Rime Born, and has a direct connection to the spirits of the Range. We can't always understand why he says and does these sorts of things."

"You do not share his trust," Haze said.

"No," the guard replied flatly. "You lied to me, and that will take time to mend. I respect the Range Keepers decision, but that is all. You will be under constant watch, and your other friends will remain in prison until further notice."

Haze nodded in resignation. "I understand. For what it's worth, I apologize for lying to you. The way the story of the Hyless was told to me I was led to believe she is very important. I couldn't risk the sensitivity of my mission to people I didn't know."

"It is something in the past that will take time to mend," Vlaire repeated. He stopped as he reached the wyvern. "For what it's worth, I respect you for looking out for the Hyless. Now get on," he said. "I will fly you down into the city."

Haze nodded silently and swung himself up behind the saddle. The wyvern was, as usual, larger than Salezz. His back was broader, and his entire body thrummed with a power that his little wyvern never had.

Vlaire pulled himself up into the saddle and settled in front of him. "This is Boar," he said simply. "Hold on."

Haze gripped the back of the saddle as the beast launched himself over the edge and into open air. His stomach leaped into his throat as they plummeted towards the white buildings below. Streets wound across the frozen waterfall below them, different levels marked with different colored windows. Houses lined the streets suspended by tall white pillars, around fifteen feet of open space between each home. White railings rose up along the edges of the streets and porches of the homes, most likely meant to keep children from falling hundreds of feet down the icy slopes.

Boar spread his wings just before they collided with the tallest peaked roof, and fluttered to a stop in the middle of the nearest cobblestone road.

"That was fast," Haze remarked as he slid down.

"You can glide down slowly if you like," Vlaire said, joining him on the ground, "but that is hardly efficient, and Boar enjoys a good dive as much as the next wyvern. I simply allow him his few indulgences."

Haze laughed. "He sounds a lot like Salezz." His heart wrenched as he thought of his mount and best friend. "Where is he being kept, anyway?"

"He isn't," Vlaire said. "He was seen up in the shelf of Tundra Falls with the rest of the wyverns. He is safe, and he has free access to hunting."

Haze's heart fell. He must have been content if he had not come looking for him yet.

Vlaire patted Boar and started towards one of the nearest houses. It was nestled back between two other homes, each almost twice its size. A small square door made of Lorgalith's dark wood swung directly in the middle of its forward wall, a tiny blue window in the top of it. More emerald green windows were scattered about the white walls of the house itself, glistening like gemstones in the dull light.

Vlaire marched up to the small house and knocked sharply on the door. It swung open immediately, a petite young woman standing inside with a small bundle in her arms. Her hair was a light blonde, tied up in a messy bun on top of her head. She wore a plain blue dress that fell to her ankles. Her eyes were a soft green, her face fair and smooth.

"Oh, hello Vlaire!" she said politely. "Lox didn't tell me you were coming by."

"Hello, Malya. The Range Keeper sent me here on official business, I'm afraid. Has Ki finished her nap for the day yet?"

The young woman looked over Vlaire's shoulder and her blue eyes met Haze's. She looked back at Vlaire. "Why?"

"Lorgalith wants this man introduced to her," Vlaire said. When the woman opened her mouth to protest, he lifted his hand. "I know it seems bizarre, as it usually does with Lorgalith, but you know his orders are orders."

The woman clamped her mouth shut and stepped aside, opening the door wider.

Vlaire gestured for Haze to enter first.

161

He stepped past Malya, who stared at him warily as he passed.

The house was quaint. A small round table with three chairs around it sat in the middle of the white room on a dark brown rug. A fireplace was nestled into the far wall, another small table next to it littered with pots and pans of various sizes. A door in the left side of the room was partly open, showing a large bed covered with red blankets. Another doorway to their right was closed off only by a light tan curtain hung over the entrance. A small bed was in the corner of the main room, to the left of the fireplace. A number of different parchments were fixed to the wall above it, a child's drawings of beasts Haze didn't recognize.

The woman closed the door behind them. "Lox!" she called. "Vlaire is here with a guest."

She stared at Haze nervously as she walked past him towards the fireplace. She set the bundle down on the small bed and it moved, a pudgy arm sticking up out of the blankets.

The curtain to their right slid open, Lox walking out of the room as he wiped his bloody hands on a towel. "Vlaire," he said politely, bowing his head. "Oh, hello again Haze. What are you two doing here?"

"Lorgalith wants him introduced to Ki," Vlaire said.

Lox's smile remained strong as he looked back at Haze, unfazed by Vlaire's news. "Oh, really? Alright, I'll bring her in."

He turned and went back into the room behind the curtain, reappearing a moment later with a young girl of about seven years. Sandy blonde hair tumbled all the way down to her waist, her eyes a bright green. A few freckles were scattered around her nose, a dress matching the color of her eyes falling to just below her knees. She looked back and forth between Vlaire and Lox, before her eyes finally settled on Haze.

"Hello," he said quietly.

162

"She can't hear you," Vlaire said. "She is deaf." He waved his hand in front of himself in an odd motion, and the girl responded with a similar gesture.

Vlaire glanced at Haze. "She says hello."

Haze walked towards her, casting a discerning eye over her features; the small scratch on her forehead, a bruised shin, messy wild hair, and dirty bare feet. Everything one would expect to see in a child.

"So, this is the Hyless," he said quietly to himself. The wheels in his mind began turning on the steps that would have to be taken to ensure her safety; given the state of her clothes and scrapes, she was obviously adventurous.

Vlaire and the woman glanced at each other. "Yes," Vlaire said, clearing his throat. "She is."

"So much trouble over a single little girl."

"She is not just a girl, Haze," Vlaire said, "She is the source of all light in the world. The reason we breathe, and walk."

Haze nodded, but he wasn't really listening. His eyes were fixed on hers, the emerald green of her gaze boring into his own. "It feels like she is staring right through me."

"A lot of people feel that way," Vlaire chuckled. "Myself included."

"How do I tell her my name?" Haze asked Lox. The young guard was standing stock still, the bloody towel motionless on his hands.

"Oh, uh, you spell out the letters like this," he said, lifting his hand and showing Haze the correct shapes.

Haze did as Lox showed him, then pointed to himself.

Ki smiled and blushed, putting her hands behind her back and looking down at her feet.

"So why exactly are you getting introduced to Ki?" Lox asked suddenly, his cheerful demeanor finally dampening slightly.

"I came here to protect her," Haze said. "Lorgalith said I was to be introduced, so here I am."

Lox nodded. "Uh huh. I see. Any other reason?" he said, scratching his head. "I mean, that sounds a bit far-fetched if you ask me, even for Lorgalith."

Vlaire stepped forward, poking at a small basket on the table and pulling out a freshly baked roll. "It's what Lorgalith wants. We can't deny him any more than we can deny her."

Lox nodded. "Right. Well. I suppose that's that, then. But still, who are you intending to protect her from, exactly?"

Haze looked up, directing his gaze at the red headed guard. His expression was kind, but inquisitive. "May we sit down? I feel like I owe you people an explanation."

Lox nodded and hurried past, eagerly pulling out the three chairs from around the table and gesturing for Haze to sit.

Haze seated himself. It was only fair that these people were given a reason for his sudden appearance in the range, and that they're minds were put at ease. And at any rate, it seemed as though Lorgalith pretty much knew everything there was to know about him anyway.

Once the two guards were seated, the young woman picked up the baby and sat on the edge of the small bed.

"My land, outside of the Mountain Range, is embroiled in the beginnings of a war," he began. "My King, Orlivan, is attempting to maintain a tenuous peace with a woman named Jaelyn, queen of the Glaistoff Empire. The previous Lord of Glaistoff was a peaceful man, but this woman incites war at the slightest provocation. She doesn't really need to be provoked at all, to be honest. I don't know the details, but somehow the legend of the Hyless was uncovered in the libraries of

Glaistoff. Jaelyn got her hands on it, and is attempting to rekindle the flames of the Havi Ut Gahdness."

Vlaire hissed angrily as Lox's eyes widened. "Are you serious?" the young guard asked under his breath.

"It is what I was told by a woman named Moxie," Haze continued. "She is a captain of Jaelyn's largest warship, but secretly serves the true Lord of Miasma City, Kinzin. She sent me here because she fears that Jaelyn and Orlivan are both going to try and take the power of the Hyless to use on the other."

"That's what the new patrols have been about," Lox said under his breath.

"What new patrols?" Haze asked in alarm. Had Orlivan begun sending patrols already?

"Well, it's true that the Seven Years of Mourning are in effect," Lox said, "but they are almost over. About six years ago, men started coming into the Range, armed with strange weapons and airships. Initially, we treated them with kindness, but it wasn't long before they made it known that they were hunting for the Hyless. The Rime Born attacked them and drove them from the Range but in the last few weeks, the patrols have picked up again. Except, instead of the people with the strange weapons and airships, they are people wielding swords and other weapons we are familiar with. Perhaps these are your people, and the ones before were Jaelyn's?"

Haze rubbed his chin. That would mean that Orlivan knew the Range was open before Galnoron had told him. He must know something that he didn't want Haze hearing about. "Why are they able to get in, anyway?" he asked. "How has the cold stopped?"

"Well," Vlaire sighed, "Ki was born almost eight years ago now. The last Hyless dies as soon as the new one is born, and until she reaches an age where she can inherit her powers, they lie dormant inside the souls of her Guardians."

"The Aurrau Von Gahdness," Haze said.

Lox nodded. "Yes."

Haze looked back and forth between the two. "Who are they?"

The two glanced at each other. "We are, as well as my sister, Oaina."

Chapter Eighteen
A Bloody Patrol

Haze stepped out of the double doors of the Gallery and breathed in the fresh air. He had slept soundly in the room they had provided for him. It was a little drafty, but the cot was soft and the blankets warm.

He took in the bright morning, the sound of screeching wyverns immediately flooding his ears as the doors closed behind him. The glistening blue creatures dove and whirled in the sky in front of him, some with riders and some without as they went about their morning business.

"Late riser, are you?" a cold voice said from his left.

Oaina was leaning against one of the wyvern statues in front of the Gallery, her hand still resting on her sword. She looked as though she had not bothered to go to sleep last night, still fully clad in her armor and her hair not the least bit awry. "Not good practice for one who is supposed to be guarding the Hyless."

Haze squinted in the light and lifted his hand over his eyes to shield them as he looked at her. "Why? Is there somewhere I am supposed to be?"

She stood up and walked over to him, his lance clasped in her right hand. She shoved it into his arm. "Yes. We go on patrol today."

She whistled and her solid white Wyvern clambered down from where she had been perched on top of the Gallery.

"Good girl," she cooed gently, rubbing under the beast's chin. The wyvern fixed Haze with a narrow-eyed glare, her blue eyes burning into his.

"What patrol?" Haze asked. "Where?"

"We have to guard the Banyeet Titans," Oaina said. "The invaders use them as home bases during their attacks."

"Banyeet Titans?" Haze asked.

"The giant trees in the plains below," Oaina said shortly. "We patrol them regularly to ward off the intruders."

Haze cleared his throat. "How often do you fight against these intruders?" He wasn't afraid of battle; he had seen his fair share of blood, but the idea of having to kill Orlivan's soldiers made his stomach flip.

"Almost daily," Oaina answered brusquely, adjusting something on her wyvern's saddle. "They are clustered at the base of the Banyeets, setting up camps usually. Or they have been, for the last two weeks or so."

Haze's heart fell. "I see."

Oaina looked back at him quickly. "If you haven't got the nerve to fight, tell me now," she snapped. "I don't want a cripple slowing me down. If you want to just stay here and play guard at Ki's door, then do that, but this is what being a Guardian of the Hyless is. Not standing quietly in the sunshine with your lance resting against the house."

"I can fight better than most you've seen," he retorted. "I was just thinking. And I certainly don't need a lecture," he added sharply. "I have spent more time with blood on my lance than most people twice my age."

"I know what you're thinking," Oaina sneered, dropping what she was doing and walking to stand in front of him. She stood so close to him, he could smell the odor of fireplace smoke wafting off of her. Her long black hair hung in thick strands over the left side of her face. "You are afraid you are going to end up killing your comrades. You fear you might have to kill someone you know." Her eyes bored into him. "I don't

168

think you have the steel it takes to be Guardian. I will be watching you, general. Should you falter for a moment, or hesitate to slay someone that poses a threat to Ki, yours will be the next life I take."

Haze looked up at her evenly. "Let me worry about what I am afraid of and what I am not," he said quietly. "I advise you not to make an enemy of me, Guardian. I didn't become the general of the Winged Demons by standing quietly in the sunshine."

She stared down at him for a moment, her eyes glinting dangerously. After a moment, she clenched her jaw and spun away, Haze catching a much better glimpse of the scar on the left side of her face as her hair spun out of the way. It was jagged and deep, the wound poorly healed. She returned to what she was doing on her saddle, and Haze slung his lance over his shoulder.

"How did you get your scar?" he asked.

"None of your business."

"I am curious," he said slowly. "I have my fair share of scars, and I have never seen one so angry as yours."

"It's none of your business," she repeated, finishing what she was doing and turning to face him. Her hair had returned to hanging over her scar. "Now come and climb on. We don't have time to waste. The last group returned from patrol half an hour ago."

Haze decided to let go of the scar for now. He knew what it was like for people to constantly ask him what had happened to his arm, and he knew Oaina must have a similar problem.

Striding past her, he swung himself deftly onto the wyvern's back, landing comfortably behind the saddle.

Oaina heaved her massive frame up in front of him, picking up the reins. "Evaala is a rougher ride than you're used to," she said flatly. "You may wish to hold on."

169

She tapped the wyvern in the side and she lumbered over to the edge of the platform. Catching her breath, the great beast launched them off the edge and into open air, winging towards the giant trees shrouded in blue mist.

She was a more comfortable ride than Oaina had said she would be. Her wings flapped steadily, falling still when she found an updraft that carried them up without effort. The scenery flew past below them, snow-capped peaks splitting the fog banks in some places. They were surrounded by the giant tree's that loomed over the Range like sentinels. The tops of the Banyeets curled out over the canyons and forests below like the heads of giant mushrooms, blocking out the sun. As they got closer to them, Haze could make out clumps of moss growing on the branches that were easily the size of entire houses. The thick blue substance grew in lines and waves up and down the branches and the trunks, creating what looked like entire cities on the black wood.

Evaala began to slowly descend towards the fog in large circles, taking them closer and closer to the first of the massive trees.

"Wait, we are patrolling by ourselves?" Haze asked.

"We are."

"But what if we run into a dozen soldiers?" he said incredulously. He had trained many of them himself; they would not be easy to overcome, especially not outnumbered six to one.

Oaina laughed coldly. "Don't worry, Hela. I won't let them hurt you."

Haze rolled his eyes. "I'll keep that in mind, thanks."

They descended into the fog, the world going completely white as the mist soaked into their clothes and immediately drenched through to their skin. They dropped through the clouds more quickly than Haze thought they would, bursting out over a dense blue forest. Normally sized trees rose from the ground by the hundreds, their branches covered in layers of thick white snow, icicles hanging down from the limbs like spikes of glass.

Haze narrowed his eyes and pointed. "What is that?"

It looked like a mushroom, or something like it, except it was as tall as the trees surrounding it, it's soft bell drooping wearily over the undergrowth beneath it. It was covered from top to bottom in the dense blue moss, growing in much smaller, yet more violent streaks across the light tan fungi.

"It is a mushroom," Oaina said flatly. "What does it look like?"

"Well, I just thought…" he trailed off. "Never mind." He didn't want to explain to Oaina how he assumed it was called something else because so far, everything else was.

They floated down into the forest, Evaala's wings brushing against the tree branches as they glided towards the snow-covered floor. They landed softly beneath one of the giant mushrooms, the sound of creatures chirping and croaking echoing across the forest.

Oaina slid wordlessly from the saddle, turning around and digging through one of the saddle bags hanging by Haze's feet.

Haze leaped down, shifting his lance on his back. "What are you looking for?"

"Our food," she said shortly. "We are going to be out here for some time. I don't like going hungry." She pulled a small leather satchel out of the saddle bag and slung it over her shoulder. "You stay here, Evaala. Be a good girl." The massive white wyvern yawned, her razor-sharp teeth glinting in the dull light.

Turning around, Oaina shouldered past him and started marching into the brush.

"Wait, where are we going?" Haze asked, hurrying to catch up.

171

"Into the places of the forest that they think we don't go," she said. "That is where they set up their camps."

"Why do you care if people come in here and set up camps?" Haze asked incredulously. "Surely they can't all mean to harm Ki?"

"We don't mind if people come in to set up camps," Oaina snapped. "Just not soldiers. They aren't welcome here, and should we find them..." she trailed off and turned to face him, stopping in the middle of the path. "We are going to kill every single one of them without hesitation. That is what we do as Guardians of the Hyless."

Haze stared at her. "You would incite a war with Orlivan over a camp of scouts?"

Oaina scowled and turned away, marching even faster down the poorly beaten trail. "He incited the war by sending them in here. Surely as a general you would know one does not send scouts into a foreign land without at least considering marching an army behind them. Or else, why send the scouts at all? Why not send..." she waved her arms around her head, "Explorers?"

Haze couldn't help but agree. He knew that Orlivan intended to enter the Range, but he couldn't simply stand by and allow Oaina to kill his men. He was their general. "That is true, but have you attempted to speak with them at all? Have you even tried to communicate?"

"No," she said flatly. "We tried with Jaelyn's soldiers, and they used the information they got from inside our city to attack it. After that, we decided that if there was any negotiating to be done, it could wait until after the Years of Mourning have passed. When the Hyless comes into her powers, we can discuss peace. Not before."

Haze fell silent and walked behind her through the thick undergrowth and shrubs. Their snow-covered branches slapped against his legs as he pushed past them, soaking into his already drenched trousers. The next

172

several hours passed in relative silence as they forged their way through miles of freezing cold underbrush, waded across half frozen streams, and climbed icy embankments.

He didn't mind too much, though. The beauty of the Range was stunning. Fish flickered in the small streams, their scales casting little rays of light through the frozen surface and making it look like the water itself was glowing. Birds and creatures unlike any Haze had ever seen flitted and scampered in the trees and hollows around them. The sapphire trees moved and whispered to each other, even though there was no wind to be heard. The giant Banyeets that towered above them groaned in response to their smaller cousins, their tops vanishing into the clouds above. The forest was filled with a myriad of different wonders, everything from the creatures to the plant life seeming to have its own kind of radiance. At one point, they came around a sudden corner in the trail and there was a clearing full of tiny blue bell flowers. To Haze's surprise, when they stepped towards them, they leaped into the air. Sprouting tiny wings that whirled on their backs like the propellers on Moxie's airship, they squealed at him as they soared towards the tree tops. Their bodies were a crystalline blue, their beady black eyes glaring indignantly out at him from under the edge of their bells. Oaina said they were Gelid Sprites, and that they were friendly for the most part. Around every corner, they found something new and fascinating. One Oaina called a Gliding Briskk, a tiny rodent-like creature that floated suspended in the air without even the smallest set of wings. It whistled and cooed at them as they passed, its purple hide flashing and pulsing brightly. She said it was warning them away from its nest. After this, Oaina grew tired of answering his questions and refused to speak anymore. So, he simply guessed as to what the beasts could be named, and began to call them things himself. The day took a turn for the worse when he nearly collided with Oaina. He had been engrossed in the scenery and failed to notice when she came to a sudden stop in the middle of the trail.

"What's going on?" he asked, coming around her to look.

He froze when he saw what had made her stop.

A giant grayish blue wolf lay in the path. The tip of every one of its hairs glistened with ice that seemed to grow on its body. Its fur was soaked in blood, a large hole in its side where it had been stabbed by something. Its purple eyes stared up at them warily, its breath coming in ragged gasps. It was at least the size of a fully-grown horse, its feet the size of small cart wheels. Its teeth were easily as long as Haze's fingers, ending in wickedly sharp points just below its upper lip.

"What happened?" Haze asked, his voice low.

"I would wager this was one of your scouts," Oaina said bitterly. "They must be somewhere close by. This creature's wounds are severe. It can't have been laying here long." She wheeled on him. "We find this on a nearly daily basis: dead or dying spirits of the Range. Your people are aggressive and destructive, and you want to know why we haven't tried talking to them? Even Jaelyn's people didn't do this!"

Haze shook his head. "I am truly sorry. I didn't know they were in here doing this sort of thing."

Oaina shook her head and drew her battle sword. She said something under her breath, then brought the massive blade down on the wolf's neck. Its breathing ceased, its body twitching briefly before falling still.

Oaina wiped her sword on its fur and sheathed it. She then turned away and wordlessly began running through the forest.

Haze was pressed to keep up as the woman jumped, ducked, and dodged around fallen trees and large boulders that were strewn across the path. He nearly collided with a giant mushroom that was leaning out into the trail, moss hanging from it in straggly vines.

"Oaina, wait!" he called. "Slow down!"

She ignored him, picking up speed as she hurtled through the forest. At length, Haze was forced to slow down. His breath came in ragged gasps, his ribs stabbing with pain. He couldn't keep up with her. She was simply too fast. Her strides were enormous, covering more ground than seemed humanly possible.

He slowed to a stop, bending over and resting his hand on his knee. He panted loudly, gasping for breath as his lungs burned with the fire of exertion.

"Damn!" he exclaimed. "How does she move so fast?"

After a few moments of wheezing, he caught his breath enough to straighten back up. He looked around himself.

Oaina had left him in a narrow part of the woods, trees thick along either side of the path that wound into the darkening forest. A few of the giant mushrooms fought for room in the tree line, their bulbous heads twisting around the trunks and limbs of the more solid growths. A solitary bird whistled a haunting tune in a nearby tree top.

He turned around and looked at the other side of the path. He was greeted with much the same sight, save for a few less mushrooms.

"Great," he said flatly. "I don't believe it. She left me in the woods by myself. This is perfect." He cursed and kicked at a stick on the ground, sending it spinning off into the bushes that lined the path.

A low, rumbling growl sounded from the underbrush as the stick rustled in the branches.

Haze froze. It would be just his luck to encounter some massive predator the second Oaina left him.

He turned slowly to face where the sound came from. A bunch of trees were grouped to together, hiding the source of the growling. The brush on either side of the trees trembled briefly, another low growl emanating from the foliage.

He ground his teeth together. He wasn't giving Oaina the pleasure of finding his mutilated corpse on the trail. How long had he been alone? Maybe three minutes?

He pulled his lance slowly from its sheath on his back and leveled it in front of him. If it was another wolf, he could kill it. Oaina had just killed one, and it had died like any other animal.

Another snarl drifted out of the bushes, their rustling intensifying by the second.

His heart pounded in his ears and he swallowed, wondering what horror might await him just out of sight. If it wasn't a wolf, perhaps it was an Algid.

The rustling grew louder, until it was little less than a roar in his ears. It drowned out the thrumming of his heart, nothing but the sound of the rattling branches scraping wildly against each other filling his mind.

If it was an Algid, he stood little hope of fighting it. His weapon couldn't hurt a cloud of fog. He braced his feet and gritted his teeth, preparing for the inevitable lunge the beast would make.

The bushes burst open, and a beast of shining blue scales leaped out onto the trail.

"Salezz!" Haze exclaimed. Relief washed over him as the wyvern barked, stomping the ground cheerfully in front of his master. "I thought you were living the high life, off hunting with your new friends!"

Salezz snorted a jet of ice at the ground and backed away, looking at Haze expectantly.

"Sorry, I have to wait here for Oaina," he said, shaking his head. "I am sure she is just waiting for a reason to tell Vlaire I need to be killed or something."

"Attempting to escape on your wyvern could be one of those reasons," Oaina's voice said from behind him.

He whirled around to see her standing in the middle of the path with her arms crossed, her expression as sour as ever. "Except I didn't," he said with an equally sour tone. "Unfortunately for you."

"Hmph." She glared at him for a moment, then pushed past him. "Come on. We have to get back to the City. I have something I must report to Vlaire."

Chapter Nineteen
Galnoron's Betrayal

Oaina had argued with Vlaire incessantly over the dead Ice Wolf. She swore that it was Orlivan's soldiers, but Vlaire wouldn't believe her. He told her that she was too quick to start wars, and that they needed to hold the little peace they had left for as long as possible. Their yelling match had ended with Oaina storming off and Vlaire flying away on Boar, leaving Haze standing alone in front of the Gallery, Salezz sitting beside him quietly.

Over the next few days, Haze went on many patrols with Oaina and Lox. They saw no more dead spirits or creatures, most of their outings in the Banyeet Titans quiet and without incident. The days he went with Lox were his favorite, because he got to see many different creatures and learn a great deal about the Range that these people had lived in for so long. The beauty was incomparable to anything he had seen outside the Mountains, but it was the animal life that amazed him the most.

Most of the animals from around the wilds of the Kingdom would flee if you approached them, or attack you if they were the violent type. These creatures, however, were nearly all friendly. With the exception of the Ice Wolves, who picked and chose their moments. When Oaina and Haze passed them on patrol, they would lift their chins lazily from the ground and yawn, staring at them curiously for a moment before settling back down to sleep. Sleeping was what they seemed to do most of the time, but Oaina said that at night, they were the most active beast in the Range. Haze could hear them howling in the late hours, the sound like a mystical battle horn that rang through the entire Range and stilled every man and beast that could hear it. Every so often, he could hear them snarling and yapping as they chased down some luckless beast, and it sent shivers down his spine. Lox said not to blame them for their violence, that they were the natural guardians of the Range and were responsible for keeping it balanced.

Then, there were the days he did nothing but lounge around town and sit by Alovere's bedside with Ki. He had still not awoken, and his wounds were now infected. Lox said not to worry. He said he would cure both the injuries and the infection in time.

Lox was by far Haze's favorite guard out of the three. He was cheerful and welcoming, his round freckled face full of light and kindness. He spoke of his wife and son regularly, always with the same ecstatic tone that implied he was as enraptured by their existence that day as he had been the last. His son, Mulwyn, was not yet a month old and doted on by both his parents, even for an infant. Haze secretly wondered if the child was going to end up spoiled when he turned old enough to reason with his parents. If how they treated Ki was any indication, their son was likely to be the most spoiled child in Hallovath.

Oaina on the other hand, was an entirely different story. From the first moment they had met, she had treated him with the same cold behavior that she did now, and she showed no sign of letting up. She had also fixed herself to him like a leech. He could barely relieve himself without her present, which was beginning to annoy him. The two weeks he had been there ought to have been enough to at least allow him to sleep in his room by himself, but that was not the case. The giant woman had set up a cot in his room by the door, and spent the night snoring like a dragon in the echoing stone room.

Haze was strangely grateful for Vlaire, most of the time. It was by his orders that Salezz was allowed to remain by Haze's side for most of the time.

The agreement was that he was not allowed to fly out of the city for any reason, or he would be escorted back by the city guards and locked up. Oaina had of course hated this arrangement, saying that Salezz should be put back out to the Falls with the other wyverns, and that if he wouldn't stay out there, he should be locked up. This agitated even Lox, who was as good-natured as it was possible to be. He told Oaina that if they needed a jail warden for the wyverns, he would send for her.

The days went by faster the longer they stayed, and Haze truly began to enjoy the company of these strange people. They devoted themselves fully to what they did, be it farming or battle or cooking. They seemed to excel at anything they tried, no matter what it was. Haze had never seen a more competent people; even Rageth would have been impressed by their devotion.

Haze was awestruck by much of the Range when they first arrived, and was thrilled every time Oaina or Lox took him out on patrol, but as the wonder began to fade, it was replaced with an uneasy fear. He was sent here to protect the Hyless. He wondered at what point that would become necessary, and when he would be called upon to fight for this beautiful place. Some part deep inside of him knew that in order to defend it, he would have to fight his own people. The thought was like a distant storm cloud, and he tried to avoid thinking on it. But the fact remained.

They had finally decided to allow Glassworn out into the city on Lorgalith's orders, and he spent much of his time in the house with Haze and Alovere. Galnoron too was released, but spent most of his time lurking about the town hall in the center of the square.

Haze watched him like a hawk, but could only devote just so much time to babysitting the wizard. He was free to do whatever he wished for most of the day, and it made Haze uneasy.

But for now, he contented himself with the various chores and jobs he could do to help Lox care for Alovere. He focused on helping Vlaire where he could, and spent the rest of his time by Alovere's bedside.

The Riders eyes were closed tightly, his skin pallid and clammy. His wounds were now infected enough to have a pungent odor to them, causing Haze to gag whenever Lox removed his bandages. Lox maintained cheerfully that it wasn't a problem, and that he was on the mend.

True to Lox's word, Alovere awoke two days later. Haze had gone down to the house immediately after Oaina had told him the news.

He was seated in a small chair next to Alovere's bed, a bowl of steaming soup in his hand. "How are you feeling?" he asked him.

Alovere winced as he stretched lightly in his bandages. "Not bad for being cut up by a machine."

"That's what it felt like? They are spirits, actually."

"Whatever they are, they have little in the way of manners," Alovere grumbled. "How is Arginox?"

"The locals are caring for him and Salezz. Free rein hunting! I know Salezz is enjoying it."

"Locals? Where are we?"

Haze glanced over his shoulder. "In a massive city in the middle of the Range. It's beautiful," he stated. "The people are very kind. As soon as you can walk, we will need to get you outside to see it."

Alovere frowned. "And Galnoron didn't know they were in here?"

"I'm not sure. He and Glassworn were just released into the city. I haven't had a chance to talk with either of them, but I don't know that we can trust him anyway."

"Just settle on trusting nothing about him, and you won't be disappointed," Alovere said bitterly. "He is a self-centered ass."

"I gathered."

"Haze." Oaina pushed her massive frame through the curtain. "Vlaire wants you to meet him at the Gallery."

Haze saw Alovere's eyebrows shoot up when he saw Oaina.

"Oh, Alovere, this is Oaina," he said, pointing to the giant woman. "She follows me everywhere and hardly lets me change my clothes by myself."

She glared at him in disapproval. "I do as I'm told, Hela, as should you. We should leave for the Gallery when you are finished here. I will be outside."

Haze sighed. "Very well. I don't suppose you have anything nice to say?"

She turned and exited the room silently.

"Hela?" Alovere asked.

Haze shook his head. "Long story."

"She is charming. She's your guard?"

It occurred to Haze that Alovere had no idea who any of the people were that cared for him. And so, like an excited boy that had been waiting to tell his father a story all day, he launched into the tale of all the events that had happened while Alovere had been unconscious. He told him about Lox and his boy, Oaina and how she had wanted to kill him, and about Vlaire and the patrols he had been taking through the Range.

182

"You wouldn't believe how beautiful it is here," He continued excitedly. "Everything has some sort of light that comes off of it. Most of the stuff here glows like candlelight! And there are these massive wolves made entirely of ice. Vlaire says they are some kind of protectors of the Range. It's like they are born with the instinct to protect the Range from people that don't belong here. Oaina and I walked right past them and they didn't even move."

Alovere frowned at Haze as he spoke. "You do remember why we came here, don't you?"

Haze looked away guiltily. "Yes, but I have been trying not to think about it."

"We don't have to do anything to it," Alovere said. "We just have to capture some beast and leave."

"But that's just the thing," Haze said immediately, "these aren't like normal animals. A lot of them are spirits! Actual, living spirits that are as wise as we are. Or wiser!" He shook his head. "We can't hurt them. What if the Hyless really turns out to have the power the legend says? We can't give that sort of information over to the likes of Orlivan or Queen Jaelyn. Wait, capture? What are you talking about?"

"What's a Hyless?" Alovere asked, frowning at him. "What are *you* talking about?"

Haze swallowed. He had said too much. "It's a creature I was sent here to protect."

Alovere raised an eyebrow. "By whom?"

Haze's mind whirled frantically. "Just a moment, just a moment. Galnoron told you that you are here to capture a beast? What did King Orlivan have to say about it?"

"He told me I was to protect Galnoron with my life. That was all. Galnoron told me we would be capturing a creature large enough to possess so much magical energy, he could use it to march Orlivan's military through the cold."

Haze cleared his throat. "Alright, it's time we shared some stories. I ended up in here because I was kidnapped by an airship crew that works with Glassworn. Moxie was the captains name. She was a rather severe person. She seemed intent on me coming down here and learning about a creature called a Hyless. She stressed that I wasn't to hurt it, but to protect it. She seemed legitimately concerned about the relations between Glaistoff and Beril."

Alovere scoffed loudly. "I wouldn't do anything she asked me to do. She kidnapped you and took you from the Kingdom! Are you mad?"

"Perhaps," Haze said quietly, "but the important part to understand, is that there *is* no cold. This is a time called the Years of Mourning. Anyone can wander in and out of this Range right now. Galnoron doesn't need to capture a beast to march any army into the Mountains, they could march in right now."

Alovere rolled his eyes. "You're thinking about it too much. We have one simple mission: Protect Galnoron. You don't have to do anything that that Moxie woman tells you, she is an enemy of His Majesty. You should simply work with Galnoron and I until we get out of here. If I can recover enough in the next day or two, we can be on our way."

Haze cleared his throat. "Ahem. Yes, about that. You have been unconscious for over two weeks."

"Two weeks?" Alovere bellowed. "That's absurd! My wounds weren't that bad!"

"They got infected," Haze explained quickly. "It was pretty bad. Lox has been treating you."

"Lox?" Alovere said.

"Ah, you're awake."

Lox's friendly tenor drifted into the room, followed a moment later by Lox himself, his fiery red hair strewn on his head from the wind. His freckled face was smudged with what looked like soot. "I heard you yell from over at the Forge. How are you feeling?"

"Like I got stabbed and cut up by a sword," Alovere said. "Thank you for watching after me."

Lox bowed his head respectfully. "It's been my pleasure. Haze has been very kind and helped us out around town with many things. It's only fair that we help cure an injured man."

"Well, I thank you again," Alovere said. "Haze tells me I was in rough shape. I owe you my life."

"There seems to be a lot of that going around right now," Lox laughed. "Ki claims you saved her life."

Alovere looked questioningly at Haze. "Ki?"

"It's this young girl that runs around the city. She is something of an orphan. The three guards are more or less her family," Haze explained.

Lox glanced at him sharply.

He could tell the young guard didn't yet trust Alovere, and without Vlaire's approval, the other Rider wasn't to hear that Ki was the Hyless. While Haze had no intention of hiding this from Alovere, but he couldn't tell him while Lox was in the room.

"I see," Alovere said slowly. "I don't know how I could have saved her life. I have never been here before."

"Ki is a mysterious little girl," Lox smiled. "It's entirely possible she meant it in a different way."

Alovere's face suddenly went white, his eyes fixed on the doorway behind the guard.

Haze followed his line of sight and saw Ki peeking from around Lox's left leg at Alovere, her face bright red.

185

"Are you alright, Alovere?" Lox asked, his brow furrowing.

"Is that Ki?" he said, his voice weak.

"Yes," Lox answered. "She has hardly left your side since you were wounded by the Rime Born."

Alovere looked back at the girl, color slowly returning to his face. "I see. Come here, girl," he said gruffly.

Lox glanced at Haze, then back to Alovere. "She can't hear you. She is deaf."

Alovere looked at him. "How do you communicate with her?"

"We sign. It is a language she came up with so we could understand her. Several of us guards have learned it over time."

Alovere swallowed. "Could I have a moment with Haze, please?"

"Certainly," Lox said. He bowed out of the room, taking Ki's hand and leading her out.

Alovere pointed to where she had stood. "She shouldn't have been standing there," he said flatly.

Haze looked at the door. "What do you mean?"

"I picked her up in a small village just outside of the Range. She was alone by a fire in a torched house. The entire village had been burned down by bandits, or an Algid or something. Galnoron was against keeping her, but I insisted. Before you ask why, I'm not telling you," he said shortly, glaring at the younger man.

Haze swallowed. "And he didn't say anything about knowing who she is?"

"What do you mean?"

Haze glanced over his shoulder. "She is the Hyless. The one the legend speaks of."

Alovere stared at the other Rider. "He must not have known that." He shook his head. "He tried to kill her."

186

Chapter Twenty
Dance Of The Hyless

"He what?" Haze said in disbelief.

"We had to climb down the face of some cliff to get into the Range," Alovere explained. "We couldn't fly on Arginox because the storms were too strong, so we were using a rope. He went first, and I followed. When it was the kid's turn to come down the rope, he used his magic or something to cut it, or make it vanish. She fell from over a hundred feet, but never hit the ground. I heard an impact like she had hit an outcropping maybe." He shook his head. "I thought she was dead for sure."

Haze couldn't believe his ears. He had Galnoron figured as a desperate type, maybe cold and calculating, but not a murderer. "And you are positive it wasn't an accident?"

Alovere nodded. "I am sure. He told me he would do the same to me if I stood in the way of his mission." He lifted his chin. "Not that he could have, but you see my point."

Haze stood up, rubbing his chin thoughtfully. "How do we handle this? If we kill him, the King will have us both executed."

"Easy," Alovere shrugged. "Tell the locals he tried to kill Ki. If the guards are really her surrogate family, I would love to see how they handle the situation." He looked back over at Ki, who had come back into the room and was standing quietly with her hands behind her back, rocking back and forth on the balls of her feet.

While Haze was sure that Vlaire would do something quite horrible to Galnoron, something else was turning through his mind.

"No," he said, shaking his head. "First of all, Oaina would kill us just for being acquainted with that slime. Second, he has something to do with this whole Hyless thing."

"What do you mean?"

Haze shrugged. "He is connected to Orlivan, that we know. But where did he come from? What does he want from the Range?" He shook his head. "We pretend we don't know anything. We let him think he has us blinded."

Alovere rolled his eyes. "How did I know you were going to say that?"

"Trust me on this one," Haze said. "I want to know what he's up to. I've had a bad feeling about him since the first time I met him. Besides," Haze winked, "why would we want Vlaire and Oaina to do our dirty work for us? I can't wait to clobber the snake."

Alovere laughed, wincing and grabbing his chest. "Yeah, that," he wheezed. "How about some food, huh? And shouldn't you be following that barge of a woman wherever she said to go?"

"Lox will bring you some soon, I'm sure."

"I hope so. I am about ready to have Arginox cook Salezz and bring him in here."

Haze chuckled and turned away, ducking through the curtain.

He found Oaina waiting impatiently outside the house, her arms crossed. "Do you think you could have made that take any longer?"

Haze smiled brightly. "I think I could have found a way if you really wanted me to."

Oaina shook her head and strode towards the middle of the street. Evaala and Salezz stood patiently on the bleach-white cobblestones, the sun glinting off of their scales. Their eyes were half closed in the light as they soaked up the warmth.

"Vlaire wants us in the Gallery," she said shortly.

"Why, what's going on?" Haze asked as he followed her out to the wyverns. He patted Salezz briefly before climbing up into the saddle.

"Just follow me to the Gallery and stop asking questions," she snapped, urging her mount into the sky.

Haze tapped Salezz and they launched into the air, following the surly guard up towards the giant ice shelf.

Oaina was in a particularly foul mood this morning. Everything he had said seemed to incite her to rage, even the slightest comment about the lack of clouds that hung in the sky that day.

A few moments later, they landed safely on the white platform beside the *Rhewddraig*. Oaina dismounted and strode towards the Gallery doors.

Haze hadn't noticed that the *Rhewddraig* had returned. It had left three days earlier for the peaks of the Range on patrol. It wasn't due back for at least five days.

He slid down off of Salezz and hurried after Oaina, the wyvern growling in dissatisfaction when he forgot to pet him.

They pushed open the creaking Gallery doors and stepped inside.

Lox, Vlaire, and Malya were all seated at a small table he recognized as the one from his room. They had dragged it out into the middle of the hall and were seated around it talking about something that had Malya's face glowing bright red. Ki stood in the center of the white carpet, her arms held up over her head in a strange pose.

Oaina stomped into the hall, her armor clanking and sword rattling loudly as she entered the marble chamber. "Alright, let's get this over with."

"Haze!" Lox called cheerfully. "Glad you could join us. You're just in time to watch."

Haze smiled as he walked towards them. "Watch what?"

Vlaire pointed at the young girl. "She is about to rehearse her dance," he said, as though Haze should know what that was.

He cleared his throat. "Okay. What kind of dance?" He seated himself beside the red headed guard.

"It is a series of dances she has been preparing for a long time," Vlaire explained. "It is supposed to unlock a little bit of her powers as a Hyless at a time. This is the last one. With luck, this could be the end of the Years of Mourning."

"I see," Haze said. "How many are there?"

Oaina rolled her eyes. "Just shut up and watch the kid dance so we can get out of here."

"Oaina!" Lox said sharply. "You know how Ki feels about her dances. Don't be so rude."

"She can't even hear me," Oaina mumbled, sinking into her chair gloomily. "I could be out on patrol. You know it's not going to work."

Haze looked at her. "Not going to work?"

"No," she grumbled. "Most of the Hyless children have gained full control of their powers by now. She is almost a full year late. She turns eight next month, and she hasn't been able to complete her dance correctly."

"She will figure it out," Vlaire said confidently. "She is the Hyless after all."

"Why can't she complete it?"

Oaina jerked her chin at the girl. "Just watch."

Ki was staring at Lox expectantly, her face glowing and split into a large smile. The guard winked at her and signed something, and she nodded.

Taking a deep breath, she began to dance.

190

She leaped and swirled across the floor, her arms flowing around her like water. Her toes seemed to barely touch the carpet as she floated lightly across the room, her hair lifting like cotton in an absent breeze.

Haze looked above him as music filtered into the hall. He could not see where it was coming from. It was as if it were melting straight out of the sky.

The skin on Ki's face and hands began to shine brightly as she whirled between the statues, the light gleaming through the stone figures and casting leaping shadows across the white carpet. The music grew louder, and Haze realized it was accompanying her dance; every move and every step was accompanied by the light strings of a violin that was nowhere to be seen. She shone brighter and brighter, the entire hall awash in the brilliant radiance that flowed from the young girl like a tidal wave.

But he noticed that though she was dancing beautifully, something was just a bit off.

Her feet grazed the ground just a moment too late, or too early. Her movements were delayed. Her brow was furrowed in concentration, her face set in determination.

Oaina shook her head as the music slowly faded away and the light began to dim. Ki slowed to a stop, finishing with a graceful curtsy. The hall returned to its normal torch-lit interior, the shadows once again falling into the corners as the dance was completed.

Lox and Malya clapped loudly, Lox leaping out of his chair and swooping the young girl into his arms as he signed something to her. He smiled proudly down at her, eyes shining brightly. Malya was signing as quick as lightning, no doubt telling Ki how proud she was.

"You did great, Button," Lox said, his face shining.

But Haze saw the tears in Ki's eyes as she buried her face into the guard's shoulder. Realization dawned on him and he looked at Vlaire. "She can't hear the music."

"No, she can't," Oaina said flatly, "and because she can't, she will never finish the dance correctly. We'll be lucky if the Hyless ever regains her powers."

"Oaina," Vlaire said, frowning at his sister.

"You know it's true," she snapped, rising to her feet. "There is no way she can finish that level of dance without being able to hear the music."

"Where is it coming from?" Haze asked suddenly.

They both turned to look at him.

"The music," he added quickly.

"From us," Vlaire answered, "from the powers of the Hyless that lay dormant in our souls. When she dances, she slowly draws them out into the world. Her dance must follow the pace of the music, or the spirit of the Hyless does not harmonize with her. Without harmony, she has no power."

Haze nodded and looked over at Ki. She was sobbing into Lox's shoulder as he held her. She knew she had failed again, and she obviously knew that it meant a great deal. He didn't know if they taught her that she was a Hyless, or if she didn't know how important this was. Either way, she looked heartbroken by her failure.

Oaina turned and stomped out of the Gallery. "Let's go," she called over her shoulder.

Haze looked over his shoulder at the girl as he followed Oaina out of the Gallery. Just before the doors closed, she sniffed and looked up at him, her tear streaked face still glowing with a faint shine.

Chapter Twenty-one
A Dark Heart

Galnoron looked over his shoulder as he cut down the dark alley that ran between the butcher shop and the seamstress's shop.

The white city was confusing at first, with its many levels and districts, but he had soon caught on to its intricacies. Over the last week that he had been allowed to roam somewhat freely, he had discovered many back passages and nooks he could use to give the two guards ordered to watch him the slip. This worked to his advantage, as he had many things to do to prepare for the attack on the city. First and foremost, he had to find out who the Hyless was.

He grimaced as he trudged down the alley, the scent of raw meat blown between the buildings by a faint breeze that floated through the town.

Haze was being awfully stingy with many of the details regarding their captors, especially regarding the Hyless. He had very little to say on any topic other than the "beauty" of the Range, despite the fact that he had spent nearly a full week with their captors before Glassworn and himself had been released.

He shuddered. The thought of spending another minute locked in a cell with that boozer made his skin crawl. As harmless as he seemed, he was nothing if not annoying. His singing and bellowing at the "bugs" in the walls were enough to drive one mad.

He drew his robe tighter around him. The weather in the cursed Range was nearly as bad as the people. He didn't know why, but he had lost his ability to use his magic inside the city, which was becoming increasingly irritating. He regained a rudimentary use of his powers if he delved deep enough into the recesses of the city and out of the more populated areas. The one time he had been forced to accompany Lox on patrol, he had found that his powers returned entirely as soon as he was outside the walls.

He smiled grimly. Lox was different from the other Guards. He had a talent for music, a kindness that flowed out of him wherever he went.

His readiness to smile was sickening.

He shook his head as he slowed down and turned around a corner, continuing down the dank alley.

The alley began to narrow, the smell of sewage and mold invading his nostrils. He knew that he could always count on finding the dark corners of the world, no matter how bright the location seemed to be. There was always the shadow on the edge, the place no one ever went save for the people with the darkest hearts, the people that thrive on the dank and cold and writhe in the sunlight as their souls reject its warmth.

People like him.

The buildings rose tall on either side of him, the cobblestone street slowly fading out from under his feet as the road burrowed into the side of the frozen waterfall itself. A few more shops were scattered sparsely along the road, carved back into shallow nests in the ice.

How anyone could run a business back here in the hollow part of the city Galnoron couldn't guess, but when he saw one of the shopkeepers step out of his tiny molding hut, he saw why.

The man was stooped and thin, what was left of his stringy hair falling around his shoulders like ancient cobwebs. His nose was pockmarked with an assortment of sores and boils, his face pale and drawn. He smiled as Galnoron passed, showing half a row of broken and missing teeth the color of blackened bread. His beady black eyes glinted at the wizard as he hurried by and pretended not to notice the man. The sign on his shop read, 'A Cure for a Cause: Give Me a Remedy, I'll Give You A Poison'.

Galnoron shuddered and hurried away from the shopkeeper. He once thought he would be that man, tending his shop with little food or money to call his own, selling false cures for false illnesses. Jaelyn had snatched him out of the jaws of destitution and given him another chance at life. While she may not be the wisest person he had ever met, he was grateful to her in his own way. Though he wasn't going to allow that to stand in his way of gaining more power: the power from the Hyless, supposedly the greatest force on the continent. His own hunt for the Hyless would not end until he held its power in his hands.

The alley finally came to a dead end, a blunt ice wall blocking his progress. Glancing over his shoulder, he checked to see if anyone had followed him.

The alley was cold and dark, the slick ice walls and floor shining in the dull light of the moon that hung in the inky sky like a watchful white eye.

He turned back to the ice and drew in a deep breath, feeling some of his magic return to him. It flowed through his veins like hot metal, warming him from the inside out.

Reaching out, he held his hand in front of the ice wall and said, "Drych."

The smooth surface of the wall buckled, melting in on itself briefly. It swirled violently for a moment, before it settled into a smooth glass-like surface. His reflection stared back at him, his yellow eyes gleaming in the dusk light.

"Jaelyn," he said.

The image of the mirror stirred, morphing in shape. It writhed for a moment, distorting his features until they were replaced by those of a woman sitting on the edge of a bed. She wore the smooth red robes of the Glaistoff Court, her long silver hair flowing around her waist like liquid steel. Her features were angular and regal. One might even say that she was beautiful, if you could see past her glittering crimson eyes.

She glared at him with a gaze hot enough to melt solid rock. "You need to stop coming to me when I am in my bedchamber, wizard."

He bowed. "My apologies, your Grace," he said smoothly, "but it is the only time I am able to slip the guards they have watching me."

"You are a sorcerer," she said coldly, "Think of something else. I tire of meeting my subjects in my nightclothes."

"Very well, your grace," he said, bowing again.

"Do you know where the Hyless is yet?"

He cleared his throat nervously. "I'm afraid not. The young Rider doesn't trust me, and isn't imparting any information that he may have. I am working tirelessly to discover its whereabouts," he added quickly, as Jaelyn's eyes narrowed dangerously, "but it's not as simple as one would hope. They have guards everywhere, and I am hardly allowed to move without at least two of them behind me."

Jaelyn's reflection stood up and paced slowly towards him, her robes brushing the floor as she walked. She stopped an arm's reach away and stared at him through the magically procured portal. "I don't care if you have to kill them. Find a way to get rid of them long enough for you to discover the identity of the Hyless before sunset three days from now. I have a few men coming into the city that night."

Galnoron frowned. "What? Why?"

Jaelyn narrowed her eyes. "I know your idea of attacking the City and burning everything to the ground appeals to your power-hungry mind, but I don't want my name stamped on the destruction of Hallovath for the rest of time. It's not how I wish to be remembered. If I can get the girl without destroying half the continent in the process, so much the better."

"Wait, girl?" Galnoron said, holding his hand up. "What girl?"

"The Hyless, you fool!" Jaelyn snapped. "What have you been looking for this entire time? A dragon?"

"I didn't exactly know what I was looking for," Galnoron muttered. "A creature of mythic and magical proportions, I suppose."

"Well, she is a girl," Jaelyn said impatiently, "and you need to have her found before evening three days from now."

Galnoron licked his cracking lips. "Very well, Your Grace, but don't you think it a little soon to try infiltrating the city?"

"Why?" she asked sharply, her eyes flashing. "Are you afraid you neglected to tell me something about its layout? Something my men need to know?"

Galnoron cleared his throat nervously. "No, it's just that I may have missed something, that's all. I have only been released for a week. There are a myriad of alleys and byways that could easily have been overlooked in passing."

Jaelyn narrowed her eyes at him. "Then you had best look closer, because you have three days to work it out. I had better know the identity of the Hyless by that point, or I might just forget to erase your name from the growing list of wanted sorcerers in Miasma City."

Galnoron swallowed. "Yes, your Grace. It will be done."

Very well," She sighed, whirling away from the mirror and strolling back towards her bed. "Leave me be and do your job. Your life counts on it, I'm afraid."

Galnoron waved his hand and the image of Jaelyn's bedroom swirled briefly before returning to nothing but a solid ice wall.

He wrapped his arms around himself and strode back towards the main city, the wheels in his mind turning frantically.

The Hyless was a girl.

He shook his head. That broadened his search, but at least he now knew the sort of creature he was looking for. It would be a challenge to find which girl it was, but he thought that he would know it when he saw it. If the legends were true, then she would most likely be surrounded by Guardians. She would have a small army around her at any given time.

He froze in the middle of the street, water from a puddle seeping into his boot.

His mind went back to the day he was released, when Lox had come and unlocked his cell. Light had flooded into the dark room, causing his eyes to water. He had not noticed it at the time, but he had had someone with him.

It was a small girl.

His stomach flipped as he allowed his magic to enhance his memory.

The image of the small blonde girl peering around the guard's leg flooded his mind. He recognized her as the girl Alovere had found in the village outside the Range. The only way she would have been able to survive that fall was if...

He cursed and stormed up towards the upper city.

He had had the Hyless in his grasp once already! She had somehow made it back to Hallovath and was once again protected by guards.

Galnoron grinned and broke into a jog. His mission had just become infinitely easier. He assumed she lived with Lox. Once he removed the guards that stood outside his house, it would be all too simple to set her up for the task force.

Things were finally coming together.

Chapter Twenty-Two
Dawnsio Golau

Haze sat beside Glassworn in the small pub the druid had found in the market district of the city. It was much cleaner than the one he frequented in Beril, and quite a bit smaller. It was owned and run by a man named Popluu, though he often insisted on being called Pop. He was a portly gentleman that stood perhaps as tall as Moxie, his bald head gleaming bright in the lamplight. A stool stood behind his bar so he was able to reach over it. His round face was bright and always plastered with a smile, belying the volume of his voice. His bellows were enough to drive even the stoutest of men from his pub when he became irritated.

Haze had decided a night of quiet was in order, and could think of no better place to get it than Popluu's Pub.

"Aren't you going to have anything else?" Glassworn slurred from beside him, his eyes crossed.

"No, I don't think so," Haze answered, shaking his head and staring wistfully at his empty goblet. "I need to get up early. I am not a fan of early mornings after late nights."

Glassworn shrugged and ordered himself another ale. "So, as I was saying," he burped, "I run into this guy the other day that told me a story about a giant fortress in the plains. Somewhere out in the Range."

"Mm," Haze said distractedly. He wasn't really listening to Glassworn. He had genuinely tried for the first five minutes of the evening, but in those five minutes the drunk must have bounced back and forth between eight different subjects. Haze had simply lost count of everything he was supposed to be remembering or picking out of the conversation, and decided immediately that there was no hope of keeping up with the druid. Losing himself in his own thoughts, Haze tried to imagine what could be going on outside the Range. Was Orlivan really preparing for war? Is that why he had scouts in the Range already?

He shook his head. If Orlivan had known the Range was open, Haze would have been the first one he told. There was never any batting around the bush with the old man. If he had discovered a way into the Range, he would have ordered Haze into it exactly like he had when Galnoron arrived. No, there had to be some other explanation. Something beyond his sight was going on in the Kingdom, and he was determined to find out what it was.

"You have a good night, Glassworn," he said, sliding his stool back and standing up.

"Going already?" Glassworn cried, lifting his head from the bar and staring at him with crossed eyes.

"I have been here for two hours."

"That's all?" the druid hiccuped. "You can't leave yet! We h-har'ly started!"

Haze chuckled and turned away. "Sorry, Glass. I gotta go."

The magician didn't answer, but laid his head silently back down on the bar.

Haze pushed his way through the double doors of the pub and out into the chill evening.

The sun had set nearly half an hour before, the entire city aglow with the light of dusk. He could see the faint glimmer of the first stars just beginning to fill the sky. Windows in the little white houses began to come to life, shedding blue and green light that danced across the face of the waterfall in a pale glow.

A thought crossed his mind, and his heart raced.

He could take Salezz out for a spin, just like he used to in Beril. Oaina was on night patrol tonight; she would never know he was missing.

Thrill rose in the back of his mind, shadowed by a twinge of fear and guilt. If he were discovered flying outside the city, he would be banned from flying Salezz and put under constant surveillance. But at the same time, he had not tasted a good breath of freedom since he arrived. No matter how courteous his captors were, they could not substitute the feeling of soaring high above the world without a care to call his own.

He bit his lip and frowned. Of course, Vlaire was still somewhere in the city, as was Lox. If either of them found him out of bounds, it would be the end of what little liberties he had left.

He shook his head and resigned himself to flying to the Gallery. If not for himself, then for the Hyless. He didn't want to think about how crippled he would be without Salezz if there were ever some need to come to Ki's aid. He had trouble enough without his arm; without his wyvern, he was worth little more than a warning sign.

He whistled, and Salezz sat up from where he lay outside the pub. He stretched, yawning widely as he climbed to his feet. The wyvern smacked his lips and blinked quickly, focusing on Haze as he walked over.

"Hey, Salezz," Haze said, patting his mount on the cheek.

The Wyrm grunted in reply, the tip of his tail twitching with halfhearted enthusiasm.

"Time to head on back to the Gallery," Haze sighed, swinging himself up onto the wyvern's back. "Long day tomorrow."

Salezz yawned again, then crouched low to the ground. With an enormous leap, he launched into the sky.

Haze's stomach took up its usual place in his feet as the wyvern soared skyward. They rose up above the roof tops, bursting out above

201

the second level of the city. The Gallery came into view, the bottom of the white platform spreading above him like a stone cloud in a darkening sky.

He ground his teeth together as the urge to fly beyond it overcame him again.

He couldn't. He knew he couldn't. He would be caught. Salezz would be taken, and he would be penned in the Gallery until Alovere was ready to fly.

He reached the edge of the Gallery platform and started to guide Salezz towards the airship dock. His hand faltered and he paused, gliding in a soft updraft next to the cobblestones. They glinted like soft pearls in the dusk light. After a moment, he pulled Salezz's reins upwards.

Abandoning any thought of being discovered, he soared above the Gallery, urging his mount higher and higher towards the top of the waterfall. The city fell away beneath him, nothing more than white splotches in the growing gloom.

He would just go to the peak of the falls, then fly back down for the night. He had no intention of going far, just high enough to look down on the city lights like he had so many times in Beril.

His heart pounding in his chest, he leaned forward and tapped Salezz with his heels. The wyvern put on a burst of speed, small wisps of clouds beginning to float past them as they reached the first layer of fog. They dampened Haze's tunic, and small droplets of water glistened on Salezz's blue scales. They skimmed along the face of the frozen waterfall, Salezz's scaly belly just missing the glass-like wall as they sped skyward.

A moment later, they shot past the top of the waterfall, gliding above the shelf of ice curling out over Hallovath like a giant claw. Salezz leveled out, opening his wings and floating silently above the edge of ice.

The Range spread out beneath them, the billowing top of the nearest Banyeet just visible in the fading light. A full moon rose in the distance, its gentle light casting shadows over the glistening blue of the falls. A soft breeze blew over them, the quiet ruffle of wind in his ears making Haze smile.

He hadn't flown this high in a long time.

He guided Salezz back down to the top of the waterfall and landed on the frozen ledge. Sliding to the ground, he patted his mount and turned to look out over Hallovath.

It was still a little too bright for all the stars to have come out, but the city was ablaze with lantern and torchlight. Emerald and sapphire dots winked up at him from the streets far below them, mixing with the dim moonlight like gemstones deep beneath the sea.

"You know, you aren't supposed to be this far from the city without a guard."

An icicle dropped into Haze's stomach and he whirled around. "Lox!"

The young guard sat astride Bard, his hands folded in his lap. He was staring at Haze sternly, an expression of exhaustion on his face. "As if I didn't have enough on my plate with patrols and caring for Alovere, you now decide to wander off and make me come chasing after you?"

Haze swallowed. "I didn't—it's just—I wasn't—"

Lox waved his hand and slid down from Bard, reaching up and lifting something from behind the saddle. Haze was surprised to see Ki in his arms as he lowered her to the ground. "Relax," he chuckled. "I didn't follow you up here. I was messing with you. We've been up here the whole time. We saw you shoot past the edge and hover up there for a bit. Pretty impressive flying."

203

Haze felt his face flush. "Thank you. Look," he said hesitantly. He tried to gauge what Lox was thinking. "I wasn't leaving or anything. I was just flying around a bit. Maybe if you could not tell Oaina about this…?"

Lox laughed out loud. "Oh, don't worry. I won't. I wouldn't wish that on a mean dog. I know an escapee when I see one, and quite frankly, the Rider sitting on the top of a frozen waterfall watching the moon rise isn't it."

Haze relaxed, feeling returning to his toes. "Thank you," he said. Then, he frowned. "What are you two doing up here?"

Lox shrugged. "This is where I take Button to practice her dances," he answered. "She gets nervous in the house, I think. She is a little uncomfortable with people watching her. So," he said, "I have been taking her up here since she first started dancing. About three years now."

Haze grinned. "She gets embarrassed? Really? But she's so good at it!"

"That's not what she thinks. She is convinced she is terrible at it, and therefore refuses to dance in front of anyone unless she is forced to. Like the other day in the Gallery," he added, poking Ki in the ribs. She giggled and stared down at her feet.

Haze fell silent for a moment, then a thought occurred to him. "Oh, do you want me to leave?" he asked, pointing down towards the city. "I can head back down to the Gallery and let her practice if you want."

Lox shook his head. "No, she already finished for the night. We were just getting on Bard to head home when we saw you."

Haze nodded, glancing at his feet. The awkward silence persisted until he cleared his throat. "It's quite a view up here," he said, turning back around to face the City again. "I have never seen anything like it."

Lox and Ki strode over to stand next to him. "Indeed. It's our favorite spot in the Range. When the sun goes down and the stars come out, their light mixes with the lanterns of the city and creates a glow in the ice of the waterfall. Any minute now, actually. It's just starting to get dark enough."

Haze nodded. Lox stood silently, Ki holding tight to his hand and casting sidelong glances at Haze.

After a moment, the awkward silence became too much, and Haze cleared his throat. "So," he said hesitantly, "What is it like being the father of the Hyless?"

Lox glanced at him. "That's an interesting question. What makes you ask?"

Haze shrugged. "I'm just curious. You seem awfully young to have an eight-year-old, and I can't imagine that mixed very well with being told that she was the Hyless shortly after you and your wife had her."

Lox laughed. "I am twenty-four," he said, "and that would have made me sixteen when Malya and I were given the honor of raising Ki. But I am not her blood father. She was born to a different family."

Haze looked at him, his eyebrows raised. "How did she come to you then?"

"Vlaire and Oaina took her from her previous home and brought her to me. Malya and I were not yet married, but we were the closest thing to a set of parents she would have. We accepted the responsibility of raising her as our own. We only recently got married and had Mulwyn."

Haze shook his head. "No offense, but why would they give an infant to a couple of sixteen-year-old's?"

Lox looked at him for a moment. "We volunteered," he said. "I had always known I was a Guardian of the Hyless, and I was the only one of the Guardians with something resembling a spouse at the time. Ki needed a family, and so we gave her one. Besides," he said, a small twinkle in his eye, "you aren't much older than me. I could argue that it seems odd a twenty-something year old soldier was made General of an elite military force. What's your story?"

Haze sighed. "I suppose I owe you one now, don't I?" He cleared his throat. "My parents were killed by druids before I could remember. King Orlivan found me in a druidic village he had just burned to the ground, and took me in as his own. He forced me to take sword lessons from Alovere, and insisted that I learn the art of combat. He made me a soldier," Haze said quietly. "By the time I was fifteen, I had been on the front lines a dozen times. When I turned nineteen, I left. I went and sold my lance to a few warlords in the Boar Mountains and made a name for myself. Three years ago, I returned to Beril and now sell my sword to Orlivan." He shrugged. "I guess I'm a General because I am his son. I won't say I have no skill, but I know Alovere is more qualified."

Lox laughed. "And you're what? Twenty-five?"

Haze glared at him. "Twenty-seven."

Lox lifted his hand. "Twenty-seven. Excuse me."

They fell silent for a moment again, before Ki made a small noise and pointed at something.

Haze looked down on the city and his jaw dropped.

Darkness had fallen completely over the Range, and the stars shone brightly above them. The green and blue windows lit by the lanterns from within the houses mixed with the moonlight trickling down from the heavens and created a violet glow that reflected off the waterfall and swirled in open air. Streams of green and purple radiance danced in the sky like magic, shifting and flickering in time with the lamps in Hallovath's homes.

"What is that?" Haze whispered.

"The waterfall is distorting the light from the houses and stars," Lox said, smiling. "We call it *Dawnsio Gol,* The Dancing Lights."

"Amazing," Haze murmured. "This happens every night?"

Lox nodded. "Unless it is cloudy or rainy. Isn't it remarkable?"

Haze nodded. "Yes. Yes, it is."

But it was more than that, much more than he could explain to Lox. A strange feeling washed over him as he stood staring down at the violet lights. When he was younger and had left as a sell sword for the Boar Mountains, he was searching; searching for what made him his own, not the soldier Orlivan had raised him to be. After years of fighting for man and beast alike, he had discovered that being a mercenary was no different from being a sworn infantry man. He was the same soldier, the same killing machine that he would always be, but here...

Here he was content. He felt no need to fight or look for what made him feel at home. He felt comfortable in the Range as a prisoner of Hallovath. In fact, if this was what being a prisoner in Hallovath was like, he would be content to remain captive for the rest of his life. For the first time he could recall, he wanted nothing more than to remain here forever, not wanting to go and discover something else. He felt as if nothing was missing from his life.

He felt at home.

****

Oaina stood quietly by the tree line that ran along the river that fed into the waterfall. Haze was seated at the edge of the falls, his legs dangling out over the city. Lox was seated beside him with Ki in his lap, and they were talking about something that suddenly made Lox burst out laughing.

She briefly considered going out and joining them, then froze. She was supposed to be on watch in the Mirror Wood. Had she not seen Haze flying above the Gallery, she would still be there. Still...

She shook her head. They most likely dreaded her showing up anyway. Best to return to the Mirror Wood.

She took a longing look at the two of them, then turned away. "Come on, Evaala," she said to her mount.

Evaala's bright sapphire eyes shone out at her from their bed of white scales.

"Let's leave them be," she said, climbing onto her wyvern's back. "We have work that needs tending."

Chapter Twenty-Three
A Complicated Past

Alovere groaned as he leaned to his right and set his bowl on the floor.

His ribs ached where Lox had run several stitches through the torn skin to keep his wound closed, though they took little effect. Every time he moved, the sutures shifted and allowed more blood to seep through. His only option was to lie as "still as death," as the female guard had worded it.

He suspected that there had to be some reason she behaved like a rabid dog, as it didn't seem possible for someone to just *be* that horrid.

She had stood around for nearly an hour the previous day and berated him about his swordsmanship. Apparently, she had seen his fight with the Rime Born and swore that he would have sustained less injuries and been less of a burden to everyone if he had just refined his art more. Fortunately, Lox had come to his aid and driven the woman off.

Lox was much more friendly than the other guard, open to conversation and questions about the village and the Range. His freckled face glowed whenever he spoke of the Range and creatures in it, giving him the look of a man that had a deep love for his home. Alovere could tell that he was holding some things back, but he was as accommodating as any soldier could be of a man he didn't know.

The most interesting thing that Lox had told him was that they weren't the first people to come to the city. There was another woman with multiple guards and strange weapons that had come a few years before. According to Lox, she was nothing but friendly, even offering to help fight against the people that were "angering the Spirits," as Lox had put it. The descriptions of the woman vaguely reminded him of the captain Haze had told him about on the Airship that had kidnapped him, but he couldn't be sure. He would have to talk to Haze about it when he came back.

He leaned up straight and looked at the little girl leaning against the far wall.

She had been seated there since he had woken up, staring at him silently. Lox had told him she was deaf, but he could have sworn she had heard him a couple of the times he had tried speaking with her. Lox had explained that she was reading his lips, and that she couldn't actually hear him. She could make vague guesses about what he was saying, but that was all.

She leaned her head back, closing her eyes.

"How are you feeling?" Lox's voice entered the room, followed by Lox himself. He had a plate in his hand, steam curling up from it.

"Wounded," Alovere replied shortly. "I almost got cut in half by an ice killing machine."

Lox chuckled. "Oh, it couldn't have been that bad! You're still alive after all. I know some people who actually *were* cut in half by a Rime Born."

Alovere grimaced. "Spare me the details."

Lox pulled a small knife from the plate of rags. "This will hurt, I'm afraid."

Alovere gritted his teeth as the man commenced to cut away the old wraps on his arm. He flinched as the edge of the guard's knife nicked his wound. "How long is she going to sit there?" He jerked his chin at Ki.

"As long as she wishes," Lox said. "If she were a disobedient child, I suppose we would have more rules for her, but she is so well behaved that she pretty much gets to do as she pleases."

"That'll go away with age," Alovere grumbled, glowering at the girl. Her eyes were still closed, her head leaning on the wall behind her. "Why is she sitting in here?"

Lox lifted away the old bandage, immediately dropping the fresh hot one on Alovere's arm before he had a chance to see the wound. "She told me that she wouldn't leave until she knows you are going to be okay," the guard said, a broad smile spreading across his freckled face. "She claims it's because you saved her life. Which," he added, "is a story I am still waiting to hear."

"Nonsense," Alovere snapped immediately. He felt his face warming quickly.

"So, she is lying then?" Lox said, beginning to cut away the bandage on Alovere's stomach.

"Hmph," he grunted, looking out the small blue window directly above him. His stomach twitched involuntarily as the cold steel of the guard's knife touched it.

The pain that washed over his body from this wound was unlike any he had felt before. The puncture wounds caused by serrated ice blades were apparently much more painful than the ones caused by the sharp edge of a steel weapon.

"It has been my experience," said the young guard, "that Ki does not lie. She is a child, and misunderstands many things, but lying is something she has always understood and never done. Whatever you did for her, she wishes to repay you. At least," he chuckled, "that is the impression I am getting."

"I did nothing any normal human being wouldn't do," Alovere stated flatly, staring out the window.

"Well, it must have meant a lot to Ki, unless you are implying that she simply likes you. Which," Lox added again with a twinkle in his eye, "doesn't seem likely."

Alovere glared down at the man as he bent over his wound. "Excuse me?" he growled.

Lox shrugged. "Well, unless you truly performed some act of kindness for Ki, the only other explanation for her behavior would be that she simply likes you as a person. No offense, but you don't exactly exude friendliness. Hence, I doubt she simply likes you. Hence, you must have actually saved her life."

"Load of dragon dung," Alovere grumbled, shifting uncomfortably. "I didn't save anyone's life." He paused and glared at Lox again as the guard finished tying a knot in his new bandage. "And there is plenty about me to like, thank you."

"Such as?"

"Such as me *not* ripping your arm off for implying that there wasn't!" Alovere snapped.

Lox nodded, picking up the bandage plate and rising to his feet. "Yes, I can see the charm you speak of. I think you and Oaina will get along just fine. Let me know if you need anything," he said, striding towards the doorway. "I am only a holler away."

Alovere grunted in acknowledgment as the guard stepped through the curtain and exited the room.

"Doesn't seem likely," he muttered to himself, swatting at his empty bowl and sending it skittering across the floor. "I'll show him likely."

He let his head flop back down on the soft blankets and stared out the skylight.

His thoughts traveled to Enial. He sighed as he remembered their last moments together before he left for this mission. He hated to disappoint her, but he needed to make sure he served his king loyally. That was the duty of a soldier. She couldn't understand what their lives would be like if he failed Orlivan. King Orlivan knew…

He shuddered, sending bolts of pain through his rib cage and arm.

He still dreamed about all the people in that village, the last village on his list before he left Jiikk. The screams haunted him to this day, echoing in both his dreams and his memory on a nearly daily basis. Dreams that came from the time when he was Javenir Bolgruust, the most wanted man on the continent of Jiikk.

He remembered the first contract he had taken as a foolish boy desperate to eat. He remembered every detail as though it had just happened earlier that morning. It had been for a farmer whose neighbor had stolen his cattle. At the time he had thought it trivial, but on a continent just off the mainland of Elliset, the populations primary source of food was meat. If someone took your livestock, it could mean the end of your entire family. Or worse, the men you owed a debt to would trade you off to the Malgonian slave traders and you would spend the last few years of your life in the ice mines of the Boar Mountains.

Alovere had accepted the contract, which was simple; kill the neighbor, make the body easily found, and leave. He was paid a hefty sum, as when the man was killed, his employer had not just his own cattle returned, but also all the livestock of the man who was murdered. The success lead to another contract, and another. In little time, he was one of the most successful assassins on Jiikk.

He sighed.

Two years after his steps into the world behind the shadows, he was presented with an offer.

His next contract was a high-ranking member of court that another member wanted silenced. What stood out about this particular mission was not the target being royalty, but the way the employer wanted it carried out. He had asked that the man be publicly burned alive in the center of the town square. Alovere had not asked why, though he knew it something to do with savage politics of the area.

When he begrudgingly agreed to carry out the mans wishes, the employer upped the pay, but there were soon more and more conditions. He said before the man was burned alive, his fingers had to be cut off.

Alovere's convictions were certainly put to the test, but exactly twenty-four hours later, the local Baron was being dragged out into the town square, his hands leaving glistening streaks of blood behind him on the cobblestones. After he had propped the bleeding man up on the edge of the fountain in the middle of the square, Alovere had gone far beyond anything his employer had asked of him. Amidst the screams of his victim and the onlookers, he removed the man's hands, and had Arginox cauterize the wounds to stop the blood flow. Next, he took his toes, then his feet. By the time the palace guards were finally getting too close for him to stay longer, the man was in thirty-five pieces. Having Arginox ignite what was left of his victim, Alovere fled before the guards arrived to find the charred corpse. It was the greatest entrance into the advanced assassinating world any eighteen-year-old could have asked for. And yet, he regretted those days of his life more than he thought it was possible to regret anything.

Especially after he met Enial.

She had waltzed into his life one day in a way he couldn't have imagined.

214

After being imprisoned for stealing, Alovere had spent three cold nights lying in his cell under an open window in the winter months. Some time had passed since his last contract, and he had resorted to stealing his daily bread.

As he was laying there shivering, the most beautiful voice he had ever heard filtered into his cell.

"Would you like some food?"

Cold suddenly washed over him, the deafening sound of cart wheels on stone filling his ears and water soaking his clothes through to his skin. He turned his head to the left and looked through a set of rusty metal bars.

He was back in his cell, reliving the first moments he met his wife. She was there in her light green dress, standing exactly as she had thirty-five years ago. A small wicker basket was hooked under her arm, the top covered with a small white sheet. Her curly brown hair was braided in a thick rope that fell down to the middle of her shoulders, her blue eyes filled with pity.

The smell of the grimy street water in his blood-soaked tunic filled his nostrils, the touch of the frigid stones in his cell sending blasts of cold straight through to his bones. He shivered violently, his teeth chattering as loudly as a blacksmith's hammer. He looked up to his right and out the open window. He saw the purple sky of Jiikk, the sun setting on a late November night. The sounds of people drawing carts past on the street outside filled his cell with the rebounding clatter of voices and wooden wheels.

"Would you like some food?" the charming voice spoke again like the ringing of soft chimes.

He turned to face her, propping himself up on his left hand and out of the small pond he was laying in. He wanted to say yes, please, but he

215

couldn't bring himself to do it. He simply stared at her silently, his body aching. She wouldn't give it to him anyway. She was just here to taunt him like everyone else that came past his cell.

The lovely young woman lifted the corner of the cloth and tucked her hand into the basket, withdrawing a large round loaf of bread. Crouching down, she extended her hand towards him, reaching through the bars.

He stared at her in confusion, waiting for her to throw it into the water.

"You have to come take it," she said kindly. "I don't want to set it down. The rats will get it."

He pulled himself to his knees and crawled across the cell to her, every joint in his body aching with cold.

Reaching out a trembling hand, he snatched the loaf and fell back down in the water with a loud splash.

She flinched back for a moment, then knelt in the water just outside his cell and watched him eat.

He tore into the bread ravenously, filling his mouth with more than he could hope to swallow. Coughing half of it up, he picked the soggy clumps of wheat out of the filthy water and shoved them back into his mouth.

It tasted like heaven.

Of course, anything would taste like heaven if you had spent the last three days freezing to death with nothing to eat at all. Unless you could catch a rat, that is. There were plenty of them, but they had grown wise to the many prisoner's state of desperation, and only came over to you after you were too cold to move anymore, at which point the tables had turned and the rat was no longer afraid of *you* eating *it*.

"I heard you are here for stealing," the young woman said softly.

He glared at her, taking another bite out of the loaf.

He hated how her eyes were so full of pity. He didn't need her pity. He didn't want it. He was Javenir Bolgruust, the finest assassin on the continent. She couldn't possibly understand how much power he had at his fingertips, or better, on the tongues of the citizens of Jiikk. "The Man of a Thousand Deaths," his employers called him, named after his ability to make his victims wish they had died a thousand times before finally killing them.

"You know, you're lucky they didn't cut your hands off," she said.

He stopped chewing and looked at her.

"My father is captain of the City Guard," she stated. "He told me what they usually do to thieves. He spared you because you are so young."

He ignored her and resumed eating.

It was true, he looked young, but he was every bit of nineteen years old. He didn't need some girl showing him pity, let alone her old man. He would survive this, just like he had survived when his parents had left him. Just like he had survived when, as a child, he was cast out of the bakery he had taken work in and left to scrounge around the streets for weeks. Just like he had survived when his second target had been a trained soldier. He always survived, he always succeeded.

He needed none of the pity this girl had to offer.

"Why won't you talk to me?" she asked suddenly. "I am showing you kindness. That was my father's supper I just gave you."

He glanced at her.

"At least tell me your name," she said quietly.

He smiled wryly to himself. Yes, that was exactly what he was going to do. Tell this girl, the daughter of the City Guard Captain, his wanted name.

217

He shook his head in amusement, shoving the last of the bread into his mouth.

The girl rose to her feet. "Well, just remember the kindness I showed you today, and remember the kindness my father showed you. In a world like ours, kindness is the only thing that gives decent people a fighting chance. Don't waste the mercy my father has shown you. When he releases you tomorrow, come by the village market. I will be there. Get some food. I will just give it to you, you don't have to steal. If my father catches you stealing again, he will have your hands."

He stared down at his grimy hands silently. Her words sunk into his heart like a weighted blade. She had shown him kindness, and because of it he was not starving. The only kindness he had ever shown anyone was a quick death, and those were few and far between.

A sudden urge to repay this girl for her gift surged through him like a tidal wave. He could give her his name, like she had asked.

No, that wouldn't do. He would be dead before morning.

"I see," she sighed. "I wish you well, stranger." She turned and started walking away.

"Wait," he croaked hoarsely, leaning up and clinging to the bars of his cell. The steel was cold in his hands, the warmth of the bread fading from his touch.

She turned around to face him.

He wracked his brain for something, anything he could give her. A word popped into his head, a word he had read in a book a long time ago, the name of some far away Sea. "Alovere," he said. "My name is Alovere."

She curtsied politely. "My name is Enial. Glad to meet you."

She turned away with a smile and strode into the darkness of the corridor outside his cell.

"Alovere!"

Pain rushed through him suddenly, the dampness of the walls and floor vanishing abruptly. They were replaced by the soft warmth of blankets, heat washing over him from a fireplace across from where he lay.

He was back in Lox's home in the Elliset Mountains, the girl still sitting silently against the far wall.

"Alovere!"

He flinched and looked to his right.

Glassworn was standing by his bed, a small wooden bottle clutched in his hand. "You would not believe what I just discovered," he whispered weakly.

Alovere winced as he sat up straighter. He looked down at his ribs, straightening the bandage slightly. "What?"

"They have drink here that makes the contents of my flask seem tame," the druid said excitedly.

Alovere narrowed his eyes at the man.

His brow gleamed with sweat, his entire body shook (with either excitement or intoxication, Alovere couldn't tell which) and his eyes were bloodshot worse than any drunkard Alovere had seen.

"You need to try it," he exclaimed, holding out the small bottle corked with a tiny blue gem. "It makes you..." he trailed off and looked over his shoulder, as if afraid someone would hear him. He leaned closer. "It makes you see things," he whispered rapturously in Alovere's ear. The stench of alcohol wafted off of him like a steaming bog, making Alovere gag. Glassworn held the bottle out again.

"No thanks," Alovere said, eyeing the stricken man warily. "I think I've seen plenty."

"Glassworn!"

Alovere heard Lox calling from behind the curtain. Moments later the guard appeared with a look of relief on his face.

"Oh good," he exclaimed. "I thought you might be here."

Alovere raised an eyebrow. "Something I need to know about?"

"Not exactly," Lox laughed sheepishly. "I think he took the wrong bottle off of my shelf this morning. Nothing serious," he added quickly, "but I need to get him to my Malya. She will start getting some fluids into him. He has been wandering all over the city babbling about seeing flying horses. Now, I don't know what a horse is, but based on the excitement with which he was yelling, my guess is that they do not fly?"

Alovere shook his head. "No, they don't," he said slowly, looking Glassworn up and down in disgust. "You know you wouldn't get poisoned if you didn't drink anything that smelled remotely spiked, you oaf!"

Glassworn looked at him stupidly. "Oh?" he said mockingly. "And what am I supposed to drink? Water?"

Alovere blinked. "Yes!"

"Come on." Lox steered Glassworn through the curtain just before he burst into a horrible rambling song with lyrics Alovere couldn't make out.

The girl was standing now, and looking at him curiously.

"What are you looking at?" he grumbled.

She walked suddenly over to his bed and stared up at him. Lifting her hands in front of her, she moved them in two simple motions, then pointed to herself.

He shook his head. "I don't understand."

She repeated the same movements, then pointed to herself. When she saw that he still wasn't understanding what she was saying, she pointed to one of the lamps, and made a brief sign with her hands.

220

"I don't understand," he said again.

She was obviously trying to tell him something, but he did not speak her language after any fashion. Some of the other soldiers had learned multiple languages in Orlivan's conquest of Elliset, but he had never had the knack.

Ki wasn't giving up. She patiently kept pointing at one thing after another and signing, until finally, when she picked up Alovere's dagger from beside his bed and did the same thing, it dawned on him.

She was trying to teach him words.

"Oh," he exclaimed. "So that is lamp," he said, pointing to the lamp and making the sign she had showed him.

She smiled broadly, showing a row of shiny white teeth with a small hole where one of her front baby teeth had fallen out.

She then pointed to herself again, and made the same two motions.

"Your name is Ki," he said, nodding. "I know, Haze told me."

She cocked her head at him, frowning slightly.

He said it again, this time slower, and making sure to exaggerate the movements of his mouth. "I know your name. Haze told me."

She smiled, rocking back and forth on the balls of her feet. Her smile faded, and she signed a few things rapidly that he couldn't hope to understand. When she saw the look of confusion on his face, she pointed to the fireplace and back to him again.

"I didn't save your life," he said quickly. "I just brought you along, that's all."

A small smile crawled across her face, and she curtsied politely. She signed what he assumed must have been her version of thank you, and hurried out of the room, her face flushing brightly.

Alovere sighed and sank back into the soft covers. His entire body ached, pounding like a headache.

Taking a deep breath, he closed his eyes and waited for sleep.

Chapter Twenty-Four
Mysterious Death

Another week came and went, and life continued as it had since they arrived. Today, much to Haze's chagrin, was training day.

He stumbled backwards as Oaina advanced, her battle sword whirling around her in a perfect curtain of steel. The edge of her blade met the hilt of his lance with a bone jarring crash, the sound of steel on steel ringing in his ears. He struggled to maintain his guard as she pushed forward, her sword dancing so fast he could hardly keep his eye on it.

Finally, she dipped the tip of it behind his left foot as he stepped back and he fell to the ground, the point of her weapon resting gently against his neck.

"You have failed again," she said, sheathing her sword gracefully and turning away. Her black hair fell in thick waves over her shoulders and face, hiding her scar. "You cannot claim to guard the Hyless when you cannot even fight against one man."

"I'm not fighting a man though, am I?" he grumbled as he pulled himself to his feet and picked his lance up off the cobblestones.

"I don't care if you are fighting an enraged fire dragon, you have to do better than that if you wish to call yourself a Guardian!" she snapped. "That level of training actually passes where you are from?"

"I should say so," he said curtly. "I'm a General, as you know."

She scowled at him. "Well then, General. Ready your lance."

Haze sighed and lifted his lance, bracing himself as she drew her sword from its sheath again.

After a brief pause, she took a breath and lunged, her sword arcing towards his neck.

He stepped to the side, spinning his lance around his back and catching the edge of her blade a hair's breadth from his shoulder. Turning it towards the ground, he countered with a lunge of his own. She easily swept it aside, and in three lightning fast moves had him lying on his back with his own lance pressed against his heart.

"Dead again," she said smugly. "Really, I don't see how you have survived this long."

He cursed and leaped to his feet. "Enough of this!" he snapped, snatching his lance from her. "It's our turn to patrol the Mirror Wood."

"General Haze!" she bellowed from behind him. "Turn and face me."

Haze rolled his eyes and turned around. "Really?"

"You do not walk away from your training if you wish to be a Guardian," Oaina said, lifting her sword. "You will fight me until I say we are done."

Haze growled and rested the shaft of his lance on his shoulder. "I am not in the mood for this."

"Are you saying you aren't in the mood for defending the Hyless?"

"I am not in the mood for games," Haze said shortly.

"You are no Guardian," Oaina scoffed. "You lack the basic skill required to become one of our lowest ranked guards."

Rage boiled up inside Haze. "I was better before—"

"Before you lost your arm?" Oaina sneered at him. "Maybe you now think that is an acceptable excuse for not serving the Hyless adequately?"

"Enough!" Haze snapped. "If you want to train me, then train me. I will not allow you to berate me."

Oaina's sword suddenly flashed forward, coming withing an inch of his eye. "Then stop me, General."

Haze roared and rolled his lance over his back, ducking low. Turning to his left, he caught the back of the hilt and brought it around by Oaina's ankles. Sweeping her feet out from under her, he flipped his lance around and caught it mid-handle. He pressed its point against the fallen Guardian's breastplate. "Enough," he panted.

She stared up at him from the ground, her eyes cold. After a moment, she shoved his foot off of her and stood up. Haze stood panting, waiting for her to start swinging in rage.

She chuckled and sheathed her blade. "Very well, Hela. Go and ready yourself. Lox will be here shortly to trade us."

Haze blinked in surprise, then turned and headed towards the Gallery. Slamming the doors shut behind him, he hurried to his room and shut himself in.

"That woman!" he seethed to himself once he was inside his modest chambers. "I have never experienced anything so infuriating."

He pulled his sweaty tunic off and swapped it for one of his dry ones. They were Lox's size, so they were a little small, but they fit, nonetheless.

As he pulled the tunic over his head, his memory traveled back to when he had first met Alovere, standing in the great hall in a war meeting with Orlivan. In the memory of a child, Alovere stood tall and strong, towering over him like one of the Banyeets. His hair was long and black in place of the waves of gray that now crowned his head. His face was as cold as ever, his hand resting on the hilt of the same plain sword Haze had seen him use for years. He wore the blood red armor he had worn for as long as Haze could remember. Six-year-old Haze had reached his pudgy hands up towards the hilt of the man's sword, but Alovere had shoved him away and told him to find his parents. He remembered the Rider's steel gray eyes staring down at him impatiently.

Haze smiled as he recalled his lessons with Alovere. Orlivan had ordered the older Rider to train Haze in the way of the sword, but it wasn't to his liking. He had always preferred the graceful subtleties of the lance. Alovere had given up trying to teach Haze once he had turned twelve and developed the habit of running off on adventures and missing his training sessions. By the time he had turned fifteen, he had tired of the older man's ill temper and fragile patience. Orlivan had put him with the second infantry, hoping to temper him. He had made four years of that, before he left to go and sell his lance to the Malgonians of the Boar Mountains. He did not see Alovere again until many years later, when he returned to sell his blade to Orlivan. He quickly rose to General, a rank Alovere had not yet been offered, and became famous as the one-armed Lord of the Demons.

He sighed as he left his room and hurried towards the doors of the Gallery. Fighting Oaina had reminded him so much of learning from Alovere. He had the same way of making you feel as though you didn't even have the right to hold a sword; his blade moved every bit as fast as the Guardian's, if not faster.

When he stepped out of the Gallery and made his way across the platform, he noticed Lox and Oaina talking in hushed voices, their expressions grave. Bard stood towering over both of them, his eyes fixed on his young master patiently.

"What's going on?" he asked when he reached them.

Lox glanced at Oaina, then looked at Haze. "I found a body while on patrol," he said.

"In town?" Haze asked in disbelief.

"Yes. It's a City Guard."

Haze looked back and forth between them. "I'm guessing there is something unusual about the body by the way you two are behaving?"

"It's been..." Lox swallowed, his face turning green. "It's mutilated badly."

Haze frowned. "I see."

Oaina turned and leaped onto Evaala. "Let's go have a look."

Haze mounted Salezz and they all followed Lox down towards the main city. The white buildings stood out against the brilliant blue waterfall reflecting the sun's rays in the early afternoon.

They floated down past the radiant structures and into the lower parts of the town. The air grew steadily colder, the light fading as they glided down into a fissure of ice beneath the rest of the city, suspended high above them. The buildings nestled in the side of the ice canyon began to show signs of deterioration as they descended; moss grew in the shady crevasses of the ancient stone structures, streaks of purple and gray nestled against the grimy white.

At length, they reached the bottom and landed in a flurry of wings and dust.

They all dismounted their wyverns and Lox gestured for them to follow him. He led them down a street that wound through the dilapidated buildings like a muddy snake, the grime and muck from the crumbling road clinging to their boots in thick clods.

"I had no idea it was like this down here," Haze exclaimed. "Hallovath seems like such a clean city."

"Hallovath is a city," Oaina said, wrinkling her nose at the gutter along the street. Dirt and grime swirled in a thick sludge that flowed down the sides of the cobblestones. "Are you saying your beloved Beril does not have the places no one dares to go?"

He shrugged. "Fair point. But it seems a little neglected for people to actually live down here," he pointed out, gesturing to one of the small houses carved into the side of the fissure.

Its domed roof drooped wearily towards its muddy foundation, emerald windows sagging in their frames. The ice walls surrounding it crept towards the edges of the moss-covered stone, slowly reclaiming their territory.

"These people don't live," Oaina spat bitterly, not even glancing at the house. "They dwell and lurk in the shadows of society. They hide from responsibility and danger, shirking their duties as citizens of Hallovath."

Lox threw a small glance at her. "What Oaina is trying to say, is that these people are rejects. Well, most of them. They refuse to work for their own living or contribute in any way, or perhaps they dabble in black magic and have been removed from the upper city as punishment. Either way, they're an unsavory sort. I *do* pity the people that live down here for no other reason than their family does, or because they lack the funds to move," he added ruefully.

Haze looked at the walls of the fissure. "How did this get here? What is this place?"

"It used to be the Keep of Hallovath before the Gallery was built. It was the center of the city before the last Hyless," Lox explained. "About a hundred years ago, construction workers dug too deep into the fissure and struck water. This part of the city flooded, and the Keep was rebuilt as the Gallery high above Hallovath. It is largely uninhabitable in the winter months, filling almost completely with water."

Haze nodded. "Why was a guard down here then?"

Lox and Oaina looked at each other.

"He wasn't. He was stationed outside my house for the majority of last night," Lox said. "He took the second shift. There was one other guard who was on shift just before this one, but we can't find him."

The walls of the fissure darkened as they walked deeper inside of it, slipping on the slight incline. At length, they reached the end of it.

Water that spread across the street mirrored the little light that filtered down through the elegant city above. It was ankle deep in places, forcing Haze to watch his step. Their path was blocked by a large ice wall, the back of the fissure. Haze could hear the faint sound of water trickling through it.

Haze sucked in a quick breath.

At the base of the wall, the mutilated body of a young man lay in the shallow water. His head had been detached and placed behind his lifeless torso, propping it up like a pillow. His hands were cut off and laid in his lap, the fingers removed and stacked methodically in their upturned palms. All the fingers were charred black, the finger nails missing completely. The stumps of his arms were burned as if to stop bleeding, the smell of scorched meat wafting off of them. Blood mixed with the water around the corpse, stretching out beneath it like a glimmering red carpet.

"Good lord," Haze murmured, his stomach coming up in his throat. "Who would do such a thing?"

"The sort of people that dwell in this sort of place," Oaina spat. "He must have wandered down here for something and gotten snatched by one of the creeps that lurk in the muck. This is probably one of their heathen sacrifices or something horrible like that."

Haze didn't agree. He didn't know why, but something about the death of this guard screamed a warning to him. "And you haven't found the other guard that was on duty last night?"

Lox shook his head. "No. He is still missing."

"Why are there guards posted outside your house, exactly?" Haze asked suddenly.

"I should think that's obvious," Oaina snapped. "The Hyless lives there, you idiot."

Haze raised his eyebrows and ignored her remark. "So, this could be an attempt on her life?"

Lox's eyes widened. "I suppose, but even the Guards are under the impression that they are there because I have Alovere in my home. Why would they mutilate a guard like this if they were after the Hyless?" He shook his head. "And anyway, who would do such a thing in Hallovath?"

"You mean apart from him and his friends?" Oaina said hotly. "I can't think of anyone."

Haze glared at her. "You slept in my chambers last night, along with every single night before that. You know I wasn't anywhere near Lox's house."

She flung her hair over her shoulder, her scar blazing an angry red in the dull light. "It could have been any of you."

"Are you implying that you doubt your own ability to keep me under lock and key?" Haze jabbed.

"I simply don't underestimate you or that wizard friend of yours! Not even the drunk!"

"That's enough," Lox interjected, frowning at them gravely. "There is a body here that needs to be seen to, and most likely a family that needs to be informed about his unfortunate fate."

Haze and Oaina both fell silent and nodded solemnly.

Gritting his teeth, Haze set about the grueling task of cleaning up the body. Gathering up the pieces of the young guard, they laid them gently in a large canvas blanket and tied it onto Bard.

Mounting the wyverns, they spurred them into the air.

As Salezz's feet left the ground, Haze felt a tingle run down his spine. Looking over his shoulder, he saw a young woman peering out at him from behind the dilapidated wall of a small house. Her hair was blonde and long, the one eye he could see peering out at him, haughty and cold. She shrank back when he turned to face her, her grimy fingers retracting around the corner of the white stone and vanishing into the darkness behind the house.

He shook his head and returned his attention to his wyvern.

They rose up through the first level of the city, then the second. The windows changed abruptly from green to blue as they rose higher. They were at the Gallery in short order, Haze glad to be out of the dreary part of the city and back in the light. Vlaire stood outside the doors of the massive white building, his expression grave.

"What happened?" he asked as soon as they landed in a flutter of scaly wings.

"We don't know," Lox answered, dismounting Bard and loosening the canvas bundle from the back of his Wyvern. "I was patrolling the main city when a girl from the Ruins approached me and said she had found a body. She looked upset, so I went looking and found this." He pulled back the canvas and revealed the body.

Vlaire's face paled. "Lord," he breathed, staring down at the jumble of limbs and charred meat. "Where was he?"

"At the end of the fissure, all the way in the back of the black magic district," Oaina said. "I suggest we start searching the newcomer's possessions," she added quickly. "You know there isn't a person in the city capable of this."

"Not in the city, no," Vlaire said quietly, "but perhaps below it."

Oaina scoffed and turned away, folding her arms over her chest.

"You don't seriously think a group of degenerates from the Ruins would have come into the main city and taken a guard off duty?" Lox asked incredulously.

"I don't know," Vlaire said calmly, "but we have to consider the possibility that this is as simple as it seems. You know the Ruins are full of…" he paused and searched for the right words. "A zealous sort of people."

"Zealous? You mean religious?" Haze asked.

Vlaire nodded. "Something like that, yes. Most of the people in the Ruins believe that the center of Hallovath never should have been moved. They believe that the Gallery of the Hyless has spiritual roots in the basin of the city. Also, they still cling to the old ways of the Guardians, which is a little more violent than our idea of how things should be."

"In what way?"

"In the way that they believe any outsider in the Range should be killed, for example," Vlaire explained. "They believe that any outsider is a threat to the Hyless and they would stop at nothing to see that the old laws of protection are upheld."

"So, this could have been an attempt on Alovere's life, not Ki's!" Haze exclaimed. "Though that still doesn't explain why they mangled the body."

"It could have been," Vlaire said slowly. "We can't rule out the possibility that Ki is in danger either. If she is, that is our top priority. For now, we double the guard at Lox's house and find this young man's poor family."

"We also need to find the other guard that was on duty last night," Lox put in. "He vanished and hasn't been seen this morning."

Vlaire sighed and shook his head. "Very well. You three find him."

232

"What will you do?" Lox asked.

"I will see to the body and family."

Chapter Twenty-Five

The Girl In The Ruins

The search went on for three days, Oaina begrudgingly allowing Haze to assist in the efforts. They scoured the city and the Ruins beneath it for hours each day but could not locate the guard that was on duty with the victim.

With their hopes wearing thin, Haze and Lox were now on patrol in the Ruins for what they had decided would be the final time. They had explored every crevice and corner there was. Haze was certain that he had learned more about the city in the three days the guard had been missing than he had in the first three weeks since he had come to Hallovath.

Haze cleared his throat as he walked next to Lox down one of the dark alleys. "So, if we find the body, what then?"

Lox shrugged. "We tell the family, as with the first one, and then begin the process of finding whoever is responsible."

"Yes, and how does that work exactly?" Haze asked. "You can't very well just go knocking door to door asking random people what happened and if they were part of it." He lifted his hand and knocked on an imaginary door. "Hello, have you mutilated anybody lately?"

"Actually, we can," Lox said, glancing at him with obvious distaste. "And that is largely what it will consist of, apart from the way you said it. We will bring anyone that we have doubts about up to the Gallery. They will be questioned thoroughly and then imprisoned or released based on what our findings are."

"And you will do this with the entire city?"

"Just the people we think may be responsible. Obviously, the baker's wife is not exactly on the top of our list, and neither is Ki, for example.

But this missing guard..." He shook his head. "It's possible he killed the first and has fled the city. So, the sooner we find him, the sooner we eliminate that theory. Also, I am afraid you and your friends will no doubt undergo some questioning. Oaina will insist upon it."

"I understand," Haze sighed. "Though I personally believe she is excessive in questioning Alovere and myself. He can barely move, and she sleeps in my chambers."

Lox chuckled. "Yes, well. Oaina is a very thorough person by nature. She would question the wyverns if we let her."

"That seems like Oaina," Haze admitted.

A glimmer of light caught his eye and his head swiveled to the left.

The girl he had seen before was standing in the middle of the alley. Her tattered dress blew around her knees, her hair hanging over her face and shrouding it from sight. The torches on the buildings around her cast eerie shadows that reached towards her body with sharp fingers.

"Who is that?" he said, looking over at Lox.

Lox looked where he was pointing. "Who?"

Haze turned to look back down the alley and was surprised to see it empty. A rat scurried through the debris of mold and stones on the once beautiful street, its eyes glinting brightly.

"Never mind," Haze mumbled, scratching his head.

Had he imagined her? She seemed real enough, standing in the alley and catching the light. It could have been a trick of his imagination, but he doubted it.

"Maybe you should get some more sleep," Lox joked. "Who was standing there exactly?"

"A young woman," Haze said. "She looked distressed."

Lox nodded. "Oh, did she? I don't see anyone."

Haze glared at him. "Alright, alright. Maybe I imagined it."

"Has Oaina been keeping you up at night?" Lox asked with a twinkle in his eye.

"Yes," Haze grumbled irritably, "and it's becoming a problem, apparently. Now I am seeing things."

"You know she only does that to make your life as miserable as possible," Lox said sincerely. "You shouldn't take it to heart."

"Let's get on with it already," Haze snapped, hurrying ahead of the other man.

He heard Lox chuckling behind him as he jogged briefly to catch up.

"Haze."

Haze froze. The voice of a young woman whispered airily in his ear, the sound sending icicles racing down his spine. "Did you hear that?"

Lox glanced at him, his face still glowing from the torment he had given Haze before. "Hear what?"

"That voice! The one of the young woman. I heard her! She said my name."

Lox smiled weakly. "No, no I didn't. I think you're getting a bit carried away."

"I heard her!" Haze insisted. "She said my name in my ear. Her voice was like liquid ice."

Lox's smile vanished. "Alright," he said crossly, "now you're going to get me spooked. That's enough of that."

"I am not jesting," Haze said firmly. "Unless you think I am seeing things and hearing voices!"

Lox frowned at him. "Like ice, you say?"

"Yes, like I could feel her speaking."

Lox opened his mouth to answer, but was cut off by a loud crash from behind them.

They both whirled around, Haze's heart leaping into his throat.

An old hand cart had fallen over, its resident alley cat yowling and pelting down one of the sides streets with its tail exploded in a ruff.

They both let out a long breath and glanced at each other sheepishly.

Lox laughed weakly and scratched his head. "Perhaps we're being a little irrational."

"I know what I heard," Haze said flatly, lifting his chin, "and there is nothing irrational—"

He was cut off as a group of men suddenly materialized out of the shadows of a nearby building. They were slouched and grimy, their faces covered in gray cloth. Heavy brown robes swirled around their ankles as they darted towards Lox and seized him from behind. They advanced like shadows of lightning and were upon the young guard in an instant.

Lox yelled and tried to pull his sword from his scabbard, but one of the men stopped his arm, twisting it up behind his back.

Haze pulled his lance from his back, charging towards the men.

Just before he reached them, something collided with the back of his head. He fell to the ground, his vision darkening as the boots of his assailants shuffled around him.

****

"Haze."

The airy voice whispered in his ear once again.

Haze's eyes snapped open, cold rushing through his body.

He leaned up and wrapped his arm around himself, shivering violently. He squinted as his eyes adjusted to the sudden wash of light pouring through the room. It looked as though he was in a tavern, a long wooden bar running the length of the wall opposite him. Stools were placed along it at regular intervals, light wear lines etched into the dark wooden seats. Lanterns dangled from the ceiling, the wicks flickering gently in a draft that came from a cracked door to his left. A group of people sat around the bar, hunched over it and whispering quietly to each other.

Haze looked to his right and nearly shot through the ceiling.

The girl he had seen in the alley was sitting on one of the stools next to him, staring at him silently through her veil of hair.

He narrowed his eyes, clearing his throat nervously. She looked vaguely familiar, though he couldn't put his finger on how. Her hair reminded him of someone else, someone he had seen before.

"Who are you?" he demanded immediately, sitting up. He winced and placed a palm on his head as it throbbed mercilessly.

He was on a rickety cot, coarse wool blankets piled around him. A fire blazed in a fireplace on the right side of the bar, a few people sitting comfortably in front of it. When they heard him speak, a few looked over their shoulders at him. Their faces were haggard and pock marked, mouths hanging open in wide toothless smiles.

"How are you feeling?" she asked quietly, a single glistening eye staring out at him from behind her curtain of hair.

"Fine, apart from the bump you gave me on the head," he said sourly, staring at her as he rubbed the back of his head. "Who are you?"

She leaned back, flipping some of the hair out of her face.

Haze's stomach danced as he realized who she reminded him of. She stared at him defiantly, one green eye glinting coldly out of a lightly freckled face. Her other eye was covered by a crude black patch, a thin scar marring the skin under the edge of it.

"Are you Ki's sister?" he asked hesitantly.

"I am Ki's mother," the woman answered shortly. "Though that is very flattering of you to say."

Haze blinked. She couldn't have even been as old as Malya. "Why do you live down here?"

"I will be asking the questions, you will be answering them," the woman snapped. "How did you come to Hallovath?"

"I am not telling you anything," Haze said flatly. "I have been kidnapped. Again, I might add. So, until we strike some sort of bargain, you are wasting your time."

The woman narrowed her eye at him. "Very well. You answer my questions, I will answer yours. Sound fair?"

Haze hesitated. He truly was getting tired of being kidnapped by women, but if she stuck to her own rules, he could learn a great deal about the things Oaina and Vlaire had refused to tell him about the Hyless. As well as things about her mother, if he was lucky.

"We take turns," Haze said warily. "One question at a time each."

"Deal. Me first. How did you come to Hallovath?"

Haze tried to think of some way to tell her without giving away any secrets he wasn't supposed to. "I came here on a mission to look for the Hyless."

"To hunt her?"

"Ah, it's my turn."

The woman grumbled and glanced over her shoulder at the men seated at the bar behind her. She seemed nervous about something, her eye shifting warily around the room.

"Where is Lox? What have you done with him?"

"If you mean the red headed Guardian, he has been returned to the New City," the woman said. "He was not harmed. Now, why were you looking for my daughter?"

239

"I was sent to protect her."

"From what?"

"From the two remaining warlords of Elliset. I believe if left untended, they will restart the tradition of the *Havi Ut Gahdness*. Now you asked two, so I get the same courtesy. What is your name?" he asked, staring at her intently.

She didn't look one bit excited about him having pointed out her error, but grumbled reluctantly, "Famau is my name. What is your second question?"

Haze thought about this for a long moment, before saying, "Why did you kidnap me?"

"I needed to speak with you in private, and without anyone from the New City knowing I was doing it. Oaina would almost certainly have my head if she knew where to find me, and would relish the act if she knew I had breached our contract."

"What contract?"

"It's not your turn," Famau snapped. "Do you believe the Hyless is truly in danger?"

Haze's heart sank as he realized he was now forced to answer a question he had been asking himself for weeks. "I don't know," he said honestly. "I know that my King would love to have any power that would help him overcome Queen Jaelyn of Miasma City, and vice versa. I honestly don't know if they have armies marching in here or if it is just as it was when I left three weeks ago. Should he decide to march on Hallovath..." He swallowed grimly. "Then there would be cause for concern, yes. What is this 'New City'? Is that what you people down here call the upper part of Hallovath?"

Famau nodded. "Yes, we have always referred to it as the New City. Those that live up there refer to it as Upper Hallovath."

"Why did you need to speak to me privately?" Haze said, narrowing his eyes. "What do you have to say to me that Lox couldn't hear?"

"Those people took my child from me," Famau spat. "I will have nothing to do with them."

"Did they take her from you because she is the Hyless?" Haze asked quietly.

He could see the pained look in her eye as she stared suddenly down at her feet. "Yes, somewhat. I knew who she was before she was born. It's something you know, carrying such a blessed child. When she was born and they discovered she was the Hyless, they told me she had to be raised by the Guardians. I was told that I could be part of it, but that there were certain rules that had to be followed. For instance, she couldn't stay at my home anymore, she had to live with one of the guards. Also, she couldn't be taught anything by me, only the guards. Well," she sighed, frowning deeply, "I briefly lost control of my wit. I took her and tried to run, but the woman stopped me."

"Oaina?"

Famau nodded. "She seized me, and when I tried to escape, she struck me with her gauntlet. I lost my eye and was banished to the Ruins until the Hyless comes of the age to accept her powers." She looked back up at him, pain streaked across her face. "I have been down here for seven years as someone else raises my child, patiently awaiting the day when she grows powerful enough to set me free."

Haze felt his heart wrench. "And you kidnapped me because you think I will tell you about Ki?"

She nodded, a tear slipping down her grimy cheek. "Please."

He blinked as everything suddenly became clear. At first, he thought perhaps Famau was a woman with an agenda or mission in mind. He thought she had kidnapped him to get at the Hyless, or to the

Guardians, but when he thought back, their entire conversation up to this point had been about the safety of Ki. She wasn't a dangerous woman.

She was a grieving mother.

He sighed, leaning up and swinging his boots to the floor. "Alright," he said reluctantly. "I will make a deal with you: I will give you news of your daughter in return for safe passage back to Upper Hallovath." He felt something like a lowlife, bartering with the feelings of an emotionally charged mother, but he needed to be sure he could return to Ki. With a dead guard and a murderer loose in the city, there was never a more important time for him to be by her side.

Famau's face lit up, and he saw her think desperately for something to ask. "What does she look like?" she asked eagerly.

"She is a nice dirty blonde," Haze said, smiling kindly. "She has a few of your freckles, and your green eyes. Her nose I don't recognize from you, so I assume it's from her father."

Famau nodded, her expression distant. "Yes, he died shortly after I conceived. He was a kind man. A blacksmith." She shook her head. "What is she like?"

"Well, she is kind. Warm of heart, for certain. She looks after Alovere, an injured friend of mine. I think she is afraid if she doesn't, everyone else will fail him," Haze chuckled. "She practically lives by his bedside."

Famau laughed and wiped a tear from her face. "What does she sound like?"

Haze's smile faded, and he cleared his throat. "Uh, I'm not sure."

Famau sniffed, looking at him imploringly. "How can you not be sure? Surely you have heard her speak?"

Haze nodded. "I have spoken with her on many separate occasions, yes," he said hesitantly, "but she speaks in a very special way. More with her hands than her voice."

Famau shook her head in bewilderment. "Why? Is that something the Guardians taught her?"

"No," Haze said gently. "I am afraid she is deaf. She can't hear, and so she learned to speak with her hands instead of her voice."

Famau's face fell and she sunk down into her chair.

"I'm sorry," Haze muttered.

He mentally kicked himself for not just saying she sounded like an angel and being done with it.

"I suppose I always knew," Famau sighed. "When she was born, I would sing her to sleep and it never seemed as though it worked terribly well. I thought there was a chance she couldn't hear me, but after a while I simply passed it off as her age. I thought perhaps she was just too young to be affected by things like singing."

"No, she is quite deaf. It doesn't slow her down though, I can assure you," he added. "Alovere found her the first time well out of the Elliset Mountain Range in a small village. She somehow managed to elude the guards and go exploring like every other seven-year-old in the world."

Famau regained her cheery expression. "That sounds like her father. He was a very adventurous person. It was all I could do to keep him in the house." She said this rapturously, as though reliving a past memory.

Haze smiled briefly. "Now I need you to tell me something in return."

She nodded. "Anything. What do you want to know?"

"How are they keeping you down here in the Ruins? Why aren't you up there still fighting to be with your daughter?"

She glanced down at her feet. "That's a long story. Do you know the Range Keeper?"

243

Haze nodded.

"Well, he saved me from Oaina. She was going to kill me, see. He told me that I was free to go down to the Ruins and stay there, but that he couldn't protect me from the Guardians if I returned to New Hallovath. He said Oaina would be free to do as she pleased."

Haze scowled. "Of course. She is probably one of the most unpleasant people I have ever met."

"I agree. But while I hold some resentment towards what she did, I know they were trying to protect the Hyless and do what was best for her. I shouldn't have reacted so drastically."

Haze stared at her in amazement. "Well, that may be the case, but I think it's justified by the fact that they were attempting to take your child from you."

Famau shrugged wearily. "Perhaps, but it doesn't change the fact that I caused us to be separated even more. That is my fault."

Haze wasn't sure what to say. He believed that directly, it was possible she could be found at fault for what had happened to her and Ki. But at the same time, most would believe that her actions were justified. After all, there had been a bunch of strange people trying to take her child from her. It didn't seem as though they could be so unforgiving of her reaction. He shook his head.

There was something missing from this story.

"Perhaps," he said simply. "Either way, I am sorry you had to endure that."

She shrugged again. "Things like that happen around the Hyless. I consider myself lucky to be her mother. Now," she said, sighing loudly, "I assume you are wanting to see him?"

Haze raised an eyebrow. "Him? Who?"

"Your missing guard," Famau said, her eye flashing. "Do you want to see him or not?"

Chapter Twenty-Six
The Cost of Past Wrongs

Alovere leaned heavily on the cane Vlaire had brought him.

His side flashed with pain as his stitches stretched. He felt a trickle of warmth as blood leaked out from under the bandages wrapped around his ribs.

"Easy does it," he muttered to himself as he worked his way slowly across the dimly lit room.

If he could just make it to the fireplace and back, he would say it was enough for the day. He had done it once already, and if he could do it again it would be a record. If Lox were here, he already would have told him to stop, no doubt.

He frowned as he took another excruciating step. Where was that guard, anyway? He had been an almost constant presence since Alovere had woken two weeks ago, and yet had not been in the house even once today. He wondered if he and Haze were being kept out late on a patrol for some reason. It had happened once before, three days ago when they were out looking for the missing guard. It turns out he had been found in pieces. The description was bone-chillingly close to what he had done to one of his first victims all those years ago.

Alovere licked his cracked lips and hobbled the rest of the way to the fireplace before turning around.

He wasn't sure what to think of it. Some part of his conscious was telling him to beware; the fact that a killing just like one he had committed so many years ago had suddenly surfaced in Hallovath had to be a coincidence. Something was going on, yet he couldn't quite put his finger on it. When Haze had told him what had happened it was as though his blood had turned to ice.

He had heard earlier that morning that two guards had gone missing, and that there was to be a search. He had thought nothing of it, as he himself had gotten a little too drunk on a late night and failed to appear at the barracks the next morning. These things tended to happen with soldiers during times of peace, but when Haze had walked in with his face as solemn as a graveyard, he knew immediately this was no late night at the pub.

He swore quietly as his side lanced with pain. Placing his hand gingerly on the bandages, he lowered himself onto the edge of the bed. He sighed triumphantly as he lay gently back against his pillows.

He had finished his walk, and without so much as a single fall. As much as Lox would have scolded him for doing it twice, he was glad he had. The heat of the fireplace on his face was reward enough, not counting how pleased he was that he was obviously recovering. His first walk had not gone this smoothly, resulting in him collapsing on the floor in a bloody heap and Malya having to haul him back to his bed while Ki watched with wide eyes. Lox had scolded him and said that if he insisted on trying to walk, he needed to wait until someone was there to help him.

Alovere begrudgingly agreed to this, but it was hardly a day later that he was up and walking by himself. The pain that accompanied each step was enough to knock him dizzy, but he did it anyway. Now, he was able to make it from one end of the room to the other twice without stopping at all. True, it was painstaking, but it was a success nonetheless.

He heard the door out in the in the main room bang open suddenly and he leaned up.

The curtain flew open to reveal Malya, her face pale. She wrung her hands in front of her, her knuckles pasty white. "Alovere, have you seen Ki?"

Alarm shot through Alovere like an arrow. "No. Why?"

Malya swallowed. "I haven't seen her for an hour."

Alovere shot to his feet, the sudden movement causing his head to swim. "Isn't that normal? I mean, couldn't she be with Vlaire or Oaina?"

Malya shook her head, her eyes wide. "No, they always tell me when they are taking her for the day. Her room is a jumbled mess, things all over the floor and the bed knocked over. I think something serious has happened."

Alovere hobbled towards the door, leaning on his cane.

"Where are you going?" Malya cried, placing a hand on his chest and pushing him back towards his bed. "You can't be going out there! You'll hurt yourself."

"Someone has to find Ki," Alovere protested. "Do Vlaire and Oaina know she is missing yet?"

Malya shook her head. "No, but I will go tell them right away. You just lay back down. Lox will be home soon and we will all go looking for her."

"Malya!" Vlaire's deep voice called sharply from the room behind her.

She pointed her finger at Alovere sternly for a moment before whirling around and exiting through the curtain.

Alovere's mind spun. Ki had spent nearly every waking moment she was allowed sitting in his room talking with him and trying to teach him to sign. It was true, not knowing where she had gone was a concern for everyone. She was a very predictable little girl for the most part.

He heard Malya cry out from in the kitchen.

Limping past the blanket, Alovere saw why.

Lox lay on the floor in the light that cascaded through the open door, his arms crossed over his chest. His eyes were closed tightly, his face pale and drawn.

"What happened?" Alovere asked immediately.

"We don't know," Vlaire said, shaking his head. "We found him on the front steps of the Gallery like this. I believe he is uninjured for the most part. He is simply unconscious."

Malya hunched over her husband, her blonde hair hiding her face. "Lox," she cried. "Wake up! Are you alright?"

"I'm afraid he has been drugged," Vlaire said uneasily. "There is no way to wake him save waiting out his sleep."

Malya looked up at him, tears tracking down her face. "Are you sure he is alright?"

"I am almost certain," Vlaire said gently. "Help me get him into your room and let him sleep this off. He will recover."

"Have you seen Ki?" Alovere spoke up, causing both of them to look at him.

"Oh, yes," Malya sniffed. "I haven't seen Ki for some time. I thought she was in Alovere's room, but he hasn't seen her either. The area around her bed is tossed badly."

Vlaire's face went white. "When did you last see her?"

"Perhaps two hours ago. I had trouble laying the baby down for a nap, and was in my room longer than usual."

Vlaire bent down and heaved Lox to his shoulder, marching him into the room opposite Alovere's. He returned a moment later without the younger Guard, his expression tense. "I will begin searching for Ki immediately. She can't have gone far on her own."

"I want to help," Alovere said stoutly. "What can I do?"

"You can stay in your room," Vlaire said sharply. "We don't want you or anyone else in your troop getting caught up in whatever this is. We have a dead guard, a missing guard, and now a missing Hyless. I think it best if you stay in your room and focus on recovering. It eliminates you from the list of people we will be questioning should this turn into an inquiry. Haze should remain out of the search as well."

Alovere looked around the room. He had not seen his young wing man. "Has he returned? With Lox?"

Vlaire blinked. "No," Vlaire muttered, "he didn't, now that you mention it."

Alovere stood up straighter. "I am coming to help," he said stubbornly. "I care for Ki as well, and now one of my best friends is out there somewhere too."

Vlaire placed his hand on Alovere's shoulder; it felt as though it were made of iron. "Listen to me. My sister would have you all locked up if she had her way. If you get involved in this, it will give her cause for speculation and there will be little I can do to dissuade her. Please, stay in your room and try to recover."

Alovere clenched his teeth. The idea of sitting in his room and twiddling his thumbs was less appealing than ever, yet he knew he wouldn't be of much use out there. He could barely move, after all. "Alright," he said begrudgingly, "but do me a favor, will you?"

Vlaire pulled his hand back. "What?"

"Find Galnoron," Alovere said quietly. "Keep an eye on him. I have reason to believe he is dangerous."

Vlaire nodded. "I already have guards searching for him and the drunk. They will be held in the Gallery until this search is over."

Alovere relaxed. Vlaire was much farther ahead than he had thought. The man was nothing if not efficient.

250

Vlaire turned and strode towards the door. "Rest up. Malya, look after him. Don't let him leave. I will let you know when we find Ki."

The door suddenly swung open before Vlaire reached it, light pouring in once again.

Galnoron stood in the doorway, his hands tucked into his sleeves and his hood pulled down over his eyes. "I hear you are looking for me, Guardian?"

Vlaire stared down at him. "Where are the guards that brought you here?"

Galnoron smiled greasily, causing every hair on the back of Alovere's neck to stand straight up. "There are none, sir. I heard a whisper that you were looking for me, so I came. Also," he added, clearing his throat waspily, "I think I should tell you something. It may concern the entire city."

Vlaire pushed past him, nearly blasting the frail man off his feet. "I don't have time. Tell it to your friend."

"I know who murdered your guard," Galnoron said loudly.

Alovere's heart froze.

Vlaire stopped and turned around slowly. "Excuse me?"

Galnoron bowed low. "Forgive me, Milord, but I thought it only fair for you to know that you are housing a very well known criminal."

Vlaire took two giant steps towards Galnoron and towered over him. "For weeks you have been nothing but silent, and now you have found my murderer, yes?" He paused. "I suppose it could have been you, given the way you sulk around like a cancer in the sunlight."

"Well, I would agree with you," Galnoron said silkily, "except I don't exactly match the picture."

"Picture?"

Alovere felt the world crashing down around his ears as Galnoron reached into his robes and pulled out a roll of parchment.

"I was fortunate enough to find this in the Ruins the other day," the sorcerer said. "A certain practitioner of black magic was able to..." he paused and glanced at Alovere. "Procure it for me."

Alovere knew there was no point in denying what that poster no doubt said about him. They were far beyond that at this point. He couldn't imagine what the man was up to, but it couldn't be good.

Vlaire snatched the poster from the wizard and unrolled it quickly. He glanced up at Alovere, then returned his gaze to the paper, his complexion fading as he read.

At length, he looked up at Alovere. His face was heavy, and his eyes cold. "This is you," he said, pointing at the parchment.

He turned it around for Alovere to see.

His heart sank. He knew exactly what it was before Vlaire had shown him. On it, a remarkable likeness of Alovere was sketched. It was a wanted poster, with a reward and a list of his known crimes. He was much younger in the drawing, yet it was obviously him. Apparently Galnoron had not been lying when he had told him so long ago that he had one of the old wanted posters.

"It is me," he admitted shamefully, "as a young man many years ago."

"It is says here on this...list, that you committed a murder much like the one seen on our guard," Vlaire said sharply, "that you are 'The Man of a Thousand Deaths.'"

Alovere nodded. "It's true. I was."

Vlaire stared at him evenly. "What am I supposed to do with this?" he said, pointing the poster. "You know I can't leave you here now!"

Alovere shook his head, his stomach twisting wretchedly. "I understand. Do what you must, but you must believe me; that was me as a much younger man. I was an assassin, highly trained and paid to kill. I left that life behind me thirty-five years ago and have not done anything like it since."

Vlaire lifted his arms above his head. "And now you are killing my guards?" he cried in exasperation.

"No, I am not," Alovere stated firmly. "I am different from who I was as a young man. Besides, I can hardly walk," he added ruefully. "How do you expect me to challenge two fully armed guards? With my cane?"

A strange feeling flowed through Alovere, coursing through his veins. It was familiar, and yet alien. It was a fear of what he had done, an old fear that had plagued him as a young boy after his first contracts. Not fear of punishment, no. It wasn't that simple. He had never feared punishment. It was the terror that consumed him as he stood beside the corpse of another man at sixteen years old, a bloody knife in his hand. Fear of having to face the families of the people he had murdered, fear that one day, he would face someone that recognized him for what he was: a murderer.

And it seemed as though the past had finally caught up with him.

Vlaire stared at him silently for a moment. Turning to the guard standing outside Lox's door, he jerked his chin towards Alovere. "Take him to Haze's chambers in the Gallery and lock him in."

"Wait!" Alovere said as the emotionless soldiers took a step towards him. They halted. "I am not who I once was," he said to Vlaire. "Lock me up if you will, it's what I would do, but watch this man carefully," he pointed at Galnoron, who leaned against the wall of the house with a confused expression on his face. "He cannot be trusted, and he already tried to kill Ki once."

Vlaire put his hands on the sides of his head. "You people amaze me!" he bellowed. "You turn on each other as quickly as wild dogs. Have you no loyalty? How can I tell who is guilty of what when you all scheme against one another?" He gestured to the guards outside Lox's door. "Lock them both up! Find the drunk, and lock him up too! They cannot be trusted, as they obviously cannot even trust each other. They are all to remain imprisoned until we locate Ki and the missing guard. Understood?"

"But I gave you your murderer!" Galnoron protested as one of the guards seized his elbow. "Why are you imprisoning me?"

"Because I don't trust you!" Vlaire seethed. "Or him! Or any of your bunch, except for Haze. And the only reason I trust him," he added, "Is because my sister has never let him out of her sight, save for today."

He whirled away and strode towards his wyvern, who stood waiting patiently in the street. "Stand outside their chambers once you have them locked in. I do not want any of them going in or out. If Haze arrives, send him to me."

He climbed onto Boar and urged him into the sky with a kick.

****

Lox sat miserably at his kitchen table, his head throbbing painfully. Malya sat across from him, feeding their son.

"So Alovere is the one that killed the guard?" Lox asked, his head booming with each word. His tongue felt like a swollen cactus and his ears sounded as though they were full of water.

"I don't know," Malya shook her head. "I don't think Vlaire does either, but he doesn't want to risk leaving him here."

"You know as well as I do that Alovere can barely move," Lox said shortly. "He has hardly left his bed since he arrived here. Ki has been with him nearly every second he has been conscious. How could he have murdered a guard and dragged his body all the way to the Ruins?"

"I know," Malya agreed, "but there was a poster with his name on it, and he admitted to being the man he was accused of."

"That only makes me trust him more," Lox said stubbornly. "Any man that admits to something that horrible while *knowing* it makes him look guilty of what he *hasn't* done has a fantastic moral compass. It simply makes me trust him."

Malya smiled weakly, bouncing the baby on her knee. "Well, I'm glad you trust him, dear, but what about our children? You really want him living in our home? He was a murderer. I know they say people change," she added, "but I don't believe that as wholeheartedly as you."

Lox grumbled and looked away. "I don't know."

It was true, he didn't know what he wanted. He didn't know why he was so upset. Anger that Vlaire marched into his home and removed his guest was certainly forefront, but that wasn't it. He had known Vlaire and Oaina for years, they were practically family. The idea that Alovere was dangerous was alien to him. He knew in the deepest parts of his heart that Alovere was a good person, regardless of what he had done in the past. Ki spent hours by his bedside teaching the man to sign and speak with her. He was a quick study, and it wasn't long before he was able to hold basic conversation with her, something only he and Malya were able to do with any efficiency.

He sighed. It would destroy Ki's world if Alovere were found to be guilty of the horrific murder in the Ruins. He supposed that was the reason he wanted Alovere to be innocent so badly. He liked the Dragon Rider, but it was Ki that motivated his sentiment. She had grown very fond of the old Rider for reasons unknown to anyone else. When he and Malya had asked her why she liked him, she had said, "He is kind."

"Lox?"

Lox snapped out of his train of thought and looked at Malya. "Yes, sorry. I was thinking."

"We still have to go look for Ki. Are you feeling well enough to fly?"

Just the thought of climbing onto Bard and wheeling over the city made him gag, but he nodded. "Yes, let's go find her. She is probably off on one of her silly adventures."

Malya didn't seem convinced, but helped him to his feet and led the way out of the house.

Bard was waiting outside, his scales glistening in the sunlight like polished sapphires.

They headed over and climbed into the saddle, Malya seating herself behind him.

Just before they took off, a loud yell pierced the silent white street.

They looked to their left to see Glassworn stumbling awkwardly along the cobblestones, his eyes wide with panic and his flask clutched in his hand with a death grip. Two guards were running behind him, trying to catch up.

But the drunk was far more agile than he looked.

He lurched and staggered in all the right places, causing the guards to just miss their grabs, or fumble awkwardly for a moment before losing their footing entirely. This continued all the way down the street until Glassworn arrived panting and wild-eyed at Bard's side. "Hello—" he screwed up his face as he tried to remember Lox's name. They had only met once, of course, and the rest of Glassworn's time had been spent in the pub. "You," he blurted finally. He glanced nervously over his shoulder, his blood shot eyes crossing briefly when he turned back to Lox. "I say, these gentlemen are insistent on capturing me! You aren't going to let them, are you?"

The two guards arrived a moment later, breathless and sweating. They bowed to him respectfully, panting as they turned to Glassworn.

"Now see here," one said crossly. "You are coming with us! Oaina's orders."

"Why?" Lox asked immediately. "I suppose he murdered a guard in cold blood? The drunken fool who can barely see in the daylight?" He winced as his head throbbed.

He wasn't much better off himself at the moment.

"Oaina and Vlaire want him locked up until Balloh is found," the guard said flatly. "She told me so herself."

"Balloh is the name of the missing guard?" Lox asked. The guard nodded. "Are you taking him to the Mirror Wood prison?"

"No, to the spare room in the Gallery."

Lox nodded. "Very well, I will take him myself."

The guards looked at each other nervously. "Uh, I don't think Oaina wanted—"

"Let me worry about what Oaina and Vlaire want!" Lox snapped. "Now go about your other duties." He reached down and seized Glassworn's arm. Dragging him up and over the pommel of the saddle, he laid him across the wyvern's back.

Water sprang into his eyes as the smell of sweat and alcohol wafted off of the man like a foul cloud. "Good grief," he wheezed.

"What do we tell Oaina when we see her?" the other guard asked hesitantly.

"I will tell her," Lox gasped, waving his hand to dissipate Glassworn's stench. "You return to your other duties," he repeated.

"But she's going to be so—"

Lox tapped Bard's sides and they leaped into the sky. His stomach lurched as he gripped the back of Glassworn's shirt. The jolting and jostling of Bard flapping his wings made him feel like he was going to lose his breakfast all over the city below him. It felt like an age had passed before Bard's claws connected with the stone of the Gallery platform, and he was able to drop hurriedly to solid ground.

Lowering Glassworn to the cobblestones, he steadied himself on Bard's flank. The great wyvern looked at him and groaned gently. "I'm fine, Bard," he said weakly. His head swam, the world shifting all around him. He swallowed, his throat like dry paper.

"Come on," he muttered, grabbing Glassworn by the back of the collar and dragging the stumbling drunkard towards the Gallery. He heard Malya dismount and follow him.

He was going to have a talk with Vlaire. Bursting into his home, seizing his guest and imprisoning all the guests in Hallovath was going over the top. He was panicking, and everyone watching on could see it. Vlaire was usually level headed, but his sister had a way of firing him up on occasion, and this was clearly one of those times. Vlaire hated hearing it from Lox, as he was so much younger than the lead guard, but there was nothing to be done about it.

He pushed open the doors to the Gallery and strode in, dragging Glassworn along with him. Oaina and Vlaire stood outside the door to Haze's room, talking in lowered voices.

"Alright," Lox said loudly, as Glassworn burped. The sound echoed across the marble hall, causing both of the other Guardians to look at him. "This is getting out of hand."

Vlaire started walking towards him, meeting him in the middle of the hall. "Lox! Good to see you on your feet."

"You can't do this, Vlaire," Lox said immediately, stopping and letting go of Glassworn's collar. The drunk tripped and crashed to the ground in a heap. "This is irrational and fueled by your sister's hate."

Vlaire frowned deeply. "If you mean imprisoning our guests, then no, it isn't. I have had quite enough of people dying and going missing. And now, the Hyless is one of them."

"Look at them!" Lox snapped impatiently. If his head felt better, he would have been more inclined to patience, but he wanted this over with and done so he could stop using his voice box. Each time he spoke, it was like a herd of angered dragons stampeded through his head. "This man is so drunk he can barely stand! Alovere is wounded so severely he can hardly move, and you think they are murdering and kidnapping people? Are you trying to throw Hallovath into a state of panic?"

Vlaire glared at him silently.

"It's foolish and impulsive," Lox continued. "Put them under guard like they have been since they arrived, and call it good enough. Focus your attentions on finding the Hyless, not chasing wild theories dreamed up by your war-mongering sister!"

Oaina snarled from over by the door, her eyes fixed on Lox with obvious disdain.

"What would you have me do?" Vlaire exclaimed. "Turn a known murderer loose in my city? He admitted to the murders of dozens of people where he came from! I can't just let him go."

"You place a constant guard on him until we find Ki and the missing guard," Lox explained. "There is nothing we can do about who he was as a young man. So, I suggest we focus on what we can do: Find Ki."

Lox could see the wheels turning in Vlaire's mind. He was clearly at war with himself. Part of him wanted to listen to his sister, no doubt, but another part of him, the part that rebelled against his older sister, knew Lox was right. Imprisoning all their guests was bound to start questions rolling among the market place and the lower city. The newcomers had been a topic of heavy discussion among the people of

Hallovath, as there had never been any strangers in the city before. If they were all suddenly thrown into prison, there would be talk of it for certain. And while he wanted the Hyless safe, Lox knew the last thing Vlaire wanted was a lynch mob.

"What you say makes sense," Vlaire admitted finally.

Lox breathed a sigh of relief. "Very good then. Let's just—"

"But my duty is to the Hyless," Vlaire continued, "and I will not allow a murderer to wander the streets of my city while the Hyless is nowhere to be found. I am no fool, and he can't be trusted. I read the full list of his crimes on that poster, and I have decided that he isn't to remain here at all."

Lox blinked. "What?"

Vlaire's expression turned to stone and he whirled around, striding towards the spare chambers. "He is to be banished from Hallovath. Him and his dragon will be sent out into the Mirror Wood where they can find their own way home. If they return, I will have the guards instructed to kill them on sight."

"But he hasn't fully healed yet," Lox protested, hurrying after the other man. "He'll die!"

"Then he won't come back, will he?"

"Vlaire, use your head," Lox said crossly. "He isn't a threat! He can barely walk!"

"As you have said. It doesn't change my mind, nor will it begin to should you continue to say it."

Vlaire stopped at the door of the chambers and jerked it open.

Galnoron shrank back from the door, rubbing the back of his head nonchalantly. Alovere was seated on the edge of Haze's bed, his back straight and eyes dead.

"Let's go, Alovere," Vlaire said. "You and your Dragon are leaving."

260

"Vlaire," Lox said angrily, "you are allowing your sister to cloud your judgment! You know as well as I do the Range Keeper believes they were sent here for a reason. You will be crossing into his territory if you do this."

"Then I will cross into it," Vlaire snapped. "I will not be the only Guardian in history who failed the Hyless!"

"You're mad! Lorgalith will hear of this," Lox said.

Alovere spoke up. "It's fine, Lox." The Rider stood up slowly, his face twisted in pain as his wounds shifted. "I will go. We all answer for the things we've done in one way or another."

"But this is dragon fodder!" Lox exclaimed. "He can't just start banishing Hallovath's guests to their deaths! It goes against everything that we are."

Alovere limped slowly towards the door. "It doesn't matter. I will fly home to my wife. I can be more than happy with that."

Lox bit his tongue before he said anything else. He knew what he had to do to put a stop to this. He had to go to Lorgalith. He was the only one Vlaire would listen to once his head had been poisoned by Oaina.

Nodding brusquely to Alovere, he turned and headed for the stairs that led up to the Range Keeper's home. Alovere wouldn't make it to his wife.

He would bleed out long before he did.

Chapter Twenty-Seven
A Parallel Truth

Lox knocked on the ornate black door, the sound hollow as it echoed down the ice passageway.

His heart thrummed in his chest, his head still swimming from the remains of whatever drug the people in the Ruins had used on him.

His mind wandered to Haze as he waited for the Keeper to open the door. If he had been taken, whoever had done so clearly had him targeted for a reason. If it were about the Hyless, they would have been better off targeting him or Alovere. Haze hardly had any contact with Ki at all. He was out patrolling with Oaina or himself too much to see Ki often, so it couldn't be about her. It had to be something about Haze himself, which meant there was someone in the Range who knew him. Someone who was trying to contact him.

He shook his head. Haze was a good person, there was no way to deny that. He flew into the Mountain Range to protect a girl he had never even met for an entirely selfless reason. Lorgalith believed that meant something extraordinary was at work.

 He was snapped back to reality as the door creaked open slowly, a cloud of black smoke billowing out the crack.

Lox coughed and waved his hand. The hair on the back of his neck stood up, and he whipped out his sword. Treading cautiously through the cloud of black and grey, he scanned the fog for any sign of the Keeper. The smoke smelled like burning feathers and cat urine, seeping into every crack and hole in the room.

He tripped on something and sent it clattering across the ice floor. It was the tea kettle, a large dent furrowed into the side of it. Flames billowed out the front of the open stove, smoke belching out above the flames at an alarming rate.

He hurried over and closed the grate, silencing the roar of the oxygen-enriched fire. Turning around, his heart sank as he saw Lorgalith lying face down on the floor, his arms spread eagle and his hot water bottle by his side.

"Lorgalith!" he cried, hurrying over and dropping his sword. He grabbed the old man's shoulders and shook him violently, coughing in the cloud of smoke. "Are you alright?"

"Mmmpphhhg," came the muffled groan.

Relief washed over Lox.

He was alive.

Whoever had attacked him was nowhere to be seen. The rest of the room was empty. The smoke began to blow out the open sides of the gazebo, no longer fed by the open stove.

"What happened?" he asked, gently trying to turn the man over.

"Hands off!" Lorgalith snapped, sitting up straight suddenly.

Lox backed away a bit. "Excuse me?"

Lorgalith didn't seem to be harmed at all. In fact, he seemed incredibly irritated that Lox had disturbed him at all.

"Here I was having a pleasant round of meditation and you run in here and start shaking me all over the place!" Lorgalith said crossly, turning to face him and rubbing his eyes. Indeed, if he had been meditating, it was the closest thing to sleeping Lox had ever seen. "Now you have gone and shut the stove!"

"It was blowing smoke out into your house!" Lox protested. "It smells horrible."

"It's incense, you cretin," Lorgalith muttered, struggling awkwardly to his feet and looking around him for his staff. Spying it on the ground a little bit away, he hobbled over to it and picked it up, straightening with a roll of his eyes. "Besides, you may have noticed that my house has no walls, so its rather difficult for the incense to even stay indoors. In spite of that, I can't say I am overly appreciative of you barging in here without permission."

"But the door—"

"The door opens itself whenever anyone knocks on it," Lorgalith snapped. "It's an enchantment I put on it to relieve me of the responsibility of hobbling over to it every time one of you goons comes knocking."

"But your tea kettle was on the floor and—"

"I was filling my hot water bottle and I spilled some on my hand. It had just boiled, so it was naturally rather warm." He scratched the back of his head. "I dropped it. It was a long way down and my back was in a fit, hence the need for the hot water bottle." He shrugged indifferently. "I didn't feel like picking it up."

Lox stared at the old man in amazement. How could someone so horribly unorganized and eccentric be the Range Keeper? It didn't seem right that such an important job should be placed on the shoulders of a geriatric lunatic. Not that anyone really knew the extent of what Lorgalith did anyway, but that was besides the obvious point that he was at least a little insane.

"Now, I suppose you are here to tell me that Alovere is being kicked out of our ever-gracious little city," Lorgalith answered his question for him, hobbling over towards his desk and lowering himself into his chair with a sigh.

Lox followed him over, standing by the end of the desk. He opened his mouth to ask how Lorgalith knew what he was going to say, then thought better of it. "Yes," he said instead. "I don't think it's right."

"It isn't."

Lox breathed a sigh of relief. "So, you will stop it then?"

"Oh goodness no," Lorgalith exclaimed, frowning at Lox as though he ought to know better. "I wouldn't dream of it."

The Guardian blinked. "B-but you agreed that it isn't right."

"That's because it isn't," Lorgalith said again, eyeing Lox as though he had sprouted a second set of ears.

Lox took a deep breath, his head spinning as he leaned on the edge of the old man's desk. "So, what are we going to do about it?"

"Nothing!" Lorgalith said giddily. "Would you grab my hot water bottle off the floor there?" he said eagerly, leaning around Lox and pointing to the small silver canister.

"I think not!" Lox snapped. "You can't just sit idly by as someone is allowed to die! You are the Range Keeper. It is your duty to look after the Range."

The decrepit old man rolled his eyes and sank into his chair. "Yes, yes. I know. That's what I am doing."

"By allowing an innocent man to be banished to his almost certain death?"

"Yes," Lorgalith said excitedly. "I admit, for a moment there I thought you weren't going to figure it out."

Lox blinked in bewilderment. This made as much sense as beating the sharp edge of a blade on a rock. Of course, he might as well have gone and beat his head on the wall of the Gallery for all the good this conversation was doing him. Just the idea nearly made him swoon. "Are you going to tell me what is going on, or aren't you?"

"I'm not," Lorgalith said immediately. Seeing the look on Lox's face, he rolled his eyes. "Alright, alright. I'll give you a hint: Just because it's wrong, doesn't mean it isn't necessary. Just because Alovere doesn't deserve to be banished to his death, how do you know that it won't service us and him in some way none of us could have predicted? Save for myself, of course," he added, clearing his throat pompously. He rubbed the top of his shining head and smiled at Lox. "Get it yet?"

Lox did not "get it." In fact, he had no idea what the old man was talking about at all. Send Alovere out into the Mirror Wood because he might do something important? That was not only unlikely, it bordered insanity. Alovere was a good person, and as much as he wished the man had not committed those crimes in his earlier life, he couldn't possibly deserve this.

He shook his head. He had to find a way to save him.

"I know you want him safe," Lorgalith said gently, his eyes soft, "but sometimes there are risks that must be taken to secure the safety of those dear to us. I know you don't understand, and I would tell you why it must be, but I am bound by the sacred promise of the Range Keeper to ensure that things go the way time intended them to, and to never speak of them. You must understand, Lox, and trust me. I would not allow an injured man to die for no good reason."

"So, he *is* going to die!" Lox exclaimed, rage building inside him. "You can't let this happen! You must do something!"

"I cannot see whether he will die or not," Lorgalith said firmly. "That I cannot predict, but he must go into the Mirror Wood. This I know as a certain fact."

"Will you not give me a better explanation?" Lox pleaded. "Tell me how I can help him! Tell me what I can do." He knew he sounded frantic, he knew he sounded like he cared for Alovere too much, but it was Ki. The thought of seeing her face when she returned to find Alovere gone...

"There is nothing you can do to prevent this from happening. It will come to pass, and there is the chance that Alovere may die," Lorgalith said flatly. "There is nothing either of us can do to stop it."

"That is not an answer to this problem! There must be some other way!"

"It is the answer, and no there isn't. You need to leave it be and don't do anything rash. If you want everything in the next few days to go the way it should and the Hyless to be safe, you need to leave this alone. I mean it, Lox," he said sternly. "I can see that you feel strongly about this, but you have to trust me."

Lox lowered his head, his rage subsiding. "Very well," he sighed. "At least tell me this: Is it likely that he will die?"

Lorgalith sighed. "It is neither likely or unlikely. It could go either way. There is a variable that could change the outcome of his banishment, but it is hidden from my sight. I only know it is there, and that it is more tragic than Alovere dying himself."

Lox nodded reluctantly. "Alright. Thank you, Lorgalith."

"Very good," The old man sighed. "Now do pass me the hot water bottle, would you?"

****

Alovere heaved himself into Arginox's saddle, spots clouding his vision as pain lanced through his ribs.

He ground his teeth together and sat up straight, trying not to notice as his stitches tore in his side.

Wind blew gently across the platform outside the Gallery, sending a chill straight to his bones.

He turned and looked down at the Mirror Wood far below the city. It was dark, a layer of fog hanging over it like a thick soup. The tops of small trees burst out of the murk like glistening blue lances, reaching for the sky.

Vlaire stood by Arginox's side, looking up at the Dragon Rider. "I'm sorry Alovere, but you have to understand that there is a lot at stake regarding the safety of the Hyless. I cannot have you here when I know what it is you used to be."

"I understand that you are cowed by your sister," Alovere said coldly, "but I also know this is how I would handle the situation myself," he sighed. "So, there is that. I hope you find her."

Vlaire nodded tensely. "We will. Now go."

Alovere thought perhaps he would have more to say to who was likely to be the last person he was going to see before he died, but now that he was here...

He shook his head and pulled on Arginox's reins, directing the great fire dragon towards the edge of the Gallery platform. He steeled himself against the inevitable hardship ahead. He knew that he had limited time before he bled to death. Lox was kind enough to pack him several changes of bandages, but had refused to come to the platform when he left. He said he was entirely too busy looking for Ki and that he didn't have time to waste.

Alovere smiled. He knew it was because the guard didn't want to watch him fly off to his death. His smile faded.

He was going to miss Lox and his family. Very few people had what it took to gain Alovere's favor, or even more rarely, his kindness. Enial was the only person Alovere would miss when he left for the longest time. Haze had run second to her after he had returned from his little adventures and Alovere had been seasoned by age. But for Lox and Ki to have spurred these feelings...perhaps it was better that he left after all.

His mind strayed to Ki, and his heart ached suddenly. He and Enial had never had children; they had not been blessed with that fortune. He knew that he had only made Ki's acquaintance a short time ago, but he felt that if he and Enial had had a daughter, that's what she would have been like. Her flowing blonde hair and green eyes were enough to steal the heart of men colder than ice, and he was no exception. He knew that there were select few things he would miss about the Range if he were lucky enough to survive banishment, and Ki was definitely one of them. She had a heart of gold, and a soul of pure kindness. He couldn't think of any person with as much natural charm as she had, save his own wife.

Enial.

He set his teeth in determination, and tapped Arginox in the ribs.

With a low groan, the beast leaped out into open air and spread his wings wide. The wind howled as they descended slowly towards the forest below. He turned as far as he could without tearing his stitches more and looked back over his shoulder.

The platform of the Gallery loomed out above the city, the glimmering blue spike of the building itself glinting in the light of the sun. He could see Lox's house tucked neatly between its larger neighbors far below him.

He took one last look at it, and turned away. He had to focus on staying alive from this point on. He would likely never see Ki and Lox again.

He sighed wearily as Arginox fell closer to the trees below. The giant Banyeet towered above him on his right. Its boughs swayed back and forth in the wind as though it were shaking its head in disapproval of Alovere's actions. The very plant life seemed to frown on his past.

He couldn't blame them. He disliked his youth just as much as the people around him. Not a day went by that he didn't regret the things he had done, or the lives he had taken. Mothers went without sons because of him, wives without husbands, daughters without fathers. He had not only murdered innocent people, he had ruined the lives of their families. If that was the only thing he learned from his time in the Range, it was enough. He knew that it was people like Lox he had killed, men that left behind wives like Malya, and children like Ki.

His insides twisted at the thought, and he pushed it away. It nestled in the back of his mind like a black widow, ready to strike the moment his thoughts strayed towards it again.

After a few hours of flying, the day grew late. He decided to descend through the clouds and settle somewhere in the forest for the night.

The mist began to flood in around him as they descended through the first layer of clouds, the top of the Banyeet vanishing behind a ceiling of white. The snow-like clouds filled in all around him, blocking his view of anything above or below his position.

Arginox growled warily, and a tingle went down Alovere's spine. The stillness of the fog draped over the thick of the forest sent shivers up and down his back, but he ignored it.

Pushing his thoughts to the side, he narrowed his eyes into the gloom. He could see nothing but mist, water droplets building up on his armor as the moisture from the clouds soaked into him. There was an odd smell that he couldn't quite place; it was like campfire smoke, only different somehow. It was more pungent, like the smell of burning hair.

The white slowly began to fade, revealing glimpses of the thick foliage beneath him. Haze had told him what the Mirror Wood was like, and he was in no way disappointed by the real thing.

The plant-life was thick and moist, water trickling down the leaves and branches of the various shrubs as fog dissipated on the leaves of the trees above and drizzled down into the wood. Mushrooms pressed out from between the trees, glowing an incandescent tan and yellow. They were easily as large as Arginox, their bulbous heads pockmarked with clumps of thick blue moss. A stream wound its way under his dragon as they descended, fish in its water glinting like candles in the current, seemingly suspended over the ground as the creek bubbled over a glistening rock bed.

Arginox fluttered to a stop by the edge of creek, his talons pressing into the soft bank. He turned his head back to his master, his glowing red eyes wide with concern.

"It's alright, 'Nox," Alovere grunted as he shifted. "It's getting close to end of day. We have to find a place to camp or we will be flying all night. I don't want to try and set up camp in the dark."

He sniffed suddenly, the smell of seared meat wafting into his nostrils. His mouth watered like a fountain as he squinted through the trees, trying to catch a glimpse of a smoke trail.

"Do you smell that?" he breathed to his dragon, as though the wyrm could answer him. "Someone is cooking meat. Where is that coming from?"

He had not eaten anything since he had been locked in the chambers earlier that morning. It was now late day, and his stomach flipped at the idea of a hot meal.

He slid painfully to the ground, wincing as a bolt of pain shot through his ribs. He cursed under his breath and shifted his armor. Perhaps he could offer some sort of payment to whoever was cooking. Haze had said there were people that lived out here in the Mirror Wood, building small houses and farming the mushrooms that grew in plenty all throughout the forest. Maybe this was a small family that had food to spare. Lox had packed him with enough dried goods to see him through a day or two, but the more of that he could save the better. He didn't want to run out before he got home. And besides, if he could secure a hot meal before he began his endless trek through the cold of the Range, so much the better.

He followed his nose across the creek and towards the tree line on the opposite bank. He limped towards the thick foliage, Arginox snorting anxiously behind him.

Pushing his way through a bristly blue bush and under a few low hanging branches, he gasped in pain as he collided with the side of one of the giant mushrooms. His head swam as his ribs throbbed painfully, blurring his vision.

Shaking his head, he pressed on, pausing briefly when he heard low voices.

"We shouldn't be stopping," a gruff voice said. It traveled through the forest like a whistle in the night, reaching Alovere's ears plainly. "We need to keep moving."

"All we have to do is reach home before tomorrow night," another man said, his voice calmer. There was something familiar about it, but Alovere couldn't put his finger on it. "We will take a little bit of time to eat and rest before we hoof it all the way back to Miasma City."

Alovere ears pricked up at this.

Miasma City? What were soldiers from Miasma City doing in the Mirror Wood? Orlivan indeed had reason to be concerned if Jaelyn's soldiers were already this far into the Range.

"They will come looking for us," the other voice said again, a hint of worry riding in it. "We should get as far from that blasted city as we can. Galnoron can deal with the rest of it."

Alovere clenched his fist. He knew that slime wizard was up to no good.

He cursed under his breath. He should have killed him on the trail! He was working for Jaelyn all along and using Orlivan's resources to do it.

"Orlivan and Jaelyn will want to launch the attack on the city in the next week," the calm voice said. "We will be back here anyway, fighting for one of them."

"Both of them!" the gruff voice spat. "Damned royals. Making nice to take Hallovath, and then turning on each other no doubt. They can't leave well enough alone."

Alovere frowned. Jaelyn and Orlivan were working together? How was that possible? They got along as well as snakes and mice. There had to be some sort of mistake.

"You know how it's going to go," the calm one said with a sharp edge to his voice. "Jaelyn has what she wants. With the power of the Hyless, she will be able to crush Orlivan like a bug. She is sending him into the city to burn out all his military. After he is spent, she will step in and deliver the final blow. The poor man won't even know that the Hyless is already gone."

Ice washed over Alovere. The Hyless gone? Ki?

He crept closer to the tree line, careful not to make a sound. He got closer and closer to where the voices came from, fire light beginning to flicker through the branches. The moss smelled thick and damp, the musky odor heavy across the forest floor.

Just a few more feet...

He slid down to his stomach, his stitches crying out in protest. Wriggling his way to the edge of the trees, he was barely able to keep himself from crying out in rage.

Zaajik sat by a fire with a soldier Alovere didn't recognize. The soldier wore the colors of Miasma City, Zaajik sporting a pair of swords from the floating city as well.

He ground his teeth together. Zaajik was working for Jaelyn! How could he have not known it?

His heart sank suddenly.

A girl sat on the ground opposite Zaajik. Her hands and feet were bound tightly and grubby lines streaked her cheeks where tears had run through the layers of travel grime.

It was Ki.

Chapter Twenty-Eight
The Hyless Athenaeum

Haze blinked into the darkness of the cave mouth.

Famau stood beside him, her arms crossed.

She had led him on a winding path through the lower part of the city that slowly took them farther and farther away from the Ruin's sparse population. She had stopped in front of a tunnel that was bored into the base of the waterfall. The edges were sharp and jagged, the melted ice forming razor-like icicles that clung to the rim of the cave like frozen teeth. The inside was black as night, the inky darkness floating just beyond the light like a malignant shadow.

"You want me to go in there?" he asked warily.

"This is called the Cave of Grasping," Famau said shortly. "It is like a library of past occurrences. I need you to see some things the Guardians will never show you."

"That's great, but I have been in one of these caves before," he said uneasily, recalling the mishap with the Algid. He shuddered. "I'm in no hurry to rush back into one."

"Well, you will rush into this one," Famau snapped. "Unless you would like to remain under my guard in the Ruins for say, the next fifty years?"

Haze glared at her. "It seems as though we should be past threatening one another."

"Oh good, you'll come along without putting up a fuss then. Let's get moving, I would like you to be back in New Hallovath before mid-day."

"Wait, you're taking me back?"

Famau rolled her eyes impatiently, as though this was something he should have figured out by now. "These tunnels lead into New

Hallovath, down by the bakery. Yes, I am taking you back to the upper city. There are just a few quick stops I want to make on the way."

Haze raised an eyebrow. "Quick stops?"

Famau stalked past him and melted into the gloom.

He hesitated.

She was gone. He could see Hallovath over his shoulder. If he ran right now, he could make it. He could tell Oaina and Vlaire where the guard was, and they would storm Famau's hideout. The guard had been saved by Famau and her people from the same fate as his comrade, and lay waiting to be transported back to the upper city. There was no need to follow her.

He shook his head. Something in the back of his mind wanted to see the library. He could learn more about the Guardians. More about Ki. Perhaps it could show him what it was that made the Guardians so willing to give their lives for the Hyless.

He sighed, and followed her into the black.

All light vanished except for what glinted across the ice floor from the open mouth. Haze began to wonder what her plan for a light source was, as they walked deeper into the cave.

The silence was deafening, the only sound being the steady drip of water from somewhere deeper inside that echoed through the tunnel like a cannon shot in the dark. The gloom was as thick as molasses, becoming so black that Haze could not see more than an inch in front of himself. Famau vanished into the ink beside him, the sound of her breathing the only indication that she was there.

He opened his mouth to ask her what they were going to do for a light, and the walls and ceiling burst into a familiar radiance. Yobes scurried along the top and sides of the tunnel like a river of starlight, illuminating the cavern in a glistening blue glow. Crystals hung like miniature chandeliers from the ceiling, their many facets catching the light of the Yobes and casting it in dancing sequins across the frozen cave floor. The cavern was burrowed into the bottom of the waterfall, so it was comprised entirely of ice, lending to the shine the Yobes and crystals emitted.

"The beauties of the Range never cease to amaze me," Haze said.

"Indeed," Famau answered indifferently. "Which is why we need to find a way to stop these other kingdoms from coming in here and creating giant cities out of our forests and killing the spirits."

Haze glared at her. "Do you even know the meaning of enjoying a moment? Or is that simply too much to ask?"

"I will enjoy many peaceful moments once my task is complete and I know that there is no way your King or his rivaling Queen can get their hands on my daughter and take all of this," she gestured to the light of the Yobes, "away from us."

Haze nodded solemnly. She was right, or course. He had always been partial to the beauty of wildlife, even to the point of letting it distract him from matters at hand, but he needed to stay focused, and above all, not stop asking questions. Famau seemed like she meant well, but he had spent considerable time with the Guardians, and he knew there must be a real reason she was tossed from New Hallovath other than fighting for her daughter. Lox wouldn't have allowed that to happen, and neither would Lorgalith, for that matter. Vlaire could be bullied by Oaina, but he didn't seem the type to condemn a mother for defending her child.

He cleared his throat. "So, what are we going to see?"

"You are going to see some history," Famau stated. "Ancient history from way back during the events of the first Hyless."

"But that was thousands of years ago," Haze exclaimed.

"It was," Famau nodded, glancing at him. Her blonde hair glinted in the light of the Yobes. "It's all recorded here, and it will be, until the end of time itself."

"And why is it that you want me to see this history so badly?"

Famau smiled grimly. "Tell me, what is the story you have heard of the Guardians of the Hyless?"

Haze recounted what Moxie had told him aboard the Laudlin. "They are powerful and stand up for the Hyless is about the sum of it," he finished. "I heard tell of four people that stood against ten thousand and were victorious."

"That is recorded here," Famau said, "but there is some debate as to how a Guardian becomes a Guardian. In all the legends, Guardians are people that rise up from positions such as bakers and blacksmiths to stand and fight for the Hyless because they alone possess the knowledge that she must survive at any cost. It is a gift given to them by the Hyless at birth. Power in a Guardian is the born wisdom and understanding of something so supernatural that most people believe it is a myth."

Haze frowned. "What are you getting at?"

"You will see," she said, rounding a corner and hurrying ahead. "We are almost there."

Haze followed her down the small side tunnel, the walls closing in and funneling them at a slight downward angle. The Yobes were even more concentrated in this area of the cave, shining so bright Haze felt as though they were still standing in the sunlight.

The tunnel eventually tapered down until Haze had to bend his head a little to keep it from brushing the ceiling, before ending at a small door nestled into the ice. It was the same black wood as the door that led into Lorgalith's gazebo, silver letters once again glittering on the surface.

"What does it say?" he asked immediately.

"I don't know, and I don't care." Famau reached forward and lifted the silver latch that held it closed. It swung inward with a weary creak, a small shower of dust falling from the top of the jamb.

Famau gestured for Haze to follow her in and stepped through the door.

He ducked through the entry and his jaw dropped.

The ceiling soared high above them, no longer just above their heads. A giant crystal hung suspended in the middle of a large round room, beams of sapphire light streaming off of it and streaking across the bookshelf-covered walls. It looked as though it were attached to the ceiling, hanging down over the chamber like a spike of ice. Yobes funneled towards the top where it connected to the cavern, the creatures flowing into it like liquid light. Tiny crystals speckled the ceiling around their larger cousin, winking down at them like stars as the Yobes trickled into their tiny crystalline cores. Bookshelves covered every wall, all filled to overflowing with dusty volumes and scrolls that Haze had no doubt recalled events that had not been spoken of in centuries. Several small tables were placed at random throughout the room, comfortable looking chairs positioned fashionably around their smooth wooden edges. They were all made of the same dark wood and engraved in silver letters of one sort or another, each one different from the next. A few books lay open and forgotten on the tables, dust collecting on their exposed pages in light gray blankets.

The sound of dripping water caused him to turn his head. On either side of the door they had just passed through, a pair of small fountains stood guard in the light. They were as tall as him and carved in the likeness of wyverns, large bowls cradled in their claws as water dripped steadily from their mouths into the vessels. Their eyes were genuine emeralds glowing a brilliant green in the light of the crystal. They looked almost sad, the melancholy drips all that were left of what used to be glorious fountains.

"What is this place?" Haze whispered.

"It is known as the Hyless Athenaeum," Famau answered quietly. "Scholars and druids who studied the Hyless gathered here for many years before the flood of the lower city a hundred years ago."

"What did they study about her?"

"It's not so much about her, as the Guardians," Famau corrected herself. "The Hyless is very simple. There is no way to determine how she gets her power or why, only that she has it. They studied the Guardians."

Haze tilted his head. "To what purpose?"

"To try and create them," she said softly, casting a longing look at one of the nearby bookshelves. "They believed that the Guardians were not a random occurrence, and that they could be chosen and trained from birth to serve the Hyless only."

"Isn't that what Vlaire, Oaina, and Lox are? Guardians?" Haze asked in confusion.

"I don't know," Famau shook her head. "It's too difficult to say. They certainly accept all responsibility for her and serve her tirelessly. But are they really the Guardians?"

She strode over to the nearest table and picked up a closed book. Haze noted that there was no dust on the cover. "I have read many accounts of the Hyless and her Guardians in the past," she said, "and each time I have come to the same conclusion: the Guardians are random. You can't make them and you can't train them. They are a unique breed of people born with the sacred knowledge that the Hyless is special."

"Are you saying you don't believe Vlaire and Lox are Guardians?"

"I don't know," Famau said again, clenching the book tightly. "But I do know this: You can't teach the knowledge that a Guardian possesses. It would be like teaching a belief; one has to believe it. In all accounts, the Guardians are strangers that appear out of nowhere for no reason, cobblers and seamstresses ready to die for a child they have never met."

"And you somehow believe that these Guardians have yet to appear this time around?" Haze asked slowly. "And that Lox, Vlaire and Oaina are just figure heads?"

"And what's worse," Famau spat, "is I think they know it! I think they are masquerading as Guardians of the Hyless so they can live posh lives in the upper city."

Haze thought this was going a bit far. Lox didn't live a posh life, and all of the Guards certainly worked themselves to the bone. Oaina, he knew, slept on the floor in his chambers, so there was no posh there. But there was something to what Famau said about the Guardians being born randomly. It made less sense, but seemed more likely given the mysticism that surrounded the Hyless. If anything, Famau had some of the facts right, but was prejudiced against the people that took her daughter from her.

"Show me some of the instances you are talking about," he said, choosing not to address her claims on the Guardians. "Let me see."

Famau turned and strode towards the crystal. Haze began to open his mouth and ask her where she was going, when she stopped underneath it. She lifted the old leather-bound volume to chest height and lowered her head.

A small stream of light swirled down towards her suddenly, touching the cover of the book. It gently lifted it out of Famau's hands, the thread of light suspending it in the air. It opened on its own, the pages flitting past like leaves in a breeze, until it finally settled on a spot somewhere in the middle, and a small cloud of blue-white appeared above it. The small cloud first formed words in a language Haze could not recognize, then took on the shapes of people, the figures cloudy and distorted. They slowly cleared up to reveal the images of three men and a woman.

The woman was short and round, her face bright and eyes brighter. She donned a kind smile and held the hand of one of the men next to her. Her partner was tall and lanky, bald on top of his head and sporting a flour covered apron and a wide, toothy grin. The other two men were obviously twins. One was burly with soot stained arms and a billowing red beard, while the other was clean shaven and slender. He wore a pair of small glasses and a long black coat, his eyes shining with a calm wisdom from behind his spectacles.

"How did you do that?" he exclaimed. "The book is flying!"

"It is the power of the Athenaeum Crystal," Famau answered. "It can show images of what is written in books. The Yobes infest the Ice Crystal and create the light and images from their own bodies. They were loyal servants of the druids of old, and still serve any who come to the Athenaeum."

"Who are they?" he asked, pointing at the sapphire images of the people.

She took a breath. "They are the first Guardians of the Hyless," she said slowly.

Haze raised an eyebrow and looked back at the image. They certainly didn't look like Guardian material. It showed a baker and his homely wife, followed by what looked like a blacksmith and his bookworm brother. "But how can that be?" he asked. "They are not warriors. These people cannot have defeated trained soldiers in combat!"

"But they did," Famau answered, "and they did it very well, from what history says."

"History says they gave their blood," Haze said.

"They died, yes, if that's what you are getting at."

Haze stared at the young woman. She stared back, her soft blue eyes seeming to search out his very soul. She looked so very kind and gentle. And she had died, along with her husband, to protect a girl they didn't know?

Famau waved her hand and the image blurred, being replaced by another. This time, it was five people, three women and two men: a farmer couple, a cobbler, a seamstress, and what looked like a merchant. Again, none of them looked like warriors.

"Let me guess," he said, "more Guardians?"

Famau nodded. "Yes, and they are the most famous ones. These are the Guardians that defeated the ten thousand by themselves. Only the seamstress had already been killed at that point, so it was just the other four left. Hence the legend."

Haze stared in amazement at the men and women. None of them were soldiers, not one.

Famau then waved her hand again, and again. Image after image of men and women appeared magically above the open book, showing dozens of people that had fought and died for the Hyless over the centuries and filling the chamber with radiance, very few of them actually soldiers. There were a couple that he could see were military; one was a Dragon Rider for certain, his mount standing behind him proudly.

The images then became more disturbing. They changed to bodies lying before the burning gates of Hallovath, spears and arrows sticking out of them at odd angles. Three people stood bloody and rigid, facing an entire army with nothing but broken weapons and solemn expressions.

She stopped on one in particular that made his spine tingle.

Two men and a woman were frozen in mid leap, their faces twisted into a snarl of defiance. They wore armor like Vlaire's and Oaina's, glinting blue in the light. In their hands they held bent and chipped swords, the edges beyond repair. They charged a battlefield of at least a thousand men, their eyes flashing dangerously. Behind them, over the woman's left shoulder, a white glow was coming from Hallovath. The Guardians looked like they moved with a power not their own as they charged the enemy ranks.

"Who are they?" Haze asked.

"That is the family Llyovek," Famau said bitterly, "the last Guardians before Vlaire and his sister. Those are his grandparents, and his grandfather's brother."

Haze felt realization dawn on him. He knew Famau was right, there was no way someone could simply decide to be a Guardian one day and be one. Vlaire and Oaina may hold the torch, as it were, but he was beginning to think that it was something to be passed on to the next group.

He wished it were simpler, but it seemed as though both Vlaire and Famau were in the right. How could Vlaire not be a Guardian if he were completely willing to put himself in harm's way for the Hyless? Did that not make him a Guardian by default?

"These people are all random," Famau said, breaking his train of thought. "Even Vlaire's grandparents were masons, that were in the process of finishing the Gallery above the city during the last Havi Ut Gahdness. These are not trained warriors. They are chosen, somehow."

284

Haze didn't answer. The more he heard, the more uneasy he became. Famau sounded less and less like a concerned mother and more like a radical rebel.

She stared at him as if waiting for him to answer, a wild light in her eye.

"I don't know what to think of it," he said cautiously. "You make a fine point. They certainly seem to be chosen at random, but if that's the case, can't Vlaire and Oaina be the chosen Guardians?"

She grumbled for a moment, kicking her foot at something on the floor. After a bit of silence, she mumbled, "Yes, I suppose." Her face fell, as though he had just confirmed her worst fears.

"But that's a good thing, right?" he said quietly. "If they are the Guardians, they will look after her. They are sworn and chosen to do it, better than anyone else in the world."

Famau didn't seem convinced. She resigned herself to a tight-lipped nod, and clapped her hands.

The book fell from the thread of light into her hands with a dull thud. Striding over to the nearest table, she dropped it onto the wood. A small cloud of dust swept off the table as she did so.

"Let's go," she said shortly. "We need to get you to the upper city. Think of me what you will, but I don't trust Vlaire and Oaina. I want you watching them."

Haze didn't move. "Now see here, I may not have a care one way or the other, but these people have been kind to me and have given me a place to stay. I won't do anything to hurt them."

"I'm not asking you too," Famau snapped. "Just watch my daughter. Make sure she stays out of harm's way, and keep the things I have said close in mind."

Haze thought about it for a moment. It wasn't much to ask; he did it as best he was able to already. All he had to do was continue doing his daily duties. Besides, Famau didn't strike him as an entirely sane person; he didn't want to say anything that would lower his chances of being returned to New Hallovath.

"Very well," he stated. "I will do that."

Famau visibly relaxed, and turned towards the door. "Thank you. Now let's get you out of here."

Chapter Twenty-Nine
To Save The Hyless

Alovere waited behind the tree with bated breath. His palm was sticky as he wrapped is fingers around the hilt of his sword. He could hear his heart thrumming in his ears.

He was too wounded to take Zaajik. He knew how the man fought; he was merciless and cold, his speed nearly matching Alovere's, even when he was healthy. He had to think of some other way to save Ki.

He had heard both of the men talking about working together under Jaelyn and Orlivan. He couldn't let them make off with the Hyless just before such a brutal attack on Hallovath.

He licked his lips, a bead of sweat rolling down his brow.

He had never felt so vulnerable before. Zaajik was considered the best swordsman in Elliset, and he was letting that thought get to him. He had never been afraid to engage someone before, least of all a man that had served under him.

Zaajik *was* afraid of him, at least a little. He feared Alovere's skill more than he should, given his age. It always made Alovere feel like perhaps Zaajik knew who he was.

The stitches in his side suddenly rang with pain.

Regardless, it was very unlikely that he would be able to best Zaajik in his current condition. He would have to find some way to talk to him and convince him to let the Hyless go. He knew that Zaajik was a self-serving person, but he wasn't entirely unreasonable. Perhaps he could make the swordsman see some sense.

He straightened up, wincing as his ribs throbbed. Clearing his throat, he stepped out from behind his tree and into the edge of their camp. Ki looked up when he stepped into the light of the fire, her eyes brightening. A smile spread across her face the second her eyes fell on him, her cheeks flushing brightly.

His heart sank. There were more of them then he had originally thought. At least half a dozen other men lay sleeping behind Ki, too low for him to have seen them from his position.

Zaajik looked up at him from his seat by the fire. His expression went from surprise, to horror as his face paled to the color of old cheese. "Alovere!" he exclaimed weakly. "How did-what—"

"What are you doing here?" Alovere asked coldly, making himself appear as confident as possible. He stared down at Zaajik, filling his expression with as much disdain as he could muster.

"We were sent on a mission by the Q—King," the swordsman stammered, wiping his hands on his trousers and standing up. His greased-back hair fell a little out of place, a strand falling in front of his left eye. He flicked it back nervously, his eyes fixed on Alovere's sword arm. "We have to grab this girl and return her to the kingdom."

"Or to Jaelyn," Alovere said bitterly, "as that would better suit your purpose?" He glared at the younger man, a little of his actual confidence returning to him.

Zaajik swallowed. "H-how do you mean?"

"I heard every word you said," Alovere snapped. "You plan to take this girl to Queen Jaelyn and stab your king in the back. You will be hanged for treason if I have any say in the matter." He lifted is chin. "If I don't kill you right here and now."

Alovere's heart raced as Zaajik took a step backwards, looking nervously from side to side.

He had him fooled.

The rest of the men had heard the commotion and now stood behind Zaajik, most of them rubbing their eyes groggily.

288

The other man that had been speaking with the young swordsman drew his blade and advanced on Alovere, his jaw set.

Alovere braced himself and pulled his sword from its scabbard.

This grunt he could kill.

"What are you doing?" Zaajik hissed, grabbing the other man's shoulder and pulling him back.

"He heard our conversation," the man snapped. "We can't let him leave!"

"Oh, so you're going to kill him, are you?" Zaajik said sarcastically. "This is the Man of a Thousand Deaths, you moron. He will slice you to bits before you even land a blow."

Alovere let out a small sigh of relief as the other man went white as a sheet and shrank back to Zaajik. As much as he hated that his identity wasn't as hidden as he would have liked, the prospect of not having to fight the young sword master made up for it.

"I will make you a deal," he said gruffly. "You give me the girl, and return to your respective kingdoms. I don't care whose. I won't report this to King Orlivan, and I will decide not to kill you here and now. Decide quickly, old men aren't known for their patience."

Zaajik opened his mouth to respond, but halted suddenly. His eyes were wide, fixed on some point by Alovere's hip.

Alovere glanced down and saw a small trickle of blood running down his armor. In all the excitement, he had failed to notice that his bandages were overdue. Blood was now seeping through the sodden material and down his side.

He felt an icicle drop into his stomach as Zaajik's eyes suddenly narrowed, taking on the look of a snake sizing up his prey. He took a slow step forward, staring at Alovere hard. His tongue flicked over his lips with a lizard-like speed.

"You are wounded, old man," he said quietly. His hand floated gently down to the hilt of his sword.

Alovere cursed under his breath. "Not so wounded that I can't defeat all of you without breaking a sweat," he said.

But Zaajik was no longer fooled. "Oh, I don't think that's the case," the younger man sneered, stalking around him like a cat around a mouse. "If it were, you would have killed us right away, or have you since become a mincer of words?"

"You don't know what you're getting yourself into, Zaajik," Alovere said, dropping all pretenses. "That girl is more important to the world than you could ever imagine. If you take her to Jaelyn—"

"My purse will weigh a great deal more than it does now, and I will be given a position among her royal guard for many years to come," Zaajik finished for him. "It's not nearly as complicated as you are trying to make it. It's actually quite simple: Take the girl, make a substantial amount of coin, and dispense with a tired old myth at the same time."

Alovere felt a familiar rage pecking at the back of his mind. The same rage that came to him whenever he was dealing with a bull-headed ass that couldn't listen to common sense. "Listen to yourself! 'Dispensing with an old myth?' Why would Jaelyn want her if it was a myth? This girl possesses more power in a strand of her hair than you do in your sword arm! You would be a fool to offer up that much power to Jaelyn. She is a tyrant."

"I don't care!" Zaajik snapped. "It doesn't matter to me who she is or where she came from, or who I have to kill to take her," he added, glaring at Alovere. "So, do me a favor and spare me the trouble of killing you. Leave."

Alovere blinked in surprise. Zaajik stood calmly, his hand on his sword. It didn't seem like the young man to spare anyone's life, let alone one who had just discovered him as being guilty of treason.

Zaajik turned away. "I am one of the greatest swordsmen alive. Someday, I will kill you, but not now. Not when you are wounded and fighting at half strength. I will be the sword master who kills the Man of a Thousand Deaths, not the used-up husk of a wounded warrior."

Alovere drew himself up proudly, ignoring his stitches as they pulled tight. "I will not be going anywhere without that girl," he said flatly. "I will leave only if I leave with *her*."

Zaajik whirled on him angrily. "I didn't say I wouldn't maim you further and *abandon* you to die!" he snarled. "Now make yourself scarce, assassin. Before I change my mind."

Alovere shook his head. "I cannot, nor will I. That girl is the only reason our world exists. I would be a selfish fool if I let you take her to the most power-hungry woman in Elliset."

Zaajik didn't hesitate. He whipped his swords out of their sheathes, leveling them at Alovere. "Last chance, Alovere. Go now, so we can have a fair duel later, or I will kill you. And if I don't, the rest of my men will."

Alovere looked at Ki. She was looking back and forth between himself and Zaajik, a look of horror on her face. He knew he couldn't leave her. It wasn't about the Hyless. It wasn't about the world. He never cared about those things.

He just cared about Ki.

Alovere set his feet, raising his sword. "So be it."

Zaajik snarled and charged, his blades moving like a blur.

But Alovere was no fool. He knew Zaajik was fast, and had expected such a forward attack. Sidestepping lightly, he raised his blade between himself and his attacker, catching the flurry of blows neatly along the flat side and turning them into the soft forest floor.

Zaajik stumbled and whirled back around. Charging, he once again tried to overwhelm Alovere with speed.

But he once again predicted the younger man's strategy and deflected them all harmlessly away from himself. He winced as he spun painfully away from Zaajik, his ribs stabbing suddenly.

He turned around just in time to catch both of Zaajik's swords mere inches from his right eye. Lifting the blades out of the way, he bent low and rammed into the younger man with his shoulder.

He sent Zaajik sprawling onto the cold, damp moss of the forest floor.

Backing away a step, he gasped in pain as spots filled his vision. His ribs throbbed mercilessly, blood now flowing freely down his side and leg.

Zaajik got slowly to his feet and turned around, his eyes wide with surprise. He raised his swords, his gaze calculating. He now knew Alovere was not as wounded as he would have liked.

"Give it up, old man," he panted. "You may ward me off for a while, but I will outlast you."

Alovere didn't answer. He just set his teeth and snarled, readying his sword.

Zaajik dashed forward, his blades whirling around him in a mesh of steel. Alovere blocked a few strikes, then felt the telltale sting of metal biting into his side as one of Zaajik's blows slipped past his guard.

He stumbled, looking down at his side. Zaajik's blade had passed through the small connecting point in his armor between his hauberk and breast plate. It wasn't deep by the feel of it.

He looked back up just in time to parry several more lightning fast blows before being struck once on the shoulder, and again in the side.

These cut deep, blood immediately issuing forth from the wounds. His ribs once again throbbed with pain, and he fell to one knee. His head spun; his body ached. Zaajik stood panting over him, leaning on the hilt of one of his swords.

"Had enough?" Zaajik gasped, taking a deep breath and letting it out in a whoosh.

Alovere couldn't concentrate, he couldn't think. It was like thoughts themselves were slipping away from him like time, his consciousness hidden behind a veil of shadow and darkness. His mind scrambled frantically, trying not to be locked out of its own existence as his life's blood poured out on the ground. He looked down at his hands. They looked alien, detached, little more than bloody gauntlets holding the hilt of a battered old sword. The hands opened, and the sword slid slowly to the ground.

He looked back up, panic filling his being as he scanned the surrounding faces for Ki. She was still seated by the fire, tears streaming freely down her face as she stared at him in horror. She looked to him for help, and he failed her.

"Zaajik," he mumbled, his voice not his own. "You can't do this. You can't hurt her, I'm begging you."

"Oh, will you let up on that?" the young man snapped, wiping his sword clean on a rag hanging from his belt. "You really came all the way out here to die for a stupid kid? What has gotten into you anyway, oh immortal assassin?"

Alovere never thought of himself as immortal. He had only ever fought to survive. He cared nothing for reputations or prestige. He just wanted Enial.

Zaajik's words became muffled in his mind as he thought of his wife, her long brown hair tumbling down her back like liquid chestnut as she smiled up at him, her countenance as radiant as ever. He longed to be home, to hold her once more before the end of his time, but it didn't seem to be part of his fortune.

"Now, I'm not cruel," Zaajik continued. "So, I won't leave you out here to die."

Alovere looked up at him. The swordsman was staring down at him almost piteously.

"I will execute you in an honorable fashion," he said quietly, "as I think you deserve that much for throwing yourself at a better man for the sake of a child."

Alovere cringed at "a better man." He didn't care much about dying, he always knew it would end like this, but a better man?

He shook his head. Perhaps he was right. He didn't even possess the power to stay at home with his wife, let alone protect the Hyless.

Zaajik moved behind him. He heard the other man draw a breath and lift his arms.

Alovere looked at Ki as he felt the tip of Zaajik's sword prick the back of his neck. She was staring wide eyed, struggling to free herself from her bonds.

Alovere smiled at her, and closed his eyes.

A loud crash cut the deafening silence in the clearing.

Zaajik's sword lifted from Alovere's neck and he heard the man stumble backwards, cursing loudly.

Alovere opened his eyes to see Lox standing in front of him, his sword in his hand and flaming hair tossed in a wild tumble on his head. Bard stood behind him, his usually soft eyes narrowed dangerously at the surrounding troops. Lox's blade was leveled at Zaajik as he scanned the clearing. "Ki!" he exclaimed.

"Lox, take her and run," Alovere said immediately, grabbing his sword and struggling to his feet. His legs wobbled like saplings in a breeze as he tried to steady himself. "You can't fight them."

"I will not let him kill you," the red head said defiantly.

Ki finally broke free from her bonds and dashed to Alovere, seizing his leg with both arms and sobbing uncontrollably.

Zaajik moved towards her, but Alovere and Lox both raised their swords. He paused and blinked uncertainly.

"Take the girl," Alovere said through gritted teeth. "My time is up. Take her home, boy."

The air was cold, mist hanging low over the trees and blanketing the clearing in white.

Lox stepped in front of Alovere, his head high. "I am a Guardian of the Hyless," he said boldly. "You are an enemy of Hallovath and a threat to mankind. If you try to harm either of these people, you will leave me no choice but to take your life."

Zaajik chuckled. "You can't beat me, Guardian or no. I can see it in your eyes; you aren't a killer."

"No, I am not," the guard said quietly, "but I must defend the Hyless."

"Well then," Zaajik smiled grimly, "it looks like you have your work cut out for you!"

Lox lifted his sword and charged.

"Wait!" Alovere yelled, reaching out and trying to grab the young red head.

There was a flurry of blows as Lox's elegantly curved sword moved in bright flashes. He battered Zaajik up and down the clearing, his face set in grim determination. Alovere's hopes rose as Lox landed a small cut on

Zaajik's arm, and another on his shoulder. Zaajik snarled, lifting his swords.

Without warning, Zaajik whirled away. Coming back at full speed, he swatted Lox's sword away and kicked him in the stomach. As Lox doubled over, Zaajik lifted is knee into the Guardian's face, sending him reeling backwards. With a loud yell, he plunged both blades into Lox's chest.

Time stopped. Alovere's heart twisted as he saw the tips of Zaajik's swords protrude from Lox's back, blood running down the edges. He had never stood a chance.

Lox's expression changed to surprise and he turned to look at Alovere, his eyes wide. With a gut-wrenching screech of metal on bone, Zaajik tore his blades from the young man's chest, and Lox's lifeless body crumpled to the forest floor.

Ki screamed and tried to run to her father, but Alovere seized the back of her dress and held her. She struggled futilely at his arm's length, sobbing and pulling desperately against his grip as she watched her father writhing and gasping for breath.

"Foolish boy," Zaajik spat. He turned to face Alovere. "It's one girl! What is wrong with you people?"

Alovere stared at Lox's eyes. Blood dripped from the corner of the young man's mouth as he gasped, gagging on his own blood.

He pulled Ki back to him. He had to focus on getting them to Arginox. He turned around, but Zaajik's men blocked the way. Zaajik stood over Lox's body as it finally fell still, the light leaving the young Guardian's eyes like a candle snuffed out by a winter wind.

"Give me the girl," Zaajik growled. "I have had enough of this for one day, I can assure you. My patience has worn thin."

Alovere looked around him for some way to escape. He would rather die with Lox than see this girl used for her power by warlords with a thirst for blood. He had to do something.

Just as he started to lift his sword, a low hiss spread through the clearing. The fog sank lower, coming closer to them by the second. Mist melted in towards them from the tree line.

Zaajik took a step back towards his men nervously, looking around them. "What is going on?" he yelled at Alovere.

Alovere had no idea.

He squinted into the tree line and felt his heart nearly stop.

Rime Born, at least fifty of them, floated through the trees and overgrown mushrooms. They glittered in the dull light like a waxed moon, their swords like spikes of silver adorning their arms. They stalked towards Ki like a creeping frost, a cold mist wafting off of them as they glided into the clearing.

"Rime Born!" one of the men yelled.

Panic broke out among Zaajik's group as the mist-like beasts began to cut into their ranks with a vengeance. One of them swooped up Ki and shoved her into Alovere's arms. It stared at him expressionlessly, and his ribs ached as he remembered their last fateful meeting. After a moment of pause, it turned and joined the rest of its brethren in the fray.

Alovere glanced at Bard as the massive Wyvern crouched protectively over his master's body, hissing at the passing Rime Born.

He shook his head.

He had to stay focused.

He turned to head back to Arginox, but Zaajik blocked his path, his swords low by his side. "I'll take her," he snarled, glancing over his shoulder as he heard his men screaming in dismay.

"I can't let you do that," Alovere said weakly. "You don't understand what is at stake."

Alovere didn't have to lift a finger. Two Rime Born saw the threat and changed their course, converging on the swordsman from different directions.

Zaajik cursed and glanced back and forth between Ki and the Rime Born. He hesitated, then turned and vanished into the underbrush.

Alovere hurried in the other direction towards Arginox, Ki bouncing up and down in his arms. She was still crying, tears running dirt tracks down her face.

He was short for breath, his vision fading as he finally reached the stream where he had left Arginox.

The great dragon stood nervously by the water, deep claw marks gouging the bank where he had been pacing. His ears pricked up when he saw his master, and he growled happily.

Leaping over the glowing water, Alovere hoisted Ki into the saddle and climbed up behind her.

"Fly, 'Nox!" he bellowed.

The great beast launched into the sky in a flurry of dead moss and leaves, piercing the mist like a scaly red arrow and bursting out above the clouds. Sunlight reflected off of the blanket of mist in a blinding white light, causing Alovere to flinch and shield his eyes. The Giant Banyeet stood behind him like an ancient sentinel, Hallovath barely visible ahead.

Ki sobbed in his arms as the wind blew over them gently, the sunlight warm and soothing.

"It's alright, kid," Alovere said. He knew she couldn't hear him, but he felt as though he had to say something. He couldn't just ignore her. What else was he supposed to do? He patted her head awkwardly, flinching when she whirled around and wrapped her arms around his chest tightly.

He gasped as pain bolted through his side and ribs. Zaajik's new wounds were causing him to lose more blood. His vision began to darken, the brilliance of the sun on the cloud bank fading slowly into various shades of green and black.

"Arginox," he groaned. "Take us to Haze."

The dragon barked a reply, and surged forward.

The flight seemed to take forever. What had taken him and Arginox only a short time to fly before now seemed as though it took near an eternity. Hallovath grew closer and closer each time he looked up, but he let his chin bump wearily on his chest as they neared the great city.

As the hours slipped past, Ki drifted off into an uneasy sleep. Her head rocked gently against Alovere's chest as her sobs became quiet sniffles drowned out by the wind.

Alovere's heart ached for her. Her father had just been murdered right in front of her trying to save an old man whose time was up anyway.

He clenched his fist around Arginox's reins. That always seemed to be the way things went. The young give themselves for the safety of the old, battles raging over the innocents of the world. Alovere knew that he would one day pay for the things he had done when he was a young man, and that the price would be steep, but he vowed that from this day forward he would no longer take innocent lives in the name of money, a kingdom, or an oath. In comparison to why Lox died, these things seemed cold and pale. Lox died in the name of the Hyless, his daughter, and in the name of a friend to whom he had shown great kindness.

Alovere shook his head. He was thinking too much. He just needed to focus on getting Ki back to Malya and the other Guardians. She needed to be watched after, there was no question about it. If Jaelyn was bold enough to send someone into the city to kidnap her, she was either very desperate, or very informed.

His thoughts traveled back to Galnoron and rage boiled up inside him again. How he longed to wrap his fingers around that snake's neck and give it a good squeeze! He only hoped he made it back to Hallovath before Oaina got around to killing him so he could savor the pleasure of doing it himself.

He urged Arginox faster, desperate to reach the city as soon as possible. The leagues melted away, and he grew tired. Allowing his chin to rest on top of Ki's head, he closed his eyes.

When he awoke again, night had fallen over the Range. He was nearing Hallovath, the glittering blue lights of the white city winking up at him out of the inky black. He saw the Gallery platform jutting out over the city below, blue torches lighting the airship dock.

Arginox glided gently down to the cobblestones, his claws clicking as he landed as softly as possible.

Alovere groaned as he swung his leg painfully over the dragon's back, lowering himself to the ground. He reached up and took Ki from the saddle, cradling her gently.

He turned and began limping towards the Gallery doors. Maybe Haze would let him in. It was unlikely they would be able to turn his General against him. Haze was far too wise for that.

He had barely reached the threshold when the door flew open to reveal Vlaire, his face scrambled in surprise. Light flooded out from around him as he blocked the doorway, streaming out onto the cobblestones. He looked first at Alovere, then at Ki. He opened his mouth to say something, then closed it awkwardly.

"What is it?" Alovere heard Oaina call from behind him in the Gallery.

Her face appeared over Vlaire's shoulder and immediately furrowed into a frown. "What are you doing here? Do you have a death wish?" Her eyes drifted to Ki, sleeping soundly in Alovere's arms and she fell silent.

She cleared her throat. "Perhaps you should come in."

Chapter Thirty
The Pain Of Truth

Vlaire's face was white as a sheet when Alovere finished his story. He and Oaina had sat Alovere down and asked him to tell them what had happened, which he did, leaving nothing out.

"Lox is dead," he said quietly. "I can hardly imagine it. The war has not even started and already a Guardian is dead."

"Foolish boy," Oaina murmured. It was the first time Alovere had ever seen her show something so akin to emotion before. Her eyes were glassy and her hand hung loosely at her side; for once, she was not gripping the hilt of her sword.

She looked at Alovere. "And they are working together with each other? These two warlords?"

Alovere nodded. "Yes. I believe Jaelyn has more power than Orlivan does, but take my word for it when I tell you that Orlivan has much more experience in matters of war. If anyone is a threat, he is."

"And you heard the man say that they will be marching on Hallovath? When?"

Alovere shook his head. "I don't know. I arrived rather late in the conversation, I'm afraid."

He jumped as the Gallery doors flew open with a loud a bang. Malya hurried into the room, her face anxious. "A guard just told me you found Ki!" she exclaimed. "Where is she?"

She was in her night robe, her hair tied in a long braid that fell to her waist. Her eyes searched the room anxiously, looking for Ki.

"She is sleeping in Lorgalith's Gazebo," Vlaire said uneasily, "but sit down, there is something we need to tell you."

Malya blinked, looking around the small table. "Where is Lox?"

"Haze a seat," Vlaire pointed to a small chair by Alovere.

Malya sat down, clearing her throat. "Did something happen to Ki?" She asked the question as if she were bracing herself against the answer, and Alovere's heart twisted.

Vlaire scratched his head. "Now, this is going to be a—"

"Wait," Alovere interrupted him.

He looked at Malya's face. She stared back at him wide eyed, searching his face for a clue as to what he was about to say. Another life he had ruined. Another life he had taken, even though he had not lifted a blade as an assassin in years. It was only fair that he be the one to deliver the news to the woman who's world he had changed forever.

"I was banished as you know," he began painfully. "Lox didn't agree with their choice," he said, jerking his chin at Vlaire and Oaina. "And so, he followed me into the Mirror Wood. I think he came to make sure I didn't bleed to death."

Malya's face paled suddenly. "Where is he?" she asked, her voice nearing panicked.

"When I went into the Mirror Wood, I found an enemy patrol that had taken Ki. I tried to save her, but I was bested by one of their swordsmen," Alovere continued.

He tried to ignore the look of terror that was slowly building on Malya's face. He knew that at the end of the explanation, he would confirm her fears. He hated that such a beautiful young mother was now paying for his crimes as a youth. Had he not murdered those people, he wouldn't have been banished. Lox would not have been murdered. Malya would have a husband, and Ki would have a father. And even now, the people around him paid for his mistakes with their very lives.

"I was going to be killed, and Ki taken to Queen Jaelyn," he said.

"Just tell me where my husband is," Malya said shortly, her voice wavering. "I'm not interested in your story!"

"He is dead," Alovere stated.

Malya's face turned upside down and tears welled up in her eyes.

"He died protecting me and Ki so we could escape and she could be home safe."

Malya didn't answer. She took a deep breath and held it for a moment before closing her eyes and letting out a single choked sob.

"I'm sorry," Alovere said painfully. "I told him to run, but—"

"This is all your fault," she said suddenly, shaking her head as sobs wracked her body. "He never should have died."

Alovere swallowed. "I know," he said wearily. "I am so very sorry. There is nothing I can do to make this up to you, but I swear I will work the rest of my life trying."

"This is all your fault!" she said again, her voice louder. "I don't have my husband here now because he was off on a fool's errand trying to save a banished old man!"

Alovere didn't know what to say. He knew she was right, but there wasn't any way he could take it back. He wished he could. He wished he could take a lot of things back, starting about thirty-five years ago.

"I will look after you and Ki with my very life, if I have to," Alovere said weakly. "I know this is my fault, and I wish with the blood in my veins that I had died and not him."

Her eyes snapped open. "You? Your fault?" She raised her voice and pointed at Vlaire and Oaina. "Not yours. Theirs!"

Vlaire and Oaina looked down at the floor solemnly.

"You sent our dying guest out into the forest because of a fairy tale that may not even be true, and my husband died trying to save him!" she screamed at the two Guardians. "You caused the death of my Lox,

304

and you failed to find my daughter! If it wasn't for the 'murderer' you banished, she wouldn't be here either!"

Alovere blinked.

Vlaire didn't answer, but stared shamefully at his feet. Oaina shifted uncomfortably and glanced over her shoulder at the room Ki was sleeping in.

Malya rose to her feet, wiping her tears. "Now, I will be taking Ki home," she said coldly, sobbing once, "and Alovere is coming with me. In spite of his wounds and his age, at least he knows what it takes to be Guardian!"

Alovere knew those words bit deeply into Oaina and Vlaire as they flinched when she said them. They stepped out of her way as she stormed past them towards the door that led to Lorgalith's chambers.

The three of them all looked at each other. They didn't have to say anything; they all knew they were equally guilty of Lox's death, in one way or another. They all regretted the decisions they had made, and they all wished it had gone some other way, any other way. Each and every one of them knew they would have happily given their life in his stead had they only been given the chance.

The Gallery doors once again groaned open. Haze strolled in, a look of surprise crossing his face when he saw them all gathered in the Gallery at this late of an hour.

His expression changed from curiosity to dread when he noticed the looks on their faces.

"Where have you been?" Oaina hissed savagely. Alovere noted grimly that her mood had plummeted due to Malya's outburst, and the rest of them were now going to be subject to her rage.

"It's a long story," he said, his tone hesitant. "What did I miss?"

Oaina snarled as another person stepped into the Gallery, A woman with long blonde hair and a patch over one eye now stood beside Haze, he expression calculating. She was grimy, but fair enough in her own way. She fixed Oaina with a melting glare the moment she stepped into the light.

"What are you doing here?" Oaina snapped. If Alovere thought her mood had been sour a moment before, it was nothing to how she looked at this woman.

"I have come to do your job for you," the other woman answered haughtily, "since you can't seem to keep your eyes on the Hyless for more than a minute without losing her."

"How long have you been listening?" Oaina roared.

"Long enough!"

"Let's not come to blows if we can help this," Haze said, casting a warning glance at the woman. "This is Famau, Ki's birth mother."

Alovere wasn't sure if it was the news that Ki had two mothers, or the loss of blood, but his head spun and he sank slowly to the floor.

"We know who she is," he heard Oaina say from behind him. "Why is she here?"

"She knows who killed the Guard," Haze said, "and she kept the second guard alive after saving him from the same fate as the first."

Alovere couldn't turn around far enough to see behind him, but he heard Oaina's familiar "harrumph." This was her acknowledgment that someone she hated had done something she was supposed to thank them for.

"Did you see his attacker?" Vlaire asked, staring at her intently. "Did you see who he was?"

"Yes," Famau nodded. "He was a robed wizard, clean shaven and cold looking. He told me to mind my own business when I found him with

306

the guard bound and laying in the water. He didn't seem keen on facing the disagreeable end of my sword, so he cursed at me and vanished into thin air."

Alovere wished he were strong enough to stand and yell out that he knew it was Galnoron all along, but he was barely able to mumble incoherently.

He heard Haze hurry over to him. "What's wrong with him? What happened?

Alovere opened his mouth to answer, but his eyes finally darkened and he fell into the swirling black of unconsciousness.

✱✱

Haze stared at his friend, the man's head hanging limply over his chest. He moaned something Haze couldn't understand.

"What happened to him?" he asked again, staring up at Vlaire and Oaina. "And where is Lox?"

The two Guardian's glanced at each other awkwardly, then Vlaire cleared his throat. "Alovere was banished under suspicion of murdering the guard, and—"

"He what?" Haze thundered. He stood up, glaring at Vlaire. "You banished *him* for killing the guard? He can barely move, let alone kill someone!"

"So, we heard," Vlaire said painfully, "from Lox. Multiple times. At any rate, after you went missing, so did Ki. Alovere was suspected due to some evidence provided by Galnoron, and so he was banished. Lox disagreed with our decision, and so followed him into the Mirror Wood. They chanced upon a task force sent by Queen Jaelyn to kidnap Ki, and Lox died trying to save her and Alovere." Vlaire sucked in a deep breath when he finished his recounting of the tale, seemingly glad it was over with.

The news struck Haze like a hammer to the heart, and he sat down in one of the chairs with a thump. He had just been walking through the Ruins with the young Guardian discussing ghost stories. It didn't seem right. Of all the people in the world that deserved to die, Lox was the farthest from them. He had been on their side since the day they came to Hallovath, always defending him and Glassworn from Oaina's moods and taking Alovere into his own home.

He shook his head, a thought occurring to him. "You said *trying* to save them? Is Ki alright?"

Vlaire nodded. "She is asleep in Lorgalith's chambers. Malya is fetching her now."

"Does she know?"

Vlaire nodded grimly.

Haze frowned, some of his fire coming back to him after the initial shock. "Why would you banish Alovere from the city? You sent them off to die, you know that, right?"

Oaina snarled and flung her hair out of her face, her scar blazing red in the blue light of the chandeliers. "Yes, we know. Malya said as much at a volume fit to shame a roaring dragon, if you must know. And yes, it's our fault, and no," she snapped, "there is nothing we can do to take it back. So, leave it, will you?"

Haze closed his mouth. He suddenly felt pity for the two Guardians. "Sorry," he said quietly. "I'm sorry that you lost a friend. I thought a great deal of him and his family myself."

Vlaire nodded silently, elbowing his sister when she opened her mouth to speak. Oaina glared at him, but remained silent.

"We need to tend to Alovere now," Haze said, looking back down at his friend.

"I stand by my earlier decision," Vlaire said suddenly, lifting his chin. "The man admitted to being a known murderer. I can't trust him to stay here."

Haze couldn't believe his ears. "Surely you can see that he is no longer a threat to anyone?" Haze pointed out. "And what is this known murderer nonsense?"

"Alovere is the Man of a Thousand Deaths," Vlaire said quietly. "He admitted to it himself."

Haze blinked. The legends of the most wanted assassin in Elliset had spread from one corner of the continent to the other. All along, Javenir Bolgruust had been serving in King Orlivan's elite force of Winged Demons. The shock swayed him for a moment, but he shook his head. "Surely you can see that he isn't a threat to you right now."

"He has to go!" Vlaire said stubbornly. His eyes and jaw were set; Haze could see there would be no moving him on his decision.

A soft clap made them all turn to face the back of the Gallery. Malya stood facing them, Ki's hand grasped in her own. Their eyes matched, swollen and red from tears as they walked slowly towards the rest of the people in the room. Haze noticed Famau immediately tense and stare at Ki. Her expression was soft as she saw her daughter walk across the room, her golden curls bouncing lightly with each step. He could feel the tension in the air as Vlaire and Oaina both watched Famau closely, fiddling anxiously with their weapons.

Malya stopped beside Oaina, looking back and forth between Famau and the Guardians. "Who is this?"

"I am Ki's mother," Famau blurted before anyone had a chance to soften the blow.

Malya blinked, her eyes fixed on Famau. She cleared her throat, lowered her head, and started to walk past. "Nice to meet you."

"I would like to speak with my daughter," Famau said shortly.

Malya stopped and faced her. "Impossible. Ki and I are going home for the evening. We have had enough for one day."

Famau opened her mouth to say something, but Oaina cut her off. "Silence, gutter rat! You came up here just to make trouble after we lost one of our Guardians! If you make one move towards the Hyless I will take your last eye!"

"As if you could protect her!" Famau shot back. "Was she not just kidnapped out from under your very nose? I would be doing us all a favor by taking her back."

"If she were safe with you, we wouldn't have taken her in the first place!" Oaina roared back.

This caught Haze's attention and he glanced at Famau. "What was that?"

"We took Ki because her mother was negligent," Vlaire said quickly, silencing Oaina. "She lived in the Ruins and was an apprentice at a black magic shop in the lower parts. Ki was not well looked after, and when we discovered that she was the Hyless, we had no choice but to take her and give her a better home."

Haze glared at Famau. This was making a lot more sense than what the woman had told him before.

"That's not entirely true," Famau protested. "I can't help that the only money I could make was from that man. I had to work there in order to support Ki! What else could I do?"

"Come to the upper city and get work where you can see the sun once in a while!" Oaina snapped. "But none of this makes any difference, because you aren't taking the Hyless anywhere. She belongs with the Guardians. That much has just become clear."

"Guardians that can't even keep her safe in her own bed!" Famau retorted.

"Which is why Alovere is leaving!" Oaina erupted. "Alovere, and all of his friends, Haze included. Ever since they arrived here, we have had dead people show up and living ones go missing! Enough is enough. They all have to go."

"That makes perfect sense!" Famau snapped back before Haze even had a chance to defend his own position. "Send away the only people that have proven they are capable of giving whatever it takes to protect the Hyless and lock her in a room by herself for the next how many years? You are mad, Oaina! You always have been! From the day you took my eye in the ruins!"

"You attacked me!" Oaina snarled. "The left side of my face will bear the marks of your black magic for the rest of my life. It was a fair trade."

Haze sighed. At least he now knew why the two disliked each other so much. Enough mangling of one another would cause two people to hate each other quite extensively.

"Fair has nothing to do with it! I was defending my child!"

And so, the screaming continued. Oaina bellowed at Famau, and Famau retaliated in kind. Vlaire stood wordlessly as the two women bickered incessantly, their raised voices echoing off the marble walls of the Gallery and out the open door into the night. Malya, meanwhile, stood listening quietly. A tear rolled down her cheek, and he could see that she was not focused on what was transpiring in the hall. Her mind was elsewhere.

"You have already lost her once," Famau shouted, "and one of your idiot Guardians went and got himself killed! So much for the power of the Aurrau Von Gahdness! She should be with her real mother. I am the only one that can care for my child the way she should be cared for!"

311

Haze flinched as Malya suddenly took a step forward and slapped Famau as hard as she could. The other woman put a hand to her cheek in surprise.

"That idiot Guardian was my husband," she said coldly, her voice like a biting wind. She pointed a shaking finger at Famau, tears welling up in her eyes again. "And you will not be taking Ki anywhere. I am her mother! She has already lost her father, and I would rather die than see her whisked off to the Lower City by you!"

Vlaire spoke up. "I think the Hyless should stay in the Gallery from now on," he said. "At least until the Years of Mourning are over. She needs to finish her dances and unlock her—"

"Ki is coming home with me!" Malya asserted, her voice cracking. "Because she is my family, not the Hyless! Stop calling her that! She didn't ask to be made this way! You don't get to treat her like an object, not while I am standing here!" She sobbed and sniffed. "While you were all gathered around the table discussing how 'The Hyless' should be managed, I was feeding her! Changing her diapers! Teaching her to walk! Helping her learn how to speak with her hands, watching her speak her first word! She is not some treasure to be fought over." She shook her head and wiped her eyes. "She is a child, my child, and none of you are taking her from me!"

She pushed past Famau and went to Alovere. She bent down, tears streaming down her face and tried to put her shoulder under his arm. "Come on," she choked, "we are going home."

"He isn't staying," Vlaire said weakly. "He can't."

"Damn you, Vlaire!" Malya screamed. "Stand up to your sister for once! This out of control! He is wounded and dying, and he needs treatment! I will not deny him what Lox swore would be his."

312

She bent back down and resumed her futile attempt at getting Alovere to his feet.

Haze bent to help her, heaving the wounded Rider to his shoulder.

Vlaire stepped between him and the door. "Sorry, Haze. I can't let you do this."

Haze felt anger well up inside him like a rising volcano, and opened his mouth to join Malya in rebuking the guard, but he was cut off by a sudden flash of light at the back of the Gallery.

Mist settled, and Lorgalith appeared in front of the stairs that led up to his Gazebo.

"Alright," he sighed wearily. "That is enough out of all of you. You are making enough racket that I couldn't sleep if all of our lives depended on it."

Vlaire bowed low, his face twisted in discomfort.

"Now, as for Alovere, he isn't going anywhere," Lorgalith said, hobbling over to the wounded man. His staff clicked on the stone floor as he crossed the marble. He laid a gentle hand on Malya's shoulder when he reached her. "I'm afraid he isn't going home with you either, milady."

"Where are you taking him?" Malya sobbed.

"He will stay with me at the top of the Gallery. His wounds are now too grievous to be cured by any natural means. I will have to see to them myself or he will die."

Malya nodded and sniffed. "Can I stay with him?"

Lorgalith cocked his head at her. "May I ask why?"

"Lox said he would help him get well," Malya said in a rush. "I intend to honor my husband's word."

The old range keeper nodded. "Very well. You may stay until he has come back from the edge, but no longer. Children need to be in their own home," he added, nodding at Ki.

"Ki is staying here," Oaina said hesitantly, her chin high.

"You madam," Lorgalith said crossly, "have done quite enough, and have danced on my last nerve, no less. But I am glad you spoke up. It is time for you all to understand your actions of the last few days."

Haze drew a bated breath. Finally, he was going to hear what had happened while he had been missing.

"You banished Alovere because you suspected him of murder and because he admitted to murder in his youth. You couldn't trust him around Ki, and so you abandoned him to his death." He frowned sternly at Vlaire for a moment, the sea of wrinkles on his forehead sagging down over his bushy eyebrows. "Had you not done so, Lox would have survived." He paused as Malya sobbed once, the sound echoing through the chamber. "For a time," he added. "Had you not banished Alovere, Ki would never have been found and Jaelyn would have plunged our world into darkness for possibly the rest of time. Lox came to me, begging me to stop you, but I could not. I knew that if I did, Ki would be lost forever. I truly thought Alovere would be the one that died," he admitted. "Alas, I cannot see everything, but Alovere's banishment and Lox's death were both necessary events. The Rime Born came to Ki's rescue, yes, but had they not followed Lox, Jaelyn's men would have made off with the Hyless." He turned to look at each of them in turn, his gaze stern. "And as for all this fighting over the Hyless, that must end. Now. We do not have the luxury of arguing over where the Hyless lays her head at night, only that she keeps it."

"Very true," a melancholy voice drawled from the dark corner of the Gallery.

They all turned to face where the voice was coming from. It was from the back-left corner of the hall, entirely veiled in darkness.

A quiet thump and curse of pain were followed by Glassworn stepping out of the gloom and under the light of the chandeliers. He winced and held his hand over his eyes as the bright light shone down on him.

Haze could scarcely believe his eyes.

It didn't look as though Glassworn had shaved a day since they arrived, his face patchy and scuffed. Had he been able to grow a beard, perhaps it wouldn't have looked so bad, but the hair was growing in thin patches and splotches across his chin and cheeks in large areas of little more than out of control fuzz clinging to his face. His eyes were bloodshot and strained, large bags hanging under them. His hair was greasy and looked as though it had been glued to his head in thick mats.

"Glassworn," Haze exclaimed. "What are you doing here?"

"I was brought up here with Galnoron and Alovere before he was banished. Galnoron couldn't stand the smell of me, so he convinced one of the guards to let me out of the cell. Now, in regards to what Lorgalith was saying," he cleared his throat and straightened up, running his fingers through his branch-like hair, "are you all seriously arguing over who gets the Hyless, when Alovere came in here and stated quite plainly that Jaelyn and Orlivan are working together?"

Haze blinked. He must have missed that part of the conversation.

Glassworn looked from one person to the next, blinking rapidly as his eyes watered. "Now I'm just a drunk, I know that, but it seems to me that you have bigger problems than where she sleeps if you are about to have two powerful warlords knocking on your gates looking for her blood."

Malya shrank back, wrapping her arms around Ki tightly. Vlaire and Oaina looked at each other, and Lorgalith nodded. "It's true. I came down here to warn you, in fact. During my meditation, I discovered something quite terrible indeed." He sighed and his face looked more tired than usual. "King Orlivan has launched his invasion. His troops are marching into the Range as we speak. We have perhaps three days before he reaches the Mirror Wood."

Chapter Thirty-one
Heart Of Ice

Cold pierced Alovere's body, jarring his senses.

He wrapped his arms around himself and lifted his head from the ground. A few rats scurried away from him in disappointment, their beady eyes glittering in the faint light coming from the nearby window.

He coughed and sat up, shivering violently. The rats darted farther away, their tails vanishing through the bars of his cell.

He rubbed his arms furiously, trying to warm up. He hated falling asleep in this accursed cell. Each time he woke up he felt closer to death. The water was now pooling nearly ankle deep on the floor, a miniature lake filling the small chamber.

"Alright, kid," a gruff voice said from outside the bars.

Alovere looked up.

A tall man was standing just outside with a set of keys dangling from his meaty hand. A small club was belted at his waist, the handle worn and cracked. His hair was short and dark silver, his eyes stern and emerald green.

"Time for you to go," he said, shoving a key into the lock of Alovere's cell and swinging the door open.

Alovere stared at him, glancing at the open door briefly.

"It's alright, you can go," the man said, more gently this time.

Alovere scrambled to his feet, his legs shaking under his weight. Water dripped from his sodden clothes back down into its main body with a loud drizzling sound. Eyeing the man warily, he took a wobbly step towards him. When the man didn't move, he lurched awkwardly out of the cell and started jogging down the hall. He didn't look back. Perhaps the man would change his mind and tell him to come back.

"Hey!" the man yelled.

Alovere froze in his tracks. Was it a trick? Was he going to use this as an excuse to execute him now? Or had he found out who he really was?

"Don't you steal anymore, you hear?" the man said sternly. "I don't want to have to cut your hands off, and I don't ever want to see you in my prison again."

Alovere breathed a sigh of relief and resumed his stagger down the corridor.

The cold stone walls seemed to go on forever, though he knew the prison wasn't that large. Corner after corner led to bleakly lit halls filled with the scurry of rats and the smell of vomit.

Desperate to be free of the confining walls, he staggered around every corner with renewed determination until at length, he reached a door that blocked his way. Turning the handle, he shoved it open and burst out into blinding sunlight. He squinted a raised his hand over his eyes.

He was in the middle of town, vendors lining up and down the shale street. He heard a man loudly commenting on the quality of the swords he was selling, and a woman asking who wanted to buy handmade clay pots. A dog yapped loudly from somewhere down the street to his right before a man yelled at it and it responded with a weak whimper.

He turned and started down the street to his left, rubbing his arms vigorously. The sun soaked through his clothes like a warm silk, drenching his body in heat. He was half tempted to close his eyes and lie down on the shale right where he was.

But he needed to get out of town before someone recognized him. He needed to find Arginox. He needed to—

"Watch it, kid!" a man yelled loudly, swerving his cart horse around him. A pile of melons stacked on the back of his cart nearly toppled to the ground. The man cursed loudly as he tried to correct the sudden movement.

Alovere put his head down and hurried off down the street.

If he could make it to the cave he was staying in outside of town, he would be able to eat and get some badly needed sleep, but he had to cross an entire city full of people. One of them was bound to recognize him. He had always used a mask when he was to be carrying out a contract in public, but he felt as though they would find something else to recognize him by; his gait, his size, or perhaps the way he held his hands when standing still.

The thought of being recognized for the things he had done terrified him.

He shuddered and crammed his hands into his tunic pockets.

Then suddenly, he heard that lovely voice.

"Alovere!"

Looking to his left, he saw Enial waving at him from behind a small vending cart loaded with bread.

He considered ignoring her and continuing on his path down the street. After all, she probably only pitied him, and that was the last thing he needed. She only wanted to help him so she could believe herself to be charitable and kind. That was the only reason people like her did kind things was to be remembered for them. It's why he didn't believe in kindness. It was never anything but a show that the entitled put on so they could claim to be good people that cared about each other.

He looked away and took a few steps away from her.

"Wait!" she called after him. "At least come and get some food."

He ground his teeth and shuffled over to her vending cart. "Why are you trying to help me?" he asked coldly. "I don't want your kindness."

She shrugged. "Because I think it's the right thing to do."

"Well take your right things to do and do them on someone else," Alovere said angrily. "I don't want you trying to help me. I have never needed help, and I still don't."

Enial put her hands on her hips. "Is that so? Then let me ask you this: If I don't give you some food, when is the next time you're going to eat? Because you look hungry. Prison is hard on people, and unless I missed my guess, you're no exception."

"You think I need your help?" Alovere sneered. Reaching out, he took one of the loaves from her cart and tucked it under his tunic. "Any help I need from people, I take. I don't accept. And *you* are no exception."

He turned away from her hurt expression and marched down the street, the warm loaf pressed against this chest.

Maybe now she would leave him alone. Maybe now she would understand that this wasn't some stupid game being played with their reputations. He had a bad one, and he didn't care. She had a good one, and it was all she cared about. He wasn't going to become some mark on her list of people she had "helped" by feeding them once in her life.

He glanced over his shoulder at her as he strode away just in time to see her sob once and wipe her eyes.

Chapter Thirty-Two
Hovvel Kell

Haze sat at the small table in the Gallery with Vlaire, Oaina, Famau, and Glassworn. Galnoron was locked in the Gallery room where they could keep an eye on him. Lorgalith had taken Alovere up to his Gazebo where he could care for him, and Malya had gone home with Ki. The rest of them set about deciding on how best to deal with Orlivan's approaching forces.

"We need to talk to Orlivan," he insisted. "He is no fool. He will listen to me if we meet with him. Why must this end with bloodshed?"

"Because you are most likely considered a traitor, if Jaelyn has had anything to do with it," Glassworn said quietly. He had shaved and washed his hair. His eyes were not nearly as bloodshot as before, but still sported large black bags beneath them. "She will have had Zaajik feed your King rumors about you fighting for Hallovath by this time. If she has him as fooled as Alovere heard, then the odds are that he will believe her. Your word will be as good as dust."

Haze cursed. Glassworn was right; if Zaajik was working with Jaelyn, there was no telling what she had fed his king in the way of lies and stories. He and Alovere were more than likely branded traitors, and Hallovath seen as a threat to the crown. It was very unlikely that Orlivan would hear anything he had to say. In fact, he was probably so disappointed in Haze right now, he would be surprised if the King would meet with him at all.

"I think we should try anyway," Vlaire said. "It is our best hope of ending this without having to fight for our lives. We have perhaps a thousand city guards. Against eight thousand?" He shook his head. "That is hopeless. We need to try and end this peacefully, if possible."

"I don't see why," Oaina growled. Her hair once again veiled her face as she leaned back in her chair moodily. Malya's outburst had permanently affected her demeanor, and she was determined to make sure everyone knew it. "We are the Guardians of legend. Let us meet them in battle and be done with it."

"You cannot fight eight thousand men!" Haze exclaimed. "I fought with them for many years and commanded most of them. Trust me when I say if the Guardians are to meet their doom, it will be at the hands of the Winged Demons." He shook his head. "You cannot meet a force of this caliber head on, and that is excluding Jaelyn's Armada!"

Glassworn nodded. "She has at least five hundred warships in her Armada, all armed with the most advanced bolt cannons in production. Each ship has a compliment of a twenty-five men or more, all capable of melee combat if necessary."

Haze swore under his breath.

They were vastly outnumbered. There was no way they could win with sheer force, not even with the Guardians.

"I have some men down in the Ruins who are loyal to the Hyless," Famau offered. "Perhaps a hundred."

"Yes, that makes all the difference," Oaina sneered sarcastically. "A hundred flee bitten gutter rats against ten thousand trained soldiers. We're saved."

"Enough!" Haze snapped. "There is too much at stake for us to be bickering back and forth like territorial wyverns. Now help me think of a real solution!"

The room fell silent for some time, until Glassworn spoke up again. "What about the Rime Born?"

They all looked at each other in surprise. In all the excitement, they had all failed to think of the great Range sentinels.

"Will they do that?" Haze asked hesitantly. "I mean, no offense, but they seem a little unpredictable."

"They aren't unpredictable," Oaina rolled her eyes impatiently. "They serve the Hyless. No one else. If you are her friend, they are yours. If you fight them in any way, they believe it to be an act of violence directed at the Hyless." She shrugged. "If we can find a way to communicate with them, I wager we would have trouble *stopping* them from helping."

"How many of them are there?" Haze asked.

Vlaire rubbed his chin. "Difficult to say. They are everywhere in the Range, and reports from patrols suggest there are at least two thousand of them. Possibly more."

Haze nodded. All they had to do was find a way to convey to the Rime Born that the Hyless was in danger, and they would fight alongside them, no question. And given Alovere's account of how they fought, they could tip the odds in their favor.

"So," he said hesitantly, "how do we communicate with them?"

"I have no idea," Vlaire said. "No one knows where they are from. Most believe they simply wander the wilds and appear only when necessary."

"I heard tell that they have a fortress in some cold flatland," Glassworn said. They all turned to face him, and he swallowed. "It was called the Great Tundra, I think?"

Oaina cocked her head at him. "That is no flatland, drunkard. The Great Tundra is very dangerous, rife with blizzards, Algids, and some of the less hospitable spirits of the Range. It would be madness to go in there."

"Besides, who did you hear this from?" Vlaire asked skeptically.

"I heard it from someone in the pub. He says they have a fortress in the Great Tundra where they dock their airship and settle themselves. He said they are ruled by a king, so to speak." He closed his eyes and blew out his cheeks. "Hovvel Kell!" he exclaimed suddenly. "That was what they called the fortress."

"The Rime Born have no king," Oaina laughed dryly. "They are beasts, little more than Algids. This 'king' would have a name, which should be in the history books of Hallovath, yet it is not." She shook her head. "Do not waste our time with nonsense. Are you going to tell us he is immortal next?"

"His name is Arglwydd Rhew," Famau spoke up.

They turned to face her.

Oaina's eyes narrowed to slits. "Tell me you heard that from a drunk in a bar so I can break both your arms."

"I read it in the history books down in the Hyless Athenaeum," she said haughtily. "He was considered very real, and still is, in fact. And yes," she laughed coldly, "he is supposedly quite immortal, and has been around since the first Hyless."

Oaina leaned back and crossed her arms. "And?"

"And he is considered the strongest force in the Range, next to the Hyless herself," Famau stated. "He has never lost a battle. The legends say he was created by the first Hyless as a last resort weapon. Him and his kind have served the spirit of the Hyless ever since."

Vlaire rubbed his chin. "So, theoretically, he could be called upon in the name of the Hyless?"

Famau nodded. "Yes, but he was never intended for war. The book was damaged, but from what I could read he was intended for something much more spiritual."

"It doesn't matter." Vlaire shook his head. "If he is real, I don't care if he was intended to lead prayer circles; we will need his help. Now," he sighed, "we only need someone with the savvy to find him."

"You can't be serious!" Oaina exclaimed. "You would waste valuable time on a myth?"

Vlaire whirled on her. "I waste nothing!" he said savagely. His eyes were fixed on his sister with obvious rage. "And you will stop destroying hopes each time we bring one up! If you have a true solution, please speak. Otherwise, keep your mouth shut!"

Oaina stared at him in surprise, then closed her mouth and nodded silently. She lowered herself further into her chair, her face flushing brightly.

"Haze," Vlaire said, turning to face the Rider. "I need you to go and investigate this. I cannot leave the City Guard, I must prepare them for what lies ahead. Can you fly to the Great Tundra?"

Haze nodded. He had hoped he would be the one to go. "Yes, I can, but I will need someone to come with me. Ordinarily, I would ask for Lox, but..." he trailed off and swallowed a lump in his throat. "That obviously isn't an option."

Glassworn cleared his throat. "I will go with you."

Haze faced him. "I don't think so, Glassworn. I need someone I can trust to accompany me."

"I will leave my flask behind," the druid said. He wrung his hands anxiously. "I will not bring it. I will remain sober the entire time." He blinked and looked back and forth between Haze and Vlaire. "Let me do this," he said quietly. "I have to help somehow. Lox was my friend too."

Haze sighed. Lox was kind to all of them, even Glassworn. He couldn't begrudge the man wanting to do something for the Guardian's family. "Very well, but you leave the flask behind, as you said. I cannot have a drunkard slowing me down. I hope this will be a fast trip. If we leave immediately, we could be there by sunset."

"Uh," Glassworn said instantly. "It's three in the morning! You don't want to sleep a little first?"

Haze glared at him.

"On second thought, I'm not all that tired," Glassworn said weakly.
****

Jaelyn sat calmly on her throne. Her legs were crossed, and her hands were folded in her lap. She breathed deeply, reminding herself of all she had accomplished over the years since Kinzin had been...dealt with.

"I am so sorry, your grace," the swordsman whimpered in front of her. He was kneeling in front of the throne, his hands on the ground in front of him and his face pressed to the cold stone floor.

"Now, Zaajik," Jaelyn sighed, standing up and walking around him. She strode down the flaming red carpet that decorated the hall of the throne room, stopping at the end of it and looking up at the guard that stood by the door. He wore a suit of concealing black armor, his helmet solid black with the a pair of Wyvern's wings etched into the front of the steel. His hand rested on a massive black sword that hung at his waist, its sheathe also covered in carvings from times past, most of which even Jaelyn didn't recognize. "Why can't you be like Vaurik, here?" she placed her hand on the side of the guards cold helm. "So reliable. So...present."

"Please forgive me," Zaajik said weakly from behind her. "Alovere got involved, and then the Rime--"

"Oh, stop talking," Jaelyn snapped, pulling her hand away from Vaurik's helmet and whirling to face the broken swordsman. "You're only making it worse for yourself. You see? This is why traitors are generally disliked; you have to be a certain kind of person to betray your

326

own kingdom and homeland, don't you? It should be noted that this typically results in both sides hating you with a passion. Fortunately for you," she said calmly, "I do *not* hate you with a passion. I simply hate you the same way I hate everyone else, and that helps us get along."
She smiled. "Don't you want us to get along, Zaajik?"
The man nodded, not looking up at her.
"Good," she sighed. "Because if I thought otherwise, I would have to have Vaurik here remove your head and send it back to your king in a box. I wonder what becomes the family of a traitor in your kingdom?"
"Beril is not my kingdom, Milady," Zaajik answered, his voice trembling slightly.
She laughed. "Oh, that is the perfect answer, isn't it? Except it doesn't help you, because neither is Miasma City. I will not taint the name of the Glaistoff Empire with traitors and snakes. So you see," Jaelyn said sweetly, "You no longer have a kingdom or a home to call your own. That means that you are already on borrowed time here, doesn't it? Only a matter of time, and your end here will come one way or the other. I would however, be willing to extend your stay if you were to bring me back the Hyless, which you have so far failed to do."
"I will not fail again," Zaajik said, his voice muffled against the stone. "King Orlivan is launching his attack against the Range as we speak. He will be arriving shortly."
"Well then," Jaelyn said, lowering herself back down onto her throne. "I suppose that means he will be wanting his trusty General at his side, won't it?"
Zaajik leaned up and rose to his feet, keeping his gaze low.
She could see how he trembled in her presence, like a leaf in a winter blizzard.
"I will succeed, your grace."

"I do hope so. And Zaajik," she said, leaning forward in her seat, "bring me Galnoron's head when this is over. That man's stay in Miasma City has officially expired."

****

It took them about an hour to saddle Salezz and pack their bags with some traveling food. Haze didn't pack much, as he didn't intend for this trip to take long. He wanted to go, enlist the aid of the Rime Born and come straight back. If he knew Orlivan, the old King wouldn't wait long before he started sending in skirmishers. Haze wanted to be as close to Hallovath as possible before this mess began.

Not long after, Haze and Glassworn leaped into the inky black sky above Hallovath, winging south towards the open expanse of the Great Tundra. Haze had heard Oaina and Lox speak of it on occasion; It was bare and bleak, nothing but miles of ice crusted plains stretching out across the Range. Blizzards were ever present, tearing across its desolate landscape and clouding what lay at its center. Vlaire had warned him before they left that the Rime Born may not be receptive to people entering their home.

According to Glassworn, the fortress struck awe into the voices of the Hallovath citizens; when he had heard it spoken of in the pub, it had always been in hushed whispers, as though speaking of it could set the frozen warriors themselves upon you. He said the only known sighting of the fortress by anyone other than a Rime Born was when the first Hyless had created it. Molded entirely out of ice, it stood guard in the center of the Tundra, housing her frigid creations until the day they would be needed.

Haze clenched his teeth.

Well, now they were needed.

The first several hours of flying were over the same terrain they were used to seeing: towering forests shrouded in light snow and mist, the sapphire tips of the trees poking through the fog here and there like icicles from a snow bank. The occasional Banyeet Titan loomed over them, their great boughs draped protectively over the forests and canyons below. They spotted a few ice wyverns winging through the branches of one of the Banyeets, glistening in the rising sun.

It wasn't until later in the day that the scenery began to change; dew draped forests began to give way to rocky canyons, boulders perched precariously on their rims. They stopped seeing Banyeet trees entirely. Eventually, the canyons leveled out to create a barren flatland, the forests vanishing suddenly at the edge of the plains. The wind was blowing harder, chips of ice and sleet blowing against their faces as they pressed into the wasteland. At length, the plain became coated entirely in ice, the wind blowing so hard that Haze was hard pressed to stay on his wyvern's back, each gust like a blow from a smith's hammer.

He pulled his tunic up to cover his face and protect it from the searing cold.

They had just passed over a frozen river when, without warning, a storm unlike anything he had experienced exploded into the icy air. It drove Salezz toward the ground, the wyvern screeching loudly as he struggled to stay aloft. Glassworn cried out and clung to Haze's waist, crushing the air out of him.

Guiding Salezz to the ground, he crash landed in the crusty snow. Salezz bent over them and lifted his wings, wrapping them around his master and the druid. The sound of the blizzard raged outside the leather-like scales, screaming like a feral animal in the night.

They were in the Great Tundra.

It was only a short time later that the blizzard vanished as quickly as it had come. The normal wind resumed: bone chilling, but not life threatening.

Their travel was slow and laborious, as they were forced to the ground every few minutes by sudden vortexes of ice and snow that battered them from all sides. Each time they took off, they were beset upon by howling winds and savage cold. It wasn't until this had happened for the tenth time that Glassworn finally spoke.

"This is taking forever," he panted. A coating of sleet covered the mask he had pulled up over his face. His silver coat glistened white with razor-like shards of ice. "It's a wonder we haven't been diced to bits."

"It can't be much farther now," Haze gasped. "We have been at this for half the day. We must be getting close. It's just south, correct? There aren't any other directions or landmarks we need to know?"

Salezz groaned loudly, the wind whipping around him as he shielded them with his wings. Haze knew the cold didn't affect him, but the wyvern was most likely getting hungry as the day waned.

Glassworn shook his head. "No, just south into the Tundra. From where we were, that is. I suppose it would be north if you were coming from the other direction."

Haze rolled his eyes. "No, Glassworn," he said sarcastically. "It would be west. I swear, I think drinking has permanently damaged your brain."

"I hear that's possible," the druid admitted, "but I find it hard to believe. I mean, I have been drinking for years and look at me. Aside from my hangovers, that is."

Haze wondered at how the man had survived as long as he had. Even in sophisticated places like Miasma City and Beril, there were dangers that befell the common man without common sense. Glassworn was the walking epitome of luck.

The wind died down suddenly, the screaming of the blizzard fading like the end of a howling song.

"Alright," Haze sighed. "Let's get on with this."

When Salezz spread his wings for them to come out, Haze's heart leaped into his throat.

An Algid floated icily in front of them, its frost-like fangs dripping in the front of its vaporous body.

"Haze," Glassworn whimpered. "It's an Algid."

"Yes, I know!" Haze snapped, trying not to move. He stared at the frigid beast, trying to think of why it was not attacking. It floated menacingly in front of them, its teeth bared in a sapphire smile. It writhed over the crusted plains, pulsing a deep blue, yet it did not attack.

"Why is it just standing there?"

"I don't know, Glassworn."

"The last one attacked us."

"The last one, you kicked."

"It was sleeping in the middle of the floor!"

"Yes! And you kicked it!"

Glassworn gasped and clutched Haze's arm as the Algid suddenly moved. It drifted slowly towards them, stopping mere inches from the end of Haze's nose. The smell coming off of it was like an early winter morning, fresh and clean. Mist swirled around gently, a whirlwind of blue and white. Drool dripped off of its bared fangs and ran in small rivulets between them as it coursed downward towards the ground. It hovered in the air in front of him, snapping in the wind like a banner caught in a breeze.

Haze frowned as a barrage of emotion pummeled his consciousness; anger, hate, and fear ran rampant through his mind. They seemed to be coming off of the Algid as though the creature was somehow conveying its feelings to them. Then, an image of Ki appeared in Haze's mind, as if thrust there from an outside force. It was accompanied by an overwhelming sense of urgency.

Haze nodded. "I understand," he whispered.

The great creature pulled back a little bit, its wraith-like body writhing and pulsing. It suddenly vanished into the sky, melting like a snowflake before an open flame.

Haze blinked and looked at Glassworn.

"Well, that was odd," the druid said. "I say, it seemed as though he was sizing us up there for a moment!"

Haze shook his head. "I don't think so. I could feel its emotions. I think it is worried about Ki."

Glassworn raised an eyebrow. "Aren't I supposed to be the drunk with hallucinations?"

Haze swung up onto Salezz. "There is no time. We have to hurry! It was extremely concerned about the Hyless. Quite frankly, I don't blame it, and I know why."

Glassworn shook his head and climbed back onto Salezz muttering quietly to himself.

And so, they resumed their tedious trek through the tundra, working their way ever closer to what they hoped was a saving grace for the Hyless.

Haze took one comfort in the brutal cold and wind; it got worse the farther into the Tundra they got, and he hoped this meant they were nearing their destination.

Three hours later, however, his hopes began to fade. The cold was still getting worse, the blizzards more frequent, and there was still no sign of the great fortress. The wind was tearing across the tundra like the edge of a knife, its cold cutting deeply into them and chilling them to the bone. Haze struggled to hold onto the reins, his hand numb and aching. Glassworn had fallen silent behind him, his arms limp around his sides. He pressed on, determined to move forward. The image the Algid had shown him was still present in his mind, a driving reminder that he had to keep moving.

Just when he had begun to think the fortress was a myth, he thought he saw something bright through the swirling snow ahead. He leaned forward, rubbing some of the snow out of his eyes with his frigid hand.

Through the blowing snow and ice, a great fortress rose up out of the tundra like a sapphire spear. Its many turrets lanced the clouds above it, vanishing into the soft white and towering above them. Its windows glistened in the dim light, scattered across its facing wall like a myriad of stars adorning a great ocean. Its battlements were patrolled by several Rime Born that stared diligently down on the tundra around them. Its sheer size put Hallovath to shame; it was many times the size of the great waterfall Hallovath called its home. Large black banners whipped in the wind above the gates like darkened dragon wings.

"Glassworn," he said, his voice cracking from the cold. "Look."

The druid moaned behind him and sat up.

Haze nodded ahead of them. "Hovvel Kell."

Chapter Thirty-Three
The Light Of The Hyless

Oaina dragged Galnoron out of the spare room and dropped him uneremoniously on the marble floor.

Finally, she was going to get to kill something.

The wizard balled up and moaned piteously, raising his hands over his head. "Wait! Don't! What have I done?"

Oaina growled under her breath. "The games you people play exhaust me! You know full well what you did!" she yelled. "You killed one of my guards, injured another, and organized the kidnap of the Hyless, which cost the life of one of her Guardians." She said the last part softly, Lox coming to her mind. "And for that, Vlaire has given me permission to do with you as I see fit."

"I didn't do any of those things," Galnoron sobbed. "I swear! You can't take Alovere's word for it! He admitted to being a murderer, how can you trust anything he says?"

"I don't." Oaina smiled coldly. "Vlaire does. As long as I get to kill one of you, I don't care where the order comes from."

Galnoron scurried away from her like a crippled crab, scrabbling and slipping on the marble floor. "K-kill me?" he moaned. "No, not me! I haven't done anything! Think about it. All the time I have been in Hallovath, have you ever seen me? No! I keep to myself! I leave you alone! I don't spend any time with Ki like Haze and Alovere do. Why do you think I would try to hurt her?"

Oaina glared at him. "Because you were the only one we didn't tell that Ki was the Hyless," she said quietly. She saw Galnoron's face fall as he realized what he had said. "Now, I am sure I could find out how you learned that she was the Hyless, but I don't really care." She drew her sword and marched towards him. "I think if I want to find out, I will just wait until after I have killed you."

Galnoron suddenly shot to his feet, backing away a step. All traces of fear were gone from his face and he returned her stone-cold gaze. "You truly think I fear you, woman?" he sneered.

Oaina paused.

This was the last reaction she expected from him. Not that it mattered, as she could just as easily finish off an uppity sorcerer as she could a cowardly wizard, but it showed how quickly his colors could change.

"I am the greatest sorcerer alive," he said icily. "You are nothing more than a pawn in a game of chess too large for your mind to even comprehend. Do you really believe that you can face Orlivan and Jaelyn with a few city guards and forest spirits?" He shook his head. "You are a fool. I control both of them, dancing them about like puppets on a string."

Oaina stopped her advance briefly. "What are you talking about?"

Galnoron's face broke into a greasy smile. "Oh, I think I will let you find out, but don't think I ever intended to let Jaelyn get hold of the Hyless. The power of the Hyless will be mine, as it should be."

"You will never take the Hyless while I breathe," Oaina snarled.

"I will do more than take her," Galnoron said. "I will take every drop of magical power she has in her body, and end her life in the process. When I am through with her, she will be nothing more than an ordinary girl, and a dead one at that."

Oaina stared at him in shock. "Steal her powers? She is the light of the world! Life would end! Are you mad?"

"Perhaps," Galnoron said, "but when I succeed, the world will be awash in the light I provide for it. Imagine those first few moments of light after she has passed and I take her gift," he said rapturously, putting his hands behind his back and pacing slowly in front of her. "After being plunged into utter darkness, unable to see, feel, or hear; the soundless scream of isolation echoing eternally in your mind as you fight against the black that looms in on you from all sides, clawing at you like a feral beast desperate for the blood of your very soul. And then..." he spread his hand open suddenly, a small orb of light appearing above his palm and hovering there. "There is light, drenching you to your core, freeing you from the beast of solitude that hunts you like a plague, freeing you from the chains of night and lifting you into the light like a sudden miracle. I will be that miracle," he said softly, his eyes distant. "People will praise me for it. Exalt me." He looked down at her and smiled. "Even worship me."

"Not if I kill you first," Oaina snarled, leaping forward.

Galnoron leaped aside lightly, a small orb of blue appearing in his right hand. He thrust it out at Oaina, and it collided with her breastplate.

She cried out and fell to the ground, liquid fire seeping into her chest. Her limbs froze, her sword falling from her hand with a loud clatter. A raging storm of heat tore through her body like a violent poison.

"It took me a while to figure out how to use my magic in this city," Galnoron said with a smile, "but I managed it. I have since been able to whisk myself home to his majesty whenever I wish. Or," he added with a shrug, "her majesty, whichever one for the day, I suppose. It's been a week now since I unlocked the rest of my powers." His eyes flashed. "Shall we give them a go?"

Oaina tried to snarl, but was unable to move. Her limbs felt like they were bound by hot irons, searing her flesh.

"We could do that," a quiet voice said from behind Galnoron. "or you could just leave in one piece."

Galnoron whirled around, his robes floating just enough to allow Oaina to glimpse Lorgalith.

The old Range Keeper leaned heavily on his staff, his back hunched and eyes narrowed.

"The Range Keeper," Galnoron sneered, his tone hesitant. "I hear you are a Time Magician. A pity you can't seem to ease its effect on you."

Lorgalith smiled. "Alas, it is a shame. However, it does allow me to live significantly longer than most Wizards, and lends me a great deal more time to hone my arts," he said, his face calm. "I would wager I have about three hundred years of experience on you. Give or take a decade or two."

Galnoron smiled. "Are you challenging me?"

Lorgalith chuckled amiably. "Gracious, no. My knee is in a poor state today and I'm not feeling up to it. I am simply telling you that if you don't leave my Guardian alone this instant, I will reduce you to dust and use you to fertilize the flower on my desk."

Galnoron blinked. "I don't think you understand the situation, buzzard. I—"

"I understand quite well," Lorgalith interrupted him. "I know that you have stolen the heart of a celestial being or other. That sort of raw power is not easily overlooked." Galnoron's face paled as Lorgalith said this, but the old man continued. "You think this lends you great strength, but you do not understand how it works. You are barely scratching the surface of its potential, while I have had centuries to master my art. Challenging me to a duel would only hasten your end, and give me even more practice." He sighed. "I grow weary of conversation when it proves itself to be witless and without any form of intellectual requirements. Shall we begin?"

Galnoron frowned. "Begin what?"

"Obviously you aren't leaving, so I assume you are going to try and kill me," Lorgalith explained cheerfully. "I won't hold that against you, as not everyone can be bright these days, but I will ask you to get on with it. I am tired, and would very much like to get back to my chair."

Galnoron looked somewhere between confused and enraged, Oaina thought. But a moment later, he had raised his hand and begun to chant something under his breath.

Lorgalith rolled his eyes. "Oh, dear."

He raised his staff and brought the bottom of it crashing down with a sound like thunder.

Galnoron was lifted of his feet and sent flying into the wall behind Oaina, crying out in pain.

In moments, he was back up, weaving his arms between himself and the the old Range Keeper, a net of shimmering purple appearing in front of him.

He yelled and cast the net, the glittering violet strands hurtling across the room at Lorgalith.

The time magician jerked his chin and the net vanished in a cloud of smoke.

"You do not understand the finer sides of magic, boy," the old man said coldly.

It was a tone Oaina had never heard the Keeper use before; dangerous, and low.

"You would do well to leave now, before you push this too far.

But Galnoron was beside himself with rage, and lifted his hands above his head.

A large red sphere began growing in his hands, quickly growing to the size of a large cartwheel.

The stone floor trembled under Oaina's knees, seeming to buckle in on itself as Galnoron called on even more power. The light in the room faded, as though the orb were absorbing it to grow larger.

"I possess more power than you could ever imagine," he said, glaring at the older man. "You do not understand what I am capable of, nor what I have given to harness this power."

"I understand more than you think," Lorgalith said softly, his eyes sad.

He stepped forward and once again struck the handle of his staff on the ground.

The orb suddenly vanished, falling to the ground in small pile of dust.

The light returned to normal, Galnoron staring around him confusion.

Lorgalith whispered something under his breath and pointed his staff at the corrupt wizard.

The sorcerer suddenly cried out in pain and clutched his chest.

"You will leave my Range," Lorgalith said coldly, as Galnoron gasped for breath. "You will tell Orlivan and Jaelyn that they are not welcome here, and that should they come here, they will answer to the greatest time magician ever to walk the continent of Elliset. You believe you posses power?" He chuckled and shook his head. "I control time itself, you power hungry little fool. You will never again set foot in my Range, or will see to it that your time is up."

Galnoron fell to the floor as Lorgalith lifted his staff and backed away. He lay on the floor for a moment, before rising shakily to his feet, a look of sheer horror painted across his face.

Oaina saw Galnoron take a step back, his brow furrowed in concern. "I will be back for the Hyless," he coughed.

"That would be unwise," Lorgalith answered quietly, his eyes flashing.

Galnoron clenched his fist. A cloud of black appeared around him, enveloping him in shadow.

With a small hiss, wizard and cloud both vanished into thin air.

Oaina gasped as she was released from Galnoron's spell. She collapsed to the floor, cold overtaking her arms and legs. It was soothing, like water over a fresh burn. She tried to lean up as Lorgalith limped over.

"No, no," he said. "Just lay there a moment. You will recover fully in just a bit."

"What did he do to me?" Oaina spat.

"I'm not sure, but it has the foundation of a simple binding spell. It will wear off presently."

"Why did you let him get away?" Oaina snapped. "He will warn Orlivan that we are ready for him!"

"Precisely why I let him go," Lorgalith answered. "A king attacking an unsuspecting opponent will be confident. One that knows he faces resistance will perhaps be more willing to talk."

Oaina nodded slowly. "Haze."

"Yes," the old Range Keeper said. "We need only hope he returns in time."

****

"Thank you very much, have a good day," Alovere grumbled as the old lady shuffled off contentedly. "Are you looking for anything particular today?" he asked the next customer in line, a young man dressed in the fine clothes of royalty.

He had made a grave error stealing that loaf of bread from Enial. He had thought she didn't have the steel to turn him in to her father, but she did. When her father became enraged and ordered his hands to be removed, Enial had asked that he be given another chance and allowed to work off his sentence at the bread stand in the market, and that is what he had been doing.

For a month.

Every day, he showed up and stood behind the little wagon, waiting for Enial to bring a fresh load of bread on her little goat cart. Together they unloaded it onto the market stand just before the sun was up, and she would take the goat and cart back home before returning to help him serve customers.

"I would like a honey glazed fruitcake, please," the young man said amiably, hanging an ornate cane from his arm.

"Yes sir," Alovere said. "Fruitcake," he grumbled to himself as he bent down and rummaged through the sweet's drawer under the table. "Fruitcake! That's what these rich people eat; honey glazed fruitcakes. *He's* a fruitcake, that's what's going on here. With extra nuts."

"I say, is there a problem?" the young man said, leaning over the cart and looking down at Alovere.

Alovere smiled up at him. "No, no problem. Just trying to find your cake is all. Looks as though we are running a little low." He spied the sticky sweet treat tucked behind a sconce and seized it. Standing back up, he set it on the table and wiped the honey from his fingers on a towel Enial had hanging from the top of the cart. "That will be three Vihl, please."

The young man dropped a few coins on the cart and picked up his cake. "Thank you, good sir," he said.

"Thank *you*," Alovere replied sickeningly. "Have a good day." He was relieved to see that the young man was the last person in line and he was now alone.

"Looks like you have this handled," Enial said from behind him.

He turned to face her. "We are out of fruitcakes, not counting yourself. I just sold the last one."

"Out of fruitcakes and its only midday!" Enial exclaimed. "The customers must like you."

"The customers don't even see me, let alone like me."

"Oh, I think they notice more than you give them credit for," Enial said, uncovering the small basket she had hanging on her arm and revealing a collection of steaming fruitcakes. "Besides, any strapping young lad serving bread has to have the hearts of every young maiden on the street fluttering," she teased.

"Strapping young man serving bread?" Alovere said in disgust. "There is nothing even remotely attractive about that."

"Depends on the maiden, I suppose," Enial said mysteriously, smiling at him. "You know you only have another week before my father claims you have served your sentence?"

Alovere blinked in surprise. He had sort of forgotten the exact date that his service ended. He supposed it must have been because he hadn't had time to think about it, or maybe he had simply not been concerned about it. "Is that so?" he said quietly. "That will be a relief."

"Mm," Enial answered him, bending down and rearranging the sweets drawer to accommodate the fresh fruitcakes. "What will you do when you finish here?"

Alovere frowned. It was something he had given much thought to, and unfortunately had not yet arrived at any sort of decision. He had been given a room to stay in at Enial's parents home. It was an attic in the stable outside, but it was vastly more comfortable than most of the places he had stayed before. They had a small cot moved upstairs, along with a small chair that he used to pull his boots on in the morning. It was nothing spectacular, but it was comfortable and it was his. He knew that when he stopped working for Enial, he would have to give it up and move back into his cave with Arginox. It was far more comfortable than the attic, by most standards, but there was something about being in the attic and listening to Enial rattle on about her day for an hour every evening that made him feel content. She was kind and didn't look down on him for the life he had chosen. It's true, she saw him as something that needed to be fixed. He had resented that at first. But now...

"I haven't decided yet," he said gruffly. "Maybe I'll hire on somewhere as a mercenary."

Enial looked up at him quickly. "A sell sword? Why would you do that?"

He shrugged. "I've some skill with a blade, and enough attitude to make it work."

"Or get you killed! Why don't you just join the City Guard?"

"I tried that three years ago. They want me to have a better education."

"So get one?" she said, sounding as though it were obvious.

He couldn't help laughing at her face. "Well, it's not that easy. You need to have enough money to pay for it, a place to live while you are getting it, and a lot of other things that I don't have." He shrugged. "So. Mercenary."

Enial sighed. "Why don't you speak to my father? Maybe he can work something out. He likes you, you know."

"A lot of good that does me," Alovere scoffed, picking up a twisted loaf of bread and flipping it in the air. "People liking me doesn't get me anywhere in life, Enial. That's what people like you don't understand."

"I like you," she blurted.

Her words gave him a start, causing him to miss the loaf of bread as it came back down. It bounced off the edge of the cart and landed with a wet flop in the mud around the wheels.

"Uh, thanks," he said awkwardly, bending down and picking the bread up. Shaking the mud off it, he wiped hopelessly at it with his sleeve. "Um, I think this is—"

"It's spoiled," Enial laughed. "We can't sell it now. Just give it here." She held out her hand.

Alovere looked at it for a moment, then looked back at the girl. Her eyes were wide, her face as pink as a sunset. "Listen," he said nervously, "I am honored that you like me. I am. But are you sure you do? I know that's a stupid question," he said hurriedly, "but I don't think you even know me, really."

Enial cleared her throat, glancing at her boots briefly. "I know you're a thief. I know you have been imprisoned for stealing at least two times."

"There. See? You don't—"

"And I know you are rude and crass," she continued.

"Alright, I get your p—"

"And that you have little respect for anyone besides yourself."

Alovere bit his tongue and folded his arms crossly.

"Also, you have a habit of making other people feel horrible or stupid, even if you are in the wrong the entire time and you know they are in the right."

He glared at her, waiting for her to say something else.

"And your face twists into incredibly rude expressions when someone begins to point out your problems," she finished, setting her basket down on the cart and smiling up at him.

Alovere thought this was a bit much, but when he opened his mouth to defend himself, his retorts were silenced by her eyes. She was smiling up at him, her face glowing like the sun. Her hands were crossed in front of her green dress, and she was rocking back and forth on the balls of her feet cheerfully.

"Well, there you have it," he mumbled quietly. "What's to like?"

"There is plenty about you to like," Enial laughed. "You're sensitive."

"Now hold on," Alovere said, pointing the muddy loaf of bread at her. "Those other insults I can take, but that—"

"Is a compliment," she interrupted him again.

"No, it isn't."

"Yes, it is."

"No, it isn't, and now you are insulting me for free!"

"Why, what's the usual cost?" she asked smugly, crossing her arms.

"A broken nose!"

Enial leaned forward and stuck out her nose. "Okay, I'm waiting."

Alovere hesitated. "That's not fair."

"Why not?"

"Because you can't do that!" he objected, gesturing at her. "You know I can't—"

"What? Hit a girl?"

"Yes!"

"Why not?"

He waved his arms around in aggravation. "Because you just don't hit girls!"

Enial leaned back and laughed out loud. "See? There is another reason to like you."

He blinked. "What?"

"You are a gentleman," she said, curtsying with a flourish. "That makes you *very* likeable."

He smiled briefly, then caught himself and glared at her. "Whatever you say." He turned and dropped the loaf of bread into the scraps bin.

He heard Enial pick up her basket behind him and start walking away.

"Enial," he called after her, turning around.

She stopped and looked back at him. A smile was still fixed on her face.

"Thank you."

"You're very welcome," she said, curtsying again. She turned and walked away, bouncing lightly across the shale street.

* *

Alovere gasped and sat up, his ribs throbbing sharply.

Bright sunlight shone in on him, drenching the emerald blankets in a soft yellow light. The sound of a tea kettle whistling filled his ears.

"I see you are awake," a voice cackled from his right.

He looked over to see an old man sitting in a high-backed chair by his bed.

He was bald, his face weary and draped in wrinkles. He wore fine gray robes embroidered in yellow sequins that hung on his body like sheets on a skeleton. He held in his hands a small flower pot, a strange blossom growing out the top of it. Its petals were different shades of blue and purple, pulsing and glowing with tiny star-like lights.

"Who are you?" Alovere asked, looking around himself. "Where am I?"

"There seems to be a lot of the identity questioning going on, hm?" the old man said cheerfully. "I think if people quit caring so much about 'who' someone else is, and worried more about what they were doing, life would be so much simpler. Don't you agree?"

346

Alovere tried to lean up, but cried out in pain and fell back down. "But I thought Vlaire and Oaina were going to banish me again?"

The old man rolled his eyes. "Ugh, yes. That. I am truly sorry Vlaire did that in the first place, but he is young and his sight is only just so encompassing. I'm afraid when he gets like this, it encompasses little more than the end of his nose. Truly, you can't blame yourself."

Alovere stared at him. "You know, you didn't answer either of my questions."

"That's true," the old man chuckled. "Then let me answer a few right now. I am Lorgalith, the Range Keeper. You were not banished again because I took you in. You are in my home atop the Gallery of the Hyless, and I intend to nurse you back to health so you can live to fight for the Hyless when the time comes."

Alovere coughed. "Why didn't you just let me die?"

"You have been having some disturbing dreams of late, Alovere," Lorgalith said gravely. "I understand that you probably think it is because of the infection in your wounds."

Alovere frowned. "How did you know that?"

"I know everything that happens inside my Range." He smiled. "It is both my privilege and my burden."

Alovere cleared his throat. "I won't ask what that means. I get the feeling you wouldn't tell me."

"You are correct!" Lorgalith said cheerfully.

"So, if my dreams and hallucinations aren't from the infection, what are they?"

"You are at war with yourself, Alovere," Lorgalith said quietly, leaning forward in is chair. The flower swayed precariously as he did so, straining towards Alovere. "The Hyless effects everyone differently. For Haze, it makes him feel at home. He has spent his life following an

347

.

honorable path, looking for where he belongs. For Glassworn, I am not entirely sure. Very powerful magic surrounds that man. But for you…" he shook his head. "The light of the Hyless shines into the darkest corners of our lives. You are reliving your past as a side effect of being too close to that light. Your wounds will not heal, nor will your torment end, until you have dreamed them to their fullest and understand them. I believe you are somehow key in the defense of this city. And no, I don't know why."

"Understand what? What could they be trying to tell me?"

"Only you can know that," Lorgalith said. "It could be anything from remembering what color you wore on the day you killed your first target to dying for the Hyless."

"You mean Ki?"

Lorgalith cocked his head and stared at Alovere. "You are a most curious individual. Everyone else sees her as 'The Hyless.' You see her as the little girl she is. Don't you think that means something?"

Alovere shook his head. "If it does, I don't know what it is."

"Well then," Lorgalith said. "You had best figure it out. Your friends are preparing for battle without you."

Chapter Thirty-Four
Arglwydd Rhew

Haze landed Salezz in front of the fortress in a swirl of white. He dropped to the ground, his boots sinking into the soft snow. The druid climbed down beside him, and they stared up at the massive gates. They were each wider than three dragons and made of solid black metal. Silver markings like the ones Haze had begun to see so much of were engraved in the metal, shining through a thin layer of ice that had built up on the gate over time. The Rime Born atop the battlements stared down at him silently.

The Fortress was massive. Haze felt like little more than a speck standing in front of it, the giant ice turrets splitting the clouds high above him. Glassworn slouched miserably next to him, his arms wrapped around himself and his teeth chattering.

"Be quiet, will you?" Haze snapped, his own jaw trembling like a leaf in a breeze.

"Easier said than done!" Glassworn retorted. "I hope they have a fire in there."

"I hope they let us in."

Haze wasn't sure what to do. He could holler up at them, he supposed, but the Rime Born didn't strike him as creatures one should be yelling at. Perhaps he could politely call up to the one standing atop the gate. Either way, he had to get their attention.

He had just opened his mouth when the gates gave a weary groan. Ice cracked and splintered, falling to the ground as the enormous metal slabs screeched open. Snow rolled up in front of them as they slid across the plains. They finally moaned to a stop, a last chip of ice falling to the ground in front of Glassworn.

A courtyard stretched out before them, barren and covered in snow. There were no footprints, or any sign of anyone having walked inside the gates for some time. A fountain stood in the middle of a large square, frozen in a frigid claw that seemed to reach out towards them. Empty homes and shops lined the edges of a large market place, snow blowing in windows with glass long broken out.

"Well," the druid said nervously. "I'm feeling pretty good about this."

Haze glanced at Glassworn and they started timidly into the yard. The snow crunched under his boots with every step, the only noise aside from the eerie howling of the wind through the eaves of the forlorn buildings.

They made it all the way into the square and stopped. They looked around, watching for any sign of the Rime Born.

Haze's heart leaped into his throat as the gates crashed closed behind them, shedding another dusting of ice shards.

Glassworn cursed and shook his head. "Should have seen that coming. Isn't that what always happens in the stories the bards tell?"

But Haze wasn't listening. He was staring straight ahead at the set of bare stairs that led up to the doors of the great fortress. There were hundreds of them climbing up towards the face of the palace like a bridge of ice. The courtyard was otherwise empty.

"Seems pretty deserted, don't you think?" Glassworn whispered. "Maybe we should go, hm?"

Haze glared at him silently and started towards the stairs.

"Now, let's not get carried away," Glassworn said, hurrying to catch up. "We need to remember that this is about the Hyless. If there is no one here, perhaps we should be getting back to her! At least if we cannot enlist the aid of the Rime Born, then we can fight for her ourselves instead of being out here freezing in the wilderness."

"Glassworn, be quiet." Haze said. "We are going to look inside the palace and make sure there's no one here. The gates opened, didn't they? And there were a few Rime Born on the battlements. They are here, and what's more, they let us in for a reason." Haze shook his head. "I am not going anywhere until I see the inside of this fortress."

Glassworn whimpered quietly and shoved his hands in his sleeves, falling in behind Haze.

Haze patted Salezz on the nose. The wyvern looked truly distressed at being left behind, but sat obediently at the foot of the stairs as his master began the long climb up.

Haze tried not to look down, the ground falling farther and farther away from him as he climbed. The stairs indeed turned into a bridge that spanned a massive canyon between the courtyard and the palace. Its jagged edges and razor-sharp rock formations made it look like the maw of a beast ready to swallow them whole should they slip. He focused on the doors that lay waiting at the end and pushed onward. Glassworn followed him begrudgingly, his head down and brow furrowed deeply as his teeth chattered fit to shame a woodpecker.

The climb seemed to go on forever before they finally reached the doors that led into the palace. They were identical miniatures to the gates that guarded the courtyard, only they sported a pair of shining silver knockers carved in the likeness of Algid fangs. Giant silver loops hung down from their canines, a sheet of ice freezing them to the doors.

Haze pulled out his dagger and dug out some of the ice, freeing one of the rings. Putting away his dagger, he grabbed the ring. Taking a deep breath, he knocked three times.

The sound was like a church bell gonging so loud that one might as well have been inside his head.

They clapped their hands over their ears as the sound reverberated again and again, bouncing off of the gaping canyon walls beneath them.

Then, everything fell silent. The wind howled a lonely tune through the fang-like rocks in the chasm below, the only sound save for the distant echoes of the final chimes from the knocker.

After a moment of silence, Glassworn turned around and started back down the stairs. "Well, I guess that's that! Why don't we get started, yes? No time to waste!"

Haze whirled to face him. "Would you just wait a minute? I thought you wanted to help the Hyless. Why are you in such a hurry to leave when this could be our only chance of saving her?"

Glassworn continued down the stairs, waving his hand over his shoulder. "Yes, well if our 'only chance' doesn't open the door, then it's not much of a chance. I'm just being realistic about this."

A loud creak sounded from the fortress and a wave of heat cascaded over Haze from behind.

Glassworn froze on the steps. His shoulders slumped and he turned back around, a weary expression on his face. "Fate has never been my friend," he sighed. "I wish just once—"

Haze ignored him and turned around. The doors were open and the warm glow of firelight shone from within. Heat wafted out of the open doors, shimmering in the frigid air like liquid glass. Haze could see a large red rug on an ice blue floor just inside, and torch-lit halls stretching as far as he could see.

"Let's go," he said.

Glassworn begrudgingly followed him through the doors, his hands rammed in his pockets and his brow furrowed.

The rug was in fact a carpet that ran the length of a hall so long that Haze could barely see the end of it. Doors were placed at regular intervals along it, the railing of a staircase protruding out from the right side of the ice a little way down the corridor. The walls were covered in not just torches, but Yobes. They flickered in and out with the dance of the torch light, scurrying here and there on the walls and ceiling. They traced intricate carvings on the walls, some of wyverns and some of Algids. There were a few pictures etched into the ice that Haze did not recognize. They were all masterfully made, seeming almost alive as the Yobes moved in the deeply grooved lines of the carvings.

A quiet snore made him look beside him.

The druid was leaning against the wall, his eyes closed and mouth hanging partly open.

"Glassworn!"

He didn't answer.

Haze reached out and slapped the drunkard, snapping him awake. The druid snorted and coughed, his eyes widening as he stood bolt upright.

"Did you really just fall asleep that fast?" Haze said incredulously.

"Sorry," Glassworn mumbled, rubbing his face where Haze had smacked him. "Very warm in here."

Haze rolled his eyes and started down the hall. Glassworn was right, though, the heat *was* nice. It soaked into Haze like a hot broth, his fingers and toes beginning to ache as the blood started flowing again.

They reached the staircase and stopped. It was made of the familiar dark wood and rose in a circular pattern high above them into the upper reaches of the fortress. The railings were exquisitely crafted, swooping down like a swan's neck at each landing and bearing the same sort of marks and carving as the walls, only in glittering silver script. They were

353

once again alight with Yobes, the blue light of the iridescent creatures giving the black stairs an eerie glow.

"Well," Haze sighed. "Stairs, or no stairs?"

"Will you consider my opinion?" Glassworn asked skeptically. "Or pretend I don't have one?"

"I will listen to what you say, and do the opposite of your suggestion," Haze said quickly. "So, yes. I would say that counts for considering your opinion."

Glassworn rubbed his chin for a moment, then his eyes lit up. "Very well then," he said smugly. "Stairs."

"Stairs it is," Haze said cheerfully, starting up the glowing flight of steps.

Glassworn blinked. "H-hey! But that's not—ugh!" he groaned, falling in behind Haze and muttering to himself.

It was a long climb before they finally reached a landing that opened up into another corridor. It was much like the first, only it had no carvings in the walls. They were instead decorated in rows of familiar statues. Haze recognized them as the previous Hylesses of the past, same as were in the Gallery.

Haze felt Glassworn tense behind him. He looked to his left and saw why.

Two Rime Born were drifting towards them soundlessly, swords sheathed by their sides. They glided over the red carpet, more mist than usual wafting off of them. Haze assumed this was because of the heat.

The two spirits stopped in front of them, their expressionless faces fixed on the Rider and his companion.

Haze swallowed. "We are here to see Arglwydd Rhew," he said hesitantly.

They cocked their heads at him, then one of them waved his hand in an obscure gesture.

"What does that mean?" Glassworn whispered to Haze.

"I don't know."

"Maybe it wants us to leave."

"I think it wants us to follow it," Haze said, frowning at the druid.

"Oh." Glassworn nodded slowly. "So, we aren't leaving then?"

"Glassworn, if you mention leaving one more time, I will leave you *here* when it is finally time to return to Hallovath," Haze said crossly. He strode after the two Rime Born as they headed for the end of the hall.

"Sorry, I just couldn't help but notice that they didn't say anything to welcome us," Glassworn stated, hurrying to catch up. "Now, where I come from, that's code for not *being* welcome."

"They are Rime Born, Glassworn. In the time we have spent in the Range, have you known one to speak?"

"Besides the point."

"It isn't, and we aren't leaving until we have seen Arglwydd Rhew. Get over it."

The Rime Born stopped suddenly, turning slowly to face them. One gestured to a door on its left, then nodded its head politely.

Haze glanced at the druid, then swallowed and grabbed the handle of the plain door. Pulling the latch, he pushed it open with a creak.

It was bright inside, light streaming in from the opposite wall comprised entirely of windows. They overlooked the gaping canyon below, a few stray wyverns dipping in and out of its many crevasses. The right side of the room was quite bare, save for a book shelf made of the black wood. It rose all the way to the ceiling, and went from one wall clear to the window on the other side of the room. It was laden with books and tomes of numerous kinds and sizes, all looking older than the mountains themselves. A chandelier affixed with dozens of candles hung from the middle of the ceiling, some of them negligently allowed to burn out completely, nothing more than puddles of wax in their holders. Dust was settled in the far corners, the mark of someone who had cleaned recently but had not been too thorough.

A light hiss sounded behind them, and they wheeled around.

A Rime Born unlike any of the others stood before them. It was faceless like its brethren, but wore a long emerald robe atop vaporous shoulders. It flowed down around where its feet would have been, the fog of cold drifting around the fabric. The robe was old and decayed, small holes chewed in the hem from mice and moth. A crown of ice was molded directly to the Rime Born's head, a part of its very being. It had ten points, each one tipped with a pearl frozen into the frigid jewelry. The crown was dirty, its host negligent in its cleaning. Carvings like the ones in the first hall adorned the entire Rime Born from head to toe, glowing softly as countless Yobes scurried along its body. It stood tall in the doorway, its head held high as it stared at them silently.

Haze knew the moment he saw him that this was Arglwydd Rhew.

He stepped to the side, his head bowed respectfully as the great creature passed through the door. It drifted to the middle of the room and turned around, to face them. It simply hovered there, looking back and forth between them.

Glassworn nudged Haze with his elbow. "Say something."

Haze thought seriously about hitting him, then changed his mind. "Your majesty," he said instead, bowing low to the Rime Born. He then froze.

He wasn't sure what to say next. Of course, he wanted help from the Rime Born, but he was unsure if this one could even understand him.

"Ask him," Glassworn whispered in his ear.

"Glassworn, shut up," Haze hissed through his teeth."

"You have to ask it," Glassworn persisted. "It's listening. The other one seemed to understand you."

"All I said was Arglwydd Rhew! Of course, it knew what I was talking about."

"Sh! He's looking at us."

Haze looked back at the Rime Born King. It had cocked its head slightly, but was as silent as ever. It stared at them in what Haze thought must have been bewilderment.

"Just ask it," Glassworn pushed. "It seems friendly enough."

"Look, you were the one that wanted to leave when we saw the gates," Haze said crossly. "Now you are telling me it's not so bad?"

"My name is Arglwydd Rhew," a deep, rumbling voice said.

They both slowly turned to face the King. He stood with his misty hands behind his back, facing them patiently. "What's yours?"

Haze mentally kicked himself. Of course, Arglwydd Rhew had heard and understood everything they had said as they stood there making fools of themselves. "Ahem," Haze said nervously. "My name is Haze, and this is Glassworn."

Arglwydd looked back and forth between them for a moment, his gaze falling to rest on Glassworn. "I know both of your names already. I simply asked to see if you would tell me the truth." He stared hard at Glassworn for a moment, the Druid swallowing anxiously. "Also, it is not considered polite to refer to a King as 'it.'"

Haze frowned. That didn't make any sense. Why would he even care what their names are? Or care if they lied about it?

"Now, you are here for a very specific reason," Arglwydd said, lifting his gaze from the petrified drunk. It was odd watching him speak; the sound seemed to appear out of nowhere, his face nothing but a sheet of smooth ice. "You wish to enlist the aid of the Rime Born against King Orlivan and Queen Jaelyn."

Haze blinked. "How did you know?"

"I'm afraid I cannot tell you that. Ask young Lorgalith and he will tell you the same thing. He knew you were going to come just as I did." He shook his head. "Though I admit, his vision is sometimes impaired by his...how shall I put this..." He paused and rubbed one icy hand under his chin. "Enthusiastic nature?"

"Young?" Glassworn snorted. "That old geezer is—" he yelped as Haze slapped the back of his head.

Haze glared at him for a moment, then turned his attention to Arglwydd Rhew. "That is correct, we wish to enlist the aid of the Rime Born. There is a great force coming that we cannot hope to defeat on our own."

"What of the Guardians?" Arglwydd asked immediately. "Are they not powerful enough?"

Haze wasn't sure what to say. Was it possible this creature actually believed the Guardians possessed supernatural powers? From all Haze had seen, they were nothing more than normal people. Oaina and Vlaire were large, but that didn't mean they were invincible, and certainly didn't mean they could defeat an army by themselves. "One of them is already dead," Haze said quietly, Lox's face coming to his mind. "Those remaining are doubtful at best. The Hyless is different; she cannot hear, and they are fearful that she may never discover her powers."

Arglwydd nodded silently, turning and pacing across the floor. He remained silent for a good while before he faced them. "Do you know who I am?"

Haze frowned in bewilderment. "I believe so. Are you not the king of the Rime Born?"

"I am, but do you know where I came from?"

Haze shook his head. "I don't."

"I was created by the first Hyless," Arglwydd said, "as were all the Rime Born. We were born of the ice that flowed freely from her soul and buried the Range in snow and cold. She created us for a terrible reason, one only she could foresee. She instilled in us the born instinct to protect not just her, but all the spirits of the Range. If one is in danger, my soldiers can feel it from forty leagues away. We are a blessing for the Range, and a curse upon ourselves." He paused. "If the Hyless needs our help, we have no choice but to respond. We cannot deny you our service, as serving the Hyless is the purpose of our existence."

Haze frowned, feeling a little bewildered. "But if you have to help us anyway, why did you make us come all the way out here to ask? Why didn't you just come to Hallovath? What's the point?"

"One learns a great deal about his own determination to see something through when he embarks on a quest such as yours," Arglwydd said mysteriously. "And it makes it easier for me to see that you truly have the Hyless's best interests at heart."

There was no way Arglwydd was going to convince him that there was something he should have "learned" from this day-long trip through the coldest place in the world, but he could see it from the Rime Born's point of view: They were created to protect the Hyless, therefore, if Haze and Glassworn had not been willing to perform this one small act in her service, the Rime Born would have discarded them as allies, or even killed them off. The idea made him shudder, but at the same time, it made him comfortable that who they were dealing with truly cared about Ki's fate.

"Thank you very much," Haze said graciously, bowing low. "We have little hope without the Rime Born."

"We must help you, as we were created to do," Arglwydd repeated. "That doesn't mean I think it wise. If you meet these armies in battle, many will die. One of them may be the Hyless herself. Why do you believe it to be your only option?"

Haze cleared his throat. "What else would you have us do? They are coming to Hallovath. They will burn it to the ground and kill any who stand in their way."

"Hide her," the old Rime Born said immediately. "Hide the Hyless where she cannot be found until she discovers her powers. If she cannot be found, she cannot be harmed."

Haze shook his head. "But that doesn't protect the citizens of Hallovath. Thousands will die in the name of the first Hyless to abandon her people! We must fight."

Arglwydd Rhew let out a sigh. "If that is your choice. But understand that the cost of war is more than lives lost. Far more valuable than a life is one's soul. You must prepare yourself for the inevitable loss of conscience during this conflict. The cost will be so much more than any of you can bear."

Haze swallowed. He knew as much already. He had tried not thinking about Lox, but he knew he wouldn't be the last to die in the name of the Hyless. He knew that shortly, it may be him bleeding out on the field of battle, or Alovere. The thought made his gut twist, but he clenched his teeth and nodded sharply. "I understand. Thank you for your aid, your Majesty."

"I will be proud to fight alongside the Guardians of the Hyless once more," Arglwydd Rhew said, bowing his head in return. "I will have the

Rime Born prepare the *Rhewddraig* to fly you back to Hallovath. It is both warmer and faster. Please make yourselves comfortable until then."

"Thank you very much," Glassworn said gratefully. "I don't think I could stand flying back through that tundra on that serpent again."

"And as for you," Arglwydd said suddenly, facing Glassworn. "I do not know why you choose to deceive one of the most powerful beings in existence, but if you come here with another lie on your tongue, I will cut it out."

Haze looked back and forth between them, his eyes wide. "Pardon me?"

Glassworn was staring at Arglwydd coolly, his expression vacant. His head was high, his eyes flashing dangerously. "Understood, your Majesty," he said, tilting his head slightly. "And should I want rebuke, I will seek you out. Until then, thank you for your service."

The two stared at each other tensely for a moment before Arglwydd nodded. "Very well. Do not wait too long to step up. The Hyless needs you."

Glassworn bowed low now, his nose nearly touching the floor as his silver coat swept the carpet. "She is my greatest concern."

Haze cleared his throat. "Should we be going now?"

"Indeed," Arglwydd said. "Wait here. I will have you escorted to the Rhewddraig," he said firmly. "Battle is upon us. We march for the Hyless."

Chapter Thirty-Five
The Laudlin's Return

The flight back to Hallovath was indeed very fast, taking only a fraction of the time it took on Salezz. The Rime Born that accompanied them on the airship were as silent as ever, though Haze felt awkward speaking around them as he was unsure whether or not the creatures could understand what he was saying. This worked out, as Glassworn seemed withdrawn since their visit with the Rime Born King, and remained silent for the majority of the flight anyway.

Vlaire and Oaina both awaited them on the airship dock by the Gallery, staring at them anxiously as they descended the ramp from the *Rhewddraig* onto the white cobblestones.

"They will help us," Haze said.

Vlaire visibly relaxed, glancing at Oaina and clearing his throat. "That's good news. How many?"

"Once gathered, Arglwydd Rhew claims there will be nearly three thousand."

Vlaire scratched the back of his head. "I have all the City Guard gathered up, about a thousand in total. They are well trained men, but have little experience. The only blades they have crossed have been with Jaelyn's patrols in the Mirror Wood." He shook his head. "They will need much guidance."

Haze nodded. "I understand. We need to discuss battle plans. Even with the help of the Rime Born we will be severely outnumbered. And out matched," he added. "Jaelyn will bring warships with her. They will be difficult for us to combat, even with the wyverns of the City Guard. How many guards have mounts?"

"About half of them. So, five hundred, give or take."

"And how many of them are very comfortable with flying?" Haze asked. He knew what new riders were like; it took years to get used to flying into thinner air, or shift your focus to battle while flying high above the ground. The slightest slip up, and you plummeted to your certain death a thousand feet below. This made new Riders uneasy before battles, and greatly affected their performance in the fray.

"I would say half again," Vlaire sighed. "These are city guards, not soldiers. Hallovath hasn't seen war in a hundred years. Obviously."

A familiar chugging behind him caught his attention, and he turned around.

He was surprised to see the *Laudlin* flying towards Hallovath, smoke billowing out of its engine compartments in the rear. Its hull glistened black in the dull light, the many bolt cannons along its rails cold and dark. Moxie stood on the prow, her hands behind her back and expression as stern as ever.

"Guards!" Haze flinched as Oaina bellowed behind him.

"What are you yelling about?" he snapped, turning to face her. "We don't need guards! This is Moxie, the woman that sent me here. She comes as a friend."

Oaina glared at him, glancing at the *Laudlin* warily. "You know that wizard 'friend' of yours had an interesting conversation with me while you were away."

Haze felt his face flush hotly. "Galnoron is no friend of mine. Anyway, what's your point?"

"I don't trust your judgment," Oaina said nastily as the *Laudlin* made berth beside the *Rhewddraig.*

Glassworn, whom Haze had quite forgotten was standing there, let out a small groan. "Oh, great. Here she comes. Just when I thought my day couldn't get any worse."

363

"Worse?" Haze exclaimed. "The Rime Born agreed to help us, Moxie is no doubt here for same reason, and you think things are going badly?"

"You be part of her crew. Just for one day," Glassworn mumbled. "Then we'll talk."

Haze could see Moxie up on deck, her voice carrying down to him as she barked out last minute orders to her crew. She then turned and started down the ramp towards him, her hands clasped firmly behind her back and her lips pursed.

"Captain," Haze said to her as she stepped off the ramp.

"General," she answered cordially, nodding her head sharply. Her gaze drifted to somewhere behind him and her eyes narrowed. "How has the dullard been behaving?" she said, a razor edge coating her words.

Haze glanced over his shoulder at the druid. "Oh, Glassworn?" He shook his head. "Fine. Drunk as ever, from time to time, but trying to help." He sighed. "It doesn't work, of course, but he tries."

"I see." Moxie looked back at Haze. "And the Hyless? Have you found it?"

"I have," Haze said, glancing at Oaina awkwardly. She was staring at him with a glare that could melt steel. "But never mind that. Why are you here?"

Moxie stood up straight, throwing her shoulders back. "I have come to inform you that Orlivan's troops are on the march. They will be arriving here by end of day tomorrow."

Haze felt his knees knock briefly. "That soon?" he asked weakly. "How many?"

"Five thousand infantry at least," Moxie said briskly. "And Jaelyn is readying her warships. I can't imagine that she will be but a day behind him."

This was happening a lot faster than Haze had anticipated. He had expected another week of patrols, and perhaps some light skirmishing on the edges of the forest before an all-out attack. "Did Orlivan's army have dragons with it?"

Moxie nodded. "Yes. Many."

Haze rubbed his face with his hand, trying to settle his nerves. So, the Winged Demons were airborne. They would be facing the very best Orlivan had to offer, many of the Riders old students of Alovere's and Haze's. He couldn't escape the feeling that this was likely to be a massacre long before Jaelyn even got involved. Of course, if what Alovere had said about her and Orlivan was true, that is probably what she wanted.

His heart ached as he thought about facing Orlivan in battle.

He shook the thought out of his head and focused on the warship captain. "What about you? Do you have any ships loyal to the Hyless?"

Moxie glanced over Haze's shoulder for a second, then shook her head. "I do not. I have captains loyal to me, but their crews may be a different story. I can guarantee the aid of perhaps ten warships. Beyond that, I make no promises."

Haze nodded. "I understand. What is your plan?"

Moxie bowed respectfully. "I have come to offer the services of my ship and crew. My Lord Kinzin has instructed me to pledge my service to you until the Years of Mourning have passed, one way or the other."

Haze blinked. "That is most admirable of you, Moxie, but you understand that this is a fight we will most likely lose?"

The airship captain drew herself up to her full height, eyes flashing. "I have come to fulfill the wishes of my lord, and die in the process if necessary. Victory or defeat, the *Laudĭin* and her crew will be remembered as the greatest warship to ever soar the skies in the name of the true ruler of Glaistoff."

Haze wasn't sure what to say. "Thank you, Moxie," he said quietly. "You honor your King."

"Excuse me," said a familiar drawling voice from beside him.

Haze rolled his eyes to Glassworn. "What?"

"Sorry," the druid said anxiously, "but milady said her 'crew'. Am I to be expected to fight, then?" he asked, fiddling with the corner of his coat.

Moxie's face turned the color of dragon fire, and she swelled up like and angry cat. "Yes!" she bellowed. "Along with the rest of your ship mates! And so help me lord should I see you drinking at any time in the next twenty-four hours, I will see you hanged from the back of my ship for a week! Have I made myself clear?"

Glassworn swallowed and mumbled something Haze couldn't hear as he backed slowly away with his head down.

"Now," Moxie said, her face slowly returning to its previous shade as she looked back at Haze. "Where do you want my ship? She's armed and ready to spew lightning and fire at your convenience."

Haze was overjoyed at Moxie's arrival, and invited her into the Gallery where they sat at the table and discussed plans. Vlaire and Oaina seemed hesitant to trust her, and rightfully so, but it wasn't long before Haze noticed Oaina's disdain turning to obvious admiration of the tiny woman. Moxie commanded the respect of everyone she faced, her entire person oozing authority. Haze had thought this would cause them to clash, but on the contrary, they hit it off rather well. Within two hours of discussion and meeting with the various captains of the City Guard, Oaina had dropped all sort of animosity towards Moxie and instead barked harshly at the guard captains that questioned her judgment.

The initial plan was simple: Moxie was Haze's hidden dagger. Neither Orlivan nor Jaelyn knew they had a fully armed warship at their disposal, least of all the largest one in Jaelyn's fleet. She would fly in with Jaelyn's fleet to avoid suspicion, and hopefully strike at the heart of the Armada once the fray began. The Rime Born and City Guard would be left to deal with Orlivan's infantry, and the Winged Demons.

Haze shuddered at the thought of facing his old comrades. They had only two hundred guards comfortable enough to face them on wyvern-back in the sky. That left them extremely vulnerable to attacks from above. They agreed that while the battle was taking place, Ki and Malya would stay in the observatory with Lorgalith. If the battle began to go poorly, Malya would take Ki and flee, hopefully hiding her until she discovered her powers.

They were just discussing where each of them would be positioned during the battle when the doors to the gallery burst open with a bang. Their heads all swiveled towards them to see Famau standing in the doorway, a sword belted to her waist and wearing a raggedy suit of old armor. It was obviously too big for her, and she had cut down some of the straps that held it in place to make the dented-up metal fit tighter. "So, where are you putting me?"

Oaina's cheerful expression vanished instantly. "In a grave if you don't stop coming in here like you own the place," she growled menacingly.

"Oaina," Vlaire warned. "We need all the help we can get." He stood up and bowed politely to Famau. "I would be honored if you would fight alongside the Rime Born."

Famau glanced at Oaina, then back to Vlaire. "Very well. Front lines, I suppose."

Vlaire nodded. "I'm afraid so."

Famau remained silent for a moment. "Where shall I wait for the mean time?"

"We don't know when the Rime Born will be arriving," Haze said, "but Orlivan will be here end of day tomorrow. You should go home until then."

The air was tense as Famau glared at them all hotly, then nodded sharply. "Alright. I will be back here in the morning." She then spun on her heels and exited the Gallery, letting the doors groan shut behind her.

"Who was that?" Moxie asked.

"Her name is Famau," Haze said as he breathed a sigh of relief. "She is Ki's mother." He had fully expected Famau and Oaina to come to blows so many times already that it felt as impending as the doom that marched on Hallovath.

"She shouldn't be fighting," Oaina grumbled, slouching back into her seat. "You know she will just die. She is no warrior."

"I wasn't aware we had the luxury of being selective," Vlaire snapped, turning to glare at his sister. "Do you have any other suggestions?"

Oaina flushed and fell silent.

Haze could see the stress this was putting on Vlaire. The Guardian knew the entire city was looking to him to protect the Hyless. He knew that the odds were terrible, and that it looked as though he could be the only Guardian in history to fail her. He looked like he had not slept the night before, dark circles smudging under his eyes. His skin was pallid and tired as he looked from person to person around the table.

Haze cleared his throat. "Orlivan will mount a full-scale attack. I know how he operates; he will hold nothing back. He will have trebuchets set up in the Mirror Wood where they are difficult to see. After barraging the city from afar for a few hours, he will start sending in the infantry. Lastly, he will unleash the Demons. They will strike at the same time from above and below."

"Good grief," Vlaire breathed. "Try to make it sound like we stand a chance."

Haze glanced at him and continued. "If we repel them, we will have a maximum of twelve hours before Jaelyn's troops arrive. She will put heavy pressure on us from above as well. She will have bolt cannons, archers, skirmishers, any troop that can attack at range."

"Okay," Oaina snapped. "So, what is the plan then? Since this sounds like a lost cause!"

Haze looked at each of them slowly. "Our only chance is an all-out offense on Orlivan's infantry," he said quietly.

Oaina rolled her eyes and Glassworn moaned piteously. Moxie leaned back in her chair and stared at him intently.

"Hear me out," Haze said loudly. "If we do not wipe out Orlivan's force on the field before Jaelyn arrives, we will be spread too thin. We are outnumbered as it is. If Jaelyn's airships attack at the same time as him it's over. We need to finish off his ground troops before she arrives and get every soldier that can fly in the air, and all the Rime Born on the *Rhewddraig*, as well."

Oaina sat up, her expression changing to curiosity. "I see. And you propose we do this how?"

369

"Evacuate the Upper City," Haze said quickly. "Send all the citizens back down to Old Hallovath. It is too deep in the waterfall for the Demons to find it easily. Then, we can have all our troops on the ground to face Orlivan without having to defend the city from attacks from above."

"But then we are vulnerable from behind," Oaina protested. "Even if what you say works, we will be putting an army of a thousand enemies behind us!"

Haze shook his head. "I used to lead those men. The second they see that the City is emptied, they will suspect a trap. They will return to Orlivan immediately."

Vlaire rubbed his chin thoughtfully. "It could work. It seems a bit unorthodox, but it sounds like a plan."

"We have to eliminate one of them before we have to face both," Haze said again. "And I don't honestly know what the Rime Born can take and what they can't. I know that against Orlivan's infantry, they will perform marvelously. But I doubt even they can stand up to dragon fire or Bolt Cannons."

Glassworn cleared his throat. "Just out of curiosity, how much of a chance do you think we stand to actually win this?"

"Silence, dunce!" Moxie barked. "Numbers are not always your friend. That doesn't mean you can't beat them."

Glassworn nodded and scratched his head. "Right," he mumbled.

A knock on the door was followed by them creaking slowly open.

Malya entered, holding Ki's hand. Her face was drawn, lips squeezed together in a tight line. She had a large bundle under arm and a sword Haze recognized from over her fireplace in her other hand.

"Hello," she said, her voice carrying like bells across the room.

370

Vlaire stood up and strode over to her, looking her over. "What are you doing here?"

"I have come to leave Ki and Mulwyn with Lorgalith," she said. "I have to do some last-minute preparing before I can move in with him as well."

Vlaire nodded. "Very well. If you need any help, let us know."

Moxie leaned over and nudged Haze. "I thought the other woman was the mother?"

Haze cleared his throat. "Yes. Well. That is a bit of a long story. Better if we just stay focused for right now."

Moxie nodded and leaned back.

Vlaire allowed Malya to pass and returned to his seat as she climbed the staircase towards Lorgalith's observatory.

He sighed loudly and rubbed his face. "Well, I suppose until tomorrow rolls around, we should prepare ourselves and get some food."

And so, they did. Each of them got their preferred weapons in order, their armor cleaned and oiled, and wyverns fed. Guards were posted in the Mirror Wood and around the city at various locations, to change hourly. Last but not least, Moxie confiscated Glassworn's flask to be certain he didn't drink himself into oblivion before they were to march in the morning.

Six hours later, Haze sat with Glassworn and Moxie in his chambers. Moxie was perched on the edge of his small cot next to him, Glassworn seated crossed legged on the floor. Haze had asked them to come so he could go over some last-minute ideas with them, but they had instead taken the conversation in a different direction.

"You know how important the Hyless is, don't you?" Moxie asked quietly, her face darkened in the gloom. "You understand what happens if she dies?"

Haze nodded. He knew. While it seemed impossible, it was cemented in his mind after his meeting with Arglwydd Rhew. The old Rime Born King's very existence seemed to solidify the legend of the Hyless in Haze's mind, and if any of the legend were true, Ki's death would bring about a total eclipse of life itself. "I believe I do, yes."

Moxie's face relaxed and she shifted slightly. "Good. So, you know how much we need to be willing to give to keep her safe? You understand what is at stake?"

Glassworn looked up at this and narrowed his eyes at Moxie.

Haze shrugged. "It's not a question of willing. Everyone that goes to battle tomorrow is willing. What matters is whether or not we succeed. As far as what is at stake, I only know that should she die, the world will be changed forever. I don't know what the world will be like without the 'spark of life,' as it is called, but I can't imagine it's good."

Moxie shook her head. "No. The texts say the death of the Hyless would plunge the entire world into chaos. From what I have read," she swallowed, "her death would be the death of all life. Should she die, so do we all."

Haze's heart sank. Then, anger boiled up inside him and he slammed his fist against the wall. It smarted and two of his fingers went numb. "How can people be so stupid," he seethed. "Of course, we hunt the only thing keeping us alive! And for what? A trophy?"

"For power," Glassworn said quietly. He shifted on the floor, sticking his feet out in front of him and resting his head on the wall. "They believe they can steal the power of life for themselves. It's what drove every man to ever hunt the Hyless. Greed."

"That's not good enough!" Haze spat. "It doesn't make sense! Why would you risk the fate of the entire world on the off chance that you might be given a vague reward no one really understands anyway?"

Glassworn blinked. "I think they understand it better than you give them credit for."

Moxie nodded. "Glassworn's right. These people would never die if they had the power of life. Anyone they knew that had died they could simply bring back. Anyone that threatened their position or hurt them, they could just take their life away." Moxie shook her head. "It would be an awesome and terrible power in the hands of the wrong person. That is why the Hyless is locked away in the Mountain Range. It gives her the best chance at surviving and fulfilling her duty to the world."

"And what exactly is her duty?" Haze asked impatiently, his temper beginning to fade. "She holds the spark of life! But why her? Why not someone else? What does she do besides freeze the mountains and make Rime Born?"

Moxie and Glassworn looked at each other. "She isn't just a vessel that holds life, Haze," Moxie said. "She distributes it. The Hyless is the only person capable of handing out life equally to everyone in the world. She is unbiased, and loyal only to her sacred duty. She breathes life into the king and murderer alike, as it is her solemn responsibility as Hyless." Moxie sighed. "She is the perfect host for such a powerful spirit. A young girl raised in seclusion and taught that all are precious in one way or another. But would it really make a difference if she was nothing more than a vessel?" She shook her head. "I don't think so."

Haze grumbled and flopped backwards onto his cot. "I suppose not."

Moxie rose to her feet, kicking Glassworn in the side. She was rewarded with a small yelp of pain as he scrambled to his feet. "Alright.

We will be on our way. Tomorrow will be a long day, I'm afraid. Rest well, General. You face the world in the morning."

Chapter Thirty-Six
The Proposal

"Sir, I have something important that I would like to discuss with you," Alovere bowed low to his reflection in the mirror. He stood up suddenly and paced back and forth twice, shaking his head. "No, that's all wrong."

"I like it," Enial laughed from the chair in the middle of his attic room.

"You like what I say no matter what it is," he said sourly. "You're not a reliable judge of quality."

"That's because you never say anything," she teased. "Besides, what are you so worried about? You know he likes you."

"Enial," Alovere said exasperatedly, "how do you think your father is going to feel when the thief he 'likes' asks for his daughter's hand in marriage?"

She shrugged. "Conflicted?"

Alovere rolled his eyes and turned back to face the mirror. "Oh, I doubt he will be conflicted. I will be lucky if he doesn't run me through on the spot."

It had been six months since Alovere had started working for the City Guard. Enial had spoken with her father and had convinced him to let Alovere join the recruits. He had proved himself to be good with a sword and quick on his feet, easily one the best swordsmen the guard had. Enial helped him with the technical part of the schooling, and her father had agreed to front the money for it. Alovere swore to pay him back for everything he had borrowed, and paid the man regularly each month from his salary.

Today was his last payment, and he intended to ask for Enial's hand in marriage.

They had spent a great deal of time together over the last few months, growing very close. He had introduced her to Arginox, taken her flying, and shown her his old cave. They spent many hours each night exploring as far out to sea as Arginox could fly without tiring, talking of little things like the market gossip and what Enial's regular customers said that day. On their way back to town, they would stop at the beach just as the sun was going down on the horizon. As its orange light danced on the sea, they would lay and watch it sink beneath the waves. Just before it got completely dark, they would dare each other to swim out as far as they could go in the growing gloom.

Before he had realized what was happening, Alovere had fallen in love with her.

"I think you worry too much," Enial laughed. "He isn't going to stab you. He likes you more than you know."

"Well, maybe there is a reason I don't know," Alovere stated. "Perhaps he doesn't want me to know because he doesn't actually like me and he just wants you to think that."

Enial rolled her eyes. "Some City Guard you are," she poked. "You haven't even got the courage to face my father and you want to help him chase criminals?"

"Criminals I will happily face," Alovere said, "but an angered father with a sword? Not my idea of courage. That's more akin to stupidity."

"Any other angered father with a sword, perhaps," Enial admitted, "but this is my father, and he is your captain. I'm telling you, it won't be that bad."

Alovere sighed and looked at himself in the dusty mirror. He wore the red tunic Enial had gotten him for special occasions over his dark leather trousers. His sword hung at his waist, the emblem of the City

Guard emblazoned on the red sheath. His dark hair was tied back, his gray eyes as cold as a December morning.

He shuddered as he thought of the man he had dragged into the town square and mutilated. His blood chilling screams still rang as loudly through his memory as if it had just happened yesterday, and not two years ago.

"Are you alright?" Enial asked, coming to stand next to him.

"I'm fine," he said weakly. "Just thinking."

He turned to face her. "I'm gonna go see him now. I might as well get this over with. Worst case scenario is he says no."

Enial smiled and stood on her toes, pecking him on the cheek. "Good. I thought you might come to that conclusion at some point. It is, after all, the only one."

Alovere stared at her in horror. "You mean you know he is going to refuse?"

She doubled over in laughter. "No, I mean that is the worst case. Good grief, you really have a problem with talking to people, don't you?"

"I don't have trouble talking to you," he mumbled, feeling his face flush.

"That's because I do all the talking. Trust me and just go. It will be fine." She dropped his small leather bag of coins into his hand and pointed at the stairs that led down out of attic.

Alovere squeezed the purse lightly and looked at Enial for a moment. Then, he wheeled around and hurried out of the room and down the stairs.

Taking a deep breath of the clean night air, he stepped boldly towards the light that shone out of her father's house window.

He sat awake at this time of night. Glaive had a small table by the window that he sat at and wrote things down. Alovere never knew what he was writing, nor did he ask. He felt it would appear nosy, but Enial said it was just because he was scared. Alovere assumed he kept logs for the prison. Perhaps inventory.

As he got close enough to the house to make out her father seated just inside, his stomach nearly came up in his throat.

Was he really doing this? A thief and a murderer asking for the hand of a City Guard's daughter. The captain of the City Guard, no less.

He slowed his pace, fiddling with the small purse of coins in his hand.

It seemed like such a trivial thing, a payment on a loan. True, it was the last payment, but it seemed like it wasn't enough to warrant asking for Enial's hand.

He cursed and kicked at a small twig on the path.

Why did he feel like he was trying to buy her father's approval? This was a payment on a loan he had taken out for an entirely different purpose, not a bribe.

Shoving the purse into his trouser pocket, he slowed his pace even further.

What if her father got angry? What if he told Alovere he didn't want him to stay here any longer?

That was what he was truly afraid of, not his blade. Should Glaive get upset enough to attack him, Alovere was certain he could handle himself.

It was his rejection that Alovere feared.

He caught a glimpse of movement in the corner of his eye and looked quickly to his right.

It was Enial's bakery, where she went to make all of the bread that they sold at the market. Her father had built her a small hut with a built-in fireplace oven so she could pursue her trade just outside his own home.

He squinted at the small building, trying to see in the darkness, but the windows were dark, and cold, no sign of movement anywhere.

He heard a loud crash and whirled back around towards Glaive's house.

The door was now open, light spilling out onto the river stone steps that led up to it. Two shadows battled with each other in the lamp light and the sound of swords clashing broke the silence of the moonless night.

Alovere whipped his sword out of his sheath and bolted to the door, throwing it open.

A man dressed in dark clothing was battering Glaive up and down the room, his sword whirling in a series of blows that the older man was having trouble blocking.

The windows on either side of Alovere burst inward, two more men leaping into the fray.

"Alovere!" the captain yelled, "run!"

Alovere felt the heat of rage building up inside his chest, the same morbid excitement he had felt whenever he accepted a dangerous mission as an assassin.

He had no intention of running.

Leaping between Glaive and the two newest assailants, he caught one of their blades on his and pushed them back.

"You would attack a man three on one?" he growled, leveling his sword at them. "Looks like you have some learning to do."

They screamed and charged, blades whirling like windmills.

He sidestepped them easily, tripping one and thrusting his sword through the other's chest as quickly as a scorpion's strike. The man fell to the ground motionless, his comrade scrambling back to his feet. Seeing his fallen friend, he looked up at Alovere, his face hidden behind a black cloth.

Glaive suddenly cried out in pain as the other assailant drove his sword into the older man's belly.

"No!" Alovere yelled, diving at him with his sword crossed in front of him.

He met the assailant's blade with a ringing clash, spinning past him and putting himself between the fallen man and his attackers.

"You will pay for the things you have done, boy," one of the dark men said, sheathing his blade.

Sweat slicked Alovere's hand as he gripped his sword tightly. He recognized that man's voice. "What do you want?"

"Nothing we can take yet," the assassin said, nodding at his companion. The other man sheathed his sword and backed away a step. "I know we can't take you by ourselves. You are, after all, the Man of a Thousand Deaths."

Alovere nearly dropped his sword. "Where did you hear that?" he whispered.

The two men didn't answer, turning away from him and striding silently from the room.

"Hey!" Alovere yelled after them. They didn't even look back.

Dropping his sword on the ground, Alovere spun around and knelt beside Glaive.

The old man coughed, blood running down the corner of his mouth.

Pulling back the man's shirt, Alovere's heart sank as he saw the wound. It was a deep gash only slightly below the rib cage, blood pouring out of it like a waterfall.

"Alovere," the man said weakly.

"Yes sir?" he answered, looking Glaive over. His wounds were severe. There was little chance of his survival, if any at all.

"Look after Enial please," he gasped. "I am not long for this world. Take her away and leave this place behind."

Alovere licked his lips. "I meant to ask you for her hand in marriage," he blurted.

Glaive chuckled, a spurt of blood issuing from his nose. "Enial told me. She thought it would be funny to torment you even though I had already said yes."

Alovere stared at the man. "You did?"

"I did."

"But I am a thief!"

"You are much more than that," Glaive said mysteriously. "I know who you are."

Alovere's stomach clenched. How was it possible? He had made certain to cover his tracks, always hide his face, never use the same method or weapon.

"I hear whispers of this man of death," Glaive wheezed. "A young boy so gifted with a blade that it is said ten men could not stand against him. A young boy with an insatiable thirst for blood and coin."

Alovere cleared his throat. "I-I'm sorry," he said simply. "I didn't mean for this to happen—"

Glaive shook his head. "I see a young boy lost in life, unsure of his true path and too scared to face it alone. Enial can give you the strength you need to do what is right and leave your life behind."

"But—"

"Never tell her who you are," Glaive said, grabbing Alovere's arm. His grip trembled, blood dripping down the back of his hand. "She must never know. You must leave Jiikk, leave this life behind, and never look back."

"I don't understand," Alovere said, shaking his head. "Why did you spare me?"

"Because my daughter loves you," he said simply. "A father will do anything for his little girl," he coughed. "Now, promise me you will take her away from here."

"Where will we go?" Alovere asked in bewilderment.

"It is a continent north of here that was discovered by a fishing vessel that got lost in a storm four years ago. It's called Elliset. It is said to be a land full of magic and riches. I meant to take her myself after her mother died." His eyes had a faraway look in them and his hand slipped from Alovere's arm. "Promise me!" the man snapped, his eyes wide.

"Alright," Alovere said quickly. "I promise."

"Father!"

Enial's scream made Alovere jump.

She ran into the room, falling to her knees by Glaive's side. "What happened?" she sobbed.

"Uh, three men broke in," Alovere stammered. "I tried to save him."

"Father!" she sobbed, wringing her hands. "What do I do? Tell me how to stop the bleeding."

Glaive smiled gently and shook his head. His eyelids fluttered briefly as he tried to focus on her. "You are such a beautiful girl, Enial," he whispered. "He will need a strong hand, this one."

"What do you mean?" Enial cried. She looked at Alovere. "Do something!"

He blinked nervously. He had seen wounds like this before. "I can't, Enial," he said gently.

Glaive's head fell softly to the side, his eyes still fixed on Enial. A slow, rattling breath escaped his lips and his chest fell still.

"Father!" She grabbed his shoulders and shook him. "Father!" She looked back at Alovere, her face streaked with tears. "Help me!"

Alovere stood up and came around to Enial, wrapping his arms around her shoulders. "Come on, we have to go. They may come back."

"No!" she screamed. "I will not leave him. He isn't dead! His eyes are still open."

"He is gone, Enial," Alovere said, pulling her to her feet. "We have to go."

She turned away from her father and buried his face in Alovere's chest, bursting into tears.

He held her close, her shoulders shaking violently with each of her sobs.

He heard a horse sneeze outside and the hair on the back of his neck stood straight up.

"Enial," he patted her back, "we have to go now."

She didn't answer. She only wrapped her arms even tighter around his torso.

Peeling her off of him, he picked up his sword from the floor and crept over to the open door.

"What are you doing?" she choked.

"They are back," he whispered, staring out into the gloom. He could see four horses tied off to the outside of Enial's bakery. They were saddled in black leather, bows strapped across the back of the saddles.

"Who are they?" Enial sniffed. She grabbed his arm. "Are they the ones that killed father?"

"Yes."

"Why?" she cried.

"Sh!"

A sword hissed out of its sheath from behind them and Alovere whirled around. Pulling Enial to his side, he lifted his blade and turned the assailant's sword into Glaive's writing table, smashing nearly all the way through it and leaving the assassins blade stuck in the wood.

Kicking the dark man in the chest and sending him flying into the hearth, Alovere seized Enial's arm and dragged her out of the house.

"Arginox!" he yelled.

He could see three more shadows hurrying along the edge of the path towards them, silver glinting in their hands.

The air was cold as it whistled by, Alovere moving faster than he had ever moved before. He pulled Enial after him, not letting her fall behind.

Within moments, the great fire dragon dropped out of the sky. He landed with a thunderous crash not ten paces away, his nostrils glowing like lanterns in the inky black.

"Come on!" he yelled, dragging her across the path to the dragon.

Grabbing her around the waist, he heaved her onto the beast's back.

A tingle ran down Alovere's spine and he ducked.

Sparks flashed off of Arginox's scales where the assailant's sword narrowly missed Alovere's head. There was a grunt of pain as Arginox brought his tail around and sent the attacker flying through the darkness.

Turning around, he hauled himself up in front of Enial and tapped Arginox in the side. "Fly!"

Arginox launched himself into the air with a roar.

Alovere looked down and saw two dark figures stumble backwards in the sudden gust of wind, their hands held over their heads.

Arginox surged higher and higher, before bursting through the clouds, moonlight drenching the puffy white mist in a soft light. Stars were draped in the sky above them, glistening as though they shared in Enial's tears.

Taking a deep breath, he tried to turn and see Enial over his shoulder. "Are you alright?" he asked.

She was silent for a moment. "Yes," she said tonelessly.

He didn't say anything else for a time. Talking to a girl that had just lost her father wasn't going to be easy, let alone the girl you hoped to marry.

"I will take care of you Enial," Alovere reassured her, though he wasn't sure how. "I promise."

She wrapped her arms around him from behind, and he felt her sobbing quietly into the back of his tunic.

Somehow, someone had found out who he was and was now hunting him.

He ground his teeth. That put Enial in danger as well.

The thought sent a wave of nausea over him.

He couldn't have that. He would have to go somewhere they couldn't find him. Her father had said something about a continent way up north, one that had been discovered by a fishing vessel.

He pulled Arginox's reins until the dragon was gliding easily north.

"Where are we going?" Enial said in a muffled voice.

"It's called Elliset."

"Have you been there?"

"No, I haven't."

Enial squeezed his ribs. "Please don't steal anymore," she said suddenly. "You have to do what's right if we are to be together. Please promise me."

Alovere bit his tongue. He would drop Enial off safely in Elliset, and return to Jiikk. He would erase the knowledge of The Man of a

Thousand Deaths from everyone that had ever heard the name. He couldn't risk anyone trying to find him and hurting Enial.

He ground his teeth together again.

He had to burn Jiikk to the ground.

"Promise me, Alovere."

Alovere swallowed, and glanced back at her. "I promise."

****

Alovere snapped awake, sitting bolt upright.

His ribs throbbed with pain, but he ignored them. He rubbed his eyes, looking around the room.

He was surprised to see Ki sitting by his bedside, her face drawn with concern.

He gazed into her green eyes, the realization of what he had to do dawning him suddenly. She sat silently, neither speaking nor signing as she stared back. She stared at him motionlessly, her expression saying more than Alovere had said in his entire life.

She had been causing his dreams. She knew who he was, what he had done, and who he was now.

She smiled gently, her head tilting to one side.

He knew what he had to do.

"Lorgalith!" he called, tearing his focus from Ki and looking around the observatory.

He spotted Lorgalith seated at his desk, his quill dancing over some parchments.

The old man turned and looked over his shoulder. "I see you have awoken. How was your dream this time?"

Alovere grimaced. "I need you to heal my wounds."

The old seer paused for a moment, before rising precariously from his seat and hobbling towards him, his staff clicking on the ice floor.

"That is easier said than done, Alovere. I do not possess the kind of magic that you require. Nothing but time can heal your wounds, I'm afraid."

"And are you not a time magician?" Alovere asked impatiently. "Can you not use your magic to accelerate my progress?"

"Or your demise," Lorgalith countered, a frown crossing his face. "What you ask is dangerous, Alovere. Should I accelerate the condition of your wounds, it could either heal you or kill you. What is it you so desperately need?"

"I need to be healed because I know the Guardians require my help. Listen," he said urgently, "my dreams were never about me. They were never about my youth. That is what I was seeing, yes, but they showed me something else, something important. I need to help my friends on the battlefield, even if it causes my death."

Lorgalith shook his head. "I think you are delirious, Rider." He shrugged. "Unless you have a better explanation, that is."

Alovere couldn't think of one. He knew what his dreams were showing him, what Ki was showing him. He knew now that Ki was not showing him his errors, or asking him to accept them. She was showing him that *she* accepted them, and while they were evil, that man was the one she needed right now.

He shook his head. "I need you to try. Please."

Lorgalith lowered himself onto the edge of the bed. "You understand that if I begin this course, the condition of your wounds may change too quickly for me to save you. If you develop an infection, it will instantly spread through your body and kill you. My magic will be accelerating *its* development as well as your recovery." He shook his head. "Given the severity of your injuries you will almost certainly die."

Alovere nodded. "I understand."

Lorgalith narrowed his eyes at him. "This has something to do with the Hyless, doesn't it?"

Alovere glanced at Ki briefly. "Yes, it does."

The Keeper's face sagged, a look of exhaustion coming over him suddenly. "These are trying times," he said. "One can only trust the Hyless and hope for the best at this point."

"So, you will help me?"

Lorgalith sighed, rolling up the sleeves of his robe. "You had better lie back. This could be a bit of a shock."

Chapter Thirty-Seven
The Beginning Of The End

Haze woke the next morning to Vlaire banging sharply on his door.

The morning was still dark, the sun not yet risen. The Rime Born had arrived sometime in the night and stood in the Mirror Wood below the city, as though they had been part of the meeting and known exactly what the plan was all along.

It was an impressive force; they stretched out into the Mirror Wood like a sea of ice and steel, glinting like glazed pearls in the pre-dawn light.

As relieved as he was that they arrived in time, Haze knew Orlivan had a force at least that size waiting on the other side of the forest.

Haze woke Glassworn and dragged him to the wyvern falls. They climbed aboard Salezz, and followed Vlaire and Boar down to meet the Rime Born. The wordless warriors ranked perfectly, their formations as flawless as polished gemstones.

He and Vlaire now hovered over them on their mounts, trying to decide about how many there were.

"It is a sizable force," Vlaire said from beside him. He was seated astride Boar, who was growling menacingly down at the Rime Born.

"It is. Perhaps three thousand. Are the City Guard joining us?"

Vlaire nodded. "They are. They should be coming—ah, here they are now."

He pointed to a stream of Wyvern Riders gliding down to mingle with the Rime Born, the scales of their blue wyverns shimmering as they descended toward the ground.

"We will wait until we see the Winged Demons flying overhead the Rime Born, and loose them once they are directly above us," Haze explained. "If I know the man that replaced me as General, he will be focused on getting inside the city. He won't be looking down."

"What do we do in the mean time?" Vlaire asked.

Haze sighed. "We need to go and parley with Orlivan. Perhaps there is a chance that none of this will have to happen."

Glassworn nodded behind him.

Haze and Vlaire winged across the tops of the trees towards the plains ahead, their nerves frayed.

Haze half hoped that there was no army waiting for them beyond the tree line; that maybe Orlivan wasn't as power-hungry as he knew him to be.

Their trip over the forest lasted only a few minutes, and the great plains opened up in front of them.

Haze's heart sank upon seeing what awaited them.

Orlivan's force was much larger than he had anticipated; at least six thousand soldiers were camped like a stain of steel and fire across the white plain, flying the banners of the Beril. Dozens of dragons and wyverns were scattered throughout the mix of infantry, marking the tents that held the Winged Demons.

He scanned for signs of Orlivan's war tent, spotting it near the front. Two men stood guard out front of it.

"Alright," he said. "I don't know how he is going to react to seeing me. Be on your guard. If Galnoron has played with his mind, then there is no telling what he may do."

Vlaire nodded, and they urged their wyverns down towards the tent.

Haze's heart hammered in his throat as a few of the soldiers looked up and pointed. He couldn't hear them over the roar of the wind, but he knew they were sounding the alarm of approaching intruders. The guards in front of the tent drew their weapons, stepping out into the open and lifting their shields. Other men began flowing towards Orlivan's tent, blades and armor glinting brightly as they formed a line in front of the door.

Salezz and Boar landed roughly on the ground, kicking up a small blizzard with their wings as they did. The world was veiled in white, hardly anything visible save for the tips of the soldier's lances shining through the cloud of snow. Slowly, the whirlwind settled back down, coating the armor and helmets of the soldiers.

A hushed whisper spread suddenly through the men surrounding them, their eyes wide with fear.

"It's General Haze."

"It's the General."

"It's the Lord of Demons."

Haze lowered himself to the ground, lifting his chin. "I have come to speak with His Majesty," he said loudly.

The men in front of the tent looked at each other briefly, before firming their stance.

"We cannot let you, sir," one of them said, shaking his head. "You are a traitor to the kingdom, and consorting with the enemies of the Beril."

"I am no such thing," Haze snapped, striding towards them. "I fight for Orlivan, and always will. Stand aside, soldier."

He tried to exude the same confidence that his men were accustomed to seeing, hoping it would dissuade them.

The men retreated a step, then held their ground. One of them stepped forward and removed his helmet.

Haze recognized him immediately.

"Horkus," he said tentatively.

The man's face was taut, and his eyes fixed. His short brown hair was as unkempt as ever, matted against his sweaty brow.

"Talk some sense into these men," Haze pleaded. "I need to parley with Orlivan before he rushes into a battle he doesn't understand."

His old comrade shook his head. "Sorry, Haze," he said painfully. "I'm under orders from Galnoron to let no one pass."

Haze's blood boiled. "That snake!" he seethed. "He is manipulating our King! He is in league with Jaelyn!"

Horkus's face fell and he shook his head sadly. "He said you would say that," he said quietly. "Please, General, you must turn yourself over to the King. Perhaps His Majesty will show you leniency."

"I am here to prevent unnecessary bloodshed!" Haze barked impatiently. "I don't care what Galnoron said about me, I am still your General! Now stand aside!"

"But you aren't their General anymore," a smooth voice said from behind the other soldiers.

The ranks parted slightly to allow a tall figure to step through. Dark hair was slicked back over a pallid face marked in thin white scars. White lips were curved into a wicked smile as beady black eyes glistened at him triumphantly.

"Zaajik," Haze growled. "Let me see Orlivan, and I will soften the blow of your sentence when you are arrested for treason."

Zaajik laughed coldly. "Interesting coming from the traitorous scum amassing an army to face his liege on the field of battle." Zaajik's face twisted wryly. "Perhaps I am the one who should be putting in a word for you."

Haze heard Vlaire drop to the ground and come to stand beside him. "We are here to parley," he said flatly. "You cannot deny us the right to meet the leader of your force to discuss terms."

"Galnoron put me in charge of the invasion," Zaajik answered smoothly. "So, I'm not actually obstructing anything. Let's hear your terms."

Haze looked at Horkus exasperatedly. "Horkus, let me see the King. Tell this oaf to move."

Horkus looked down at the ground silently.

"You will have to think of a way to win back the loyalty of your Demons that doesn't involve ordering them about under the flag of an opposing nation," Zaajik said, rolling his shoulders and cracking his neck. "Now, I suggest you leave. I am under orders to kill you on sight, after all." He drew his sword and started towards Haze. "Unless you think you can take me with one arm."

Haze snarled and crouched low, his lance ready in front of him.

"Stop!" a familiar voice barked into the crisp morning air.

King Orlivan shoved his way through the cluster of soldiers out front of his tent, his aging face wrinkled into a frown. "What is going on?" he said sharply, staring at the soldiers.

His gaze fell on Haze, and his expression softened. "Haze," he said weakly.

He looked as though he hadn't slept in a week; dark circles were carved under his eyes and stress lines ran the length of his face. He wore a full suit of battle armor, his massive broadsword belted at his waist.

"Your Majesty," Haze said, bowing low.

Orlivan's face hardened again, and he lifted his chin. "Why are you here?" he asked, his eyes searching.

Haze could tell the old man wanted nothing more than to hear that this was all a simple misunderstanding, that Haze was still his son, that the battle would never happen. Haze could see his own thoughts and wishes reflected in the King's wise old eyes.

"I am here to beg you not to attack Hallovath," Haze said. "There is much in the Range that you don't understand."

Galnoron appeared suddenly at Orlivan's right, his hood low over his face.

Haze resisted the urge to hurl his lance through the wizard's eye, and remained focused on the King.

"So, help me understand!" Orlivan snapped angrily. "Why is my General committing treason against the crown and amassing an army against me?"

"You marched an army on Hallovath. We are simply responding in kind."

"We?" Orlivan growled, his expression pained. "What have you done, boy? I raised you! You are like my son. You should share this final victory with me."

"You have been fooled, My Lord," Haze said angrily. "Can you not see that Galnoron is playing with your mind? He is controlling you with his left hand, and driving the sword of Queen Jaelyn at your heart with his right. Hallovath is a peaceful place; it is not a threat to your rule or your people. Attacking it will only lead to unnecessary violence!"

"Do not mock me!" Orlivan snapped. "You accuse not only Galnoron, but myself of being gullible enough to fall for basic trickery! While you betrayed me for—for a group of Magicians and Spirits!"

Haze wasn't sure what to say. He had come here to face Orlivan; to tell him how he was wrong in coming here and attacking the people of the Range. He knew there was nothing more important than him succeeding in appeasing the old King, and he didn't even know where to begin.

"Please," he said quietly, "Trust me as you once did. This cannot happen. The price will be more than you can imagine."

"I can't believe you have fallen for this nonsense!" Orlivan said incredulously. "You of all people know the dangers of magic and the people who use it!"

"All due respect," Vlaire cut in, "but this is a parley in which we wish to discuss the terms of your immediate surrender. Not Haze's childhood."

Orlivan narrowed his eyes at Vlaire. "Who are you?"

"I am Vlaire, Lord of Hallovath," he answered boldly. "You are trespassing in our lands and hunting its spirits. Now you stand outside my city with an army and are preparing to destroy my home and kill my people." He shook his head. "You have made a grave error, but I am willing to afford you forgiveness should you surrender and withdraw your army from my mountain range immediately. How would you like to commence?"

Haze closed his eyes and sighed. "Vlaire..."

Orlivan glanced at Galnoron briefly. "You are clearly outmatched," he said. "We have you outnumbered, and more troops are on their way. You should be considering how best to change my mind, not threaten me."

"If I may have a word," Glassworn said from behind Haze.

Haze tensed as Glassworn slid down from Salezz and landed on the ground behind them.

"Glassworn, this isn't the time. Really, am I going to have muzzle you two?"

"Milord," Glassworn said, ignoring Haze and stepping in front of Orlivan. Putting his hand behind his back, he bowed with a flourish. His silver coat swept the snow and ice as he bowed. "Make no mistake, I would greatly prefer that this confrontation end without conflict or loss of life, but I must correct you on your statement."

The druid was calm and composed. His face was relaxed, his left hand held behind his back in perfect posture as he stared at Orlivan evenly. Haze noted the bags under his eyes were gone and his complexion had cleared up.

"And who are you?" Orlivan said angrily. "I tire of nameless subjects addressing me as though they have the right!"

"I am His Majesty Lord Kinzin Arlegius," the druid said calmly. "Rightful ruler of the Empire of Glaistoff, and the last Druid of Val Ek Song."

Haze blinked as gasps swept through the soldiers around them. His face went numb as he tried to believe what he had just heard.

"You are dead," Orlivan said weakly, his face paling. "It's not possible."

Kinzin nodded. "Indeed, the world presumes me dead, as I wished it to. I could not risk my identity being discovered while my sister holds my throne. I have been devising a plan to retake my kingdom and put an end to her tyranny, but her madness has escalated beyond my control. She rekindled the fires of the Havi Ut Gahdness, and I'm afraid my focus then changed to keeping the Hyless safe. Unfortunately," he added, "you now threaten my position. I cannot allow you into the City of Hallovath. I urge you to withdraw your troops and reassess your relationship with my sister."

Orlivan half smiled, some color returning to his face. "Even if what you say is true, a single king cannot stop me. Your army belongs to Jaelyn now, and she is a strong ally of mine."

Kinzin folded his hands inside his sleeves and squared his shoulders. "That is not entirely true," he said, directing his gaze skyward.

Haze's looked up, and his mouth dropped open.

Dozens of airships melted through the fog, black hulls gleaming in the dim light. Bolt cannons glistened on the rails, charged and ready to fire. There were at least two hundred of them, prism motors chugging merrily as they lowered themselves down towards the battlefield.

Haze recognized the *Laudlin* at the front, Moxie just visible from the ground, her hands behind her back in perfect posture.

"The true soldiers of Miasma City are loyal to their King," Kinzin said, his chin high, "not the impostor that calls herself Queen."

Orlivan cleared his throat, glancing up at Kinzin's armada. "It seems you have fooled us all. Well done. But it doesn't change the threat Hallovath poses to my kingdom. I cannot allow them to hurt my people."

"It is not your people being harmed, Milord," Kinzin said, "but the people of the Range. Two men were brutally murdered by soldiers trying to steal the Hyless. One of which was a young father of two. The other, a City Guard posted outside his door."

Orlivan glanced at Galnoron. "What is he talking about? What is this 'Hyless'?"

"Nothing, my Lord," Galnoron answered quickly. "He is creating lies as an excuse for battle."

Haze finally found his voice. "Your General," he said, jabbing a finger at Zaajik, "was found in the Range conspiring with Jaelyn's forces. They had kidnapped a young girl known to be the great spirit of the Mountain Range. Alovere saved her and brought her home at the cost of another young man's life."

Orlivan frowned. "Nonsense. My men wouldn't act without my authority." He glared at Zaajik, who pretended not to notice. "I'm sure there is a logical explanation for all this."

"Yes," Kinzin said. "Galnoron has pulled the thickest of wools over your eyes. He has stolen the loyalty of your men from you, and your kingdom is next. He works closely for Queen Jaelyn, and will stop at nothing to please her for what he believes will be his own personal gain. He is responsible for the death of my wife and unborn child, and will be the cause of your death as well, if you let him."

Haze blinked.

He had forgotten that Lord Kinzin's family had been murdered. He had heard the stories, but had always heard Kinzin had died with them. He suddenly realized that Kinzin had not only lost his throne, but everyone dear to him as well.

The druid stood facing the King, his expression calm.

"Your Majesty," Haze said suddenly, "I don't ask you to withdraw immediately. Simply postpone your attack on Hallovath. Examine the details yourself," he pleaded. "Come to the city, meet the people, and hear their stories. Examine Galnoron closely. If you find Hallovath to be as dangerous as Galnoron says, I will lead your force against it myself."

Vlaire looked at him quickly, but Haze ignored him.

Orlivan fiddled with his sword hilt. "You swear to me upon our bond as father and son that what you say is true?"

Haze bowed. "I swear on my life."

Haze noticed with satisfaction that Galnoron's face reddened as Orlivan looked at him.

"Tell me Haze," Orlivan said, now staring hard at Vlaire, "how many friends do you have?"

"Two. Alovere and Horkus. I allow Rageth to believe he doesn't count."

"And how many men do you trust?"

"Very few."

Orlivan nodded at Vlaire. "Do you trust this man? You believe what he says?"

"I do."

Orlivan sighed, his face sagging. "Very well, I will postpone the attack."

Relief washed over Haze.

Orlivan nodded at him and turned to walk back towards his tent. "Come, my boy. We have much to discuss."

Galnoron's face twisted with rage and he flipped his hood down quickly. Zaajik looked at Galnoron in surprise and laid his hand on one of his swords.

"I do not think it is wise, my lord," Galnoron said quietly. "He is—"

"A soldier I raised and trained myself from a boy," Orlivan interrupted him. "I have been his father since he could barely lift a sword, and he has never trusted a soul as long as I've known him. If he trusts this man, I will need to examine him myself."

"But your Majesty—"

"That's enough, wizard!" Orlivan snapped, turning to face him. "Can you not see that we now face a King? A fleet of airships? Not to mention I take it rather to heart when I am lied to and fooled by a disreputable wizard with a hunger for power! I will see the city myself before I attack it, and you will keep your mouth closed. Zaajik!" he snapped. "Put Galnoron in irons and see that he doesn't leave his tent."

Haze felt a surge of victory as Galnoron glared at Orlivan like a cobra.

Zaajik looked back and forth between Galnoron and Orlivan, his hand still on his sword. His expression was cold and emotionless.

"Are you deaf, man?" Orlivan bellowed, whirling on Zaajik. "Seize this wretch!"

Haze felt something in the air change suddenly. It was like a wind that was at first warm and soft, but had turned abruptly harsh.

Galnoron gave a slight nod in Zaajik's direction.

In a flash, the swordsman's blade was out of its sheath.

Haze yelled, tearing his lance out of its scabbard and hurling himself towards Orlivan.

Time seemed for a moment to slow down, Zaajik taking a smooth step forward.

Orlivan's eyes widened, and he grabbed at his sword, but he wasn't fast enough.

Haze was powerless as he watched Zaajik plunge his blade into the King's chest.

Haze screamed and launched himself forward.

Galnoron flicked his hand, and a sudden flash of pain sent him flying back into Salezz's flank, his head rapping against the Wyrm's stone-like scales.

He leaned up, his head spinning.

Zaajik whipped his sword out of Orlivan's torso and wiped it neatly on his victim's hauberk. It was spotless and sheathed before the King's body had fallen to the ground.

"Orlivan!" Haze cried, scrambling back to his feet and leaping forward again. His lance was gripped firmly in his hand, the frigid metal burning into his palm.

Vlaire seized him from behind, dragging him towards Salezz. "We have to go," he said urgently.

Horkus was staring dumbfounded at Orlivan's body, his face white as a sheet.

"Don't just stand there!" Galnoron was yelling. "Get them!"

A few of the soldiers moved towards them hesitantly, Zaajik turning to face them. "Anyone that refuses to attack answers to me," the man said coldly.

The soldiers rushed them just as Vlaire hauled Haze effortlessly onto Salezz's back. Lord Kinzin hurried over, throwing himself up behind Haze as he urged his wyvern into the sky.

The soldiers grew smaller and smaller beneath them as they rose through the cold air, followed closely by Vlaire and Boar.

Chapter Thirty-Eight
The Battle for Hallovath

Moxie bared her teeth as she saw the Rime Born begin their advance. She had just watched as the swordsman killed Orlivan. Haze and Vlaire were now landed on the ground in front of the approaching force of frozen warriors, their weapons drawn. Oaina landed next to them, her battle sword glinting in the light.

"Alright boys," she yelled, whirling around and stalking across the deck. "It's time to serve your King! Let's get some Boltcannons loaded and power in our engines." She gripped the iron rails of her beloved warship. "Lets ride some lightning!"

****

Haze looked around him as the Rime Born marched past, stalking coldly towards Orlivan's approaching infantry.

Vlaire stood beside him with his hammer in his hand and his expression flat.

Oaina stood ahead of them, her teeth bared and knuckles white on the hilt of her sword.

Famau melted out of the ranks of Rime Born and came to stand beside them.

"What's the plan, people?" she asked loudly over the hiss of the Rime Born.

"It's a full-on attack," Haze yelled back, his mind still reeling. "Crush them as quickly as we can before Jaelyn arrives."

Kinzin slid down from Salezz and slapped him on the flank, sending the wyvern shooting back into the sky with the others. "This is it, then," he said calmly. "You will all need to stay focused. If Jaelyn is reported as being a day out, then she is half that at least. Expect early company."

His face was hard, his hair tumbling in the wind and coat whipping wildly.

Haze tried to do as the King said, but Orlivan kept springing to his mind. His father lay dead across the battlefield, killed by one of his own soldiers.

The sound of Orlivan's troops yelling began to drift across the plains, the infantry pounding across the snow-packed earth.

Vlaire and Oaina looked at each other, then back at Haze.

"For the Hyless," Vlaire said quietly.

Haze nodded.

Together, they charged the ranks of enemy soldiers.

The familiar rush of blood tore through Haze's body as they drew closer and closer to the glittering spears of their enemies, the thought of who would be first to die coursing through his mind like electric fire.

They were now close enough to make out the individual weapon of each opponent; axe, sword, glaive.

He thought of Orlivan, and his blood boiled as they drew so close that he could make out the infantry's eyes; wide, and terrified.

He yelled as his feet pounded across the snow, Rime Born thundering on his left and right.

With a final burst of speed, he launched himself forward.

The clash of steel on steel rang through his ears as the two forces met with a sound like metal thunder, the shriek of pain following closely after.

His body jarred as his lance came into contact with the belly of the soldier in front of him and he twisted it free, letting the man fall to the ground. Vlaire blew past him on his left, plowing into three men like a wild bull and sending them tumbling like broken dolls.

He was followed closely by his sister, her face set in a frown. Her hair flew wildly, revealing her angry red scar as she pulled her sword between herself and her enemies. A battle cry tore from her lips as she whipped it over her head like an axe, lifting five soldiers off of their feet and sending them flying back into their comrades with a scream. She turned, her eyes glinting dangerously as she fended off attacks from her left.

The ground trembled under his feet, and Haze looked to his right.

Lord Kinzin stalked across the battlefield like a violent storm, a blizzard writhing around him in a cloud of razor-sharp ice.

Haze had never seen so much raw power; each of his movements lifted dozens of men into the air, sending them streaking across the sky. Explosions of ice and snow erupted wherever he pointed his hands, freezing his unlucky adversaries into pillars of ice. Scores of men backed away in terror, fleeing from the path of the raging Druid King.

Famau was like a feral cat. She leaped from one soldier to the next with deadly efficiency, leaving a trail of slit throats and gaping puncture wounds in her wake.

He narrowed his eyes into the swirl of metal and blood ahead of him and saw a familiar face.

Zaajik spun out of the way of a Rime Born's attack, drawing both of his swords across its neck and sending its head tumbling across the ground. He spun left and right, Rime Born falling at his sides like brittle grass as his blades danced seamlessly around him in a mesh of steel.

Grinding his teeth, Haze cut down a soldier blocking his path and made his way towards the swordsman.

Another infantryman leaped in his way, and he dispatched him with a quick thrust to the throat. He ducked under a Rime Born's swinging arm just in time to catch one of Zaajik's swords on the hilt of his lance and turn it into the ground. A spray of ice chips leaped into the air where it gouged the earth.

Zaajik stumbled backwards, trying to catch his footing. He caught his balance and smiled at Haze.

"Hello, General," he sneered.

"I am no general of yours," Haze spat. "You disgrace the name of the Demons!"

The battle raged around them, the clash of steel and screaming men deafening. He could see Oaina in the corner of his eye making her way towards him as she blasted three more men back into their own ranks. Vlaire struggled to hold back half a dozen spearmen, his hammer whirling around him like an angered wasp.

"I disgrace much more than that," Zaajik laughed, "but at least I didn't betray them. I stayed to fight with the Demons as you marched off on your own personal mission. If only you knew how much of a toll that took on your beloved King."

"You killed him!" Haze yelled. "You murdered your own King!"

"He was no king of mine," Zaajik said, shaking his head, "but from the way that conversation went, I would say he was more than that to you."

Haze bared his teeth.

"I hear tell Orlivan didn't know what to do with himself when you abandoned him for a myth," Zaajik continued, "that the old man was heart-broken when his esteemed General left. King Orlivan the Weak; a fitting title for the history books."

"Enough!" Haze snapped. "You will not speak his name!"

Zaajik lifted his arms and yelled over the din of the battle. "Then come and silence me, 'Lord of the Demons'!"

Haze lifted his lance and charged with a yell. He covered the ground between them quickly, his fury lending speed to his strides. It was as if the entire battle melted away from around him, nothing but Zaajik's sneering face floating before his eyes.

He parried the swordsman's first strike, ducking under the next. Flipping his lance over his back, he caught it and drove the tip towards Zaajik's heart. It was knocked aside by one of the other man's curved swords, and Haze spun away. Turning back around, he charged once again.

His every movement was fueled with rage, his lance darting towards the swordsman with lightning speed.

But Zaajik was equally fast. He spun away on his toes and brought one of his blades to stop Haze's mere inches from his body.

No matter how hard Haze tried, he couldn't seem to break through the man's defense. It were as though Zaajik were lighter than air, his attacks consistent and fluid. Just when Haze thought he was getting the better of him, Zaajik would counter with deadly power and accuracy; it was like parrying a volley of arrows as his swords blurred around his body.

Suddenly, Zaajik leaped forward, swords whirling. Haze wasn't able to bring his lance to bear fast enough, and one of the blades hummed dangerously close to his neck. He stepped backwards, trying desperately to counter the swordsman's attacks.

But it was no use. Zaajik was too fast. His swords twirled like a tornado of steel until he suddenly lifted both of them high over his head.

He brought them down with a yell, and Haze's lance snapped in two.

Stumbling backwards, Haze caught the half of his lance that had the blade on it. Lifting it, he redirected another one of Zaajik's blows into the air.

For the first time in three years, Haze tried to catch himself with his left arm. It was instinctual: He reached out for the ground with his phantom limb, but his fall wasn't stopped.

His vision suddenly blurred as the flat side of Zaajik's second sword connected with his head.

He fell to his side, his hand pressing into hard-packed snow.

The cold radiated through his body and his head violently.

He blinked furiously, trying to regain his vision. He could see Zaajik walking slowly towards him, his features fuzzy and contorted.

"Not as impressive as I was told," he drawled, the clash of metal nearly drowning out his voice. "I was told that you could defeat a thousand men with one hand behind your back."

Haze couldn't stop himself from smiling as he remembered his and Rageth's old joke. "I only have one hand," he mumbled, his vision beginning to clear.

"Not for long," Zaajik said, sheathing one sword and leveling the other one at Haze's good shoulder. "What do you say we make you flush on both sides, General?"

Haze looked around him.

Fire swept across the battlefield, Rime Born melting like icicles in its path. The Winged Demons had never flown into the city; they were raking the battlefield with their dragons, pools of the melted warriors forming around the enemy infantry.

His heart sank.

There was never a chance of winning this. It was never meant to be. They were outnumbered to a staggering degree, and Jaelyn had not even arrived. It had ended so much faster than he thought.

"It was nice knowing you, Haze," Zaajik said, snapping Haze back to his own demise.

The man lifted his sword. "Tell Orlivan I was happy to take care of the family he left behind."

Haze tried to move, but his body ached with pain. His head swam when he tried to sit up, reaching uselessly for his lance.

A shadow flitted across Zaajik's face, and the swordsman paused.

A thunderous screech announced the arrival of a massive fire dragon crashing to the ground in a storm of ice and snow. Its mouth was open in a raging snarl, a blue flame glowing hot in the back of its throat.

Zaajik stumbled backwards, lifting his hand over his eyes.

The snow settled slowly as a Rider clad entirely in blood red armor slid to the ground. He drew a plain, double edged sword and stalked slowly towards Zaajik.

"Return to your Score!" Zaajik snapped impatiently, glaring at the red Rider.

The soldier lifted his hand and unbuckled the strap holding his helmet on. He lifted it off, and Haze's heart thundered.

"I don't answer to the likes of you," Alovere snarled, letting his helmet fall to the ground.

Haze looked him over.

He stood tall and strong, showing not a sign of his grievous injuries. His face was flushed and healthy, iron-gray eyes narrowed at Zaajik.

"Alovere," Zaajik said, his face paling as he drew his second sword again. "Come for a rematch, old man?"

Alovere shook his head, his eyes flat. "No. I've come for your life."

Haze saw Zaajik swallow nervously and lift his swords in front of him. "I bested you once," he said weakly. "I will do it again."

"You bested an injured old man defending a helpless girl," Alovere said. He lifted his chin, his eyes glinting. "I am the Man of Thousand Deaths."

The Rider advanced on Zaajik slowly, his sword still hanging loosely in his hand. The swordsman lifted his blades to attack, and Alovere's flashed up. It bit into Zaajik's neck like a steel viper, blood spurting from the wound. Alovere stepped lightly to the side, his blade dancing out once more and sinking into Zaajik's shoulder.

The swordsman cried out in pain and stumbled away from his adversary. His swords flailed desperately in front of him, trying to ward off his attacker.

The older man waited calmly as Zaajik's movements slowed, his blades drooping wearily towards the ground as his blood stained the earth. When Zaajik fell almost completely still and the tips of his swords rested on the frozen plain, Alovere stepped forward.

He plunged his sword into Zaajik's chest briefly, then tore it free and allowed the swordsman to fall lifelessly to the ground.

Haze stared at Alovere as the man wiped his sword clean and sheathed it calmly.

He then turned to Haze, his face wrinkled with concern. "Are you alright?" he asked, his voice barely audible over the roar of the battle.

Haze nodded, struggling shakily to his feet. He picked up the sharp end of his lance, trying to keep his balance.

"I think so. Caught a pretty tough one to the head." He stared down at Zaajik's body.

The swordsman's eyes were wide with terror, caught open in his final moment of life.

Alovere looked down at him. "The one life I don't regret taking," he said bitterly. "Now gather yourself. Jaelyn's forces are almost here."

Haze shook his head. "How are you down here? How are you not injured?"

Alovere glanced at him. "Lorgalith fixed me up, somewhat. I'm still not perfect, but I can fight."

Haze nodded. "Did you get a look of how we were fairing on your way down?"

Alovere's lips pressed into a thin line. "Not good. We need some men in the air to counter the Demons, *now*. They will have all the Rime Born melted into puddles in hours if we don't beat them back."

Just as Alovere spoke, a group of the Demons dove towards them. There were about a dozen, all Dragon riders. Their mounts dove with open mouths, flame glowing in the backs of their throats.

"Cover!" Haze yelled, looking around him for somewhere to hide. There was nothing but scattered shields and bodies, nothing that would provide cover from a raging fire dragon.

Just before the Demons reached them, a loud chugging filled the air. A streak of lighting passed in front of them, followed shortly by an enormous black airship.

The *Laudlin* yawned into view, blocking out the sun with its black balloon and coming between Haze and the approaching Demons. Bolt Cannons opened fire on deck, spewing lighting and death at the Riders. They vanished in a spray of red and screams.

Haze could make out Moxie standing on the prow, her brow furrowed and hands held tightly behind her back as the *Laudlin* made off toward its next target.

Haze and Alovere bolted over to Arginox and leaped on, Alovere urging his mount into the sky.

They got a much better view of the battle from high above it; Rime Born were struggling across the entire scene, weakened by the onslaught of dragon-fire from the Demons. Oaina was penned in by twenty or so lance men, bellowing and swinging her sword around herself desperately. Her opponents were too terrified to move in close, and so surrounded her and kept her at lance-length. Vlaire was nowhere to be seen. Famau was battling alongside Kinzin, who was apparently unaffected by anything his enemies had to offer. Teeth bared, he unleashed vortex after vortex of angry blizzards that tore through the enemy ranks like clouds of falling stars.

"Go to Oaina," Haze yelled over the noise of the wind. "She needs our help."

Alovere didn't answer; he simply directed Arginox down towards the woman circled by glittering steel.

They entered a steep dive, the wind tearing Haze's helmet off and sending it whirling through open air.

They landed with a crash just outside of the circle of men and leaped off of Arginox, weapons in hand.

They were met by half a dozen soldiers that broke free from the circle and charged, their weapons high.

Ducking under a blow directed at his head, Haze drove his shortened lance into the bottom of his opponent's jaw, spinning away and squaring himself at the next attacker.

Alovere moved with a grace Haze had never seen before; his blade danced like a steel minstrel around his crimson figure, followed closely by spurts of blood and screams as four men dropped like flies around the old warrior.

Haze dispatched his own adversary with a quick thrust to the chest and hurried towards Oaina.

A familiar chugging filled the air as another airship dropped down towards them, Boltcannons glowing.

Haze frowned. Something wasn't right.

Alarm rushed through him as he saw the flag of Miasma City flying from its prow. He looked past it and saw a sea of black sinking through the clouds, crimson flags flying and cannons glowing.

Jaelyn's Armada had arrived.

"Lookout!" he yelled, shoving Alovere to the side.

The Boltcannons barked loudly, bolts of lightning tearing into the ground where he and Alovere had been standing moments before. The soldiers standing around Oaina scattered, allowing her to dash out of their midst.

"Oaina!" Haze cried. "The airship!"

Oaina stared at him, frowning in bewilderment.

Haze pointed at the airship above her, and she turned to look.

Its cannons were glowing, trained directly on her.

She lifted her arms and roared defiantly, staring down the dark machine. Haze's heart sank as the cannons snapped, bolts of lightning streaking towards the Guardian.

Vlaire appeared out of nowhere, bowling through the spearmen that blocked his way. His face was stained with blood, a gaping hole in his leg where something had torn through the armor. His hammer was gone and his hands empty. With his mouth open in a snarl, he plowed through three more men advancing on Oaina. Bellowing like an enraged bull, he leaped in front of his older sister.

The bolts tore into his body, and he vanished in a spray of red.

"Vlaire!" Haze screamed, leaping to his feet.

Oaina stood stock still, a dumbfounded expression on her face. She was covered from head to toe in her brother's blood, drenching her in a crimson blanket.

Haze ran towards her, Alovere hot on his heels.

The spearmen were once again advancing on her with weapons raised.

Before Haze cold reach her, her expression changed. Her eyes glinted with rage, and she lifted her sword. A battle cry tore from her lips, and she charged into the group of spearmen.

Three lances caught her in the side immediately. She yelled and whipped her sword overhead, two of her attackers falling to the ground in half.

Haze's legs pounded the ice furiously trying to reach her.

Another spear sank into her ribs, and she tore it free. She threw it like a dart at the nearest soldier to her; it passed all the way through him and impaled his comrade behind him.

Haze felt Alovere's fist close on the back of his armor, and he reeled back. He fell to the ground, Alovere leaping in front of him.

"It's too late," the old Rider said breathlessly.

Haze watched as Oaina whirled her sword, bellowing as her opponents washed over her like a tidal wave. Nothing but her sword was visible as it whipped over her head, eventually vanishing into the sea of blood and metal.

Haze cursed and slammed his fist into the ground.

"Get up," Alovere snapped, glancing over his shoulder.

Airships darkened the sky. The Rime Born were all but defeated as the enemy infantry gathered itself together.

"We have to fall back."

Haze nodded and stood up.

They ran back to Arginox, Bolt Cannons tearing the ground up at their heels.

Leaping on the mighty fire dragon, they sped into the sky.

Haze looked down and saw Kinzin retreating slowly, his opponents too nervous to rush him. Famau was nowhere to be seen.

Remnants of the City Guard stood around Kinzin as he retreated, their shields high. The Rime Born were completely gone. Puddles strewn across the battlefield mixed with blood, creating crimson pools that reflected the light of cannon fire with each shot.

Haze scanned the sky for the *Laudlin*, but was unable to find it amid the storm of Jaelyn's Armada.

A loud horn sounded, the horn of the City Guard. Kinzin and his comrades turned and fled towards Hallovath, the druid occasionally pausing long enough to turn and launch another swirl of ice at the attackers.

Haze shook his head.

The battle for Hallovath was lost.

Chapter Thirty-Nine
The Guardians Of The Hyless

Haze and Alovere landed in front of the Gates, dismounting immediately. A handful of city guards stood wearily before the massive metal doors, all leaning on their weapons and panting. There were perhaps twenty all together.

Kinzin rested his hands on his knees, blood dripping from a small cut on his brow.

"Where is Moxie?" Haze asked immediately.

Kinzin shook his head. "I don't know. Vlaire and Oaina?"

Haze flinched. "Dead."

Kinzin's face fell and he stood up straight. "Famau, too. Galnoron ambushed me on the field and she took the brunt of his attack for me."

"Then the city is lost," one of the guards said loudly.

Haze turned to face him.

The man glanced nervously at his comrades. "The Guardians are dead, are they not?"

Haze nodded grimly.

The sound of marching drew his attention forward. The enemy infantry stomped towards them, renewed by Jaelyn's reinforcements. Brand new weapons glittered in the hands of Miasma City's finest, their armor a dark green and trimmed with yellow. They were only a few hundred paces away. Hundreds of airships hung in the sky like obsidian chandeliers, their decks alight with glowing cannons.

The men drew closer and closer, now only a few dozen paces away.

"How are we supposed to fight thousands of men?" another guard said. "And airships, too?"

The enemy force stopped suddenly, a throw's distance away from the gates.

Haze swallowed nervously.

"Why aren't they attacking?" someone said at the back of the group, voicing everyone's thoughts.

Haze narrowed his eyes as the ranks parted and a familiar face made his blood boil.

Galnoron stepped forward, a dark object dangling from his right hand. He stared at them coldly, a small smile lifting the corner of his mouth.

"People of Hallovath!" he yelled.

He tossed the strange object forward. It tumbled across the ice, rolling to a stop in front of Haze.

His stomach flipped as he looked down at Oaina's head, her scarred face staring up at him with lifeless eyes.

"Your Guardians are dead! You cannot hope to defend your city."

A murmur broke out in the soldiers behind Haze.

"But fear not," the wizard continued, "for I have an offer for you."

Haze clenched his fist.

"Give us the Hyless," Galnoron yelled, "and no more of you shall be harmed. The time for myths is over; your Guardians cannot save you now."

There was dead silence as the wizard's words sunk slowly into their minds.

For a moment, Haze considered it. Not because he was weak; not because he was afraid to die, but for the people and families that waited for them inside the walls of Hallovath.

He shook his head.

Orlivan wouldn't have yielded here. Orlivan would fight until his last breath, like Oaina and Vlaire.

One of the guards cleared his throat. "It's one girl," he said timidly, voicing what the rest of the soldiers were thinking. "For the lives of everyone in the city? Let's just hand her over."

"Only if you go with her, fool," one of the other guards said savagely.

"Aye, he's right," another guard said. "I have family in Hallovath! Why should they have to die for a girl we barely know?"

"Silence!" Haze hissed. "We will do no such thing."

He knew Malya was well gone by now, and Ki with her. All they had to do was stall Galnoron long enough to make sure they made a clean escape.

"Don't be foolish," Galnoron said. "You are dying in the name of a legend that has not been seen or heard of in five hundred years! Just give us the girl, and we will be on our way. You can return to your normal lives."

"I say we give them the girl," another guard spoke up. "Even if she is the Hyless, what's the point of dying for her? She's a single kid. We are talking about saving hundreds of lives! There are citizens in this city!"

Haze opened his mouth to rebuke the soldiers, but a soft laugh cut him off. He turned to look at Alovere.

The old Rider stood with his sword in his hand, his face tired as he held a hand to his side.

Apparently, his wounds were not entirely healed.

"Just a girl? Is that who you think you're fighting for?" he asked quietly. He stood up straighter, his face twisting in pain.

Leaning on his sword, he turned to face the rest of the guards. "Life flows through that girl like a river. It flows through her, and into you," he said, pointing at one of the soldiers.

The man shifted nervously.

"We do not fight for a simple girl. We are not fighting and dying for a nameless myth. Should this child die, all life will be snuffed out; color will vanish from the world. Your children will die and your wives will suffer." A few of the guards looked at each other as he spoke. He shook his head. "You do not fight for the Hyless. You fight for your brothers, your sisters, your wives, and your children. We do not have the luxury of quitting; we were not blessed with the right to give up and roll over! You think you're Guardians are dead?" he chuckled and shook his head. "I am looking at them! You, men and women who rose up and faced the impossible! You, who have fought and died for her already, and do you know why? Because we must! We are destined to protect her with our very life's blood if necessary." He raised his voice, and stood up straighter. "We fight and we die for the life of all mankind. The Hyless is not a myth to be laughed at, she is real, and is waiting inside the walls of this City, just as helpless as your loved ones. We now face an army of men who care nothing for those we love! They have come to take the City and all with it, but they did not count on us. We will not stand by as power-hungry fools take the lives of our friends and family! We will fight them!" He lifted his sword into the air, now yelling as loud as he could. "And we will die! Here! Today, with the names of our families whispered on our dying breath, we will give our lives in the name of life and light. We do not die for a nameless girl: We die for Ki!"

Time slowed.

Alovere turned around, his sword grasped firmly in his hand. He leaned forward and took the first running steps towards the enemy force.

Thunder erupted around Haze as the City Guards bellowed a battle cry. Weapons raised, they tore after the old Rider, screaming the name of the Hyless.

Kinzin opened his mouth in a roar, his hands lifted towards the sky. The ground trembled under the druid's feet, geysers of snow and ice erupting into the air as a dark cloud formation rolled in overhead.

Adrenaline rushed through Haze and he lifted his lance. With a yell, he charged after Alovere.

Haze focused on nothing but the ranks of the enemies, his lance gripped tightly in his hand.

Galnoron backed away a step, his face a mixture of confusion and fear.

Haze knew he was about to die. Except for once...

He felt honored to do so.

****

Lorgalith stood at the edge of the Observatory staring down at the old Rider in amazement. He turned and charged the enemy ranks with his sword raised. He was followed by two other men: the druid, and Haze. The small stream of city guards followed shortly after, battered weapons nearly as high as their battle cry.

Realization dawned on him as he stared transfixed at the scene below. Tears sprang into his eyes as he watched them charge towards certain doom, blood smeared faces grim with determination.

"Behold," he whispered to himself. "The Guardians of the Hyless."

A thump behind him caused him to turn around.

Ki burst into the room, her face furrowed in fear.

"Ki!" he exclaimed. "You are not supposed to be here!"

She ran past him to the edge of the Observatory and looked down.

419

She stared at Alovere for a moment. Her eyes widened as she saw him charging the soldiers of Miasma City.

She burst into tears and whirled around, hurrying to the center of the room.

"Ki," Lorgalith signed, hobbling over to her. "You need to leave. Where is your mother?"

Malya burst into the room, her face rigid with terror.

She relaxed when she saw Ki. "She vanished right in front of me again as we were going over the falls," she said hurriedly. "I don't know what happened."

Lorgalith opened his mouth to answer, but stopped when a breeze blew suddenly across the Observatory. It had not come from the open wall overlooking the forest; it had flowed from Ki. It was soft and warm, like morning sun.

Her eyes were closed, her hands held in front of her. She poised lightly on her toes for a moment, her hair flowing around her shoulders.

Then, she began to dance.

Music filtered into the room out of thin air, gliding around her in a liquid light. Her hair shone like stars as she whirled around, leaping and spinning across the frigid floor like a leaf on a fall breeze. Each step was perfectly in tune and followed the music flawlessly as the tear-stricken girl danced with all her might..

"She is doing it," Malya said excitedly. "She can hear the music!"

Lorgalith shook his head. "No, she cannot. This is the power of the Guardians."

Malya frowned at him. "Pardon me?"

Lorgalith smiled. "She isn't dancing to the music. The music forms to her dance. It comes from the Guardians who charge the battlefield in her name, ready to give their lives, and she in turn," he said softly, "Is

420

dancing to save them. It just like the legend. This is the awakening of the Hyless."

****

Haze charged side by side with Alovere and Kinzin, broken lance held ready. They were no more than a few dozen paces from the enemy ranks, their faces easily visible behind their helms. Airships floated over them, their cannons charged and ready to fire. The archers of Miasma City had arrows drawn and trained on Haze and his companions.

Now less than a dozen paces away, Haze gathered and prepared to hurl himself into the onslaught of arrows. He would take one down with him at least.

He stumbled as the ground shook suddenly, the massive cloud bank rolling in over Hallovath like a curtain of black. Streaks of lightning danced across the sky as the cloud formed a vortex centered over Jaelyn's airships. A bolt of lightning tore through one of their hulls like a flaming lance, the ship tipping slowly towards the ground as its crew tried desperately to put out the sudden fires on deck.

The enemy troops shrank back in terror, staring at Haze and Alovere as though they were on fire.

With renewed strength, Haze threw himself forward, leaping at them with teeth bared.

He froze.

He was stopped, suddenly motionless in midair. The enemy troops stared back at him like statues, mouths frozen open in gasps of horror. He tried to turn his head to see Alovere, but was unable to move. He tried to move his arm, but it didn't respond.

The airship falling from the sky had stopped falling. The smoke trail was frozen above it, the explosion of flames seized just outside the hull in a paralyzed flash.

421

A blink of light lit the battlefield, blurring Haze's vision.

When it cleared, he couldn't believe his eyes.

Ki appeared in between them and the enemy infantry, her hair swirling around her head like golden mist. Her face was set in determination as tears ran freely down her cheeks. She held her hands in front of her, fingers splayed.

The ground trembled, shaking and leaping like an angered wyvern.

Shoving her hands forward, she frowned in concentration.

The enemy force inched back. The frozen men stared at her in horror. The entire army slid backwards, their boots grinding into the snow.

She shoved again, a bead of sweat appearing on her brow. The army once again slid a few inches.

Haze's heart rose as Ki shoved again and again, each time pushing Jaelyn's army back a little. Her eyes were set, her hands trembling as she struggled to hold them back.

Another flash lit the battlefield, and panic tore through Haze's body.

Galnoron appeared suddenly behind Ki, his face twisted in rage. Lightning crackled around him as his teleportation spell faded.

Haze struggled to free himself, but was frozen in time. He tried to call out, to say something, anything, but his voice was cold and unresponsive.

Galnoron took a step forward and seized Ki by the hair.

Haze fought desperately against his invisible bonds as the wizard shoved the girl to her knees. Her eyes were wide with surprise as she struggled against him, frantically battling to free herself.

The sorcerer placed his hand on her chest and yelled something in a strange language.

She fell still, her mouth dropping open. A small beam of light rose up from the depths of her throat. It flowed like a trickle of silver out into open air, vanishing in the cold November frost.

Light began to fade. The green armor of Miasma City's soldiers began to turn a dull gray. Ki's locks faded from brilliant gold to a dull metal color, her eyes following suit. The flames frozen outside the falling airship turned to white, the glistening black hull fading to a dull glint.

Haze tried to scream, a soundless action that tightened his chest.

The light that flowed out of Ki suddenly stopped. The tail end of the radiance floated out of her mouth, and dissipated into the air in a light mist. Her eyes closed slowly, and Galnoron let go of her hair.

She fell to the frozen plains, her arms twisted awkwardly beneath her.

Haze couldn't move. He couldn't think. The light began to fade quicker than ever, all color bleeding out of the world. The brilliant sapphire boughs of the Banyeets lost their crystalline shine, fading to a pallid iron color. The sky darkened, the clouds that swirled overhead changing to a deep black, white lightning frozen in their midst like veins in a vaporous gemstone.

Galnoron yelled suddenly, the sound of his voice carrying across the plains like the snap of a cannon. The ground trembled once again and a black light oozed out of the wizard like blood from a wound, eddying around him in a soft spiral. He lifted his hands above his head, a white orb appearing between them. "Behold!" he screamed. "Your new Hyless!"

Haze struggled violently.

His rage boiled over as he watched Galnoron turn slowly to face them.

His eyes glowed a bright yellow, contrasting with the world of gray that now surrounded them.

They had failed. Failed to protect the Hyless. Failed to stop Galnoron. What sort of horror the man had planned, Haze could only guess. He stared at Ki's body, her pale face cold against the snow packed ground. Her eyes were open and lifeless, seemingly gazing at him, sightless and empty.

He tried to curse, to scream at Galnoron and tell him to fight him like a man, to pick up a sword and face him. His voice seized in his throat, the muscles tightening like a bowstring.

"You will never be a Hyless," a cold voice tore through the silence. It boomed across the battlefield like a war horn, vibrating Haze's armor.

A burst of color appeared next to Galnoron, a vivid ice-blue. Light streamed from the strange creature, warming Haze's limbs and allowing him to fall to the ground. He could move again, his hand cold on his lance.

The color slowly took shape. A tall Rime Born materialized beside the sorcerer, an emerald green cloak draped over its broad shoulders.

Arglwydd Rhew faced Galnoron, his emotionless features fixed on the sorcerer's face. "I was created to protect the world from people like you."

"You cannot stop me, Rime Born!" Galnoron bellowed, the orb of light growing out of control over his head.

"No, I cannot," the Rime Born King answered simply. "Only the Hyless can. I was created to absorb her powers should she ever be stripped of them by the likes of you. What you feel is not the power of the Hyless flowing through your veins, but the side effects of taking her life. Her strength went directly to me."

The orb shimmering above Galnoron's head vanished with a small pop and the black mist seeped into the ground.

He took a step back as the frozen King reached out with a claw-like hand.

"I am here to end your rampage, wizard."

A blast of radiance coursed over Galnoron, surrounding his body in green light. It whirled around him in a violent storm, the wizard lifting his hands and crying out in pain. Arglwydd's tattered cloak whipped in the storm light, radiance shining through its moth-eaten holes.

Haze watched in amazement as the sorcerer slowly stooped forward, his fingers becoming bony and hooked. His face sagged as he instantly aged, the wrinkles on his shaved head multiplying by the dozen. He looked to be older than Lorgalith himself before his eyes wearily closed, his chin sagging down to his bony chest.

The light suddenly vanished, and Galnoron's emptied husk fell to the ground beside Ki, bursting into a cloud of dust.

Haze's invisible bonds suddenly vanished, and he leaped to his feet as Alovere bolted past him.

The old Rider was at Ki's side in an instant, cradling her head in his arms.

"I commend you, Guardians," Arglwydd Rhew said, bowing his head as he turned away from Galnoron's empty clothes. "I regret to inform you the battle isn't over yet. I have been gifted the powers of the Hyless for a short time, though my body cannot contain them for long. The enemy force is breaking free from Ki's spell."

Haze had noticed it too. A few enemy soldiers were twitching convulsively, trying to move. One or two dragons were able to blink. The airship that had frozen mid fall had suddenly dropped a few feet before stopping once again.

"What do we do?" Alovere looked up at Arglwydd. A single tear rolled down his cheek as he stroked Ki's hair. "She...she's gone."

Arglwydd stepped towards her. "No. She is stripped of what makes her who she is. I will return her powers now, but you must stand back. Once returned, the Hyless will be at full strength. She may not yet know how to control it."

Haze touched Alovere's shoulder. "Come on, Alovere. Let him do what he must."

Alovere took one longing look at Ki, and laid her gently back down in the snow. "Alright." he nodded, wiping his eyes. "Let's go."

They hurried back toward Kinzin, who was in the middle of breaking free from his enchantment. He fell to the ground, landing flat on his face. Haze couldn't help but remember this was Glassworn's most frequent position of choice.

They turned around and watched with bated breath as Arglwydd Rhew knelt beside Ki, laying his hands on her side.

A soft glow emanated from his fingertips and color slowly returned to Ki's hair. Golden light danced from one curl to the next, quickly reclaiming its territory among the gray locks.

Moments later, she took a sudden breath. Her chest rose in a wild gasp and a gust of warm air rushed over Haze and his companions. She sat bolt upright and her eyes snapped open.

They shone a bright emerald green.

Color flooded back into the world, the rush of light warming Haze to his very core. The green armor of the Miasma City soldiers glinted brightly. The fire erupting out of the side of the airship blazed to life, its flames a vivid yellow. The Banyeets once more shed their sapphire light across the Mirror Wood, their boughs swaying gently in the soft breeze.

"Protect your Range, little one," Arglwydd said gently, standing up. He turned to face Haze and Alovere. "Look after the Hyless for me. I have fulfilled my use."

Haze stepped forward as Arglwydd's fingers began to deteriorate. "What do you mean?" he said, staring at the Rime Born. "What is happening?"

Arglwydd stared at him. "My body is ravaged by the power of the Hyless. My time is at an end. Tell young Lorgalith the Hyless is in his hands."

"Wait! Can't Lorgalith help you?"

Arglwydd shook his head. "I have served the Hyless. Two thousand years I have waited for this day. I would not allow him to help me even if he could."

The great King lifted his hands and slowly drifted apart, his body turning to shards of ice. They formed a small cloud that hovered above the plains for a moments, before writhing suddenly and exploding in a flash of blue light.

Haze covered his face with his hand briefly. When he lowered it, Arglwydd Rhew was gone.

Alovere dashed forward, falling on his knees next to Ki. "Are you okay?"

She leaned forward and wrapped her arms around his neck, sobbing hysterically.

Haze hurried over. "Alovere," he said, nudging the other man's shoulder. "They are all breaking free."

The enemy force was indeed free of Ki's spell, shaking their heads and gathering their bearings. The airship had resumed its fall, gliding slowly towards the frozen plains.

Alovere nodded and stood up, scooping Ki into his arms. "Let's get her out of here."

But Ki had something else in mind.

She struggled free of Alovere's arms and ran to face the enemy force. She lifted her bare foot and slammed it firmly into the snow with her hands in front of her.

Haze felt the air change direction and blow towards Jaelyn's troops. Snow lifted from the ground. Clouds lowered themselves down towards them, reaching with gray fingers towards the infantry.

Ki took a breath. A wave of energy blasted off of her and knocked Haze to his knees. Her hair shot straight up as though a hurricane had formed directly under her feet. Her little green dress flapped wildly in the wind as she took a slow step forward. She stretched a hand out to her side, and one of the great mountains of the Range split open with a thunderous crack.

Haze could see blue sky beyond it, and the familiar green of the continent reached his eyes.

She stretched the other hand out and the ground heaved violently. The enemy soldiers suddenly shot back towards the split in the Range. Airships piled together in a jumble of cannons and metal as they were swept backwards by an unseen force.

The infantry screamed and tumbled across the frozen ground before being lifted into the air and launched backwards towards the opening in the Range. The entire sea of men and airships vanished from sight as they blew farther and farther away. Ki's face was drawn with concentration she stared hard at the bright green of the continent beyond the Range, staggering wide-eyed as power raged around her. She took a shaky step forward, tears streaming down her face. She leaned towards her enemies, her mouth wide in a deafening scream.

Her hands clapped together in front of her. The mountain snapped shut with a thunderous clap, closing off the outside world and its people from the Elliset Mountain Range.

The air stilled and the clouds parted, allowing sunshine to trickle through onto the snow below. The tops of the mountains were revealed as the fog melted away. Haze watched as shimmering white and blue crept across their peaks, freezing them over in a deadly cold.

An ice wyvern winged through the clear sky, letting out a hesitant screech as it flew past.

"The Hyless has returned," Kinzin murmured from beside him. "The Years of Mourning have passed."

Chapter Forty
To Release a Friend

Haze patted Boar gently on the nose. The wyvern looked at him with wide eyes.

It had been three days since the defeat of Jaelyn and Galnoron, and it was time to move on.

Lord Kinzin had vanished the day before without a word to anyone. Haze could only guess where he had gone. Alovere had left for Beril, saying he would return shortly with Enial. He intended to spend the remainder of his life in Hallovath, looking after Ki.

Haze and Malya stood atop Tundra Falls where Lox used to take Ki to practice her dances. Evaala, Boar, and Bard were perched on the edge of the waterfall and facing them patiently.

Though they couldn't give the Guardians a proper burial without their bodies, Haze and Malya had decided to release their wyverns instead. The saddle that was almost a permanent fixture on Boar's back now lay on the ground.

The wyvern stared at it in confusion.

"It's alright, big boy," Haze said rubbing his nose. "You are free to go."

The wyvern stared at him for a moment, then turned and fell from the edge of the waterfall. Free falling for a moment, he spread his wings and glided out over the city, shimmering like a sapphire.

Haze moved to Evaala.

The wyvern glared at him coldly, then turned and leaped out into the air.

Haze smiled. It seemed very much like Oaina.

He halted at Bard. The giant wyvern stared down at him, his eyes round and soft.

Malya stood by his side, her eyes filled with tears. Ki was holding her hand and sniffling quietly.

"You're a good boy, Bard," Malya sobbed. "You come back whenever you want, okay?"

Bard turned and nuzzled his head into her ribs gently, his expression concerned.

Malya unbuckled the leather saddle and let it fall to the ground. "Go on, Bard," she choked. "Go with your friends."

The giant gazed at her for a moment before turning his eyes to Haze.

He cleared his throat and rubbed the wyvern under the chin for a moment. He then backed away a step. "Go on, Bard. Let's see some wings."

The Wyrm turned away and lumbered to the edge of the falls. He looked over his shoulder at them briefly, and jumped gracefully into the air.

Malya burst into tears, covering her face with her hands.

"It's alright," Haze said gently, rubbing her back. "He will be back."

Malya nodded, her hands still covering her face.

"Alovere will be back soon," he said. "He returned to Beril to get his wife, and he said he will be moving to Hallovath to look after you and Ki."

"I know," Malya choked, wiping her eyes. She looked up at him. "Thank you for this, Haze."

He nodded. "It's the least I can do. You lost your husband and friends. I know how that feels."

He staggered as a gust of air nearly pitched them off of the top of the waterfall.

Salezz tore past them, winging down after Bard and Evaala.

Haze smiled as the little wyvern spun gracefully in the air.

His smile faded as a small light began to shine from the beast's scales. He continued barrel-rolling over and over as the light grew brighter, until he looked like a shining arrow streaking through the sky.

With an explosion of light, his wings extended out, growing more quickly than a raging flame. His head sprouted horns, and his tail grew a row of spines the size of Haze's arm. He roared, a jet of ice blasting out into the open air. With a loud hiss, the light faded away to reveal the largest wyvern Haze had ever seen.

He dwarfed even Bard with his elegant wings sweeping wider than the length of Moxie's ship.

He wheeled back around, heading towards the top of the falls.

Haze and Malya stepped back as he landed in front of them, his wings flapping furiously.

He gazed down at Haze, his eyes narrow and warm. His forehead was broader, and sported a pair of elegantly curved horns that swept upward in a gentle spiral. His chest was wider than a tree trunk, glistening brightly in the sunlight. His tail flicked around his feet as he perched in front of them, awaiting his master's approval.

Salezz had finally had his last growth spurt.

"Hey, Salezz," Haze said softly, stroking the wyverns nose. "Pretty impressive, little guy."

He snorted in dissatisfaction, and Haze and Malya laughed.

When their laughter died away, Malya looked up at Haze. "What will you do now?" she asked. "Return to Beril?"

Haze shook his head. "I don't think so," he said. "I have other duties to attend."

Malya frowned and sniffed. "Like what?"

Haze looked out over the city of Hallovath and sighed contentedly. "I am a Guardian of the Hyless."

The End